WVAL 3/22

All Girls

Emily Layden

Emily Layden is a graduate of Stanford University, and has taught at several girls' schools in the United States. Her writing has appeared in the *New York Times*, *Marie Claire*, *Billfold* and *Runner's World*. *All Girls* is her first novel.

Praise for *All Girls*

'The pages turn fast and the girls are complex, compelling and written with incredible tenderness. Layden excels at rendering the everyday details of boarding school life'   Kate Elizabeth Russell, *New York Times*

'An exciting, innovative debut from a fresh and assured new voice'
Taylor Jenkins Reid, bestselling author of *Daisy Jones and the Six*

'Sexual awakening and institutional reckoning intertwine in Emily Layden's rich, kaleidoscopic debut'
Elizabeth Ames, author of *The Other's Gold*

'Astutely captures the claustrophobic and toxic culture of conformity among teenage girls'   *Observer*

'Diving into the unprocessed underworld of adolescence, Layden creates space for a conversation about feminism and the unsung difficulties of surviving in a male-dominated world. Intelligent, evocative, and empathetic'   *Kirkus*

All Girls

Emily Layden

JOHN MURRAY

First published in Great Britain in 2021 by John Murray (Publishers)
An Hachette UK company

This paperback edition published in 2022

1

A CIP catalogue record for this title is available from the British Library

Paperback ISBN 9781529330106
eBook ISBN 9781529330113

Printed and bound in Great Britain by Clays Ltd, Elcograf S.p.A.

John Murray policy is to use papers that are natural, renewable and recyclable
products and made from wood grown in sustainable forests. The logging and
manufacturing processes are expected to conform to the environmental
regulations of the country of origin.

John Murray (Publishers)
Carmelite House
50 Victoria Embankment
London EC4Y 0DZ

www.johnmurraypress.co.uk

I stepped from Plank to Plank
A slow and cautious way
The Stars about my Head I felt
About my Feet the Sea—

I knew not but the next
Would be my final inch—
This gave me that precarious Gait
Some call Experience—

EMILY DICKINSON

Here

There are no major highways into the northwest corner of Connecticut that comprises Litchfield County. Travelers from the more densely populated suburbs of New York—from Westchester and Long Island, from Danbury and Greenwich—find themselves frustrated by the path of winnowing thoroughfares, turnpikes and interstates splitting again and again like capillaries from an artery. No matter the starting point, the final approach to Atwater requires navigating Litchfield's web of two-lane county roads, flanked in most cases by farmland and medium-thick deciduous forest, the only signage suggesting lowered speeds around particularly treacherous curves. In this corner of New England—like the PCH in certain parts of Southern California; like the pavement that cuts between oil fields outside Odessa—these are the roads meant for windows down and music on loud. This is where teenagers wrap themselves around telephone poles.

The vandal—if vandalism is what you wanted to call it—clearly knew this when she considered her options. (Unlike the question of whether the act was vandalism, there was near-unanimous agreement that the culprit was, in fact, a she.) She clearly knew that families dropping their daughters off at school had their pick of county routes to zig and zag across, like ants to the nest. She might have also known that the nearest billboards were at the interchanges and highway overpasses near Waterbury and Hartford; she might have further estimated the number of students who drove that way and decided: *Not enough.* When she placed her order with Vistaprint—the label was printed neatly on the back of each poster board—for one hundred eighteen-by-twenty-seven-inch signs and one hundred stands, it was with the understanding that the best approach was a scattershot one, shrapnel blasted across the entire county. She likely researched Connecticut laws and local ordinances regarding yard signs and public property and determined that what she was planning was *probably not* illegal, not exactly, but that it was best to plant the signs under the cover of darkness on a night as close to Opening Day as possible.

And so when the residents of Kent and Goshen and Roxbury woke one morning in late August, the day the boarding school at the heart of their suburban-rural community was set to open for the academic year, and made their way to the little main streets and intersections that held their corner stores and gas stations, they found their roads peppered with little black rectangles, low and squat and set thirty feet from the pavement. It wasn't until they passed two or three that the words coalesced into meaning, the *r*s and *p*s sorted and organized by a fogged morning brain. Longer still it took to identify the purpose of these campaign signs in a nonelection year, and so the phrasing of the placards planted like seeds in a fifteen-mile radius from The Atwater School settled confusedly onto the surrounding community. A RAPIST WORKS HERE, they read, the message positioned next to a sepia-toned photo of a schoolhouse steeple, haloed in black like an antique portrait.

They were gone almost as soon as they'd popped up, lingering only for a day or two, so that those that remained withered like mailbox balloons after a birthday party, wilted and random, more frequent the farther you traveled from campus. They guessed the school came around and tore them up, or maybe it was their neighbors for whom the vulgarity of the signs was too much: Who wanted to look at that word every day? Who wanted to think about that kind of violence? Because of this, few of them had the chance to look up the URL that slugged the bottom of each sign, the one that might have directed them to a petition to extend Connecticut's statute of limitations on rape and sexual assault, a kind of activism that might have struck them as surprisingly reasonable given the shock of the headline and the tabloidishness of the signs. In time, the townspeople for whom Atwater was a kind of ivory tower would decide the words on the yard signs weren't meant for them, not really, and the act of vigilante justice would fade in their memories to a kind of sad and misguided prank. They were used to this kind of thing, the whispers of scandal that accompany the very, very privileged. It was never any of their business.

Orientation

Orientation

Lauren Triplett has vomited in a lot of public places: on the sidelines of a soccer field; in the parking lot of a Dunkin' Donuts; at Six Flags; at Disney World; once, even, at the edges of a black-diamond run on a mountain in the Adirondacks, orange-pink throw-up melting the powder on contact. And now: Somewhere on the Side of the Road in Rural Connecticut.

Her mother has not bothered to get out of the car. Susan Triplett has a spectacularly weak stomach of her own, and while a person might think that would make her *more* sympathetic to her daughter's propensity for motion sickness, in fact it does not.

Instead, Lauren's dad hangs a few feet off, hands on his hips: "Sorry, kid."

Lauren spits, her hands still braced against her knees. She eyes her shins for flecks of stray vomit. She'll need to find a place to brush her teeth. Did she pack mouthwash? That would be easier. "Not your fault," she says, her eyes not quite meeting her dad's as she peels herself up, unfurling her vertebrae one at a time. "How much longer?"

"Not much. Fifteen minutes."

Lauren nods. A large SUV zips past them, its draft shaking the Tripletts' own Forester and kicking up dead leaves settled at the shoulder. "I hope that's not one of my classmates."

Her dad shrugs. "No way they got a good-enough look."

Lauren rolls her eyes. "Not helpful."

As they climb back into the car, Lauren's mother extends a hand into the back seat, passing a tin of mints in her daughter's direction. "D'you guys see that?" she says, nodding her chin toward the windshield.

"Hmm?" Lauren's dad starts the car and checks his mirror.

"There," her mom says, pointing now, the tin of mints aimed at a small poster twenty yards up the road.

Her dad sighs and shakes his head. "What do you think that's about?"

"I hope it doesn't have anything to do with your school," Susan says.

The mint opens Lauren's nasal passages, and she chokes back a sneeze.

"Mom," she says, by way of rebuke.

"I'm just saying. These places are all dealing with this stuff now."

"Sue."

"What?"

Her father turns on his blinker and eases the car out onto the road. They are quiet as they roll past the sign, all three of them engaged in a kind of mental matching game. The tower in the photo is perfectly nondescript, as though the sign's creator did a standard image search for steeples and selected randomly from the algorithm's assortment. There could be another prep school here, Lauren thinks. She remembers from her search that there are a dozen of them in western Connecticut, maybe more, all multisyllabic and old-moneyed: Westminster, Canterbury, Loomis Chaffee. But as their car draws even with the yard sign and Lauren cranes her neck toward the window, tapping her nose accidentally against the glass, she feels the familiar sink of disappointment, of a false hope not borne out. When she decided to apply to Atwater, her desk at home was covered with marketing and admissions materials from the school, thick-papered pamphlets and flyers and viewbooks dipped in navy and white. Almost all of them featured a low-angled shot of an open-air steeple, looming like a fortress watchtower. After she was accepted, she kept the viewbooks and flyers and pamphlets in their haphazard pile like a casual reminder. She absorbed them through the periphery of her mornings and evenings every day for months.

She would know that clock tower anywhere.

The truth is that this whole thing, really, was Grace's idea. Grace's mom and grandmother and great-grandmother (and probably great-great-grandmother, back and back until before women were even allowed to go to school) all went to the same all-girls boarding school in Massachusetts. It was never a question that Grace would, in eighth grade, apply there as well. Grace was Lauren's best friend, but Grace—knowing that she would leave their prison-compound-like middle school in upstate New York for the hallowed halls of a historic boarding school—always treated their friendship like a temporary arrangement, like Lauren was a placeholder until Grace could make *real* friends, the ones she'd have for life. Grace's mother went to Napa every year with her classmates; Grace's grandmother, in her late eighties, never missed Alumnae Weekend.

It was a whole world Lauren knew nothing about. Her parents went to public high schools and respectable-but-public colleges and graduate schools. It wasn't like they were poor and Grace was rich—in their modest-size town, they lived in the same subdivision and their moms went to the same gym and the biggest difference Lauren could see was that Grace's family went to Nantucket in the summer and Lauren's went to Cape Cod. But Grace's family had something Lauren's dad called *pedigree*, and it set their otherwise identical suburban lives apart from one another.

By the start of eighth grade, boarding school was all Grace would talk about. When her locker got stuck, she'd roll her eyes and say that *next year* she wouldn't have to deal with nuisances like *lockers*. When she was bored in study hall, she'd say that *next year* she'd have "frees." Pushing iceberg lettuce around her sectioned lunch tray, she'd longingly sigh: The food's going to be so good *next year*.

And so one day during study hall Lauren googled "best boarding schools" (the predictive search added "in America") and started scrolling. Grace's school was on all the top-fifty lists, as high as number twenty-seven on a list of the most *elite* boarding schools, whatever that means. They were all beautiful. Most of them were in New England, although there was one in Santa Barbara where each student had her own pet horse. Literally. They called it the Horse Program, capital *H*, capital *P*, just like that—and it was, according to the website, an essential bonding experience for the freshman class. For the most part, though, the schools looked less like world-class resorts and more like baby colleges: small campuses nestled in leafy valleys or below lazily rolling hills with neatly arranged quads and coordinated Gothic or colonial architecture. At some of them, the students wore uniforms—plaid skirts and sweater vests for the girls; blazers for the boys—but at others the students dressed like Lauren's classmates on their better days: jeans, sweaters, combat boots.

"Lauren?" The girl in front of Lauren is very tall, and she leans over and forward slightly as she says her name. She is also impossibly beautiful, so ridiculously flawless that Lauren is temporarily speechless. Her skin is smooth and poreless. Her eyes are almond-shaped and flecked with gold. Her hair is curly in the way of hair let out of loose braids, deeply parted, and tossed over one side. Lauren had been expecting the girls at Atwater to be pretty, but Standard American Rich Girl pretty: tall and white with Hamptons tans and shiny hair. This girl, the one saying Lauren's name with a question mark, is *movie-star gorgeous*.

"I'm Olivia Anderson," she continues, extending a hand from a long and lithe arm. "I'm your Proctor."

"Um, hey," Lauren says, jostling the duffel bag she has over one shoulder to reach toward Olivia. Olivia's palm is soft and the smooth kind of dry, like baby powder.

"A proctor? What's that?" Susan stops riffling through the trunk of the car and stands next to her daughter. "Hi," she adds, extending her own hand. "I'm Lauren's mom."

"Hi, Lauren's Mom," Olivia says. She smiles like an old friend: big, generous, knowing. "Every Hall has a kind of leadership team," Olivia explains, "made up of a Dorm Parent and two upperclasswomen: a Proctor and Peer Educator."

"I thought this was the underclass . . . women dorm?" Lauren's mother asks, fumbling her way through a valiant attempt to speak Olivia's language. Twinned lines tunnel between her eyes, creasing the skin behind the bridge of her sunglasses.

"It is," Olivia says, "with the exception of the student leaders."

She pauses, assessing Susan's furrowed brow. "Can I tell you a secret?" she says, leaning in slightly.

Lauren can't tell whether the question's directed at her or her mother. In the beat she takes to consider, Susan answers, also leaning in: "What?"

"We say we want to be student leaders because we want to help 'foster community,'" Olivia says, her voice hushed, grinning, "but the truth is: we really just want to live closer to the dining hall."

At this, Lauren's mom cackles, her head craned back. She reaches an arm out and rests a hand on Olivia's shoulder, and in the brief moment that Susan's head knocks back, her sunglassed eyes tilted to the clouds, Olivia half winks at Lauren.

"Anyway, as I was saying: your Peer Educator is a junior who runs bimonthly health and wellness programs during Hall Meeting. On our floor, the Peer Ed is Tate McKenzie." Olivia cranes her head over Lauren's shoulder, scanning the parking lot. "I'll introduce you when I see her. The Dorm Parent is a faculty or staff member assigned to live in the Hall apartment, and she's the adult in charge of things like sign-outs and chores and nightly check-in."

"And who's that?"

"Our Dorm Parent is Ms. Daniels. She teaches history." Olivia directs her gaze at Lauren. "She's chill. You'll really like her. And then, finally, there's me, your Proctor. You can come to me for anything: directions to your classes, insider info on teachers, where to find the best Korean food in a hundred miles—anything. So," she says, pausing as if coming up for air, "can I show you your room?"

It is clear that Susan Triplett is thoroughly charmed. She thinks she and Olivia are already confidantes, old friends. Her voice lowered, she asks, "Do you know anything about those yard signs? The ones"—here she drops to almost a whisper—"about the rapist?"

Lauren is temporarily stunned. Her eyes widen so quickly that she can feel her lids tuck into the farthest reaches of her ocular bone. "Mom," she hisses.

"Oh, those," Olivia says, pursing her lips into a tight, bemused smile. "So upsetting, aren't they?"

Susan nods emphatically.

"I don't know much about it, to be honest. I haven't even seen one yet. They popped up this morning, I guess, and we—the Proctors—got to school a couple of days ago."

"I see. But you've heard about them?"

Olivia's eyes flicker to Lauren, and Lauren imagines they say: *Your mother is a handful, isn't she? I see why you wanted to come here.*

"Mom," Lauren says. "Drop it."

"Oh no, it's fine!" Olivia flashes Lauren's mother her biggest, most generous smile. "The administration told us about them this morning and said we might get questions about it. They're still fact-gathering, but Admin plans to send out a letter to parents as soon as they have the correct information."

"So it does have to do with Atwater," Susan says, and for a moment Olivia's face contracts, confused.

"Well, yes. It appears that way, given the photograph."

A snapshot of Lauren's desk at home slides across her brain, the glossed cardstock reflecting the lamp glow, obscuring the image.

"But I don't really know much else about it."

Susan Triplett looks chided, although Olivia continues to smile warmly at both of them. When Lauren's mother does not press the issue, Olivia's shoulders seem to drop and her smile transforms into a grin. Grabbing a bag from the trunk, she begins to rattle off a series of expectations regarding dorm life (she uses that word, "expectations," and it is not until much later that Lauren learns that "expectation" is Atwater code for "rule"). Study hall is from seven to nine. Quiet hours begin at nine thirty, but some of their hallmates may like to get to bed before then and they should be respectful of that. Check-in is by ten on weekdays, eleven on weekends. Lights-out is at ten thirty during the week—"which sucks, I know," Olivia adds sympathetically—and eleven thirty on weekends. Do not empty your personal trash in the common-room trash; bring it outside to the dumpsters. Do not leave dirty dishes in the common-room sink. Chores are typically completed on Sunday evening after study hall, and will be assigned by Ms. Daniels.

Although the details are businesslike, Olivia talks as though she has known Lauren and her family for years. She seems to listen with her entire being. When she is not pointing out landmarks and holding doors open and motioning directions, she looks Lauren directly in the eyes. Lauren imagines the conversations they'll have by the soft glow of their desk lamps, late into the night.

When she thinks about it now, Lauren wants to say that on the scale of decisions, coming to Atwater was really a shrug. Her best friend was leaving, and so Lauren thought maybe she should, too. When she first asked her father about boarding school, he laughed. When he realized she was serious, he kept laughing, adding a "no-fucking-way" for clarity. The no-fucking-way was his mistake: he should have known his daughter had inherited his stubbornness and that his refusal to even have a conversation would turn a passing idea into a capital-*G* Goal. She applied to six schools—not a halfhearted number like three, and not an insane number like ten. Four of them were girls' schools. She got in everywhere, and Atwater threw the most scholarship money her way. (Not very much, her dad would remind her.) It was her mother who diligently printed out the suggested packing list and who drove to Target almost daily during the final days of summer, buying extra of nearly everything (four towels instead of two, six washcloths instead of four; ten days' worth of socks and underwear; double packs of toothpaste and deodorant and, humiliatingly, the hundred-count box of tampons). Shopping was how Lauren's mother expressed her love, which was not to say that she took Lauren to the mall or that they went on day trips to New York City like Grace and her mom, but rather that a to-do list that involved spending money was Susan Triplett's love language.

She kept everything in the guest room, where the Target bags accumulated as if it were Christmastime (the guest room was off-limits to Lauren and her brother, Max, during the holidays). As the days until move-in shrunk to the single digits—four, then three, then two—Susan unpacked each shopping bag, organizing the items into two large Rubbermaid-type containers because, she said, they would pack easier. She said this from her knees in the guest bedroom as she smoothed out a towel, folded it in thirds lengthwise, and then rolled it tightly, like a sleeping bag.

"Bryce! This must be your roommate!" The woman standing in the doorway of Lauren's new room is thin with spindly ankles and tight, radiant skin. The few wrinkles she has strike Lauren, somehow, as the *right* kind of wrinkles: a delicate crinkling at the corners of the eyes, barely there curves parenthesizing her lips. "Come say hello, why don't you."

"Mom," says the girl as she emerges from behind her mother's shoulder, "I'm not five. I know how to introduce myself." She steps around the woman angling her hip in the doorframe and extends a perfectly manicured hand with the same certainty as Olivia had in the parking lot.

"Hi," she breathes. "I'm Bryce." Unlike Olivia, Bryce *is* Standard American Rich Girl pretty. She has straight brown hair and perfect bone structure and a smattering of neat freckles across her nose. While so many of Lauren's friends from home are middle-school skinny, Bryce is naturally thin, grown-up thin. "You must be Lauren. Olivia told me your name when she showed us to our room. Where are you from?"

"Albany," Lauren says, and when Bryce's little nose wrinkles confusedly she adds, "upstate New York."

Bryce nods. "Oh, cool. I'm from Danbury, but my dad lives in Chappaqua. That's upstate, right?"

"If you're from Manhattan, it is!" Susan waves from the hallway. "It's so nice to meet you. I'm Susan, Lauren's mom."

"Lillian Engel," Bryce's mother replies.

The two moms shake hands, and Lauren feels a reflexive embarrassment at her mother's mere existence. She cannot imagine her own mother in tight cropped jeans and minimalist sandals; Lillian seems sophisticated in a way Lauren's mom never has.

"Is it okay that Bryce took this side of the room?" She motions to her right. "I'm sure she wouldn't mind switching to over by the window if you wanted," she adds.

Their room runs long and narrow and parallel to the hallway, one bed positioned against the wall that buffers the hall and the other against the exterior, beneath the edge of their window. Although they are technically on the first floor, Lathrop is built into a hill; rooms in the back of the building stand a story higher above ground than rooms in the front, so Lauren and Bryce still have a view.

"Oh, no," Lauren says. "It's fine."

"Lauren's bed at home is under a window, too," Lauren's mom adds. "Right, sweetie?"

"Excellent," Mrs. Engel says, her hands clasped as if in prayer.

Lauren is not much help as they do the actual moving in. Her dad shuttles things up from where the car is parked. Her mother unpacks: she lines the dresser with floral-printed dresser paper; she finds the outlet behind the desk; she organizes Lauren's shoes on the floor of her closet in neat rows. Lillian Engel does not get on her knees and line her daughter's underwear drawer with floral-printed paper. It makes Lauren embarrassed, and she finds herself hurrying her mother through the last bit of unpacking.

The rules are the rules: Parents must leave by 4:30 P.M. on Move-In Day, and so at quarter past Lauren stands in the parking lot with her mother and father with the confused feeling of an anticlimax. They hug and remind each other that she'll be home in just a few weeks, over the fall Long Weekend. Lauren's mother holds her a beat too long, and Lauren is gripped briefly with the cynical suspicion that this goodbye is performative. Not wanting to make a scene, Lauren pulls her phone out of her pocket and taps into her messages as the car pulls away.

> Just said bye to Sue and Brett. How's your move-in?

Lauren waits in the parking lot until her parents' car is out of sight, disappeared down the hill they drove up hours before. When Grace doesn't respond, she's left with no choice: she slides her phone into her back pocket and turns back toward the dorm.

That night they have their first Hall Meeting. Olivia and their Peer Educator, Tate McKenzie, and Ms. Daniels review dorm expectations and lead them through some icebreakers. They begin by sharing "roses and thorns": something that has gone well—a rose—and something that went or is going less well. They'll do this each night for the next three days, and most of the thorns will involve getting lost, and most of the roses will involve not getting lost. Lauren tries to remember her hallmates' names: Natalie Howard is pretty like Bryce and spends the week in coordinated athleisure; her roommate is Brianna Heller, but she's from Texas and within a month they'll be calling her "Tex" instead. Macy Grant and Jade Wright share the room across the hall from Bryce and Lauren, and Lauren thinks she'll like them, based on the fact that they, too, don't say much during Hall Meetings.

At the end of the meeting, Ms. Daniels takes a deep breath and lowers her tone to something Lauren recognizes as more teacherly: empathetic but stern, nurturing but authoritative. She's pretty, Lauren thinks, with clear skin and honey-blond hair. She could be a college student, in her faded Williams crewneck.

"I want to give you guys a little bit of time to finish unpacking before lights out," she begins, "but I need to say one more thing before we wrap up Meeting." She looks around the room, leaning forward off the edge of the couch she shares with Olivia and Tate, who each lean back and train their eyes on the ground at their feet.

"This is a hard thing to talk about, and I want to say in advance that I'm sorry that we have to have this conversation on your first night at your new school. I hope it doesn't dampen your enthusiasm for being here, because I promise you that this is a special place and that you're going to love it." She smiles. She has straight white teeth and tiny dimples. "Some of you may have driven past some disturbing yard signs on your way to school this morning. Like campaign signs you might see during an election, but not. Am I right?"

There is a beat before someone volunteers. "Yeah," Tessa DeGroff says, a little bit too loudly for the stillness that has settled over the group. Tessa is from D.C., the daughter of lawyers-turned-lobbyists.

"Anybody else? Or just Tessa?"

Lauren wonders if Ms. Daniels knows her name, too. Around her, her hallmates nod, one after another, in half shrugs and chin flicks.

"Right. Well, I want to tell you everything I know about the signs, but I also want you to know that it's not much. They were planted overnight, and the administration just hasn't quite had enough time to sort it all out. But I can tell you that they were likely placed by an alum, not a current student or a staff member."

"A recent alum?" Tessa asks.

"Not a recent graduate, no," Ms. Daniels replies. "But there is an alum who has made an accusation of sexual assault against a faculty member she worked with as a student. And she is—clearly—unhappy with how the school has responded to this allegation." Ms. Daniels pauses, and Lauren watches how she seems to chew on the inside of her lower lip, curling it in slightly.

"So . . . but . . . the teacher still works here?"

Ms. Daniels holds her response for a moment. "The individual in question has a long history of service and dedication to the school and its students. We do not have any reason to believe that the alum is telling the truth about this."

"When did this alum graduate?" Daphne Martin, Tessa's roommate, is from London, and—accordingly—has an accent that endears her to the entire hallway.

"I'm afraid I can't answer that question. We cannot provide any details that might identify either the alum or the faculty member. I know that must be frustrating and confusing, and I'm sorry. I don't mean to begin our relationship here in a way that seems to lack transparency."

Next to Ms. Daniels, Tate picks at her cuticles, her middle finger flicking against the curved corner of her thumbnail.

"So what's the school going to do?"

"For now, they are trying to work with the alumna to get a clearer picture of her motive and desired outcome. Once they have more information, they'll communicate their findings and next steps to the broader community."

There's a beat of quiet, and Ms. Daniels scans the room again, her eyes wide and unblinking.

"Was it rape?" Tessa has tiny, deep-set eyes.

Ms. Daniels cocks her head to one side, her shoulders rising with an outsize inhale. "I don't think I can answer that question, either. I'm so sorry."

"So, what *are* you telling us?" Tessa asks, her voice short and sharp. Next to Lauren, Bryce leans forward, her lips pursed, undeniably intrigued.

"Can I say something?"

Lauren realizes why Olivia Anderson's voice feels so familiar: She sounds like a politician, or a television anchor, firm and even-paced.

"Of course," Ms. Daniels says without taking her eyes off Tessa.

"This school is my home. Three years ago, I sat in this very common room and listened to my proctor—Delaney Mathis—tell us about all that we had to look forward to. And not just our classes and sports, but also all these traditions that sounded so exotic to me at first"—Olivia uses her hands when she talks, and when she says "exotic" she elongates the *oh* in the middle—"like Ringing and Fall Fest and Vespers and Founder's Day." She pauses, turning her mouth into a kind of pleading smile. "I remember the only one I recognized was prom. It was like I'd dropped into a fantasy world, you know? I felt like I'd have to learn a whole different language to survive here."

Lauren has already started to pick up on the Atwater shorthand: Trask is the arts center; Avery is the library; most faculty live in the on-campus housing in "Professorville." They live in Lathrop; the upperclasswomen live in Whitney.

"So what you're saying is that Atwater is magical," Tate adds.

"Well, I'm supposed to be a cool and jaded senior now, and I don't want any of you ruining my reputation, but—"

"Oh, don't worry, nobody thinks you're cool." Tate winks.

Olivia reaches across the couch and gives her Peer Educator a shove on the shoulder. Tate pretends the blow is more than it is, bouncing off the couch arm on her other side. Around her, Lauren's classmates laugh a little nervously, reasonably sure they're in on the joke. It only works because Olivia is so obviously, untouchably cool.

"But yeah," Olivia continues, "I'm saying that I'm sorry your first night here hasn't been like when Harry falls through Platform Nine and Three-Quarters, because that's what you deserve."

Between them, Ms. Daniels uncrosses her legs, resting her socked feet back on the carpet beneath them. "I know this might be difficult to process, and I want you to know that these two"—she waves an arm across the couch, gesturing vaguely at the young women on either side of her—"are here for exactly this kind of thing." Ms. Daniels pauses.

"Well, not *exactly* this kind of thing," Tate interjects. "More like, this kind of social-emotional processing."

Lauren wonders where someone would learn a phrase like that—"social-emotional processing"—and then she realizes: Here. Atwater.

"Yes, that. If any of this has been at all triggering for any of you, I want you to know that my door is open," Ms. Daniels says.

"And so is mine," Tate adds.

"Mine too, except not right now, because I'm going to bed."

The room laughs.

"I'm serious," Olivia says, and even Lauren laughs this time.

That night, Lauren stays awake for a while, her body alert to the sounds of her new home. The blinds cord catches in the late-summer breeze, and the plastic taps gently against itself in a rhythm too irregular to ignore as white noise; footsteps pad up and down the hallways, personless shadows skirting in the hall light that creeps beneath the base of their door. She tries to imagine this as a place where a girl could be raped, pinned down, a hand over her mouth to muffle her screams. Eventually her ears catch the thrum of the cicadas, like cheap toy-store whistles or a band of the world's tiniest maracas, the same night symphony she hears in upstate New York, and she is able to fall asleep.

The three days before classes begin is called Opening Week. It's a mix of orientation and bonding activities and, for those students who play a fall sport, preseason practice. Lauren takes her French placement exam and receives a perfectly adequate score. She makes the varsity field hockey squad, but the team is so much obviously worse than the public school at home that she has a hard time feeling all that triumphant. She knew this when she applied—that Atwater was not one of the athletic powerhouses; those were the coed schools in New Hampshire and Maine that recruited postgraduates to play on their football and hockey and basketball teams—but still she found the lack of talent during tryouts vaguely alarming. *It's sort of a cliché, isn't it*, she thought, as Chloe Eaton flubbed a free hit, *the girls' school that isn't any good at sports*. But the idea is too complicated to wrangle in the middle of all the rest, and she sweeps it from the synapses of her brain.

In the afternoon on the second day, they play a game that involves rubber chickens. Outside on the Bowl, they're organized into circles according to Hall. Their Proctors distribute bean bags among them, beginning with just two to a circle. They pass the bean bags to one another per Olivia's rules: You cannot pass to either of the people next to you, nor can you pass back to the person from whom you just received a bean bag. You have to say the name of the person to whom you are passing. The little pouches feel damp and dusty in Lauren's hand, the first dirty thing she's touched at Atwater. Olivia allows them a minute or two to get into a rhythm, and Lauren finds that they more or less pass in a pattern—she receives from Jade Wright across the circle to her left, and passes on to Daphne Martin to the right—until Olivia hurls a rubber chicken at Natalie Howard, who—in her surprise—lets the chicken smack against her chest and fall to the ground. Macy Grant, who had been in the habit of passing a bean bag to Natalie, tries to withdraw her pass mid-throw, and sends the bean bag in a lame arc halfway across the circle.

"Oops!" she says, embarrassed.

"New rule!" Olivia explains. "When I throw a rubber chicken at you, you have to catch it and throw it back to me, outside the circle. I'll also be adding more bean bags."

They look at one another, squinting in the afternoon sun, all a little nervous and none wanting to be the next Natalie (or Macy, for that matter). At Olivia's urging, they start passing their bean bags again, one at a time, and then Olivia begins tossing rubber chickens into their midst. She has a mesh bag of a half dozen of them, and in the course of their game four or five make their way into rotation. At first the chickens mess up the rhythm: they come at the same time as a bean bag, so the receiver of the chicken also gives a bad pass; they cause rule violations (through some combination of bad luck and timing, Brianna Heller's only option is to pass to the person right next to her, which is against the rules). Each time they make a mistake, Olivia pauses and allows them to regroup.

Eventually she explains that the game is a metaphor. The bean bags represent your daily routine, she says: classes, homework, practice, meals, chores, et cetera. The chickens are the things that interrupt your routine: The flu, a migraine; a fight with your parents; special events, like Atwater traditions. Success in boarding school—and in life!—is a matter of managing the interruptions, of planning for the unplanned-for.

Olivia smiles at them. "Get it?"

At meals Bryce and Lauren sit together with a group of freshmen, and Bryce narrates the dining hall. Bryce, as it turns out, is Atwater's version of Grace: the fourth generation in her family to attend Atwater. Partly because she has been tagging along at Alumnae Weekend since her infancy and partly because her grandmother spent a decade on the Board of Trustees, Bryce is an encyclopedia of Atwater lore. A cluster of juniors sit together by the windows in the back corner; from the way Bryce talks about them—and the way her new classmates lean in, committing the details to memory—Lauren has the sense that these girls are who she might have classified as the popular girls at her school back home. The one with the long, matte-brown hair and lived-in eyeliner is Sloane Beck, and she was a professional dancer before her father shipped her off to Connecticut. She goes before the Disciplinary Committee every year but she will never, ever be kicked out of school because her family has promised to donate enough money to name a building once Sloane graduates. She's sitting next to Brie Feldman, who has curly blond hair and a doll-like complexion; Brie's roommate is Chloe Eaton, a round-faced Marylander with dimples and a deep tan. Sloane's best friend is Blake Trude, another dancer, who takes the train into the city twice a week and most weekends to dance with a company uptown. People who don't know that Sloane played the role of Marie in the New York City Ballet's *Nutcracker* at eleven think that Blake is the real prodigy, and that the story Sloane tells about her father forcing her to give up professional dancing is just a cover for the fact that she just wasn't good enough to cut it in New York.

The seniors filter in and out of meals, wandering in long after the initial rush. Unlike the other grades, they do not eat in large groups, twelve girls packed around a table meant to sit comfortably only eight. They eat in pairs or trios or even, sometimes, alone, with a book or a newspaper in hand, and never with trays—only plates. The fact that they are rarely witnessed as a group makes it harder for Lauren to keep track of them. Although they arrive straight from practice, Collier Ludington and Addison Bowlsby look like they have not broken a sweat. Their skin gleams like Gwyneth Paltrow's. They are the kinds of girls Lauren assumed she would meet at boarding school; they are, it seems to Lauren, older versions of Bryce. Hitomi Sakano joins Louisa Manning, a junior and co-editor of the school paper, at a table near the front of the dining hall. Hitomi is the daughter of two diplomats, and the newspaper's fiercely incisive Opinion editor. When Olivia Anderson comes to dinner—still in her soccer gear, baggy shorts with a hooded sweatshirt and knee-high socks scrunched down around her ankles—it's with Emma Towne, who is not *not* pretty but who, next to Olivia, looks like an average high school senior. She has soft features and brown-almost-blond hair. Bryce explains that Emma is Olivia's girlfriend, and they've been dating since their sophomore year. They are most definitely *not* Atwater's first on-campus same-sex couple, but they might very well be the first couple to live that identity completely out in the open, with the full knowledge of faculty and staff. Their relationship has created some challenges for Atwater, Bryce says, and when Lauren asks for elaboration Bryce explains that, well, for example, if Bryce were dating someone, she could not have him sleep over in her dorm room, because boys are not allowed to sleep over. (They are not even allowed in the dorms.) But girls are allowed to have sleepovers, and so far no exception has been made for Olivia and Emma.

Atwater has a rotating schedule, and at Hall Meeting on the third evening it's explained to her. There is no possible way to memorize it save a photographic memory. Every Monday is the same. Tuesdays are different from Mondays, but every Tuesday is the same. Wednesdays are different still, but every Wednesday is the same, and so on. She prints out copies of the schedule and tapes them to her agenda and to the inside of her notebook and takes a screenshot to keep in her phone for easy reference. There will be a special schedule on Opening Day (which is the last day of Opening Week) to accommodate the Opening Assembly. She takes a picture of that one, too.

After meeting, she and Bryce linger in the common room, comparing schedules. They have half of their classes together. Bryce doesn't know much about the new English teacher, Ms. Ryan, but they've seen her around: She's the Dorm Parent on the second floor of Lathrop, where she lives in the faculty apartment with her husband, Owen. She is young and pretty, petite with big eyes, and graduated from Yale two years ago. Lauren wonders about the presence of Ms. Ryan's husband in the dorms: Do the girls on Ms. Ryan's hall still walk back from the bathrooms in their towels, like they do on Lauren's hall, even though Owen might see them?

For French, Lauren has Inès DuBois, the actually French French teacher. Ms. Daniels is also their history teacher. To fulfill her art requirement, she signed up for Drawing and Painting with Mr. Breslin. Bryce says she should think about switching to Photography with Mr. Zarzynski.

It's easier, she says. Plus, Drawing and Painting is for the, you know, *art kids*.

Although Ms. Ryan's husband is objectively handsome, it's Emmett Morgan, Lauren's algebra teacher, who is the mutual crush of almost every straight student on campus. At twenty-four, he has the wide-shouldered softness of an overgrown frat boy. He played lacrosse at Dartmouth and spent two years at a failing start-up in San Francisco. Atwater has an unofficial policy against hiring single men, Bryce explains, but they got in a bind last year when the previous algebra teacher quit just weeks before the start of the new school year. Emmett is both the son of a former trustee and the best they could find with no time to actually search.

"But," she says, "the timing couldn't be worse."

"What do you mean?" Lauren asks.

"Well, with this rape accusation, you know?"

Lauren doesn't know. She wrinkles her nose. Bryce looks around the common room, confirming that they're alone. Their hallmates are all busy with late-stage unpacking: organizing their books on their shelves, hanging twinkle lights from their windows, tacking pictures to their walls in neat rows.

"Look, I don't know the entire story, because my grandmother isn't on the Board anymore—but she still hears things."

"So you know what happened? With the—the yard signs?"

"I mean, I know the gist. It's weird that they're calling the girl an alum, because *technically* she didn't graduate."

"What do you mean?"

Bryce slides a teal Lululemon scrunchie from her wrist and twists it twice around a bun fastened at the nape of her neck. Her hair tendrils around her ear, and she tucks the stray pieces away from her face. "This alum—or almost-alum, I guess—says that she told the school she was raped in the fall of her senior year, right after it happened, and that they kicked her out."

Lauren feels like she's missing something. "That doesn't make any sense. Why would they do that?"

"I don't know. I mean, some things don't add up, for sure. First of all, she didn't and has never pressed charges against this guy, which my grandmother says is in part because her case is so shaky that no lawyer worth his salt would take it."

"She's suing the school, though?"

"Threatening to, I guess."

"Why? I mean—what does she want?"

"I don't know," Bryce shrugs. "But anyway, that's why it's kind of awkward about Mr. Morgan. They stopped hiring single male teachers after exactly this incident in the nineties—again, unofficially—and it's just not an ideal moment for them to start back up."

"Because it doesn't look good?"

"It just doesn't look like they're taking any of this all that seriously," Bryce says.

Before bed Lauren calls home for the second time. The first time was only briefly, when she could not find where her mother packed the razors (she put all the extra toiletries in the small duffel bag beneath her bed, including the supersize Tampax box). She calls again because she promised on the first call that she would make a second call to let them know how everything was going. They switch briefly to FaceTime so she can show them her room; she points out that they've already seen it, to which her mother replies, "But not all *moved in*!" Already they have begun to speak different languages: Lauren finds herself using words like "Dorm Parent" and "Proctor" and "Hall Meeting" and as she does her parents say things like, "Now what does she do again?" and "Was that the pretty Black girl we met in the parking lot?" and "Is your 'hall' the same thing as your dorm?" And Lauren finds herself getting frustrated and so she tells them she has to go brush her teeth and get ready for bed, even though it's nine forty-five and the truth is she already flossed, too.

"Wait—sweetie?" Lauren recognizes her mother's tone, the way she speaks when she's been looking for a window to say something.

"Yeah?"

"Have there been any updates about the . . . you know . . . the sign we saw when we dropped you off?"

Across the room, Bryce is embroiled in detangling a set of necklaces that she hangs, one by one, from a golden jewelry stand—a doll-size garment rack. If she heard Lauren's mother through the speaker, she does not react. Their room is coming together, Lauren thinks: It's clean and organized but not *sterile*, like Leah Stern's room down the hall. There are places where their things mingle side by side as if they'd planned it: Two towels rumpled on the railing across the closet door above two sets of kicked-off shower flip-flops.

"No, Mom," Lauren says. "Not really."

As soon as she hangs up she feels vaguely guilty. It is the same sensation she has when she squishes a bug that is not a spider, or when she's caught not washing her hands after peeing, or when Charlie, their golden retriever, comes into Lauren's room with a toy and she is too busy to play.

In bed she pulls her comforter up around her shoulders, tucking her elbows in next to her ribs, her face and her hands the only parts of her body outside the covers. She pulls her phone close to her nose and opens Instagram.

Grace has blond hair and blue eyes, high cheekbones and tan skin. She's pretty on paper, but in reality she looks a little bit young, frozen in sixth grade, soft at the edges. This is painfully obvious in the picture she's posted, her face framed on either side by two girls who look a lot like Bryce: button-nosed and symmetrical. They're outside in the deep blue of a late-summer night, glowing in the not-quite dusk. It's one of those almost-candids, all three girls laughing, Grace's mouth directly at the camera, her hair falling across her forehead.

we hate it here, the caption reads, punctuated with a yellow heart emoji.

Lauren holds her thumb over the image square for a beat, thinks about coming back to it later. Instead, she moves her finger to the comment box and types:

omg sameee

She watches her comment fall in line; a beat passes, and a red alert pops into the app's right corner.

gracelostinspace: miss u lady!
Laurennotatriplett: miss you too!
gracelostinspace: tell me everything!
gracelostinspace: do u love it

Lauren types, deletes, retypes. There was a time when Grace would have gotten all the details Lauren's mother didn't: about Mr. Morgan, about Ms. Daniels, about Olivia and Tate and Bryce. She would have asked her if she thought the girl who planted the yard signs was telling the truth.

Lauren imagines Grace on the other side of the screen, in her own bed in her new school in Massachusetts, the one that was her destiny, watching the ellipses dance in their DM. There's only one way to answer now, Lauren knows.

Laurennotatriplett: it's perfect

Atwater Families,

It was my great pleasure and privilege to welcome our community to campus for Opening Week. The festivities marked the start of my twelfth year at Atwater, and yet the thrill of these first days has not worn off: from the enthusiasm of the new freshmen to the wisdom of the seniors, I love watching and guessing how this cohort will shape the semesters to come.

These celebratory days before classes start play a critical role in establishing the broader tone for the year, which is why I was particularly sorry to have them marred by an act of vandalism. On your drive to campus on Opening Day, you might have noticed a scattering of yard signs targeting Atwater; I want to reassure you that we are treating the placement of these signs with the appropriate seriousness, and that we anticipate no further interruption to our school year and our students' lives.

Moving forward, I want to state very clearly two things: first, we intend to execute a thorough investigation of the incident to determine with certainty the perpetrator and their motivation; second, Atwater has always been and remains a place that prioritizes above all else the safety of its students. I believe that there is no faculty better equipped to help lead our students in social-emotional growth and discovery, and that we are well prepared on campus to guide our student body in the processing that might naturally accompany something of this sensitivity and complexity.

Our students pride themselves on their capacity to manage their multitudinous responsibilities with diligence and dedication. As the key adults in their lives, it is our job to continually model this behavior. I believe we can empathetically navigate this moment without losing sight of our ultimate, perpetual goal: the providing of a world-class education. I look forward to partnering with you in this effort.

Be well,
Patricia Brodie
Head of School

Initiation

Her entire life, Macy Grant has been what teachers call "a math/science kid," traditionally excelling inside the clean, black-and-white logic of numbers and facts. This is why it is frustrating to her—sitting at her desk with a small headache forming at the inner edges of her eyebrows and sweat beading where her hair slips from her ponytail at the base of her neck—that her algebra homework is currently not going very well. She wants to blame the late-September heat, a death rattle of summer that marinates the campus in stale humidity and renders any real focus impossible; she also wants to blame their teacher, Mr. Morgan, who despite being very, very cute, is not—in Macy's opinion—all that great at the teaching. But she has the hollow feeling that this particular homework disaster is neither the weather nor Mr. Morgan's fault, at least not entirely.

"Is that the algebra homework?" Lauren sits cross-legged at the edge of Macy's bed, her body wedged into Macy's window, shoulders pressed against the screen.

Macy slumps into her desk and wipes her forehead, grunting her confirmation. "I'm so fucked."

"Bryce says we'll get used to it," Lauren says, unconcernedly, quoting as she often does her self-assured roommate. Bryce is exactly the kind of person Macy expected to meet at boarding school—a fourth-generation legacy from the expensive part of Connecticut, delicate-featured with a blue-blood name—but she is not the kind of person Macy expected to become friends with, if that's what they are. On the other hand, Macy developed a quick kinship with Lauren, who hung around the dorm in mesh shorts from her old school and camp-issued T-shirts, her blond hair in a braided ponytail.

"So I was thinking," she continues, extricating herself from the window frame, "I'm going to run for class council. Not anything too important like VP, but maybe secretary? I just figure that Wellesley is going to want to see a commitment to leadership, and it's never too early to begin catering your résumé to the experiences your top choice values. . . ." She trails off, and Macy thinks: This, too, sounds like something Bryce would say.

"Do you actually want to be on class council, though?" Macy asks. "I mean, you'd be great, obviously, but I don't think you should do it if your heart's not really in it."

"My heart is in getting into Wellesley," Lauren says flatly. "And our cocurriculars will play a very important role in our college prospects. Speaking of, have you given the *Heron* any more thought? I overheard Louisa talking to Ms. Doyle at lunch and it sounds like they're putting out their first issue soon. I think they stop accepting new members once they start printing."

Macy twists her ponytail away from her back. It was a therapist who'd recommended that Macy try writing as a way to "manage obsessive thoughts," and Macy's own mother who'd suggested that journalism might be a way to combine this recommendation with Macy's natural inclination toward facts and puzzles. Although she hadn't shared all this, Macy had still made the mistake of telling Lauren that she was considering joining Atwater's student newspaper, the not-daily *Daily Heron*, and Lauren had refused to let go of the idea.

"Can you explain to me again why you're worried about college right now? You do know that it's still the first month of our freshman year, right?"

"Have you really *not* thought about college?" Lauren asks.

Of course they'd all thought about college, at least as a concept, because college was part of the reason they'd come to Atwater: the name alone a guaranteed résumé-booster, a way to get your application to the top of the pile. Macy shrugs.

"I figure running will be a big factor in my choice," she says lamely, although it's the truth.

"Yeah, but there are *no* guarantees. Addison is a quadruple legacy at Georgetown and apparently she's freaking out that she might not get in."

"Can't her dad just donate a library or something?"

Macy whips around. Her roommate, Jade, stands in the doorframe, her muscled shoulders peeking out from the armholes of a cutoff hooded sweatshirt, the kind of wildly impractical and impossibly cool piece of clothing only Jade could pull off.

"Hey kids," she adds, flashing what Macy has come to see as her trademark smirk.

"Hey," Macy smiles.

"I mean, seriously. Have you seen that girl's Insta? It's literal hashtag Rich Kids of Instagram. Look!" Jade pulls her phone from her pocket and thumbs quickly through her apps, clicking into Addison's profile. She holds it out for Macy and Lauren to see, her arm extended across the room in their direction. The senior's grid is an endless stream of luxury vacations: Hawaiian beaches, Tahoe sunsets, wildflowers in the Tetons. "You're telling me this girl can't just buy her way into college?"

Although they'd known the seniors barely four weeks, a fascination with them had blossomed immediately among the freshmen, Macy included. It was Bryce who provided them with entrée into their world: not only was she on the tennis team with Addison and Karla Flores and Priya Sandhu, but she also seemed to speak their language, a shared vocabulary of the best restaurants in every major city and the best hotels in every resort destination. Macy places an index finger to Jade's screen, scrolling past matcha lattes and açai bowls.

"Seems like it to me," Macy says, the little hole in her gut hollowing further as she thinks about her own family's inability to finance a more compelling college application. "I know her grades aren't the best, but I'm sure she'll be fine."

"Well, Bryce was saying that Priya and Addie were talking about the whole"—here Lauren lowers her voice—"rapist thing, and that they're, like, a little worried that it's going to hurt their admissions prospects."

Jade whistles. "*Hoo* boy, I don't even know where to start with that. Number one, college makes people insane. Number two, 'rapist thing'?"

Lauren shrugs, a little sheepish. "What are we supposed to call it?"

She has a point, Macy thinks. All the available phrasing seems too clinical—"accusation," "allegation"—or simply too adult: A "scandal" is a thing that happens to politicians and professional athletes. Plus, they hadn't heard anything at all about the signs or the reason for their placement since Opening Week, when they'd all received a vague email from Mrs. Brodie outlining the situation: *We are working with our alumnae and our Board to develop a clearer picture of the circumstances that led to the vandalism, and look forward to reporting our findings to the community.* Despite the Head of School's claims, though, they knew almost nothing more than what Ms. Daniels had told them on the first night.

Jade shakes her head. "Number three: If I'm understanding you correctly, the seniors are worried that this woman's *rape* might prevent them from getting into their dream school?"

"Okay, well, when you put it that way—"

"What other way is there to put it?"

"It's not *all* the seniors, for starters," Lauren says, a bit of an edge to her voice. "I think that some of the tennis girls were just talking about college and saying that, like, the whole thing has sort of hurt Atwater's reputation. So when an admissions officer sees their applications, the first thing they'll think is, 'Oh, that's the school where the girl was raped,' not, you know, 'Oh, that's one of the best schools in the country.'"

"Do you think that's really true?" Macy asks.

"I don't know if it would actually, consciously impact an admissions *decision*, but I can totally see there being a subconscious gut reaction. Like word association, almost. And maybe it's not even 'That's the school with the rapist.' It could be 'That's the school with the crazy alum,' if they don't believe her, or just 'That's the school with all the drama.'"

"So people outside Atwater are talking about this?" As far as Macy knew, there hadn't been so much as an erroneous comment on Atwater's

Facebook page about the incident; it certainly hadn't been in the local papers, which the school had delivered each morning courtesy of the donation of an alumna who believed quite staunchly in the power of print journalism.

"I think the boarding school community is very small," Lauren says. After a beat, she adds: "What I want to know is, why would this alum have planted those signs? I mean, it *is* kind of crazy. It seems totally predictable to me that it would have only alienated her further."

Macy has noticed a tendency among some of her classmates to try on the linguistic costume of an adult woman, yoking together big concepts and tight construction in a distinctive pitch and clip. In the end they always oversell it: It's the inflated self-importance that gives it away. "It's hard to say without knowing exactly what she wants," Macy says.

Jade nods. "Although, if you're trying to be, like, a trustworthy and sympathetic witness, you probably don't commit regional vandalism. You, like, wear your hair in a middle part and button your Ann Taylor blouse all the way up." Jade mimes the buttoning, pinching her fingertips together at the neck.

"I told you, you've been watching too much *SVU*," Macy quips, then adds: "Maybe it wasn't her."

"But who else could it have been?" Lauren asks.

Jade shrugs. "Maybe Addison wants something besides her grades to blame when she doesn't get into Georgetown."

Lauren is appalled. "It was absolutely not Addison Bowlsby!"

Jade laughs and puts her hands up in surrender. "Easy! Of course it wasn't Addison. Speaking of: What's the deal with Friday?"

As if on cue, Macy's heart quickens. She feels a thudding inside her chest, a pounding she never notices in even the toughest workout, not when her heart rate reaches two hundred beats a minute during repeat two hundreds.

"Bryce doesn't know any more than we do," Lauren says. Although Initiation itself is among Atwater's worst-kept secrets, what actually happened between the freshmen and the seniors on the first full moon of the fall trimester was under lock and key. The secrecy seemed to be part of the whole thing, creating suspense and fear.

"Maybe it'll be some super-fucked-up sorority-girl shit." Jade raises her eyebrows. Macy thinks she's joking, but she can't be sure.

"Like what?"

"I once read about a sorority that did something called a 'Sharpie party,'" Lauren chimes in. "They made the pledges get completely naked, then circled all the parts on their bodies that needed 'improving.'"

Jade snorts.

"Do you really think it's going to be that terrible?" Macy asks.

"I really doubt it," Jade says.

"Plus," Lauren adds, "the school is under a lot of scrutiny right now. I don't think they'd allow anything too risky."

Macy opens her mouth and then closes it again. This is not good enough for her. She craves the exact logistics, not only the big questions like *What's the difference between Ringing and Initiation?* but also where will they be going and when do they have to leave and what do they tell their Dorm Parent, Ms. Daniels, and how long will it take and will she still be able to get eight hours of sleep on Friday because they have a race on Saturday? And also: Does everyone do it? Like, *literally* everyone?

Lauren jumps off Macy's bed, tugging slightly on the hem of her mesh shorts as she stands. "I've gotta do the English reading," she says. "See you guys at breakfast?"

Jade nods.

Macy manages a smile. "Yeah."

That night, Macy can't sleep. Her mind spirals. She plays out scenario after scenario, like an attorney prepping for questioning, a flowchart of possible pathways blossoming inside her head. She sees herself inside a house of undefined ownership—the country home Addison's family bought in Litchfield for when they visit from California, maybe, although of course Macy has only heard about the house, never seen it—stripped naked, lined up between Lauren and Jade; in the next image, Macy sits in Ms. Paulsen's office, her parents on either side of her, the stiff wood of one of Atwater's spindle-back chairs pressing into her shoulders. Ms. Paulsen tells her that she is in violation of a half-dozen Atwater rules, chief among them signing out of campus under false pretenses. She is forced to leave campus immediately, without so much as returning to her room for her clothes or her sneakers or to say goodbye to Jade.

When her alarm chimes at six thirty the next morning, Macy cannot say whether she slept, and if the stream of consciousness she traveled eventually meandered into dreams.

Despite Macy's IEP and her accommodation plan and Scullen Middle School's fairly stellar reputation as far as suburban public schools go, her teachers regularly cold-called on Macy or otherwise asked her to do things that functioned as triggers. And even though her parents *did* blame the teachers and the administration, Macy did not, because by the end of eighth grade almost everything was a trigger: she could not recite French from memory and she could not deliver a presentation to the class and she could not be asked to read out loud and she could not do projects that did not come with a very, very clear set of expectations, like how many points each component was worth and how each component would be graded and whether the rough draft would be graded or if it was just a checkpoint and if it was just a checkpoint, then how many *points* completion of the rough draft was worth. It never helped that her parents were constantly having meetings with her teachers or with her principal, because that only increased Macy's sense that she was a mounting burden to her teachers, a drain on their time and resources and mental energy. She did not want to schedule a dozen extra help sessions per week because her parents believed that one-on-one time would help Macy to feel more comfortable with her teachers. She did not want her teachers to develop alternative assignments or independent studies.

She wanted to be normal. And if she could not be normal, then she wanted to be ignored. But her grades were inconsistent and she was so obviously unhappy and her parents were frustrated with the school and did not think that a high school four times Scullen's size was likely to improve the situation. They spent spring break that year touring Lake Forest and the Lab Schools and St. Ignatius but none of Chicago's best day schools seemed like a fit for their family, who'd have to drive Macy an hour each way, adding two hours to an already exhausting day. They talked about selling the house in Naperville and moving to Chicago proper, but Macy didn't want to move somewhere where her runs would be relegated to streetlight intervals or wind-battling tempos along the Lakefront Trail.

When they visited Atwater, Macy could picture herself running along the country roads that carved up rural Connecticut; she liked the small network of trails that snaked through the forest behind campus. As her parents asked questions about individualized education and Atwater's Academic Resource Center, Macy pieced together routes in her head: Four miles in the rough square of roads around the school, then three by taking the forest trails at their widest; out-and-back tempos on the rolling hills of the county road that stretched in front of campus. Nestled behind the gym and out of sight on a regular Admissions tour, Atwater's track was its only disappointment: the centers of the lanes worn thin, the blue coating chipped away, cracked at the outer edges—it had to have been thirty years old. Standing in the middle of lane three on the backstretch, the polyurethane hard like cement beneath her feet, Macy hung her head.

"We're just waiting for a name donor," the coach explained, reading Macy's mind. Ms. Brown was a math teacher with short blond hair and the weathered look of someone who's spent decades outside, skin stretched thin over cheekbones carved by sun and wind over thousands of miles. Macy liked the way her blue eyes wrinkled at the corners and the way she talked with her hands. Her parents liked her because she talked about looking out for girls' well-being and how she didn't believe in putting high mileage on developing bodies.

When she got home Macy punched Atwater's zip code into Google

Map Pedometer and traced routes around the Litchfield Hills, counting the miles, using street view when she could to check the grade or to be sure a particular county road hadn't widened to a kind of highway.

Mr. Morgan lectures with his textbook in his hand, the teacher's edition, his tie loosened and his hair a little bit ruffled. It is very clear that he is flying by the seat of his pants, the lesson developing in the moment. Macy has not spent a lot of time around high school or college guys, but something about the way Mr. Morgan carries himself reminds her of an adolescent boy—or, at least, he does *not* carry himself the way the adult men in her life (her dad, her grandfather, her teachers at Scullen Middle School) generally do. He's explaining point-slope equations, telling them how to find the equation of a line when they're given the slope (m) and an unknown point on the line (x_1, y_1). There's a formula to follow. In theory it should be uncomplicated. It *is* uncomplicated. It's still September; this is just foundational stuff for the rest of the year, Mr. Morgan reminds them most days, apologizing for how simple and straightforward this all is.

But Mr. Morgan also likes to cold-call. While his back is turned to the class, the textbook in one hand, scribbling away on the chalkboard, he'll say, "Macy, can this be simplified?" Which is exactly what he does now.

Macy has the familiar sensation of a rock settling into her stomach suddenly, the same weight she feels in the minutes before a race. The longer she takes to answer, the more eyes turn to her, Jade's and Bryce's and Lauren's and Leah Stern's, even—Leah, the only other freshman on the cross-country team, whose eyes rarely land anywhere besides her feet and the floor and the paper in front of her and sometimes the board. Macy is jealous of Leah, of her obvious weirdness, the childish way she dresses, her ponytail with the middle part, her refusal to speak to anyone. Mr. Morgan never calls on Leah.

Mr. Morgan turns from the board, over his right shoulder. "Macy?" he asks again.

"I don't know," she says, which is sort of the truth, because she was paying attention but *not* paying attention, watching the world around her, watching Mr. Morgan move across the board, the steps of the formula laid one after another, but none of it was actually settling into her consciousness, making a home inside the grooves of her distracted brain. It was all white noise.

"Come on," Mr. Morgan says, smiling. He has the teeth of a white-collar serial killer, the villain in a suburban psychological thriller: fluorescent white and pin straight. "You've got this," he adds.

But Macy does not have this. She tries to look over the formula again, to backtrack to the start of the problem at the top left corner of the board. But her face is hot and she feels her armpits dampening and the class around her starts to fidget: She hears a pencil drop on the floor and a desk creak as someone shifts her weight and the scratch of an eraser across rough paper and the click of a calculator out of its sleeve.

Mr. Morgan smiles at her. "I get it. Wednesday morning, first class of the day, hard to focus. But hang in there, guys! Five more minutes and then I'll give you time to get started on your homework. Who can help Macy out?"

Bryce pipes up from the back row with the correct answer. Macy sinks into her chair. She tugs at the front of her shirt, caving her chest inward, pulling the fabric away from the sweat that pools under her arms.

At lunch, Macy feels too sick to eat. Her stomach cramps and unfurls, cramps and unfurls. She hardly remembers it now, but her parents say that she was a picky eater even as a small child. For weeks at a time she'd refuse to eat anything for dinner other than buttered pasta, oil-slick shapes slipping around in a bowl like fish out of water. Around the same time, she decided on toast for breakfast: buttered, like the pasta, with nothing else—no jam, no peanut butter (*never* peanut butter); no cinnamon and sugar. Lunch was a struggle, because what she liked could not be packed in a lunchbox and consumed three or four hours later: mac and cheese, grilled cheese, cheese quesadillas. Her dad convinced her that cheese sandwiches were just dry, cold grilled cheeses, and so for months in second grade she ate two slices of neon-orange American cheese on white bread.

From the get-go it was too much for Macy's mother, who shopped at Whole Foods and drank tea instead of coffee and who slathered DEET-free bug spray and mineral-based sunscreen on her daughter in the summer months. She lay awake at night, staring at the ceiling, imagining refined sugars and preservatives marching through her daughter's little body like invaders, chewing away at the synapses in her developing brain, setting fire to her neurotransmitters, planting like grenades the seeds of insulin resistance and dementia. She tried sneaking greens into the foods Macy *would* eat: puréed zucchini folded into banana bread; butternut squash roasted and puréed and stirred into stovetop macaroni and cheese; cauliflower steamed and mashed and used to replace half the potatoes. She saw a therapist, where she talked mainly about her own eating issues and her own mother's—Macy's grandmother's—exacting standards, and the therapist, misunderstanding the severity of the situation through no fault of her own, tried to help Katie Grant feel as though she was projecting some deeply rooted anxieties onto her own daughter.

Jade smacks her tray on the table next to Macy. "Nice lunch," she says, eyeing the two pieces of wheat toast cooling on Macy's plate.

"I'm not feeling so hot."

"You should go to the Health Center," Bryce chimes in.

"Then she'd have to miss practice," Jade says, rolling her eyes. "God forbid."

Macy spots Leah Stern, sitting across the dining hall with seven or eight other girls, her head bent over her tray, physically inside the circle but not at all a part of it. The dining hall's round tables meant that no one ate alone, that sometimes different friend groups had to share a table.

Macy looks up at Bryce and musters a smile, chewing a piece of bread until it reaches the consistency of baby food.

The afternoon passes in a fog. In history, Ms. Daniels lectures about belief systems, and Natalie Howard—thinking it would be funny, which it is to most of Macy's classmates—asks about the flat-earth theory, and even persuades Ms. Daniels to show a clip from some YouTuber about exactly this. In Drawing and Painting, where Macy is the only freshman, Mr. Breslin has asked them to each contribute one item to a still life of objects that represent power. Macy presents her old Garmin, the rubber-plastic strap torn and rusted where it connects to the watch face.

"Ahh, time," Mr. Breslin says. "As relentless as the ocean!"

Macy had actually intended the watch as a kind of symbol of her training, which makes her feel strong and therefore *powerful*, but she doesn't correct him.

At practice they run eight by four hundred, starting every three minutes, and Macy finishes each interval nine or ten seconds ahead of the next-fastest runner. On the way back from the track she texts Jade—still feeling sick, don't wait for me for dinner—and takes her time ascending the gentle hill to the gym and then down again to Lathrop. She notices how the sun is setting earlier; in the twenty minutes since practice officially ended, the sky has burst into flames, the underbellies of the clouds to the east bright pink above the sunken sun. It's too flat in Naperville for sunsets like this: It drops evenly to some far-off horizon, an expanse of blue-to-gold ombré that parallels the land.

Back in Lathrop, she tosses her bags on the floor next to her bed and slumps into her desk chair. She opens her computer with the intent of checking her email, doing the kind of mindless tabbing around that comes after a couple of hours away from the internet, but when she opens Chrome and finds herself presented with the Google search bar she pauses. She types into the long rectangle the first thing that comes to mind: "high school initiation." From there, she ends up on a website dedicated to high school football, in the bowels of a forum with an almost psychotic level of emoji usage for a group of (she assumes) adult men. The tone is all wrong: gleeful, almost; nostalgic.

So she opens a new tab and googles "hazing" instead, and when predictive search offers to add "deaths," Macy goes with that. The headlines are a nightmare. *4 Members Sentenced in Pledge's Hazing Death. Police Say 9 Charged in Hazing Death. When a Hazing Goes Very Wrong.* Most of the stories have to do with fraternities and most of the deaths are related to alcohol poisoning, at least loosely. In one, a freshman falls down the stairs and the other fraternity members do not think to call an ambulance to check for any kind of internal bleeding. By morning, he's dead. In another, a student's underlying heart condition could not handle the task of carrying a backpack full of sand around campus for a day. In several, the victim choked on his own vomit. In several more, the deceased's blood alcohol level was .44, or .47, or .38, five times the legal limit.

There seems to be a trend in the articles against chronicling the details of the actual rituals, so Macy tabs over to Reddit, where she does a blanket search on hazing. Here is the specificity she's been looking for: adult diapers, worn around campus all day; a case of beer in ninety minutes; testicles hooked by the pick of a hammer; branding with twisted hangers; phone sex listened in on; something called a gallon challenge, an allegedly impossible task involving a gallon of milk; something called a "soggy biscuit"; something called a "rainbow party." She cross-references with Urban Dictionary. It cannot possibly be real, Macy thinks. But how can it *not* be real? Who would make this stuff up?

"'Former child actor arrested in fraternity hazing ritual'?" Jade's voice cuts through the thick fog that's descended upon Macy, clouding space and time.

Reflexively she snaps her computer shut, the metal and plastic smacking like a trap.

Jade laughs from over Macy's shoulder, reaches down, and peels the screen up again. "What are you doing?"

"Just messing around," Macy says, but only because saying nothing would be worse.

"Is this about Friday?"

Macy shrugs. "No. I just—I don't know. You know how it is. In six more clicks I'll be reading a recipe for an Instant Pot casserole."

"What's an Instant Pot?"

"Like a Crock-Pot? But faster? I think? My mom has one."

Jade raises an eyebrow. She takes a step back, leaning against Macy's bed. "Is this what's been bothering you today? Initiation?"

"What do you mean?"

Jade tucks into herself, curving her shoulders, eyes on the floor. It's an unusual posture for Macy's roommate, whose default setting is a chin-out swagger Macy only *just* started to see as less-than intimidating. "You didn't eat anything today. When Mr. Morgan called on you in math . . . you should have known the answer to that question."

"I wasn't paying attention."

"Yeah, I know, that's sort of my point. You just seem like something's off. You can tell us, Mace."

"*Us?*"

"Me. Bryce, Lauren. *Your friends.*"

"So have you guys been talking about me? Having secret conversations—*Ooh, what's wrong with Macy? She's so stupid, I can't believe she didn't know how to solve that equation. . . .*"

The look that flickers over Jade's face—her eyebrows, her lips, the movement of her head, subtly—is one Macy has seen before. It's the universal reaction to a disproportionate response.

Still, Macy cannot help herself. "You're here on *scholarship*, Jade. You think you won't be the first to go when we all get caught?"

"Watch it, Macy." Jade's voice is even.

"No, *you* watch it, Jade. Hazing is *against the law.*"

"Did you figure that out on your little research spree?"

"I did, actually."

Jade issues a quick sharp half laugh, half sigh. "God, you know what? You should join the *Heron.* You'd fit right in."

"What is that supposed to mean?"

"Anjali Reddi is the most self-righteous person on this campus, and Louisa Manning isn't far behind." She pauses, collecting herself. "It's just—you're being ridiculous. Listen to yourself. Against the law? First of all, we're the ones *being hazed*, so even *if* this were to reach the status of legal prosecution I doubt we'd be the ones held to account. You don't charge the victim. Second of all, do you really think that anything that dangerous or demeaning would have survived generations? You read about a bunch of hazing-related deaths, right? And I'm guessing they were all at frats? Boys falling down stairs, everybody too drunk to realize how seriously they were hurt?"

Macy is quiet.

"Yeah. That's not what's going to happen here, Mace. Think about it logically. We have Dorm Parents. When the seniors party they go to Addison's country house. When anybody else drinks they do it in the woods or in their rooms in groups of, like, three or four. Whatever you're imagining just *isn't possible.*"

"It doesn't have to be dangerous. It just might be embarrassing."

"Embarrassing? So you're embarrassed. And guess what? I'll be embarrassed right along with you. And Bryce and Lauren, too. All of us." Jade pauses. "But you've gotta get it together, Macy. I am being very patient right now because you are clearly going through something, but you are losing your shit over nothing at all. It's a silly tradition. There are going to be, like, two hundred more of them in our four years here."

"Well," Macy says, "maybe I'm not cut out for this place."

"No, Macy. You can tell me you're not cut out for this place when your grades are in the tank or when you're pulling your eyebrows out over college applications. You cannot tell me you're not cut out for this place because you're intimidated by a stupid tradition. Now, it's late, and I've got homework to do, and we're not going to talk about this again until whatever happens on Friday happens." She walks over to her desk, grabbing her computer from its resting spot. Just as she reaches the doorframe, she turns to face her roommate. "And, when you're ready, you're going to apologize to me for saying that thing about my scholarship. And you're never going to use it against me again, or—I swear to God, Macy—that's the end of our friendship."

The next morning, Macy climbs out of bed as soon as there's enough light to justify the hour as dawn. She changes quickly and quietly, fumbling for her clothing in the half-darkness, using her phone light to find a matching pair of socks in her top drawer. She grabs her sneakers in her hand and pads out of her room barefoot, twisting the knob as she closes the door behind her.

Outside, the sun shoots across the Bowl, throwing long, amber-tinged shadows on dewy grass that was just twenty minutes ago a muted gray. The brightness confuses her, causing her to briefly question her outfit selection. Fall morning runs are always hard to dress for—crisp but not cold, with stretches of sun-drenched road that can get, after three or four or six miles, uncomfortably warm. With the sun rising fast, Macy wonders if she should ditch the light long-sleeve she wears over her tank top—but she doesn't want to risk waking Jade, or running into Ms. Brown, and the confrontation either would entail. A little extra sweat won't kill her, she thinks, so she kicks her legs a few times, rolls her hips once, twice, and begins.

Her loop is straight out of campus, down through the gate and right up 126. The roads are quiet, and when Atwater is safely behind her—around a turn and beneath a few rolling hills—Macy is able to relax into her stride. She focuses on her breath, which is even but rattling slightly, at the end, from the cold. A small cloud issues on the exhale. These are the mornings she loves. The chill shakes out the tiredness in the first three minutes, but it's warm enough that she has a good sweat going by the second mile. She turns her attention to her stride, running through a mental checklist: Arms low? Forward lean? Chin down? Forefoot strike?

After about a mile she hangs a right, and then another right a half-mile down that road, completing the smallest, narrowest side of the long, thin rectangle she's running. Cars have a tendency to whip around these generally traffic-less county routes, so Macy is careful to hug the shoulder, her ankles threatening to slip where the blacktop cliffs into dirt and grass. She's in a rhythm now, two and a half miles away from school, the midpoint of her run. Her mind is empty, clear, meandering meditatively.

Macy and running were love at first sight. The coaches at her local high school held a summer running camp—they used it as an opportunity to scout up-and-coming talent, hooking promising middle schoolers before they had the chance to get good at one of America's more popular youth sports: soccer, lacrosse, basketball—and Macy decided to give it a shot. A husband-and-wife duo who'd led Neuqua to a dozen state championships in the last twenty years, the Keatings disguised their running in games: Interval training masqueraded as red light-green light; long runs took the shape of particularly grueling battles of capture the flag. Macy showed up that first Monday morning, undersize and underweight, her sports bra barely necessary beneath a ten-dollar camisole tank top, dirty-blond hair tucked into a frizzy bun—and Mr. and Mrs. Keating saw four years of championships and a scholarship to Duke or Michigan or, if her grades weren't quite up to snuff, Oregon.

Running gave Macy a singular focus. When she ran—just three or four miles at a time then—her mind didn't exactly go blank, but it hummed along, churning through thoughts in the same fleeting way it did under a hot shower at the end of a long day. But it was the feeling she got *after* running that she started to crave most: blissful, linguine-legged exhaustion. That summer she would finish her half day at running camp and then retreat to the couch for the afternoon, her only priority to nurse the weariness she felt bone-deep. The two weeks of camp were the first time Macy remembered feeling somewhat at peace.

When seventh grade started, she applied for the athletic director's permission to compete on the high school cross-country team. Middle schoolers were technically allowed to play their sport at a higher level than the middle school modified team, but they needed to pass a basic fitness test to ensure that they were physically mature enough to train alongside young adults five years older than them. Macy had no trouble with the push-ups and sit-ups and twelve-minute running test; it was at her physical with her pediatrician that the problem arose. Her iron was low. So were her B12 and vitamin D levels. Her hair was growing abnormally thick on her forearms, her doctor said, holding one up by Macy's wrist for her mother to see. Is she eating a balanced diet?

Macy's mother's chin quivered, an ugly wrinkling that made Macy embarrassed. She burst into tears, babbling about how Dr. Shapiro must think she's such a bad mother but *she won't eat anything, she just won't, only beige foods for years now, I've never seen anyone so picky in my life.* . . .

Dr. Shapiro, bewildered and too busy to spend more than seven minutes with each of her patients that afternoon, reached for a Kleenex and gave Macy's mother a pat on the shoulder before turning to Macy.

"If you want to run," she said, "you have to eat. Have you ever had Ensure?"

Macy shook her head.

"It's a nutritional supplement traditionally for the elderly. They sell it at the grocery store. It comes in little blue-and-white plastic bottles. I need you to drink it at least twice a day, three times if you can stomach it." Turning back to her mother, Dr. Shapiro added, her voice stern: "And this is only a stopgap. She needs a balanced diet."

As Macy turns right back into campus—Professorville to her right, the Head of School's house at the end of the oak-lined drive to her left— she keeps her chin down, not wanting to catch the eye of anyone who might be out this early: swimmers coming back from morning practice or faculty walking their dogs or even Vinny and the maintenance guys mowing the lawns. She jogs around the back of Lathrop, where she's less likely to catch an upperclasswoman wandering across the Bowl on her way to an early breakfast.

The rising sun hits the back of the building, bathing the small parking lot behind Lathrop in warm golden light. Macy lingers in it for a little bit, walking in tiny circles as her heart rate slows and the muscles in her legs cease twitching. She takes a seat on the blacktop—still cool from the night—and begins to move through a series of lazy stretches. She has her left leg wrapped over her right and her right elbow hooked over her left knee when the back door of Lathrop clangs open.

Louisa Manning is the kind of girl who looks serious and studious even in sweatpants, and this morning is no exception. She scampers down Lathrop's back steps with her head down and a novel tucked underneath her left armpit, an apple in one fist and a to-go coffee mug in another. Unlike Anjali Reddi, whose dark hair is looped into a sleek topknot,

Louisa's shoulder-length blunt cut is tousled in the way of models going for a bed-head look. The *Heron*'s editors are far enough away from where Macy sits that their conversation reaches her as little more than a melancholic murmur, and Macy hopes that this distance will mean they ignore her. But instead of heading left around the building toward Whitney, they head to the right, in Macy's direction, cutting at a diagonal across the lot—

"Hey." They slow to a stop a few feet from where Macy sits in a frog stretch, easing her knees toward the ground.

"Hey."

"Macy, right?" Louisa asks. Next to her, Anjali taps into her phone.

Macy nods.

"Were you out for a run?"

"Just a few miles. Trying to shake off yesterday's workout."

"Kit says you're fast," Anjali adds without looking up from her screen.

Macy never knows what to say to this.

"She also says that you're thinking about joining the *Heron*?" Louisa peers over the top of her horn-rimmed glasses.

Macy picks at a piece of blacktop wedged between the tread of her shoe. "I mean, I was thinking about it."

"What's holding you back?" Anjali slides her phone into her back pocket.

Macy does not say: *Because I don't even know where the* Heron *room is and I don't know anyone else on the staff and I don't know what I would write about and I don't know if anyone would like my writing, anyway.* Instead she says: "I just have a lot going on."

Louisa drops her chin and raises an eyebrow.

"It only gets worse," Anjali smiles. "You should think about it, at least. We meet on Mondays during club block."

Macy nods. "I'll think about it."

"Good. And I'll see you on Friday, right?"

Looking down at her thighs, Macy imagines a large, black circle drawn oblong along the fat that sheaths her adductor. Her chest swells; a lump lodges in her throat. "I guess so," she manages.

"Cool," Anjali says, beginning to turn on her heels.

"And let me know if you wanna talk about the *Heron*," Louisa adds.

Anjali ticks her chin up once, a quick nod. "Later," she says, like an afterthought.

Macy smiles and lifts her hand in a small wave. She watches the friends from her place on the pavement until they disappear over the hill in the distance.

Despite the extra workout, Macy eats neither breakfast nor lunch that day. She avoids the dining hall entirely, her stomach cramping as though her body is engaged in some wholesale organ rejection. In biology, Ms. McCann explains the difference between smooth and rough endoplasmic reticulum. Next to Macy, Bryce is furiously drawing the organelle on her notes and labeling it exactly as it appears on the slide at the front of the classroom. At the lab table in front of them, Leah Stern rotates on the top of her stool, spinning slowly to the left, then to the right.

Macy begins to scribble *RER—proteins* and *SER—fats, hormones*, but as she does so she notices a small nick in the cuticle on her right thumb. She sets her pencil down and draws her hand toward her stomach. She traces the nail of her index finger along the half-moon of her thumbnail, feeling where the dry skin that overlaps at the base of the nail peels away from the shell. She moves her fingers across one another until she feels the nail of her index finger catch against the frayed cuticle, and then she gets to work. She chips and twists, flicking and picking at the skin until she has a hold on it—and then pulls, dragging the skin from where it meets the nail. It comes easily at first, following the natural curve of the nail bed, dead skin shearing easily from the living—but then it grooves away from the nail, and suddenly the flap Macy holds pulls toward her knuckle. She tries to redirect, angling the skin back toward the nail itself, but it's too late: the blood blossoms in tiny droplets that swell into one another like raindrops forming a puddle.

It does not hurt, but Macy exhales quickly anyway, loud enough that Bryce turns her way. Macy drops her finger into her lap, discreetly rolling her thumb into the hem of her shorts, using the fabric like a tissue, willing it to stem the tide.

Practice that afternoon does not go well. It's an easy steady-state run, four miles on the roads Macy ran that morning, plus drills and core. The muscles along the sides of her spine threaten to spasm, flexing in tiny little pulses like tremors before a major earthquake. Leah Stern's half step is particularly annoying, a bad habit that pushes the pace and ruins the workout for everybody else. Macy can't resist trying to close the gap Leah creates, and the result is that the team finishes the run strung out over a hundred yards rather than together as a pack. Macy's breathing catches in her throat.

The cycle of her insides eating themselves continues. By the time she gets back to Lathrop after practice she feels as though she might have explosive diarrhea, which happens sometimes when she is extraordinarily dehydrated. She can't bear the thought of dinner, but she scrounges in the storage bins under her bed for the packets of powdered electrolyte mix her parents packed for her. She watches it dissolve in a tiny water tornado, slumped against the side of her bed.

The rest of the school is in the dining hall—lingering over teas and decaf coffees, knees tucked into chests, treating the minutes between dinner and study hall like stolen time, the rare half hour during which they are accountable to no one—and so Macy has the bathroom to herself. She leans over the trough sink, so far that her hip bones knock into the hard porcelain, causing her to wince. She positions herself so that her face is mere inches from the mirror, turning her chin slowly left then right, surveying the landscape. The pores on her nose seem to widen the longer she looks. She counts a smattering of blackheads at her chin. She begins by flicking a nail across a small whitehead near her eyebrow, listening to the tiny *pop* as it bursts. She examines the damage—minimal, none really, just a little red mark where there used to be a microscopic mountaintop of pus. Leaning closer to the mirror, she places her forefingers on either side of the tip of her nose and then drags them in opposite directions, stretching the skin, before moving her fingers toward one another again. She watches as strings of discharge sprout from her pores, long and thin and solid enough to stand on end, like tiny bacterial beanstalks. She works until her nose is red and swollen and sore before training her fingertips on her chin.

This only ends one way, Macy knows, and despite her experience and the fact that she can hear her therapists' gentle preaching rattling inside her brain—*picking is a "body-focused repetitive behavior" and a "physical manifestation of your anxiety"*—she makes the same fatal error: she goes for a pore on her cheek that is not quite ready, and her fingers slip and her skin, weakened under the duress of the last twenty minutes, peels away beneath her nails, leaving a raw red crescent shape in its wake. *Fuck*, Macy thinks, and she steps away from the mirror abruptly, repulsed by her own insatiable compulsion. *Fuck fuck fuck*. Now she will have a scab. Now the situation is so much worse than when she walked in here, a pinprick carved into a crater.

She's staring at her face when the bathroom door swings open. Leah Stern is wearing pink plastic shower shoes and a teal bathrobe patterned with pink and white ice cream cones. In her left hand she holds her shower caddy—also a bright green-blue—and with her right hand she clutches her bathrobe closed at her chest. She looks like what Lauren calls "sheltered": like she hasn't seen much of the world; like she is nearer to twelve than thirty.

"Hey," Leah says.

Macy wonders how bruised and battered her face looks. Does Leah know she's been picking? "Hey."

Leah stands still for a minute, and Macy feels as though she is supposed to say something else, anything else, to compensate for the alarming spectacle of her skin.

"Ready for Saturday?" Macy asks, a heat diffusing from her ears.

"I guess. Sounds like it's a tough course." Leah doesn't lift her response like a question, but she doesn't move for the shower stalls, either.

"I think so. I almost want to skip the walk-through. I'd rather not get all worked up about that hill at mile two." Of course Macy would never skip the walk-through.

Leah nods but does not agree.

Maybe it is their surprising normalcy that makes her do it—the remarkable fact that the air does not combust with awkwardness—or maybe it's because of the adrenaline that slicks through her veins, her body's response to shame. But she has barely thought it through before the words are out of her mouth: "I hope that whatever they have planned for us tomorrow night doesn't keep us up late."

Something in Leah shifts. "Initiation?"

"Yeah." Macy groans and rolls her eyes.

Is it disappointment? Embarrassment? Leah turns to the showers as she answers, pulling back the curtain on the second corral. "I don't think I'll be participating in that."

"Oh." Macy pauses. She notices that Leah has a large whitehead at her temple, red-rimmed and pulsing, and is briefly overtaken by the desire to squeeze it. "Too bad. It'll be fun. You should think about coming."

Leah raises a single eyebrow, slightly. "Thanks. I don't think it's really my thing, though." She places her shower caddy with a thud on the shelf inside the stall. There's a metallic scrape as she slides the curtain shut behind her, leaving Macy alone under the white lights of the bathroom.

When Macy wakes the next morning it is as if from a nightmare, with the vague malaise of something not quite right. It takes her a minute to remember, and then there it is: Leah and her casual "it's not really my thing." She moves swiftly through the stages of anxiety, replaying the conversation again and again. She can sense her brain doing what it always does, shifting the lens, applying a filter, cutting and splicing. The more she replays the reel the more Leah's dismissal sours, drips with scorn. What she really meant, Macy knows, was that it shouldn't be anybody's thing. Macy wonders what it would cost to be like Leah Stern: to feel that unburdened by her classmates' expectations. To half-step her teammates on group runs. To exist mostly in a world of her own making. She could start tonight, she thinks. Whatever Initiation is—they still don't know, they still haven't been told where to be and when and what to wear and what they'll have to do and for how long—she could just say no, just skip it, just sit this one out. They would leave her alone, like everyone leaves Leah alone.

She pretends to sleep while Jade pads around the room, listening to her roommate's morning routine: drawers open and shut; the closet grinds on its rails; a zipper crunches. She can hear Jade slide on her backpack, the weight shifting against one shoulder and then the other. She is careful to shut the door quietly behind her, easing the latch into the strike so gently that the click of closure is barely audible. It is a tender enough gesture that Macy knows her roommate has forgiven her, and she tucks herself deep into her comforter, hiding inside the shame that flushes hot across her chest.

All day long, Initiation looms. Every time Macy spots a cluster of seniors together—Addison and Collier walking across the Bowl during morning break; Priya Sandhu and Karla Flores sprinkling sunflower seeds over their salads at lunch; Olivia Anderson's head in Emma Towne's lap, Olivia's legs dangling off the end of a bench outside Whitney in the early afternoon—she assumes that they are fine-tuning their plans for tonight, plotting and scheming down to the last detail. She hates them. She indulges in long fantasies of interior monologues, losing herself during biology and algebra in the exact phrasing that would make Addison and Collier see the error of their hierarchical ways.

Meanwhile, Macy's friends have started to doubt the whole thing. At lunch—where Macy makes herself a plate of salad but does not eat so much as a safe-colored chickpea—Lauren muses that the whole thing is just psychological torture, a bit of a mindfuck to keep the freshmen from feeling too comfortable.

"Maybe the torture itself *is* the initiation," she says.

"Unh-uh." Bryce shakes her head and demurs through a mouthful of turkey sandwich. "My mom said it's real."

"Did she tell you what it is?"

Bryce shakes her head again. "Just said to have fun and watch my feet."

"Watch your feet?" Jade perks up. Jade loves clues.

Bryce shrugs. "Whatever that means."

In between English and history, Macy runs back to Lathrop. She scrounges underneath her bed, pulling the storage bins and baskets one by one from where her parents puzzled them into place until she finds what she's looking for: a case of Ensure, purchased just for emergencies. She downs half a bottle right there, leaning against her bed frame, the liquid chalky in texture and muted in flavor. Before she throws the bottle in the hall recycling she peels off the label and shoves it deep inside her backpack.

At practice, Macy does her best to avoid Leah altogether. She hammers harder than she should on their shakeout to prevent Leah from half-stepping. In the end-of-practice huddle, Ms. Brown smiles and says, "Nobody roll an ankle tonight, okay?" and Kit laughs and Tasha Lyons says, "No spoilers, Coach!" and Macy feels suddenly violently nauseous, like she might vomit in the middle of the circle. The bus leaves at eight tomorrow, Ms. Brown adds, but the race isn't until eleven, so maybe bring something light to snack on: a banana, a granola bar, et cetera. As they disperse, Carol Brown puts a hand on Macy's shoulder, holding her back.

"You ready for tomorrow, Mace?"

Macy shrugs. "A little nervous about the hill at mile two."

Ms. Brown smiles, her eyes big and crinkly. "You'll be fine. You won't set a PR but I think you can still finish in the top three. Just hold your move until after the hill." She pauses, and Macy can tell she wants to say something more. She has a wild fantasy that Ms. Brown is going to tell her about Initiation, to confess exactly what's coming, because she doesn't want her star runner to blow it tonight—but when Ms. Brown speaks again all she says is, "You've seemed a little off this week," and Macy feels her heart drop with a thud into the bottom of her stomach.

"I'm sorry."

"Don't apologize. Is everything all right?"

Macy feels like she might cry. Her throat swells. The muscles around her eyebrows seem to spasm, clenching and unclenching. But she is so sick of being a source of trouble, a constant burden, always, and the whole reason she came here, to this northwestern corner of Connecticut, a thousand miles from home, was so that she *wouldn't* be a burden, so that she could have a fresh start, no more teachers eyeing her warily, nervous about her triggers and the parent phone calls and the meetings and the IEP and the e-mails from psychologists and psychiatrists.

"I'm fine," she manages. "Just a busy week, I guess."

It's obvious that Ms. Brown doesn't believe her. She tilts her head to one side, takes a minute before she speaks. "It can have a cumulative effect," she offers. "The first couple of weeks are like a vacation, you know? It doesn't hit you right away that this place is your new reality. But you'll be okay, Macy. This is the right place for you."

It is enough to make Macy's insides puddle at her navel, her body a shell.

Dinner comes and goes. When Jade is in the bathroom, Macy sneaks another Ensure from under her bed. She makes a mental note to find a garbage in the gym or over in Trask to dispose of the wrappers. The last of late summer hangs deep orange over the hills when Macy climbs into her bed, hoping that she can fall asleep and morning will come and the whole thing will have been as Lauren guessed: a ruse, an experiment; psychic torture. In the distance, a peeper chirps, maybe the season's last survivor.

She wakes to a thundering. It takes her a moment to process where she is, to orient herself in the slash of gold light that cuts underneath their door. Jade's bed is neatly made, her roommate nowhere in sight. She is able to separate the cacophony that rumbles outside her door into its discrete parts: Shouts, laughter; the stampede of feet; fists banging against doors. She has the feeling of being six or seven and playing hide-and-seek, her body stiff with giddy and irrational terror.

Macy is thinking about curling deeper into her comforter, imagining telling her friends tomorrow that she just slept through it, when her door creaks open and Tasha Lyons's head peers around the corner. "Hey, speed demon. You in or what?"

"I didn't think I had a choice."

Tasha's voice is not altogether impatient. "Believe it or not, it's not that much fun to haze someone who doesn't want to be hazed."

Macy doesn't know how to respond to this.

"You should at least come watch," Tasha says.

"Will it take a while?"

Tasha lets out a kind of exasperated laugh. "You'll be just fine for tomorrow morning." After a beat, she adds: "Come on."

Macy climbs out of bed. "Do I need shoes?"

Tasha shrugs. "You heard Coach."

The thundering is beneath them now, echoing and reverberating in the stairwell and sifting in from the cracked windows in the lounge. Macy follows Tasha down the hall and stairs, closing in on her classmates. They smack against the fire exit, and—

The first thing Macy notices is the moon, low and swollen and so bright it blots out the stars. In groups of two and five and seven Macy's classmates stampede across the silver grass. They undress as they run, unhooking bras and stumbling to peel off socks. Fully clothed seniors swarm among them, some with their phones out, flashes bursting like fireflies.

"Where are they going?" Macy asks.

"Only one way to find out." Tasha smiles. It's not an order.

Back home in Naperville, Macy would find herself night running in the winter months, when the sun sets early and rises late, daylight a matter of just eight or ten hours. She was never allowed to stray from their neighborhood, where her parents could be sure that despite the darkness she'd be safe. She'd run lollipop-shaped loops around the network of cul-de-sacs, again and again and again, until her watch read forty or fifty or sixty minutes.

She glances at Tasha, who nods encouragingly.

Her classmates have a two-hundred-yard head start on Macy, but she closes the gap quickly. In seconds she's somewhere in the front-middle of the pack, following the leaders she can't see over the hill at the gym and down into the forest. As they crash through the brush, she catches a glimpse of Linda Paulsen, their hard-nosed Dean of Students, keeping watch at the mouth of the path.

Fifty yards into the woods, they cut from the trail. Macy tears at thinned branches, her arms shielding her body. Twigs snap beneath her feet. The group slows, working through obstacles.

"I'm gonna get poison ivy!"

"There's no poison ivy here!"

"What about ticks!"

"Fuck!"

"Sorry!"

"WATCH THE STUMP!"

Their feet hit dirt, then rock. Macy hears the smack of water on skin before she realizes where they are. The creek empties into the Housatonic a half mile down the road. Her team brought her here on the third day of practice, to cool off after mile repeats in the August humidity.

She realizes that she is the only one still dressed. It's worse than being naked. She peels off her T-shirt and shorts, the latter tangling on her sneakers. She steps out of them, stacking them neatly on a rock set back from the shore.

The water hits her like knives, splashing at her waist.

"Doesn't count unless you dunk!"

The stream sears across her forehead, pinching her temples in a vise. She brings her hands to her face, sweeping water from her eyes and nose.

The seniors hoot and shout. Someone sprays champagne from the shore. To her left, Daphne and Lauren wrestle one another into the water. Someone yells at them to watch the rocks. Bryce crouches in the tide, her breasts marbled beneath the clear waves. Jade thrashes toward Macy. With her right forearm she cups the river and tosses it in her direction.

"You made it!"

Macy laughs, squeezing water from her hair. The moon has risen fully now, and out of its halo the stars squint above the trees. She dances above the jagged rocks, shifting her weight from one sharp edge to another. She nods at her roommate, electric with their mischief, relief barely outweighing all the rest, terrified and thrilled and triumphant all at once.

In the morning, Macy is slower than usual to wake. She stays in her bed for an extra minute, warm beneath the comforter she brought from her bed at home. As she bounds down the stairs to the dining hall, she realizes she feels rested for the first time in weeks. Her prerace jitters are thoroughly under control: not a trace of faint nausea, no frantic trips to the bathroom. The stairwell smells like eggs and maple syrup, and she plans her meal: Oatmeal, she thinks, and a banana, and small cup of black tea. She makes a mental note to grab an extra piece of fruit in case she gets shaky from the caffeine, which happens to her sometimes.

Between the late night and the fact that it is only 7:30 A.M. on a Saturday, Macy is not surprised that the dining hall is sparsely populated: a handful of upperclasswomen, sitting alone at random tables, crouched over their newspapers. She underestimated how much she would like the school's ban on cell phones in the dining hall; there's something charming about this view of her classmates bathed in morning light, hunched over steaming coffee and the morning news.

Jade and Lauren sit at a table in the corner. She realizes immediately that something is wrong from the way they share a paper, their heads almost touching. Suddenly the image in the dining hall is an ominous one, each unfolded newspaper a land mine waiting to explode as soon as Macy is close enough to read a headline. She imagines what they say before she can actually see them, her subconscious splicing together language from her frenzied research: *HAZING SUSPECTED IN STUDENT DEATH; STUDENT DROWNED—HAZING TO BLAME?*

She would have known, wouldn't she? If someone had fallen? If someone hadn't made it home last night? It was dark, and the shore of the creek was rocky; Macy herself felt her ankle flop on a larger-than-usual stone. It would have been easy, she imagines, for someone to have tripped and fallen face-first into the water. She's heard about deaths like this, she's sure of it: accidental drownings in mere inches of lake or pond or stream.

Jade senses Macy before she announces her arrival at their table. "Did you see this?" she says, turning her body away from the table so that the paper is in full view.

It takes Macy a moment to unscramble the words that stretch across the front page of the morning's *Hartford Courant*. When they do, the first thing she feels is a profound relief. A smile squeaks between her lips, and for a wild moment she thinks she might laugh. It bubbles in her chest.

"Honestly, I can't believe they kept it out of the news for this long," Jade says.

RAPE ACCUSATION ROCKS
LOCAL PREP SCHOOL

Next to her, Lauren takes a drag of her coffee and shakes her head. "My mom is going to lose it."

"Your mom reads the *Courant*?"

A former student at the all-girls Atwater School in Canaan is seeking legal action against the institution over its mishandling of an accusation she made while enrolled, the *Courant* finds. Karen Mirro, 38, was a senior at Atwater in the fall of 1995 when she says she was raped by a male faculty member in his on-campus apartment.

"Why is she suing the school and not this guy?"

"'Because Mirro was eighteen at the time,'" Lauren reads, "'the alleged rape falls outside Connecticut's statute of limitations for sex crimes.'"

"But that just means he can't be prosecuted, not that he can't be *sued*," Macy explains.

"True," Jade says, nodding. "I mean, the school is a bigger fish, right? More money."

But something about this doesn't sit right with Macy. She thinks about Linda Paulsen, arms folded at the edge of the woods, her presence at Initiation a kind of tacit permission, adult supervision. "Maybe she feels like it's partially the school's fault," she offers.

Lauren looks up from the paper, wrinkling her nose. "Hmm, you might be right," she says, skimming the article quickly. "Sounds like she's saying that they expelled her as retaliation." She clears her throat and reads aloud: "'Mirro contends that her expulsion was handed down in retribution for her allegation against a beloved faculty member—'"

"Does the article name the teacher?" Macy interrupts.

"Unh-uh," Jade shakes her head. "But we've got a date now. Shouldn't be that hard to figure out which of the current male teachers were also employed here in '95."

Macy nods.

"I've gotta tell Bryce," Lauren says, sitting up abruptly. "Can I take this copy? You guys can grab another one from the stand?"

Jade lifts her elbows from where they hold down the paper and turns up her palms. "Be my guest."

"Oh, hey, Mace—Louisa Manning is sitting in the back. You should go talk to her about the *Heron*," Lauren says, by way of parting.

"Don't you have to get ready to go?" Jade interrupts Macy's sizing up of the dining hall.

Without looking at Jade, Macy says: "I thought it was going to be about last night."

"What?"

"When I saw you guys reading. I thought—I thought maybe something happened last night."

The look Jade gives Macy isn't wholly confused. She pauses and tilts her chin in Macy's direction. "Well, you weren't *totally* wrong about some shit going down this weekend, I guess."

Macy cringes. Shame flares in her gut. But she knows it's meant as an olive branch, and so she forces a laugh. "Can't say I didn't tell you so," she says.

"Hey," Jade adds, lifting the paper again, "don't forget to grab something to eat. Can't race on an empty stomach."

Macy grunts noncommittally. Instead of turning and heading for the hot food bar—she probably would have been overdoing it with the oatmeal, anyway—she heads for the back of the dining hall, weaving through the round tables toward the double doors that spill into Lathrop's foyer. These are off-limits during dinner for reasons Macy hasn't completely figured out (probably to maintain an orderly flow of traffic through the food stations), but weekend brunch is a more leisurely affair. Plus, there's not a single faculty member in sight. As she walks, the *Courant* beams up at her from every occupied table.

Louisa is wearing an Atwater half-zip above heathered gray sweatpants. Her feet are tucked beneath her; her Birkenstocks are kicked off at odd angles on the floor. She is so engrossed in the newspaper that she doesn't look up as Macy approaches.

"Louisa?"

"Mmm?" For a second, Louisa keeps her head lowered. When she lifts her chin to Macy, she taps her glasses up the bridge of her nose. "Oh, hey."

"Hi."

"So how was Initiation?"

Macy shrugs.

"Yeah," Louisa says, leaning back in her chair. "Lotta fuss over nothing. So—you coming to meeting on Monday?"

"Actually, that's why I wanted to talk to you—"

Louisa sits up, unfolding her legs. Her feet search the floor beneath the table blindly, tapping in the direction of her sandals until her toes find the cork bottoms. She wriggles beneath the leather straps. And then she taps the *Courant* in front of her. "You want to help us get to the bottom of this?"

"Well, I'm not a great writer," Macy says, and then, just in case Louisa might misinterpret her honesty as fishing-for-compliments self-deprecation, she adds, "I'm much better at math and science."

Louisa nods like she's thinking it over. She curls her bottom lip slightly inside her top, as if she's biting it inside her mouth. "I bet you're a hell of a researcher, then," she says, after a beat. "And I bet you don't give up easy."

Does she know about how Macy's mind refuses to let a single thing go? Macy's therapists were always telling her to *interrogate her anxiety*: to look beneath the "superficial obsession" for a root cause. Although she might be fixating, for example, on the failed joke in the group text (the one to which her friends only replied "ha"), the problem was not her sense of humor but rather a profound insecurity within those friendships themselves. But it was rarely this simple: What possible good reason was there—for instance—for the meltdown over the birthday cake she made for her dad's fiftieth birthday, the one she tried to decorate to look like the tie-dye T-shirt he wore on Sunday mornings but that instead came out looking like muddy water, too many colors of frosting swirled too close together? *It's dirty like Dad's shirt, too,* Macy's mother had said, trying for laughter when logic failed. But there was Macy, heaving with sobs at her disaster of a dessert until she gagged and then literally vomited.

"Don't you think that having all the facts would make us feel a little bit better?" Louisa adds.

Maybe her behavior this week wasn't a total mystery. Maybe she knew—somehow—that something felt unsafe about this place, and she only *thought* the danger was Initiation: an irrational obsession sourced from a rational worry. *What do people see when they look at me,* Macy always wondered. *What do they know?* Is it possible that in Macy Louisa perceives a worthy ally, somebody else with good instincts and an ability to trust her intuition?

Of course it's probably not anything like that. Louisa probably just thinks of Macy as an endurance athlete, dogged and gritty. She probably just thinks of Macy as a runner.

To: Atwater Parents Association <<APA@TheAtwaterSchool.org>>; Atwater Alumnae Association <<AAA@TheAtwaterSchool.org>>
From: brodiep@TheAtwaterSchool.org
Date: Oct 5, 2015, 4:27 P.M.
Subject: From the Desk of Patricia Brodie

Atwater Families and esteemed Alumnae,

By now, I imagine that most of you have read the article published in the *Hartford Courant* on September 26. For those of you who have not—and in an effort to fully acknowledge the content of the article, and to recognize and assuage any concerns that we as a school are evading conversation on the matter—I've linked to the piece below my signature. I am reaching out now in an effort to provide some context for the reporting and to explain our decision-making surrounding the matter over the course of the last three months.

We were first made aware of the allegations outlined in the story in July, when the Board of Trustees was contacted by attorneys representing Karen Mirro. We did not make the news public for two very simple reasons: first, it was important to us to protect the confidentiality of the involved parties; second, and most practically speaking, the legal contours of the case prohibited us from doing so. Although the *Courant* has entered the story into the public discourse, these two points remain true. Nevertheless, we've heard from many of you who feel that the school has been less than forthright in its communication; your feedback matters to us, and we intend to reexamine our policies and procedures for gaps in transparency. We welcome your suggestions, which you may send to my attention or to the Board.

Every day, we talk to our girls about the importance of collaboration and the sustaining power of community. We hope that you will join us in our efforts to learn and grow, and that together we can contribute to Atwater's two-hundred-year-legacy of leadership in the advancement of women and girls. Should you find yourself on campus, my door is always open.

Be well,
Patricia Brodie
Head of School

RAPE ACCUSATION ROCKS
LOCAL PREP SCHOOL

By Amanda Lucas

Updated September 27, 2015, 7:32 A.M.

FALLS VILLAGE, CT—A former student at the all-girls Atwater School in Canaan is seeking legal action against the institution over its mishandling of an accusation she made while enrolled, the *Courant* finds. Karen Mirro, 38, was a senior at Atwater in the fall of 1995 when she says she was raped by a male faculty member in his on-campus apartment. Mirro alleges that the school failed to investigate her claim, and that she later faced retaliation for her accusation.

According to documents obtained by the *Courant*, Mirro states that she reported the rape to school administrators, who encouraged her to take a leave of absence to tend to her mental health. She declined this course of action. One month later, Mirro was found smoking cigarettes in the woods behind campus. Possession of nicotine products on school property was then and is now a violation of a school "Fundamental Standard." According to Atwater's website, a Fundamental Standard is a "pillar of the school's community expectations," and violation of a Standard may result in dismissal from the school. Mirro was offered the opportunity to withdraw from Atwater to avoid the appearance of an expulsion on her official disciplinary record, and she left campus in November 1995.

Mirro, whose representatives declined to comment for this story, claims in her suit that although expulsion was delineated as one in a course of possible consequences for her behavior, it was uncommonly administered. She contends that her punishment was handed down in retribution for her allegation against a beloved faculty member, who, she maintains, was allowed to remain on campus.

Because Mirro was eighteen at the time, the alleged rape falls outside Connecticut's statute of limitations for sex crimes. In seeking recourse through a civil suit against the school, Mirro seeks damages in an amount equal to the cost of her treatment needs both previously incurred and forthcoming.

Atwater is ranked among the top girls' schools in the country, with an alumnae network that includes senators, cabinet members, Silicon Valley executives, and countless industry pioneers. School officials did not immediately respond to a request for comment.

Vol. CCII,

Issue No. I

The basement of Atwater's main academic building is, technically, a fully functional educational space: the southern wing houses a series of low-ceilinged classrooms, filled with standard rectangular tables and chairs; the corridor that runs beneath the front of the building holds the tech help desk and the facilities hub and a copy room; a donor paid for an old computer lab to be converted into a small black box theater for drama classes. The hallways throughout are peppered with random furniture: sagging couches lugged from dorm lounges, clustered in twos and threes around faded antique rugs. Along the walls above the polished concrete floors, generations of students have pieced together fragments of murals: portraits of distinguished alumnae; the Litchfield Hills rendered in the style of *Starry Night*; a cluster of animals, exploding from a central source like flower petals, an elephant's ear blossoming from the mane of a roaring lion.

It's here where the staff of Atwater's student newspaper meets once a week, in a room at the very end of the wing that runs below the building's northern edge, through a door beneath a rounded alcove. At some point, someone painted a series of birds in flight in inky black above the archway, seven winged shadows curving up and away from the doorframe. Louisa Manning likes to think that it was a member of the *Heron* staff who did it, maybe the newspaper's art director in the nineties, someone with the skills to tattoo the cement bricks with precision but with the writerly morality of a journalist—the tiny crows a relative of the heron but also symbolic of the First Amendment itself: freedom of speech, freedom of the press; freedom.

Last year in English class, Ms. Edwards asked Louisa's class to write about their favorite place on campus. Louisa, a sophomore at the time, wrote three pages about the *Heron* room, from the birds in flight to the cracks in the cement walls to the row of old desktop computers they use for layout, one of which is missing the "K" on the keyboard. She wrote about how it smells like mold and old pizza—usually because there actually *is* old pizza somewhere, graying on the coffee tables pushed between the couches or stacked in boxes on top of the trash bins—and how one time they found a dead mouse in the closet that had, probably, been dead for years, half its carcass subsumed by the fraying carpet, a mass of bones and synthetic fibers knotted together over time. She wrote about how you might think the room would be dark and airless, but that because they meet in the afternoons the setting sun catches in the aboveground windows that graze the room's ceiling, filling their work space with rays of warm evening light two-thirds of the year. In the end, what Louisa wrote in response to Ms. Edwards's assignment was unmistakably a love letter, and she tacked it to the bulletin board in the *Heron* room, next to the clips they saved of particularly hilarious or otherwise egregious typos (like the time they forgot to fill in the copy of an entire article and so where they'd meant to run a story on student pressure they'd printed a feature comprised of Latin placeholder text instead) and outtakes from their headshots and random memes and several cut-ups of *Peanuts* strips featuring a creatively frustrated Snoopy, tapping away on his typewriter atop his doghouse.

The room is why Louisa is always the first person at *Heron* meetings: Because there is literally nowhere else on campus that she'd rather be. Now that she's a coeditor, arriving early seems like the responsible thing to do—but in Louisa's mind, that's just icing on the cake. Normally, she uses the quiet time to get a little homework done, but today Louisa can't focus on anything but the meeting. She runs through the to-do list in her head: Final copy edits with Anjali; layout tweaks with Mia; the finishing touches on their editors' letter; plans for the announcement at Morning Meeting on Thursday, when their first issue will drop. She always has a slightly caffeinated adrenaline buzz during print week, but this time she feels it more acutely than ever before.

"I had an idea." Louisa hears Mia before she sees her, their senior art director announcing her arrival in a droll pitch that matches her Doc Martens and her frayed denim.

Louisa first met Mia Tavoletti when she joined the *Daily Heron*'s writing staff as a freshman. Mia was a sophomore and editor of the Opinion pages, forever filing her stories late and complaining that the name *The Daily Heron* was stupid because (1) they weren't a daily, and (2) the *Heron*/ "Herald" wordplay was the "least original thing in the entire universe." But the truth was that—even if she showed up late, and even then only to sit at the outer edge of the group with her legs dangling from the table—Mia never missed a meeting. When Riya, a senior and art director at the time, would be stuck in the *Heron* room doing layout late the night before deadline, Mia would order a pizza and sit with her.

"What are you doing here?"

"What do you mean?"

"I mean, you've literally never been early to a meeting before."

Mia flings her backpack onto the chair in front of her computer. "*That's* because we've never done anything this interesting before."

Louisa rolls her eyes.

"Don't give me that look. Listen, I know you think this whole enterprise is like some noble civic duty, but I mean—come on." Mia taps her login into the computer and clicks open InDesign.

"What's your idea?"

"Right." Mia spins around in her chair. "So I know that we decided that we weren't going to include all the data from Macy and Bryce's survey in the print issue, but I think we should make a graphic of the full results for digital."

Louisa cocks her head to one side. Usually, the *Heron*'s digital version is just a PDF of the print format, accessible as a download from a link they distribute the day the issue drops. They were always talking to their faculty adviser, Ms. Doyle, about launching a proper website, but Mrs. Brodie had "reservations about a public-facing enterprise."

"That would change how we do digital, wouldn't it?"

Mia nods. "Well, I was thinking about that, because we only have three days."

"Two, really." They sent the file to their printer on Wednesday night.

"Sure. Whatever. Anyway, not enough time to build a whole new concept. But, realistically, I have enough time to design a graphic and insert two new pages into the file."

Louisa raises an eyebrow. Issue in and issue out, Mia's procrastination is the editor's chief source of anxiety. More than once, she's emailed the file to their printer literally one minute before their deadline. But Mia has a point here, in that the survey the freshmen developed might be worth the stress this time: 278 of Atwater's 342 students responded to Bryce and Macy's questionnaire, and although the Google Form was hardly scientific, there were some compelling numbers (e.g., although Louisa had never been sent an unsolicited dick pic, apparently over 30 percent of her classmates had).

"And! I know you're going to say that I barely get layout done in time as it is, *but* I can add the graphic *after* I've sent the issue to the printer, because the PDF doesn't have to be ready for public view until the morning."

"So you'll pull an all-nighter for the sake of data journalism?"

"It would be my honor to make such a sacrifice." Mia puts a hand to her chest.

Louisa laughs. "Okay, let's talk about it after meeting. And let me run it by Anjali."

As the room slowly fills—the new freshmen, Macy and Bryce, both staff writers, are the next to arrive, followed by Brie Feldman (Arts) and Kit Eldridge (Sports), and finally Hitomi Sakano (Opinion) and Anjali—Louisa looks over the outline on their whiteboard. They've done theme issues before—they did one on climate change last year, with contributing pieces by alumnae who worked as environmental scientists and in environmental policy, and one her freshman year for Atwater's bicentennial—but this one is different, and not just because of the topic.

There's the interview Brie did with the alumna filmmaker who made a documentary about sexual assault in the military. There's the feature Kit wrote about Title IX and the interview she did with an alumna who works as a counselor to victims of sexual assault. The Opinion section is twice as long this issue, in the format of letters instead of editorials, from alumnae who believe Karen Mirro. She and Anjali pitched the issue as one designed to explore how Atwater equipped its young women with an understanding of healthy relationships, and although Louisa wasn't sure they had delivered on *exactly* this, they had created something that reflected their community's understanding of sex and sexual violence. It placed the *Hartford Courant* article and Karen Mirro's case in the broader context of a cultural issue. In a world where the lens that framed the conversation about sex was always chosen by the grown-ups, this was their chance to say: *This is what it looks like to us.*

Anjali sidles up next to Louisa. She wears a Brown crewneck sweatshirt. Before she speaks, she pushes her sleeves up to the crook of her elbow, like a male senator signaling that he's getting ready to work. Anjali's sister is a junior at Brown, and Anjali is applying early decision in a few weeks. Louisa read her essay, about how everyone assumes she is quite literally from India, or at least the daughter of immigrants (in reality, she is the granddaughter of immigrants on her father's side). It was funny but, in Louisa's opinion, a little bit done-before. But it was just Brown, and so it was probably fine.

"All right everybody," Anjali yells. "Listen up!"

From her usual spot in the back by the computers, Mia smacks the table loudly. "Hey! Listen to Anjali."

The room quiets. "Thanks, Mia. Okay, so, we've got forty-eight hours to get this thing in shape. You know the drill: Get with your editing partner and do a final round of copy edits. Make sure you've loaded your work into InCopy before you leave today, so that Mia can get cranking on layout."

"Bryce and Macy," Louisa adds: "We need to talk to you about your survey."

Brie and Kit make a low *ooooohing* sound, like middle schoolers when a classmate is sent to the principal's office.

"Real mature, guys," Louisa chides. "This is a finishing touches day, everybody, and I don't need to explain how important this issue is. We want it to be good."

"Don't we always want it to be good?" Brie asks.

Louisa raises an eyebrow. "Of course. But we all know that the administration hasn't exactly invited our input on this particular subject. This is our opportunity to be heard."

"Right," Anjali chimes in. "Not to get all sentimental or anything, but: We could make some real change with this."

In the back corner, Mia rolls her eyes.

"All right," Louisa jumps in, before Anjali starts to moralize about student voice and institutional transparency, her favorite topics this year. "Let's get to work, everybody."

In a few minutes the room has settled into its usual murmur of productivity, keyboards clacking intermittently, low-level conversation here and there, the groan of the furniture as someone shifts her weight. Louisa and Anjali take their usual spots at the table next to Mia, and Louisa pulls up her browser to their draft of the editors' letter. Unwrapping a granola bar, Anjali scans the language.

"I dunno, I still think it's too . . . restrained," she says.

Louisa reads the introduction: *For over two centuries, Atwater has worked to advance the progress of women and girls . . .* "Well, we said we wanted to write something neutral," Louisa argues.

"Yeah, I know, but I think that, ultimately"—Anjali pauses, chewing, her cheek protruding as she digs for a piece of granola wedged in her back teeth—"we didn't exactly produce an issue that is *neutral*. It's fairly reported, sure, but it definitely sets out to establish that the school, you know, needs to . . . I don't know, step up as a leader in this particular . . ." She searches for the word: "realm."

Louisa nods, mulling it over. Anjali is a little bit prone to drama— again, this is why Brown makes sense for her—and that's why they make a good team as coeditors. Louisa is more restrained, more disciplined, more reasonable. Anjali is impulsive, bighearted, always looking for a cause.

"Hey, gang!" Ms. Doyle teaches American Lit in addition to advising the *Heron*. She's tiny—five foot two, 115 pounds, if Louisa had to guess—with chin-length brown hair that falls across her face when she speaks, which she does animatedly. Unlike most female teachers who carry their things in tote bags, Ms. Doyle uses a backpack—urban and slightly masculine, squared off at the corners, a Japanese brand Louisa has never seen anywhere else. She has a high-pitched voice and piercing blue eyes.

There's a chorus of return greetings—*Hey, Ms. D; What's up, Ms. Doyle?*—that Ms. Doyle waves off as she settles her backpack onto an empty chair and unwinds her scarf.

"How're things?" She directs her first question to Anjali and Louisa.

"Louisa and I are just tweaking our letter," Anjali says, and Louisa resists the urge to glare at her coeditor. "We think it needs to match the tone of the issue a little bit more."

"Mmm." Ms. Doyle nods, thinking. In the pause that opens between them, Louisa sizes up their adviser. She notices that her eyes are red-rimmed, and that the circles underneath are darker than usual—something beyond the general perpetual tiredness of most people Louisa's parents' age. So she is not all that surprised when Ms. Doyle takes a breath and says, "Listen, girls: I need to talk to you both."

Louisa feels her stomach somersault, like when she was a little girl and her elementary school teachers would catch her reading during math, a chapter book propped inside her desk, the fear that she was in *real* trouble quickly usurped by embarrassment that she was so *uncool*, so afraid of disappointing her teachers.

"What's up?" Anjali asks.

"Can we step outside for a minute?"

"For sure," Anjali says, and they rise from their chairs and follow Ms. Doyle out into the hallway alcove.

"I'm so sorry, girls," Ms. Doyle begins. "I know you've put a lot of hard work into this issue, and—there's just no easy way to say this . . ."

Anjali and Louisa exchange a glance. It's clear to Louisa that Anjali is experiencing the same mild panic that floods Louisa's bloodstream.

When Ms. Doyle finally speaks, Louisa has the disorienting sensation of déjà vu, as if she's inside her own dream: "Mrs. Brodie has decided that it is not in the best interests of the school to publish this special issue of the *Heron*."

"What?"

"I know that you both wanted to produce seven issues this year, so canceling this current issue might require adjusting that goal, but I really think—I think these are circumstances beyond your control."

"It's not just about printing an extra issue," Anjali squeaks, and her voice chokes at the edges, caught in her throat. She looks like she might start crying.

"I think we feel really proud of *this* issue," Louisa says, trying to finish what her coeditor cannot.

"I know that," Ms. Doyle says.

Louisa waits for her to say more; when she doesn't, Louisa asks: "Why?"

Ms. Doyle brings her left hand to her forehead and rubs her temple briefly before tucking her hair behind her ear. "The school is really under a lot of scrutiny right now," Ms. Doyle says, repeating a phrase Louisa has heard ricocheting around the halls since Karen Mirro's yard signs appeared on Opening Day. "I think there's a desire that we present a unified front."

"What does that mean?"

Louisa extends a hand to Anjali's shoulder, a kind of sympathetic but warning tap.

Ms. Doyle nods. "It means that the school newspaper cannot publish the letters of alumnae who support Karen Mirro," she says.

"So we'll cut that section," Louisa says. She had concerns about the portion anyway: They'd sourced the letters via the private Facebook group for *Heron* alumnae, and although the responses themselves were sent to and filtered through Ms. Doyle, Louisa was nonetheless concerned that the feedback they'd received represented a degree of groupthink, something their adviser was always cautioning them against. They hadn't received a single letter that articulated support for the school's handling of the scandal, either in 1995 or now. Three of the letters claimed to be from Karen's classmates.

"I offered the same compromise to Mrs. Brodie. I also suggested that we print some articles that present a more balanced view of the reality . . . letters from alumnae who believe the school always provided a safe environment for them to learn and grow, for example; an interview with an attorney who has defended people against false accusations of rape and assault—"

"That doesn't happen," Anjali spits.

"Well, it *does*, but I'll admit it does not happen all that frequently—"

"Less than ten percent of accusations of *reported* rapes are false," Anjali says. "And only about twenty percent of rapes are reported to the police. It's in Brie's article."

"—but I thought it might help Mrs. Brodie to see that we weren't trying to . . . undermine the school in any way."

"We're *not*," Louisa says, hating how her voice sounds when she pleads.

"*I* know that. And, honestly, I think Mrs. Brodie knows that, too. But she is in the difficult position of having to defend the school's reputation right now, and I think that means that she is extra cautious about doing anything . . . controversial."

Anjali's jaw hangs half-open.

"So—so this is final?" Louisa asks. "Can we meet with Mrs. Brodie and try to change her mind?"

Ms. Doyle shrugs. "I can't tell you *not* to reach out to the Head of School. But I can tell you that I'm not sure it will do any good."

"We've never had to get her permission before," Anjali argues. "I mean, this seems like a violation of the First Amendment."

Ms. Doyle laughs, quietly, a sympathetic chuckle. "Unfortunately, school newspapers are subject to a lower level of First Amendment protection. *Hazelwood versus Kuhlmeier*," Ms. Doyle says, emphasizing the *cool* in the last name. "1988 Supreme Court ruling."

"Well, that's bullshit," Anjali says, and Louisa briefly wonders if her coeditor means the ruling itself or the ease with which Ms. Doyle called it up as evidence.

"Maybe," Ms. Doyle says. "But it's the world we're writing in."

"I mean, the *Heron* isn't some piece of marketing material. If it was then Communications would produce it."

"I know," Ms. Doyle says. "Listen—I think there's a way that some of the work you've done for this issue can be incorporated into a new one. Brie's piece, for example—it's really a standard alum profile. We can definitely hang on to that one."

"What about the survey? Eighty percent of the school participated in it. Does Mrs. Brodie know about that? That she's effectively just disappearing their feedback?"

Ms. Doyle sighs, so deeply and exaggeratedly that it reminds Louisa of a breathing pattern they learned last year during a workshop on "mindfulness": inhale for five seconds, hold for one, exhale for eight. "Mrs. Brodie would like to hold on to that information for sharing at a faculty meeting later this year. Perhaps I can persuade her to invite you ladies to present the data." Normally, it is quite an honor to be a student guest at an Atwater faculty meeting, and one bestowed on only one or two students per year—or sometimes none at all.

Anjali blinks, unmoved by Ms. Doyle's half-invitation. "So—that's it?"

"What are we going to tell the staff?" Louisa asks.

"I'll take care of that," Ms. Doyle says. "You guys shouldn't have to explain this."

Louisa came to Atwater from Pittsburgh via Dubai. In eighth grade, her father—an engineer and executive for a major oil company—was reassigned again, and they were heading back and deeper into the American West when Louisa made her father promise that if she started over at some high school in Wyoming that she wouldn't have to move again in two years. When her father couldn't promise that—when he said, actually, that it was really unlikely they'd be in Wyoming longer than eighteen months—Louisa announced that she wanted to go to boarding school. At first, her mother had flat-out refused: they could have separated the family long ago, let Louisa's father continent jump while Louisa and her mother stayed put in the town house in Shadyside or, before that, the oversize craftsman in Seattle. But they had decided to keep the family together, because wasn't that the most important thing?

So Louisa made a list, and sent emails to admissions representatives at schools, and within two weeks she had prepared a presentation for her parents that she delivered on a Tuesday night after dinner. She chose all-girls schools not necessarily because she believed in the confidence-building benefits of a single-gender education (as their websites promised) but simply because she thought her more traditional Korean parents might be more open to the idea if she took sex out of the equation. There was Miss Hall's, nestled in the Berkshires in western Massachusetts, a reasonable safety school for her; there was Foxcroft, in Virginia, which was maybe a little too Southern culturally and where every girl learned to ride a horse; there was Miss Porter's, in central Connecticut, the most prestigious of the all-girls schools; there was Ethel Walker, also in Connecticut, another school where every girl learned to ride a horse. And, finally, there was Atwater, tucked in the Litchfield Hills, where white-collar lawyers and Westchester bankers sent their daughters instead of Manhattan's Chapin or Brearley or Spence. Louisa liked Atwater from the start: its proximity to the city, for one ("Just a quick train ride away," the admissions counselor told her), and that the girls didn't have to wear a uniform.

At first, the compromise was that Louisa's mother would get an apartment nearby, and Louisa would be among the small cohort of Atwater's day students, a group that mostly consisted of the children of successful creative types who'd decamped from New York lofts to farmhouse fixer-uppers but whose careers still necessitated proximity to the city. In Louisa's mind, this was an obviously laughably ludicrous idea. (Why couldn't they just stay in Dubai, then? Why hadn't they stayed in Pittsburgh? If they were going to do that, then she wanted to look at other elite day schools: Castilleja near San Francisco; Harvard-Westlake in Los Angeles. If that's the plan, she argued, then she reserved the right to begin her research from scratch, choosing any place in the world.) For Louisa, though, the whole experiment wasn't just about the ability to stay put for four years, to see one high school all the way through; she liked the *idea* of boarding school, liked the bubble-like insularity of one in the middle of her changing world. In a lifetime defined by traveling in tow, boarding school would be a destiny of her own choosing.

In the middle of study hall, when she should be working her way through *The Scarlet Letter*, the conversation with Ms. Doyle clangs around Louisa's brain. She rehearses an interior monologue of all the things she should have said, a lengthy list of all the reasons this issue of the *Heron* deserved to be published. On her computer, next to the tabs she has open for her homework—Atwater's online learning platform, PowerSchool, which provides real-time reporting of her GPA, so she can watch the decimals fluctuate out to the hundredths as her teachers enter grades; dictionary.com, so she can look up words like "sepulchre" and "sumptuary" and "phantasmagoric" as she reads; Shmoop, not because she isn't doing the reading, but because it helps her to read more quickly if she scans a summary first—she has open the *Heron*'s shared-drive folder, where the staff keeps their writing until they load it into InCopy.

She clicks open the editors' letter. Anjali was right, she thinks: It's too detached. In her effort to write something neutral, she said nothing at all. There is no mention of Karen Mirro or her allegation; as far as the letter is concerned, the *Heron* staff chose to run this special issue without any particular inspiration or impetus.

Louisa doesn't know if Karen Mirro is telling the truth. Before they thought of the special issue, the plan was to write a feature on her allegation. It would be a real piece of investigative journalism. Louisa had spent hours in the library poring over yearbooks from the midnineties, hunting for any clues: what clubs Karen did, what sports she played, who her friends might have been based on group photos in the collages that peppered each book. She wanted to know what kind of girl Karen was—was she a jock? A loner outsider? An artist? Did she get drunk in the woods behind campus? Did she go to New York during the weekends?

The 1996 yearbook in particular became a focal point of Louisa's obsession: she spent long stretches staring at the space where Karen's picture should have been, as if the slim rectangle between *Kimberly Michaels* and *Melissa Moody* might suddenly open like a chasm, a maw of answers. She studied like a map the class picture taken on graduation, desperate to ask each girl cradling a red rose in a long white dress what she knew about their erstwhile classmate. Was she someone who deserved to get kicked out, someone for whom smoking cigarettes was just an unfortunate last straw, an anticlimax in a series of greater offenses? And what about the man Karen said raped her: Did they know who he was? And what happened to him?

And maybe this is where she should have known, should have realized what was coming: Ms. Doyle guided them away from a feature on Karen herself and the allegation. If the *Courant* hadn't broken all the details with the resources of an entire fully funded newsroom, she'd said, then it was unlikely that the *Heron* could do it with a half-dozen writers inside four weeks. Plus, she'd added: Even if they were to cultivate leads, they were likely to reach a number of dead ends due to the confidentiality that governed the case's ongoing legal proceedings.

Ultimately they decided, together, to do an issue on sexual assault and healthy relationships *generally*. They'd talk to psychologists and lawyers and public health experts. They'd survey the Atwater student body to gauge their understanding of and feelings about sexual violence. They might not know what happened to Karen Mirro, but they were vaguely aware that the laws of forward progress dictated that the landscape should have improved in the twenty years since her accusation; had it? And if not, why not? It was smart: A trapdoor into the controversy. Ms. Doyle herself had helped them open it. And then she shut it.

A bubble blinks in the top corner of Louisa's screen, alerting her to an iMessage from Anjali.

How r u feeling?

Annoyed?

Same

> I just keep going over it in my head.

tbh I don't blame Ms. Doyle tho

> Really?

This surprises Louisa. Between them, Anjali is the hot-tempered one.

Yea I mean I think she seemed pretty upset too

U know?

> I guess so.

> I still think she should have stood up for us though.

Maybe she did tho

We don't know what Brodie said

> Do you think there's anything else we can do?

> We still have time

Louisa watches the ellipses appear and disappear as Anjali types, deletes, retypes.

Maybe we *should* ask Brodie for a meeting?

She has office hours on Tuesdays

Louisa considers this. She can count on one hand the number of conversations she's had with Patricia Brodie: she spoke to her at an Accepted Students' Day after she was admitted; at the end of each academic year, Mrs. Brodie visited the *Heron* room to thank the staff for its service to the school; and during her sophomore year, Mrs. Brodie sat in on Louisa's history class and held her back afterward to express how impressed she was with Louisa's questions. It was generally Louisa's understanding that Mrs. Brodie did two things for the school: she made the rules, and she visited alumnae to ask for money.

Okay.

* * *

Mrs. Brodie's office is cavernous. It is also, technically, from what Louisa can tell, at least three rooms in one. Her assistant, Ms. Hanifin, has her own office that functions as a kind of waiting area for visitors, which is where Louisa and Anjali sat in spindle-backed chairs for twelve minutes while they waited for Mrs. Brodie, who was—predictably, Ms. Hanifin said—running behind schedule. From Ms. Hanifin's office they were ushered by Mrs. Brodie herself into the Head's office, which was at least twice the size of any classroom in Schoolhouse (although, it should be noted, not any larger than the science classrooms). The back of the room features a three-sided picture window, from which Mrs. Brodie and her guests can see the forest and the Litchfield Hills, alight as they are now with the full spectrum of fall foliage: amber-tinged maple leaves and bloodred oaks and bright, Crayola-yellow poplars. In front of the window, facing into the room, three tables are puzzled together to make a kind of three-sided desk; to the left of the desk as they walk in, a round and heavy-bottomed table centers four chairs like those Louisa and Anjali waited in. Beyond the table, another door is halfway open, revealing in the shadows the contours of Mrs. Brodie's private bathroom. This makes sense to Louisa, who finds herself imagining how awkward it would be for everyone involved if Mrs. Brodie had to poop in a stall in one of the regular bathrooms. She realizes she's smirking, imagining the absurdity of Mrs. Brodie pooping, and she curls her bottom lip beneath her teeth, biting back the nervous laughter that threatens to burst forth.

Mrs. Brodie seems to fit the room she occupies, which is not to say that she is cavernous but that she is equally impressive: tall, thin, with angled cheekbones and beady, dark eyes. Today she is in her standard uniform—a kind of androgynous set popular among serious and still-working women in their sixties and seventies, khakis beneath a turtleneck and a red cardigan, topped with a patterned silk scarf tied in a loose knot, centered at her sternum. Louisa imagines that Mrs. Brodie was pretty in her own way, once, in the way that skinny and angular people are.

Mrs. Brodie slides a chair from where it's nestled at the edge of the round table, and motions for the girls to do the same. She places her palms in her lap and leans back in her chair and smiles at the girls; as if by reflex, Louisa smiles in return.

"Thanks so much for making the time, ladies. I know how busy you girls are." This opening statement strikes Louisa as absolutely ludicrous. As busy and overextended as Louisa perpetually feels—in this very moment she is reviewing the to-do list she keeps shelved in the back corner of her skull, a running tab of homework and projects and pages to read and emails to answer and summer program deadlines—she knows they are not, in fact, any busier than the Head of School.

"I also want to thank you both for all the time and effort you've put into the *Heron* over the years," Mrs. Brodie continues. "A vibrant and widely read student newspaper is absolutely essential to our community health and identity. Would you believe me if I told you I still keep the front page of our bicentennial issue on my fridge?" She says this with such wide-eyed delight that Louisa leans back slightly, the back of her rib cage crunching against the chair. And then Mrs. Brodie allows her face to drop, her smile to shift to a frown, her eyebrows to inch toward one another. "Now," she says, "I understand that you're feeling a little disappointed about changing direction for the first issue."

Louisa notices that Mrs. Brodie does not use any specific noun to direct the change, as though the *change in direction* is happening of its own accord, as if by magic. Next to her, Anjali shifts forward in her seat, cocking her chin at an upward-tilting angle.

"We worked really hard on this issue, Mrs. Brodie. We believe that it's fair, and well reported, and well reasoned." Anjali and Louisa had gone over their talking points during lunch. They were to focus on the quality of the writing and the judiciousness with which they'd selected their features. At some point, they would pivot to the significance of the topic matter, which they would pitch as relevant regardless of the Karen Mirro situation.

"I believe you," Mrs. Brodie nods. "And I wish we could all share in your work. I really do."

"If we cut the alumnae letters," Louisa interjects, "the issue will be free of any reference to Karen Mirro or the ongoing . . . um, case." Louisa didn't know if a lawsuit was technically a *case*, but it seemed against their best interests to use the word "scandal."

Mrs. Brodie nods again. Louisa looks at Anjali. "And yet," she begins, lowering her chin and peering over the top of her tiny, delicate, wire-framed glasses: "It wouldn't be hard to make the connection, yes?"

Anjali and Louisa exchange a look.

"What if . . ." Louisa pauses, the nervousness of a new idea pulsing at her temples: "What if its relevance *is* exactly the reason—from a public relations perspective—to publish it?"

Anjali's head whips in Louisa's direction, her eyebrows raised. Louisa has veered far off script.

"And what do you mean by that, Louisa?" Mrs. Brodie drops her chin a degree more.

"If we cut the Opinion section, with the alumna letters, then the issue could be received and interpreted as an effort on the school's part to cultivate a healthy and safe environment"—Louisa realizes her sentence has brought her to a cliff, and the cliff is the word "sex," which she would rather die than say in this room to Mrs. Brodie—"where, um, relationships are concerned."

Actually, Louisa does not have a hard time imagining Mrs. Brodie having sex. She's old, sure—maybe sixty-five, sixty-eight—but she's really kind of elegant, and it's sort of fascinating to imagine a time when she might let her guard down.

"So," Louisa continues, emboldened by the fact that Mrs. Brodie has not yet interrupted her or otherwise kicked her out of their office, "in a way, publishing the issue supports the idea that Atwater is a place that protects and nurtures not only the academic growth but also the social-emotional well-being of its girls." Louisa remembers that phrase—"social-emotional well-being"—from the Peer Educator application, which she thought about submitting before she was named coeditor of the *Heron*.

"Have you considered joining our debate team, Ms. Manning?"

Louisa knows this kind of compliment. Adults always do this: tell her she's smart, precocious, exceptional in some way unrelated to the task at hand—before denying her whatever she's really asking for. "I think I have a full plate as it is," she says, to be polite.

"I'm sure you do. While you make a compelling point, Louisa, I believe that Atwater has other policies and practices we can point to as fostering an environment that—as you say—nurtures the social-emotional well-being of our students."

Louisa can hear the air quotes around the last phrase, as if Mrs. Brodie is mocking her.

"In fact, I would argue that a newspaper issue dedicated to—what are you calling it? Sexual health?—may actually be a *detriment* to the emotional health of many of your classmates, who might see the obvious connection and feel confronted by a topic they find confusing or even triggering."

Anjali can't help herself: "So *that's* why no one is talking to us about Karen Mirro? Because it might be *triggering*?"

"Ms. Reddi, I understand that you're upset right now. I would suggest that you talk to your Dorm Parent or one of the school counselors if you find the topic of sexual assault an emotional challenge."

"It's not the topic. It's the fact that nobody tells us anything," Anjali snaps. "It's the lack of information that presents an *emotional challenge*."

"I think what we're trying to say is," Louisa begins, afraid that Anjali has crossed a line, "we think that this is a really important issue—one that does a service to the school. And it's really *good*, too. It's the best one I've been a part of."

There is a long pause while Mrs. Brodie adjusts in her seat, her shoulders bobbing as she shifts her crossed legs. "Has either of you ever heard of a sand mandala?"

Anjali shifts her head to one side, raises an eyebrow.

"No? Sand mandalas are a Tibetan Buddhist tradition. Tibetan monks construct these gorgeous, massive—I mean, really *huge*"—she spreads her arms wide, gesturing at the circumference of the table—"designs out of grains of colored sand. First, the monks draw the mandala—mandalas are these incredibly intricate, ornate, symmetrical designs that typically symbolize the complexity of the universe. So the monks sketch the mandala, and then—instead of painting it—they use straws and funnels and teeny tiny scrapers to lay millions of infinitesimal grains of colored sand on top of the design. It takes them weeks or even months to finish one. And the absolute focus and steadfastness required? I mean, you can't even sneeze!

"And when you look at a sand mandala from a distance, you can't even tell that it's made of sand—it looks like paint.

"But then, after all that—after hours and hours and hours, one grain of sand at a time—they destroy it. Just wipe it all away."

"Why?"

"The destruction of the mandala is meant to symbolize the transitory nature of things, the idea that everything that passes across this earth does so only fleetingly. But I like to think that the whole thing is also about valuing the process over the product, you know?" She pauses, waiting for some kind of affirmation from the young women in front of her. "You ladies are like the monks, you see: You did the work, with diligence and dedication. You built your issue, grain by grain. And now . . ."

"And now we have to destroy it," Anjali says flatly.

Mrs. Brodie tilts her chin toward the ceiling, her eyes searching the beams above. "You're better for the work," she says. "And now you have to share that wisdom with the school in other ways."

Louisa loses a game of rock-paper-scissors with Anjali, and so it's her job to send the news to the *Heron* group text. She does this as she walks back to Whitney, long balloons slipping into the chat as quickly as she steps.

> Hey guys. We just met with Mrs. Brodie to
> appeal. It's a no-go. I'm really sorry, and I

just want to say that I'm so proud of the work
everyone put in on this issue. We'll meet on
Monday as usual to regroup.

Noo :'(

that bitch

This is some bullshit

what did she say

Louisa thinks about the sand mandala.

The same stuff Ms. Doyle said.

So sorry L.

we should just publish it anyway

Yeah!

I mean what could they do? Fire all of us?

lol probably

Hah

But seriously

Don't delete any of your work. Leave it loaded in
InCopy. I want to hang on to it.

Why

K

I still believe in the concept, so maybe it's
something we can revisit when this whole thing
is over.

sounds good

*   *   *

In a typical school day, most Atwater students do not check their school email more than once or twice. Very few of them have it linked to their phones, because the Outlook app is, in a word, "annoying," and so they prefer to just check their mail from their computers. Anyway, nothing distributed via email is ever all that urgent, and so there's no real reason to have it an icon-tap away.

This is how Louisa knows something is wrong when she wakes up the next morning to a barrage of texts telling her to check her email.

From Anjali: Omg check your email
From Hitomi: What is this email!

On the Heron group chat:

Everybody check your email!!!!!!!

omg who did this

A and L was this u guys

o shit

Louisa crawls to the front of her bed and reaches across the floor to her desk, where her laptop sleeps in its charger. Pulling her computer back into her lap and nestling into her pillows, she flips open her screen and enters her password. In seconds she's on her email, where the most recent message—sent at 12:02 A.M.—is from brodiehatesthe1stamendment@gmail.com.

Louisa immediately feels sick. She is struck by a number of entirely improbable and yet—in her panicked state—plausible scenarios: Did she sleepwalk last night, in her dreams building an anonymous account to smear the Head of School? She's read about fugue states; maybe one happened to her? Can anyone account for her whereabouts at 12:02 A.M.?

Inside the email is a single link, and Louisa recognizes the URL before she clicks. It's the same format they use when they distribute the digital version of the *Heron* to the school after it goes to print. With her breath caught in her chest, she clicks through, some tiny corner of her brain still hopeful that it isn't exactly what she knows it is, her hope alive as long as the page loads.

But there it is: the entire issue.

STATE OF PLAY: GIRLS AND SEX

THE DEFENDER: ONE ALUM'S FIGHT AGAINST MILITARY ASSAULT

TIME FOR A CHANGE? WHY WE NEED A TITLE IX FOR THE MODERN ERA

There's the graphic Mia designed (*Getting Help After Sexual Assault*), a flowchart of pathways for how to report and how to find support. There's Macy and Bryce's survey, the private lives of 280 of her classmates folded into graphs: a pie chart cleaved in half to reflect the 50 percent of students who reported talking to their parents about consent; another sliced to account for the places Atwater girls learned about sex, with a triangle sized at 18 percent to represent the number of students who cited "porn" (a number that seemed low to Louisa, if she was being honest, although she allowed that "learning about" sex from porn was different than merely watching it, which even she had done once or twice out of curiosity). A bar graph ranked the places an Atwater student was most likely to seek help if they or someone they knew were in an unhealthy relationship: "a friend" towered like a skyscraper (193 of the 278 responses) over "a family member" (46 responses) and "a trusted nonrelative adult" (28). Even now, Louisa feels the familiar swelling of pride at a job well done.

She scrolls back through the PDF, looking for—she can't help it—any mistakes, any misspellings or misplaced punctuation or dropped quote marks. Usually, she and Anjali (and sometimes Hitomi) do a round of copy edits once the files are all loaded in, one last polish while Mia waits impatiently to finish layout. It becomes a bit of a competition between the three of them, who can find the most errors.

Louisa feels her heart in her throat. On the second page of the file, on what would be the first inside page of the newspaper if they had gone to print, at the very top, beneath the words "FROM THE EDITORS":

>Four weeks ago, the *Hartford Courant* broke a story about this place that we call home: A former student named Karen Mirro alleges that she was raped by an Atwater faculty member and that she furthermore faced retaliation for reporting the assault. Since then, Karen's junior-year head-shot has hung in the *Heron* room, tacked at the center of a corkboard we use for planning. It wasn't hard to find: she lives in the yearbooks, where we'll all live one day, frozen in time for future generations. In 1995, she had long, curly, honey-blond hair. She played soccer. She was a member of Spanish Honor Society and Key Club.
>
>For a little while, we thought we could solve the mystery of Karen Mirro and whatever happened in the fall of her senior year. But the more we talked, the more we realized that we didn't just want to know the specifics of Karen's story. We wanted to know what would happen if it were one of us, in 2015. Would we tell? How would the school react? Who would they protect?
>
>We'd been prepared to write a letter saying that—despite countless interviews and hours of research—we hadn't answered those questions. We'd been prepared to say: this is the landscape, but our concerns are still hypotheticals; the best we can do is lay them onto one another and make an educated guess. But then we were told not to publish this issue. And that makes us wonder whether we understand more than we originally thought.

She reads it three more times, until she can recite it from memory. She recognizes the words as her own. She knows that she wrote them last night, during study hall, in a blind rage, when she couldn't focus on her actual homework because she was too angry with Mrs. Brodie. Even now, she marvels at her own restraint, the rhythm at the end of the last graph, the gut punch in the kicker. Louisa has always loved a good kicker.

What's funny, too, is that this piece isn't even *really* how she feels. The self-righteousness of it almost makes her laugh, wildly, a kind of horrified outburst. If she was feeling self-righteous about anything last night—which she was—it was about Mrs. Brodie's infringing on their free speech. She spent a half hour in the middle of writing that letter googling the First Amendment rights of student newspapers, spiraling deep into the bowels of legal journals whose language was so dull as to be rendered incomprehensible. The way in, she realized, was not through vague and lofty legalese but rather a tug on the heartstrings: as they'd learned in researching this issue, one in three women would experience some kind of sexual violence in their lifetimes. Shouldn't Atwater, protector and defender and supporter of women, want its student body to know about this? Shouldn't they want to educate a generation that could fix the epidemic?

That's what she wanted the letter to communicate. And then somebody—not her, she was sure of it now—pulled the document from its file in the *Heron* shared drive, uploaded it into InCopy, finished the layout, loaded the whole thing into a PDF, and distributed it to the entire school.

She does not respond to any of the texts that pile up on her phone, the little red icon ticking ever upward: twelve unread messages, then thirteen, fourteen, group chats firing without her. Instead, she climbs out of bed, dressing quickly: tapered sweatpants, a T-shirt, a navy Atwater half-zip, the school crest in bright white curlicues above her right breast. It occurs to her that it's probably cold out, on this late October morning, and wraps a chunky, cable-knit scarf in two loops around her neck. She grabs her phone and darts out.

She keeps her head down as she crosses the Bowl, too unprepared for the questions she knows will come: *Did you see it? Did you do this?* She has never broken a single Atwater rule—not one that counts, at least—but she knows that the truth is not enough in this case. She makes it all the way downstairs—through the side door of Schoolhouse, down the back stairs, past the sagging couches and the portraits of distinguished alumnae and the roaring lion, through the alcove beneath the fluttering birds and into the *Heron* room.

For some reason, Louisa is surprised to find it empty. She half expected—she realizes now, embarrassed, ridiculously—to find the culprit sitting there, at Mia's desk, the completed file downloaded on the screen in front of her. But instead the room is empty, and it smells musty and like cold cement and the only lights are those that flicker from the computers and the scanner and the printer and the graying dawn that seeps through the ground-level window.

For two years, Louisa has always found her answers in this room. When she didn't have any friends in her first few weeks at school, she joined the *Heron*. Feeling far away from her parents, her relationship with her own mother strained by miles and misunderstanding, she learned to rely on Ms. Doyle. Knowing that she lacked leadership skills and that she would need them for her college applications (and for life, after that), she lobbied to become coeditor, slowly taking on more and more responsibility for the paper during her sophomore year, nurturing her friendship with Anjali so that she, too, would advocate for Louisa's promotion.

Maybe it's for these reasons—in combination with some deep-seated belief in her journalist's ability to sleuth it out—that she begins to tear apart the room. She rifles through the stacks of pages they'd accumulated in research—photocopies of yearbook entries, printouts of the *Courant* story, ripped sheets of loose-leaf scribbled with random notes, saved and set aside *just in case*. She reads and rereads again the notes on the whiteboards, looking for any new additions or changes to their outline. She logs in to one of the desktops they keep for layout, searching wildly for digital footprints.

She can see that the file was last saved at 11:32 last night, but she has no way of knowing who did so. (Surely there is a way, but Louisa—a writer who wants to major in English, whose ability to fix a glitch on her iPhone extends to turning it off and on again—has zero computer skills beyond those required for daily life.) And anyway, wouldn't the culprit have been savvy enough to log in under someone else's name?

What if it was her name? How would she prove that it wasn't her?

It would be a vast overstatement to say that even one-half of Atwater's students read the *Heron*. The staff does its best, issue in and issue out, to promote their work, making announcements at school meetings and distributing new issues far and wide, leaving piles of them in every dorm common room and scattered on the tables in the dining hall and in Avery and in the lounges in Trask. They post flyers in the bathroom stalls— PICK UP YOUR COPY OF *THE HERON*—and locker room mirrors and on every single bulletin board they can find. But the only people who read it seriously—besides the devoted alumnae in the *Heron* Facebook group, where Mia always posts the PDF—are teachers and friends of the staff and maybe some weird loner outsiders like Leah Stern and Gretchen Myers.

All along, it turns out, the solution was to envelop the paper in scandal.

Breakfast is dominated by the leak. Girls huddle in pairs and three-somes around the dining hall, reading and rereading. The first two classes of the day are usurped entirely by the issue, which everyone—thanks to Lou-isa's letter—knows was not supposed to be published. There is a renewed run on the yearbook archives in the library during morning break, this time not for the chance to size up Karen Mirro herself—that happened after the *Courant* article; they all know her blond curls and soft, round face—but to find and appraise the women whose letters are included in Hitomi's Opinion section *("LET KAREN MIRRO TELL HER STORY," ALUMS SAY)*. They want to know what kinds of bodies these reasonable-sounding voices inhabited, as if a person's high school head-shot could cement or undermine their authority. Stephanie Vandenburg, who wrote that "Karen has a right to finally be heard," was the prettiest. Amy Fishkin, who said "Atwater's commitment is first and foremost to the safety and well-being of its students," had short, dark hair, and looked thirty in 1995. Heather Hawkins—"the school has a duty to operate with transparency"—wore overalls.

The faculty are told to ignore it, but compliance with this mandate depends on the individual. The young teachers—the ones who want to be cool, who want to be *liked*, like Ms. Ryan and Ms. Daniels and Ms. Trujillo—all let their students run away with their gossip.

In Spanish I, Ms. Trujillo tries to engage with her students: "Are you worried about sexual assault?" she asks.

She's met with shrugs and raised eyebrows until Tessa DeGroff says, "Probably eventually we will be, just like we'll be worried about accidentally getting pregnant and cervical cancer," after which Ms. Trujillo leaves the girls to themselves.

But Louisa Manning doesn't know any of this, because she hides in the Health Center under the guise of a migraine through third period. Normally Louisa is not one of those students who exploits the weary kindness of the nursing staff, but she figures that if there is any day to engage in some light manipulation, the day she has been framed for insubordination against the Head of School is one. Finally, during lunch, she makes her way back to her room, where she plans to get changed and then find Ms. Doyle and try to explain.

Her room, though, is already occupied.

"Where the fuck have you been?" Anjali bolts up from where she's been lying, legs outstretched and wrapped at the ankles, on Louisa's half-made bed.

"Health Center," Louisa grunts.

"Seriously?"

Louisa shrugs. Anjali waits.

"So?"

Finally the orb that has sat lodged in Louisa's throat bursts. She has always been a silent, steady crier—a weeper rather than a sobber—but the release of the tears that stream down her cheek is no less profound. She

feels like she can breathe again, like the fact of her suspicions confirmed—
that it certainly *looked* like she did it, even if she didn't—is so much better
than the wondering.

"I mean, you can't cry about it!"

"I didn't fucking do it," Louisa says, quietly.

Anjali blinks. "What?"

"I didn't do it. I know it looks like I did it because you and I are the
most likely suspects and that's *my* editor's letter in there, but I didn't do it!
I wrote the letter after our meeting with Mrs. Brodie when I was angry
just as, like, I don't know—a way of processing!"

"Dude. I know you didn't do it. Mia did. She already turned herself
in. Ms. Doyle has been looking for us—she told me to come find you."

Snot channels into the groove above Louisa's lip. "Mia?"

Anjali leans back. "I know, man."

"I just—I never got the impression that she cared all that much about
the *Heron*."

"Me neither. But, the more I think about it, the more it sorta makes
sense—she's a little edgy, you know? And she's butted heads with Admin
before over stuff she does with Flawless." ***Flawless—with three aster-
isks, just like the Beyoncé song—is Atwater's feminist club. "She can be
a bit of a crusader. Plus, I just don't know who else would be competent
enough in layout to get it done that quickly."

"Huh." Louisa nods, thinking it over. Something doesn't fit for her.
"So . . . is she kicked out?"

"Of school? No, no way. I mean, I don't know, but they won't kick
her out for this. It'll just make everything worse, you know? But she's off
the *Heron*, so that sucks. We'll have to find someone else who can learn
InDesign in, like, four weeks."

Louisa nods again. Anjali has had a jump start on processing this revelation, but for Louisa it still feels like whiplash. "When does Ms. Doyle
want to see us?"

"ASAP."

"Okay. Um, give me a minute? I'll be right back."

"Sure," Anjali says, returning to her phone.

Mia's room is downstairs and down the hall, at the end of the second floor in a long and narrow single that requires all the furniture to be stacked on end, her bed wedged in the back corner, her desk at the foot of her bed, her dresser in the front of the room next to the door. Mia is exactly where Louisa expected to find her, seated at her desk, one foot on her chair with her knee tucked beneath her chin, scrolling Reddit.

"Hey," Louisa announces her arrival.

Mia turns in her chair. "Oh, hey."

Louisa leans against the doorframe, not clear whether she's invited in, unsure if she even wants to stay.

"I just . . ." She didn't have a plan. "Why did you do it?"

Mia cocks a head to one side, so that her long dark hair falls from its place behind her ear. "I don't get a thank-you?"

"Mia, you put *my* letter in there. Everyone on staff knew I wrote that, so everyone thought I did it."

Mia's jaw drops, her eyes widen. She hangs her head and massages her scalp, then pushes her mess of modelesque straight hair back away from her forehead. "You didn't do it."

"What?"

"I only *told* Ms. Doyle I did it."

Suddenly it clicks for Louisa, who drops her shoulders, curving her vertebrae into the jamb. "You thought I did."

"Yeah."

"Why would you do that for me?"

Mia shrugs. "I just figured the paper needed someone with enough balls to send an email from an account named 'Brodie Hates the First Amendment.'"

Louisa laughs in spite of herself, in spite of the moment.

"Plus, the paper doesn't really matter to me all that much. No offense or anything."

"Okay, but—you shouldn't get in trouble for something you didn't do. We'll tell Ms. Doyle it wasn't either one of us."

Mia laughs, and Louisa has the embarrassed feeling of not getting the joke.

"Right now, I'm probably just looking at getting kicked off the paper. They don't want to make a bigger deal out of this than they have to. But if I say I lied to cover for someone else? You know how this place feels about *honesty*." Mia rolls her eyes as she says it, as though the truth is such an overrated thing. "I could actually get in *real* trouble. And then Linda Paulsen would launch a full investigation of the paper. It's easier this way. Plus, like I said: you want this person on your staff, whoever she is."

When Louisa was younger—right at the cusp of old-enough-to-know-better—she *begged* for a little sister. When asked what she wanted for Christmas and birthdays or for gifts held aloft as bribes for various elementary accomplishments (completing a season of rec soccer in Shadyside, for entering and winning the school science fair, for doing her first and only piano recital), Louisa always, always said: a baby sister. She watched her parents have conversations in low voices at the kitchen island; she saw how they exchanged glances in the front seat of the car. She knew that although her family was a unit of three, that her parents, too, were a unit, separate from her. It was crushingly lonely.

She's never asked her mother why they stopped at one kid; she has no idea if there were miscarriages or IVF or even if her pregnancy with Louisa was notable in any way. She knows now, at sixteen-almost-seventeen, that people have reasons. But she never quite outran the desire at the core of the ask: someone to have a private world with; someone to tell her secrets to.

"Who do you think it was?" Louisa asks.

Mia tilts her chin up, cradling it in an open hand, picking absentmindedly at a tiny scab of a zit near the back of her jaw. "No clue," she says, finally.

The *Heron* staff is too small to be cliquey, but it's a random enough assortment of girls that their relationships for the most part exist only in their basement lair. For two years, Louisa has thought of Mia Tavoletti as not serious enough for her, a little too much trouble.

Maybe she was wrong, she thinks now, although she knows it's too late to matter. Maybe they could have been friends.

To: doylen@TheAtwaterSchool.org
From: rogers.meg@hvis.org
Date: Oct 25, 2015, 10:38 P.M.
Subject: Call for Alumnae Letters

Dear Ms. Doyle,

I do not expect you to remember me: I was a student in your eleventh-grade American Literature class in 1994–95, but not a very good one (at least per Atwater's standards). I'm happy to report that I pulled it together a bit at Skidmore, and then went on to get my MSW at NYU. I live in the Hudson Valley now, where I work as a school counselor at a small independent day school. I have a daughter, Penelope, who just turned three.

I'm reaching out because I am aware that you are the faculty adviser for the *Heron*, and it came to my attention just recently that your students are seeking alumnae input for an upcoming feature on Karen Mirro. I hope that I'm not too late, as I would very much like to contribute.

Karen was a close friend of mine: We were both artists, and became good friends our sophomore year when we worked on set design for the musical. We roomed together as juniors, and lived in adjacent singles in Whitney for the first semester of our senior year. Although we had common interests, I suspect we were really drawn to one another because of our shared apathy for academic achievement.

Shortly after returning to campus for the start of our senior year, Karen told me that she was dating an older man. She said that she could not tell me who because he was married. I never questioned the authenticity of her story, and I am embarrassed to admit that I never cautioned her against such a relationship, either. I was seventeen (Karen had turned eighteen that August), and it was thrilling to me.

Karen often left Whitney after lights-out to rendezvous with this man. One morning over breakfast in early November, she told me that things had gotten "a little weird" the night before. I asked her to elaborate, but for the first time she wasn't as willing to give me all the salacious details. I remember her shrugging, speaking in fragments, and tugging the cuffs of her sweatshirt down over her knuckles. I patted her on the shoulder and said—and the memory of this has only sharpened, my own inadequacy seared into my brain—"he probably had a fight with his wife." Three weeks later, she got caught smoking in the woods with Heather Hawkins, who'd never so much as cheated on a vocabulary quiz. You know how the rest of the story goes.

I've thought a lot about that dining hall conversation in the years since. I was twenty-one the first time a man got "a little weird" with me, and then twenty-three. Both times I characterized the incident to friends in exactly that way, either because Karen had given me the language or because it was the natural way to describe the confused feeling I had that maybe I'd played some role in my own hurt. I'm not saying that what happened to Karen happened to me, or vice versa: What I'm saying is that we were both very young, and it was 1995, and for both of these reasons we did not have the vocabulary we have now to describe such experiences.

Karen was the wiser, more experienced one within our friendship. I'm sure she knew I thought there was something glamorous about her affair, and to say what she has said now would have ruined the facade. Although I am ashamed by my own teenage narcissism, I want to be kind to both of our younger selves, and understanding of all that we didn't know. Karen and I have lost touch, and the opportunity has long passed for me to tell her all this. But I'd still like to try to be a better friend, and it seems speaking up for her right to share her story— equipped as she is with the hindsight of adulthood and the knowledge afforded by a changing landscape—is the least I could do.

Please let me know if this is still possible, and, if so, to whom I would address my thoughts.

Meg Rogers

Class of 1996

Fall Fest

There was no chance of doing any AP Biology that day. Any time Mr. Gregory said "ATP," Kit Eldridge, dressed in a teetering wig and a brass-buttoned coat as Alexander Hamilton, shot up from her seat and began reciting the preamble to the Constitution: "We the People, in Order to form a more perfect Union, establish Justice, insure domestic Tranquility, provide for the common defence, promote the general welfare, and secure the Blessings of Liberty to ourselves and our Posterity, do ordain and establish this Constitution for the United States of America." When he asked them to write, from memory, the steps to cellular respiration, Brie Feldman, dressed as one half of the Mario Brothers, shouted, in a squeaky voice with a bad Italian accent, "Let's go!" and then began playing, from her phone, music from the Mario Kart video game. In the back, dressed as Belle from *Beauty and the Beast*, Sloane perched at the edge of her lab stool, her heels cocked against the ground. She began class with a fully choreographed rendition of "Belle (Reprise)."

Mr. Gregory is the perfect Atwater teacher for Ringing. Through each interruption he is patient but undeterred. He claps politely and then returns to his slides. The young and new teachers are always too young and too new to know how to handle it. They try to play along or they ask overeager questions, wanting to be in on the joke. The veteran teachers like Mr. Gregory have a kind of mild disinterest, an okay-let's-get-this-over-with kind of attitude. It endears them to their students, who find indifference—especially among their male teachers—motivating. They love him for it.

In the back of the class, Chloe Eaton is wearing a unicorn onesie, the horn-adorned hood drooped on her back. She ordered it online for $60 plus overnight shipping, and while she might normally be grateful for the opportunity to wear a onesie to class, right now she just feels awkward. The costume Priya picked for Chloe—but which Chloe paid for, because Ringing expenses are the responsibility of the junior class—is the least imaginative and the least original, chosen at random at the last minute. It's not even embarrassing: it's just boring. She's supposed to leave small piles of glitter in her seat in every classroom ("Unicorn poop!"), but Linda Paulsen vetoed that particular prank after first period, complete with a brief tirade about how Ring Dares that unreasonably burdened the janitorial staff were unfair and "privileged," and that, as an Atwater alumna herself, she expected more from them.

Chloe had never really looked forward to Ringing, the custom through which Atwater juniors earn (via successful completion of a series of dares, most of which involve a costume and an element of performance) and are bestowed their class rings. Of all the Atwater traditions, it gave her the most anxiety: What if no one wanted to be her Ring Sister? Or, what if someone would be her Ring Sister but, you know, it was someone who chose her out of default? What if she was the only junior left without a Ring Sister, and so Paulsen had to pair her with the only senior who hadn't yet been proposed to?

In the end she proposed to Priya because they were both part of the same tangled knot: Priya was friends-but-not-best-friends with Addison and Collier just like Chloe was friends-but-not-best-friends with Blake and Sloane. Blake asked Collier; Sloane asked Addison. (Honestly, she thought Sloane would ask Karla Flores, who greeted Atwater with the same kind of regular indifference as she did, but there are varying strategies to this sort of thing.) She wasn't like Louisa Manning, who had an actual best friend in the senior class (Anjali Reddi), or like the theater kids, who all hung together regardless of grade. She could have asked a senior on the field hockey team, like Isabelle Baldwin or Ashley Witt, but they were the kind of not-very-close that results from actually knowing one another. Which is to say: they had made a conscious decision not to be friends. The whole ordeal—choosing and proposing to a Ring Sister—was the closest thing to actual dating that Chloe had ever experienced: Blake and Sloane ran interference with Collier and Addison, sniffing out who remained of the seniors, then presented the list back to Chloe; then, like matchmaking couriers, circled back to Collier and Addison to confirm mutual interest or agreement. Finally, they landed upon Priya.

In a school that largely lacked promposals, Ring Sister proposals took on all the related fanfare. Classes ground to a halt, unable to withstand the deluge of interruptions and speculation. Louisa Manning wrote an editorial for the newspaper, five hundred words on her friendship with Anjali Reddi beneath the headline, *ANJALI, WILL YOU BE MY RING SISTER?* Blake persuaded the kitchen to decorate a cake with the same question for Collier; Sloane went for maximum audience, using the student-announcement portion of Morning Meeting to propose to Addison. Even Kit Eldridge, with her West Coast hippieness that tends to buck tradition, proposed to Karla Flores via the hand delivery of a massive cornucopia of fall flowers, dahlias and black-eyed Susans and garden vines cascading out of an antique silver vase. Kyla Moore stood behind the opposing team's goal during a home soccer game, holding a giant sign directed at Olivia Anderson. Brie persuaded someone on the maintenance staff to code a message to Emma Towne in the pool scoreboard. For ten days the proposals interrupted field hockey games and extra help sessions and Atwater's weekly formal dinner—and then it all stopped for a month, until mid-November, when Ringing occupied the already-distracted week before Thanksgiving break.

All of this is to say that, sitting in the back of biology in her unicorn onesie, Chloe has not been looking forward to this week. Her phone faceup on the desk, shielded by her classmates and the depth of field from Mr. Gregory's largely indifferent eyes, she swipes through Snapchat, where every other post has *RINGING* scribbled across it in neon pink or fluorescent yellow. She taps over to her own post from this morning and watches her pinched fingers sprinkle glitter, raining from in between her neatly manicured nails before the video rewinds and plays in reverse, the iridescent flecks sucked back up into her hand. It's mesmerizing. It's the best thing to come out of today. (This is affirmed by her messages, which are flooded with video replies in the form of hearts and thumbs-up and *100* emojis.)

Next to her, Sloane repositions her notebook closer to Chloe. She's scrawled something in the top corner in handwriting that is like Sloane herself: tight, elegant, unfussy. *What's tomorrow?* it reads.

Chloe gives her head the tiniest of shakes. She doesn't know. She reaches for her own pencil and scribbles a response: *You?*

Jasmine (from 'Aladdin'), Sloane writes.

Chloe looks up from the paper and Sloane rolls her eyes.

Disney princesses all week, I guess.

Chloe shrugs, but as she turns her attention back to Mr. Gregory—diagramming the citric acid cycle now—she notices her lungs filling properly for the first time today.

When she gets back to her room that night, there's a bag positioned on her bed with a card propped in front of it, waiting expectantly. She takes the time to unpack her own backpack first, plugging in her laptop and setting it on her desk, stacking her books on the hutch above, scanning her planner to assess the night's homework: a chapter in *The Awakening*; twenty pages on secession for APUSH. She can skim both in under an hour. Finally, she picks up the card, flips it over, running her hands along the milky smooth envelope. The card inside is blank save for three attentive letters at center—*PKS*—in a kind of stern and serifed font. Inside, Priya's looped handwriting is hasty and crooked: "For tomorrow!!" it reads. "—P."

The instructions seem unnecessary, the lack of personal touch almost insulting. *No shit*, Chloe thinks, before imagining that Priya wanted the chance to use the monogrammed stationery that gathered dust most of the year. Still, would it have killed her to write another sentence? *Can't wait for Saturday*, maybe? Or, *Super pumped to be your Ring Sister!* Maybe she could have signed it that way, *XO, Your Ring Sister*, instead of that trying-too-hard —*P*. (It's a rare initial that holds up to the single-letter nickname. *B*, for Blair or Bea or Bianca, works; so does *S*, for names like Serena or Sienna or Simone. *P* for Priya is not one of them. Neither is *C* for Chloe.) She slips the card back inside the envelope, putting both aside, and turns her attention to the bag itself. Whatever it is barely fits in the bag; that it is Chester-the-Cheetah orange and soft is immediately apparent, and the realization comes before Chloe has it a third of the way out of the bag.

"Another onesie?"

The voice is behind her, and Chloe whips her head over her shoulder to see her roommate standing in the doorway, clutching a steaming paper cup close to her chest.

"Apparently."

"That's sort of boring," Brie says. "But I guess at least it's comfortable?"

Chloe holds the body-shaped blanket up against herself, matching its shoulders to her own. "I guess so. The booties are a little annoying. I have to, like, shove them into Uggs . . ." She trails off.

Brie places her tea neatly on her desk before striding over to where Chloe stands. She pinches the fabric between her thumb and forefingers, the polyester gliding between her fingertips, and makes a low whistling sound. "Man, no chance I'd stay awake through APUSH if I was wearing that. What else is in there?"

Chloe plunges her hands again into the depths of the bag, fishing around beneath the onesie. When her hand emerges, it's clutching a single-serving-size cup of Frosted Flakes.

"'They're *grrrreat*!'"

"I guess I'm Tony the Tiger. . . ." Chloe peers into the bag again. "There must be a dozen of these in here, all Frosted Flakes."

"What are the instructions?"

"Add milk."

Brie snorts. "No, idiot, like—what does Priya want you to *do* with the cereal? What's the dare?"

Chloe turns the cup over in her hands, rattling the flakes inside against their plastic container like a small percussion instrument. "I don't know. . . ."

"After the glitter was vetoed, I doubt chucking cereal into the air will be allowed."

"Yeah, definitely not."

"Oh—look. It says something on the bottom."

Chloe looks at Brie, then flips the cup over in her hand. *EAT*. "Eat? When?"

"See if the same thing is written on the others."

Chloe turns the bag upside down, and single-serving packs of Frosted Flakes rain down on her bed, clattering against one another. As they tumble onto her comforter, rolling away from each other like bumper cars, they catch black lettering across the bottom of each, and the words piece together like an impressionist painting—*EAT* across every single one.

"Damn," Brie says. "That's a lot of Frosted Flakes."

The next day, any time Chloe might have normally eaten in public—sipping coffee at breakfast with Brie; at snack; during lunch—she eats Frosted Flakes instead, hunched over the little plastic-paper cups, the blue paper top peeled partway so that it half covers her face. By the afternoon she is starving—a matter not necessarily of lacking calories but of lacking nutrition, of substance, of fiber—but isn't willing to risk Priya or one of Collier's lackeys catching her at the snack bar or ordering in. She skips dinner entirely, unable to bear even the thought of tonight's acorn squash and green beans and roasted turkey. She sits in their room instead, and sneaks a protein bar from Brie's stockpile, eating only half of it because it, too, like the Frosted Flakes, tastes like chemicals and sugar and the headache that set in two hours ago and which now rages between her eyebrows. She starts fantasizing about breakfast, about Atwater's designer egg McMuffins (served on little ciabatta rolls instead) and maple sausage, neither of which she'd eaten since her freshman year, because only freshmen and a certain kind of upperclasswoman eat from the hot-food bar at breakfast.

On Wednesday, she wears a onesie printed to look like wizard robes, carries a wand, and casts a spell every time a teacher says "homework." Some of her classmates have read the books a dozen times over and try to engage with Chloe using obscure references and a language that sounds like inside baseball. Chloe would have to admit she hadn't read the series, eliciting at worst horror and at best an offer to binge-watch the movie adaptations this weekend. Most of the time, though, a classmate would just whisper longingly—"I'm so jealous"—and Chloe would think, Don't be, someone wears this every year.

She doesn't have to wear a onesie on Thursday—the costumes in general were fading in presence and originality by the fourth day—but she *does* have to carry around a small speaker and project music as she walks from class to class. ("Your personal soundtrack!" Priya's note read, with a link to a playlist of pop icons Chloe listened to only as a passenger in other people's cars.) This is mostly fine, except the teachers hate it and three times yell at her to turn it down.

Friday offers, per tradition, a break. The following day is Fall Fest, an all-school carnival of sorts, during which Chloe and her classmates will perform their last Ring Dare. Having survived Fall Fest, Ringing would conclude on Sunday evening at Ring Dinner, where Priya would finally present Chloe with her school ring.

As a freshman and sophomore, Chloe loved Fall Fest. The school brings in food trucks—the high-end artisan ones that served things like banh mi tacos and grilled cheese with smoked Gouda and caramelized onions—and a bouncy-house slide. There are quintessential New England autumnal things like pumpkin carving and bobbing for apples and paper cups of steaming hot cider and, across the street through the Atwater gate, a corn maze. Chloe has never been entirely clear on what combination of money and neighborly sensibility led to the Darrow family carving up and lending out to a bunch of teenagers a wide swath of their cornfield every November. She isn't even sure if the Darrows made the maze themselves, or if Atwater hired the men and machines that arrived in late October and mowed and trimmed and left sweet-smelling piles of mashed leaves and stalks in their wake. Some of the more competitive Atwater girls—the best athletes, like Kyla, a sprinter and jumper bound for Division I—would try to persuade a teacher or janitor to let them up into the clock tower, where a high, clear vantage point would help them solve the maze before racing through it on Saturday.

Mostly, though, the maze is a place to hook up. The other best part of Fall Fest—besides the grilled cheese and the tacos and the cider dough-nuts—is the fact that Atwater buses in students from other boarding schools in New England and upstate New York. (For years, they'd only invited students from a boys' school in New Hampshire, but due to a stu-dent outcry that the practice was "heteronormative matchmaking," At-water now welcomed students from an all-girls school, too.) Each of the classes handled this differently. The seniors, Chloe had noticed, reacted coolly, many of them in relationships or, after three years at Atwater, having established friend groups with these students who visited regu-larly. The freshmen were nervous and excitable, most of them traveling in unfriendly and impenetrable packs and living vicariously through the handful who managed to spend five minutes alone with a boy in the corn maze or the pool hallway. (Chloe's freshman year, both Sloane and Blake hooked up with boys from Salisbury.) The sophomores had a little more savvy, knew how to flirt in the safety of a large group. Last year, Chloe had traded numbers with a boy from Westminster, and they'd texted for a few weeks before naturally falling out of touch. Juniors, of course, had Ringing.

The whole point of finishing Ring Dares on Fall Fest was precisely because of Atwater's guests. It was timed for maximal humiliation. On the day of the year when you wanted to wear your cutest, most New England–y fall outfit—when every other Atwater girl would be dressed in camel sweaters and Barbour jackets and jeans tucked into Hunter boots—you'd have to run around in, say, snow pants. When every other Atwater girl would have her long hair in soft curls or a perfectly untidy bun, you'd be wearing a clown wig. It was a nightmare.

"Think about it this way," Brie was saying to Chloe, chatting reasonably from across the room while she dug through her closet, tossing clothes in a pile over her shoulder. "If a guy still talks to you while you're doing dramatic readings of nursery rhymes while dressed like a mime—"

"Is that what you have to do?" Chloe asks, horrified.

"What? No. I'm just saying. Hypothetically. If he's game for our shenanigans"—here she stands up triumphantly, having finally found what she was looking for—"then you know (a) he's into you, and (b) he's a keeper."

"So . . . what's Emma got you doing?"

Brie snorts. "A bunch of us have to do a flash mob."

Immediately Chloe feels her stomach sink, the kind of weighty and sudden disappointment she felt when she didn't make the varsity field hockey team as a freshman even though she knew, deep in her heart, that she wasn't actually good enough. Still, she had hoped. Brie and whomever else would be shielded from embarrassment by the comfort of a mob. It was so easy. Fun, even. She groaned with jealousy: "Who else?"

"Hmm . . . Sloane, Blake, Kit, Kyla . . . I don't know who else. Honestly I'm surprised you're not doing it too, since Priya is friends with Collier and Addison."

It *is* weird, Chloe thinks, especially since Priya hadn't been all that original with her dares all week. Chloe had interpreted it as lazy half-heartedness, but (she thinks) if Priya was really being lazy and half-hearted about all this, wouldn't she have wanted to tag along in a group dare? It would have saved her the effort of thinking up something on her own. . . .

"So what's the song?"

Brie walks over to her phone, scrolls and taps for a minute, and then, as a percussion-laden backbeat announces itself in their tiny dorm room, steps into the center of their floor and begins to perform a sloppy, stilted, weakly memorized choreograph to Beyoncé's "Run the World (Girls)."

"Stop, please—" Chloe shields her eyes, laughing, feigning horror. The more she protests, the more Brie digs into it, swinging her hips wider, kicking her legs higher, finally sashaying over to Chloe and grabbing her by the wrists, pulling her off her bed and into the beat with her until they collapse onto the ground.

Her back against the carpet, Chloe speaks to the ceiling. "You really need to practice a little more."

Brie reaches across and smacks her roommate lightly on the shoulder. "Anyway, my plan is to stand in the back and let Sloane and Blake have the spotlight."

"Smart."

"So, what's your dare?"

"I don't know yet."

Brie rolls over onto her side, propping herself up on her elbow. "Hmm. Well, maybe you should practice the dance just in case."

"You just want someone to make you look good."

"Excuse me? Did you see those moves? I look so good I'm gonna make everybody else look *bad*." Still lying on her side, she shimmies her shoulders a little.

Chloe loves this about Brie, the way she doesn't get all worked up about Atwater traditions and pomp and circumstance. Whenever she calls home, Chloe's parents ask about Brie, and her dad always says that "that Brie has a good head on her shoulders." It is true that Brie has a way of impressing parents, with a kind of old-soul maturity that radiates an even keel. She is probably right. Priya probably forgot to tell her about the dance, and tomorrow morning Chloe will wake up to a not-so-apologetic text that demands she learn the flash mob routine by the afternoon.

"All right," she says, rolling over and standing up suddenly. "Am I gonna have to do that foot-stomp thing? Because I've seen the music video, and I don't think I'm coordinated enough for that."

Chloe's first thought the next morning is that it is a perfect fall day. She and Brie like to sleep with their windows open as long as possible, and buried under the comforter she feels the fresh cool of the season filtering across the room. A New England fall, she learned her freshman year, has a kind of morning chill you can smell. On the twin bed across from her, Brie is still sleeping—although the rest of Whitney is, it seems, wide awake. She listens as her classmates run from room to room, and knows that—for many of them—the best part of the day has begun: *getting ready*. In hindsight, she'd wish she'd stayed like that forever: The gold autumn light sifting through Atwater's flimsy shades; the cool, wet, fresh-smelling air diffusing into the warmth of a room shared by two bodies; the vague mechanical sounds of industrial equipment and facilities staff in the distance, hard at work setting up the day's festivities.

Instead of doing this—instead of enjoying one extra, optimistic, quiet-but-not-lonely moment—Chloe rolls over and reaches for her phone, resting facedown on top of her desk next to her bed. With the tilt of the screen, her display lights up, rectangular bubbles covering the picture of her dog, Stanley: messages from Kit and Sloane and Brie (she must have gone to bed after Chloe) and, there at the bottom, a single message from Priya Sandhu.

She has the sensation of having read the thing before she actually has, as though she has subconsciously absorbed the content of the message by merely displaying the words in front of her. It is not unlike the times she's tried Sloane's Adderall, when her senses become so supercharged that she needs to read a thing several times to absorb the words *in order*, from left to right, top to bottom. She feels suddenly hot and sweaty, too, also like when she takes Adderall.

Hey, sorry I forgot to tell you about tomorrow. I
know some of the girls are doing a flash mob but
I figure it's too late for you to learn the dance.
Plus, this'll be more fun! I dare you to make out
with a Westminster guy in the corn maze.

She'd sealed the message with two kissy-face emojis, little hearts bursting from their puckered lips.

Chloe hasn't kissed a boy since the only boy she'd kissed. It happened two summers ago, after she spent most of her first year at Atwater embarrassed and trying to hide the fact that she hadn't yet kissed anyone, never mind all the other things the girls would ask during a game of ten fingers. She and Tyler Mandell had been friends since elementary school, it happened in Andrea Flynn's parents' finished basement after they'd both had a couple of beers, there was a lot of teeth knocking and, after, Chloe was mostly just grateful it was over, in both the literal sense (i.e., kissing Tyler) and the bigger, metaphorical sense: she was no longer years behind everyone else; during a game of ten fingers, no one ever asked, "Never have I ever kissed *five* boys." The question was just "Never have I ever kissed a boy," and now Chloe had.

Lately, though, she'd sensed she was falling behind again—not behind girls like Sloane, who lost her virginity during their sophomore year to a senior at Collegiate and who had since had sex with a guy from Horace Mann and another guy from Collegiate, but behind girls like Brie, who gave head for the first time last summer and who could talk about what she liked a guy to do when he fingered her, because it had happened enough times for her to have developed an opinion about it. Maybe it was because of the rogue newspaper release and the flyers Mrs. Brodie had the *Heron* staff hang around school ("How to Talk to Survivors" and "Getting Help at Atwater") and the lesson their Peer Educator had given on affirmative consent, but it seemed like everybody was having versions of sex now, or at least talking about it.

In the bed across from her, Brie stirs beneath her comforter, finally rolling over and catching Chloe's eye. She smiles contentedly, beneath shut eyes, and snuggles into the cocoon of her duvet dramatically.

"Morning," Brie says, her voice raspy with sleep. "Guess what day it is."

Chloe sits up and places her phone facedown on her desk, as it was when she woke up. "How many cider doughnuts is too many cider doughnuts, do you think?"

The visiting schools would start arriving around noon, and although normally Chloe likes to arrive places at a time her mother calls "fashionably late"—even though it had nothing to do with fashion and everything to do with being able to assess the social scene, to survey the room or party for the already-formed cluster of people she knew—Mrs. Brodie had given her usual very stern speech that Atwater should be "a good host" and be at Fall Fest to "welcome their guests." Plus, she'd added, anyone who was late would earn an infraction.

So when they had finally finished getting ready—after Blake finished straightening the back of Brie's hair; after Blake had, after trying on three different sweaters from her own closet, finally borrowed something from Kit; after Kyla had refused to be talked out of wearing sneakers—they headed out of Whitney and toward the Bowl.

Chloe remembers once when her dad had asked her, only half kidding, if she and her friends coordinated their outfits when they went out together.

"It's like there's an official Chloe's Gang uniform," he'd said, laughing at his own joke, imagining the exaggerated capitalization.

She'd been short with him, looking up from her phone to offer a terse "What are you talking about?"

Her mother quickly slid into Chloe's corner, chiding her husband with an eye roll and a "*Rick*, stop that." But descending into the Bowl now, Chloe can't help but see her dad's side of things: Atwater looks like an army of preppy, slender, perfectly groomed lumberjacks—plaids beneath field jackets or quilted vests or fisherman knit sweaters above denim tucked into boots. It isn't normally like this at Atwater, she thinks defensively—when she first visited, Chloe was struck by how the school not only didn't have uniforms but also that, for all she could tell, it seemed to neither have a dress code: there were girls in skirts and sweaters and riding boots but also in jeans and sweatshirts and team uniforms and faded or ripped or torn black-on-black-on-black ensembles—but Fall Fest was almost a themed party, like the spring luau or the winter rave. Plus, the rare presence of *visitors*—specifically male visitors—tilts the balance.

Or maybe it's just Chloe who thinks that way. Walking out to the Bowl, she sees that the anticipated arrival of their guests hasn't caused her classmates to shrink to the edges of the circle, to cluster in gangs of three and four, arms on hips, waiting to ensure that when the moment came they looked cool and casual and even a little expectant. Instead, Chloe hears shrieks in the distance, puncturing the air that gently hums with the machinery that powers Fall Fest: the bouncy slide, the food trucks, the kettle corn. She imagines that some of the freshmen are already on their second go through the corn maze, trying to improve upon their time. The rest of the ninth graders—at least, she spotted Lauren Triplett and Bryce Engel, and a trio of girls who looked small and eager the way freshmen still do in the fall—are clustered around a large metal basin, hands gripping the edges, listening as Mr. Banks gesticulates his way through the directions for bobbing for apples. (Which is, again, an activity no one besides the freshmen would participate in.)

Although some teachers—like Mr. Banks—are tasked with manning activities, many simply mix and mingle with the students, enjoying Fall Fest as if it is a regular street fair and this is the real world. Ms. Daniels and Ms. Trujillo stand in line at Whey Station, a bright yellowy-orange truck that sells mac and cheese and grilled cheese. Mr. Morgan, who is twenty-four and built like Adonis and who isn't a great math teacher but who has, nonetheless, a kind of endlessly dreamy bumbling charm, stands at the front of a booth playing a game that involves tossing little plastic rings over heavy metal bottles. He's positioned in a kind of mid-squat, grinning and floppy-haired, side-arming each ring like a small Frisbee and tossing his head back when it inevitably misses its mark. Ms. Ryan and her husband move among the crowd, clutching steaming paper cups, their heads cocked slightly toward one another.

There is a little cluster of picnic tables near the ring of food trucks, and each year the seniors claim them as their territory. In general, seating is discouraged at Fall Fest—until later in the afternoon, when, tired or bored or paired off, they'll find their way to the edges of the Bowl, where park benches pepper the sidewalk looping inner campus, or else simply fall to the grass a few feet from the games and trucks. For now, though, Fall Fest's makeshift cafeteria belongs to the seniors—at least a certain cohort of them—who make room for their group by sitting not only on the table benches but on the tabletops as well. They tuck into one another, crossing and angling their dangled legs to squeeze tighter together, wrapping one arm around another before placing a single elbow on a single kneecap or crossing their arms in front of their sweatered torsos.

Priya sits near the end of the actual bench, a few bouncy-haired heads down from Collier and Addison. She wears dark denim tucked into boots and a turtleneck sweater. At least there's this, Chloe tells herself: At least *she* knows better than to wear a turtleneck on a heavily photographed day. For a second, Chloe thinks they make eye contact—she drops her eyes quickly, then feels the immediate embarrassment of being so obvious about her avoidance.

She hadn't responded to Priya's text, nor had she told Brie (or Sloane or Blake or Kit or anyone) about her new dare. Telling them would mean she'd have to explain why she was nervous about it, which would mean explaining that, actually, she hasn't hooked up with anyone in over a year, and in fact she's only ever hooked up with one boy, once, which would be to offer clarification on something she was just kind of leaving to assumption. As they did their hair and makeup, Sloane and Blake practiced the dance in the Whitney hallway, and Brie offered once again to teach Chloe the steps, and so she tried for a few minutes before Sloane lost interest and Blake announced an outfit dilemma. She could just tell Priya she never got the text—but it was such an obvious, familiar lie. She could slide herself into a big group and physically *go through* the corn maze with a boy from Westminster and then, later, tell Priya that they'd hooked up—but Chloe knew that whatever she did or said she'd done tonight would filter through the school in a matter of hours, and then across New England via text or Snapchat or Twitter and ultimately back to whichever bewildered boy she named as her partner. The only other option was to bail on a Ring Dare entirely, which was obviously not an option at all.

She met Aidan Beiers during last year's Fall Fest, when Sloane and Blake—both of whom had boyfriends somewhere else, who were doing it for sheer sport—engineered a coed race through the corn maze near the end of the day. He was skinny like a runner, with a sort of concave chest and shoulders that slumped slightly, and the natural tan of someone who spends a lot of time outside; he had light brown hair that—like all the boys Chloe knew—was slightly longer at the top, for styling into that kind of pushed-back, swept-over look celebrities usually wore to awards shows. He was good-looking, basically, if a little bit young. Chloe—who would not call herself skinny, and not in the body-dysmorphic way, either (she isn't fat, but she has the kind of thighs and butt that make her well suited to field hockey)—had a hard time initially with Aidan's thinness: She couldn't imagine the way their bodies would fit together; she imagined those moments in movie sex scenes when the guy would pick up the girl and gently back her into a wall, and think, *Aidan would never be able to do that to me.* But she needed his thinness, and his middle school face, too, because it was what separated him from flawless and placed him within Chloe's reach.

Nothing happened between them. The group Sloane and Blake put together naturally coupled off—Chloe almost felt sorry for the boys who ended up with Sloane and Blake, whose casual flirtatiousness did not betray the simple fact that they each had a boyfriend and would not, therefore, be hooking up with any of Atwater's male guests that day—and Chloe and Aidan, the stragglers in the group, ended up together. He was new to Westminster, and Chloe asked him how he liked it and how the cross-country team was doing and where he was from and, thankfully, the walk through the maze really only lasted long enough to cover the most informational kind of small talk. He asked her for her number after they crossed the street back onto Atwater's campus. Texting him had made her the center of their friend group's attention for a brief while, as they helped her compose each message, agonizing over the connotation of each piece of punctuation.

All week, Chloe had been secretly hoping he'd text her. She'd leave her phone unattended for extended periods of time, imagining that the longer she went without looking at it, the surer she'd be to return to a message from Aidan. At Brie's urging, she'd drafted (and then deleted) dozens of messages to him, alternatively flirty and casual and sometimes both flirty and casual. ("If you want something, what are you doing to make it happen?" Brie had asked, sagely and patiently; then, later, less patiently: "Do you even want to see him?") The fact that he *hadn't* texted actually made Chloe *more* anxious about seeing him: she wasn't sure how to act around him when they were inevitably reunited. It had even occurred to her that she should pretend she didn't remember him, or maybe—and, until yesterday, this had seemed the most likely—she would just do her best to avoid him entirely.

But now she needs Aidan, or at least Aidan is her best bet, and as they wander through Fall Fest she feels the vague nausea of nervous anticipation. She is only half listening to Brie ("Am I in the mood for sweet or savory?" she had said a minute ago, and Chloe assumes she is still trying to decide which snack to eat first) when the first bus rolls around the loop, swinging into the Lathrop parking lot.

"Look," she says, interrupting Brie.

"Hmm? Oh—looks like Salisbury?"

In Chloe's imagination, the arrival of a guest school at Atwater always played out like high school dance scenes from movies set in the 1950s: the girls and boys cluster on separate sides of the gym, whispering to one another and waiting for someone to bridge the divide. In reality, it—both high school dances and the arrival of guests at Atwater—is nothing at all like this.

Instead, the bus pulls up, groans to a stop, opens its doors, and fifty or so Salisbury kids empty out onto the loop pavement and descend upon the Bowl, and a small pack of Atwater girls stride casually across the grass, waving, a couple of them tapping into their phones, like friends who used to go to summer camp together. Then they turn and rejoin the carnival, one cell pinching wide to swallow another, the process repeating each time a bus rolls in.

He finds her while she is sitting with Brie, splitting a cider doughnut (sweet, Brie had decided). Chloe feels a hand on her slouched shoulder and immediately a weight settles into her gut, filling the space between her sternum and her pelvis.

In the year since they'd last seen each other—since they'd met—his face has thinned out, a product of the several inches he has apparently grown in that same time. His skin is smooth and tanned, and he's gotten a haircut. As she tries to parse all the things that are different about him from the Aidan she'd stored up in her memory and in her iPhone, it strikes her: he looks suddenly like a man.

He stands with two other boys, one about average height, the other still waiting for the growth spurt he's long been promised, both with the distinct hunched-over thinness of runners, both in quarter-zip fleeces.

"Hey."

"Hey."

"This is Carter and Luke," Aidan says, waving generally at the taller one and then the shorter one.

Chloe nods and smiles.

"Hey! I'm Brie," her friend says, leaning forward and shaking Carter-and-Luke's hands. Chloe marvels at her easy sociability. "So how was the drive?"

Brie guides them through the small talk: the drive was fine but long; the cross-country team is doing well but Carter is having an issue with his Achilles; they spent their summers on the Cape (Aidan) and the Vineyard (Luke) and in the Hamptons (Carter); they commiserate about SAT prep and the barely survivable workload of junior year. All the while, Chloe has the vague sense that Aidan is trying to catch her eye, trying to communicate something indelible to her and only her—she feels his eyes on her, the urgency of him, but is too nervous to meet his gaze. Or maybe—it seemed likely, even—she imagines it, because she has so inflated their non-relationship that she's completely lost touch with reality.

But then Brie suggests they take a walk and Chloe stands from where she's been sitting and slides in front of Aidan, who motions for her to go ahead of him and places his hand on the small of her back, gently, just for a second. She did not imagine it.

In the end it would seem obvious, like she should have pieced it all together: the lack of communication, the casual expectation, the furtive and hungry touching. And the way she never questioned it, never even threw a flirty-but-menacing barb his way; when she replayed the tape, later, the moment Aidan put his hand on her lower back, she'd turn and raise an eyebrow, as if to say, *Excuse me?* Even in her imagination, the best she could do was scowl.

As they wander through the food trucks and game stalls, balls clanging against tinny metal and carnival bells dinging, their fivesome naturally stretches out to a staggered line: Brie leading the way, chattering over her shoulder about the day, sometimes referencing her friend in the back ("Chloe always says these games are rigged—but that's kind of the point, right?"); Carter and Luke behind her, mostly not talking but sometimes one of them holding up his phone in the cocked-elbow way boys do to add to their story; Chloe and Aidan bringing up the rear, Aidan a half step behind her but close enough for her to feel his warmth.

At some point—when they pause to take a picture, or as Brie is using her training as an Atwater tour guide to embellish upon the history of Fall Fest—Chloe stops short, and Aidan's body bumps into hers. As he separates himself from her, Aidan takes her hips in his hands, gently placing them on the soft parts of her torso above the widest part of her pelvis.

"Whoops—sorry," she mumbles over her shoulder, apologizing for the accidental touching but also just filling the space between them. She can still feel the exact places where his hands rested on her hips.

"My bad," he says as she turns to look at him—still not squarely, still over her shoulder—and as they make eye contact he smiles with his lips shut. It is a smile that suggests that it was not *his bad*. "Hey, you want a cider?"

"Oh, yeah, I'd love one, thanks—"

Aidan's body angles back toward the cider cart, as though he is motioning for them to walk in that direction together. "You aren't going to make me walk back alone, are you?"

"What, you can't carry two ciders?" Brie pops her head over Chloe's shoulder, grinning widely. Chloe exhales for the first time since bumping into Aidan.

"Actually, no. I'm afraid this hand"—he holds up his left hand as though taking an oath—"is merely for show."

Brie laughs. "Is that so?" Chloe has always been jealous of this, the way Brie can always play along, never missing a beat or filling her turn in the conversation with laughter instead of words.

"It's true. It's a rare congenital defect. My left hand is utterly incapable of carrying hot beverages." He looks at Chloe sideways and raises an eyebrow. She feels herself smiling, almost automatically, as if Aidan's smirk is itself infectious.

"I guess you've got to give the man a hand, Chloe."

"Literally."

"Hey," Brie says, with mock severity, "don't get any ideas."

The boys laugh, and Chloe feels as though she missed the innuendo. Or maybe she was imagining it altogether.

Aidan motions toward the cart. "After you."

It's only awkward for a few steps, as Chloe runs through topics of conversation, abandoning each small-talk question as soon as it floats into her throat. She knows better than to bring up something they've texted about—nothing says *I'm obsessed with you* like quoting a nine-months-old text conversation. She takes her cues from Aidan's own indifference.

The line at the cider cart is long, as it has been throughout the afternoon. At the end of the day, someone—the Dorm Parents, probably—will box up the leftover doughnuts and shuttle them around to the dorm common rooms, where they'll stiffen and crumble and be picked over by dozens of noncommittal hands. It is almost enough to ruin cider doughnuts for a person.

"So," he says as they sidle into the line, "where've you been?"

Chloe did not believe that boys actually said things like this, but here is one, saying it to her. She almost giggles; she bites the inside of her lower lip to halt the smile that threatens to crack across her face.

"What do you mean?"

He smiles and bumps his left hip gently into her right. "We stopped talking."

She can't help it. A single loud "Hah!" bursts from her mouth.

Aidan looks horrified. "What?"

"Nothing. I just—I guess it takes two to text."

For the smallest of instants, Aidan's eyes widen beneath raised eyebrows, and Chloe feels her face grow hot with the embarrassment of having said the wrong thing; of having been too loud and too aggressive and unvarnished.

"I just mean—" she begins, before Aidan holds up two hands.

"No, no, you're right. My bad, too, I guess." He smiles. "So can I buy you a doughnut and hear about all those texts you would have sent if I hadn't been such a jerk?"

"Well, the doughnuts are free, so . . ." She trails off, feeling her heart quicken. Maybe she was getting it right, after all.

"Can't sneak anything past you, can I?"

They grab their doughnuts and cider and make as if to head back toward their group, where Brie holds court among Aidan's slouched-over friends, but as they walk Aidan tilts his chin across the Bowl in Whitney's rough direction.

"You know, this is my third Atwater Fall Fest, and I've never had a tour. I don't know what any of these buildings are."

"Well, that one is Whitney—the upperclasswomen dorm. You're not allowed in there, so don't get any ideas."

"Jeez, I didn't think I was being so obvious." He grins again, in that unnerving way of his: it seemed to tell Chloe she only *thought* she was in on the joke.

"You wouldn't be the first visitor to make a beeline for Whitney," she says, even though it isn't exactly the truth, or at least not the truth based on Chloe's experience.

"So how about an open-air tour, then? Exteriors only."

For only the third or fourth time that afternoon, Chloe looks directly at Aidan, his dark hair gleaming in the perpetual gold of a fall day. There is something in the way he carries himself—the way he hunches his shoulders but keeps his chin out and up—that makes her feel a little uneasy around him. But the truth is that Chloe always feels a little uneasy around boys, as if they can tell by looking at her that she has so little experience in the things that mattered.

But Chloe wants—*needs*—that experience, and the only way she is going to get it is by saying yes to a moment like this one, where she will be alone-but-not-really-alone with a boy she hardly knows for some extended period of time.

"Okay," she says. "But you should know that it's Brie who's the official tour guide, not me."

"I'll keep my expectations low."

As it turns out, Chloe is an okay tour guide. Somehow—certainly not by choice, certainly not intentionally—various Atwater trivia has seeped into her consciousness, so that she is able to embellish her tour with various historical and cultural anecdotes: there are the steam tunnels, long closed, of which there was originally only one, built so that women could sneak underground to the gym, which was originally built to look like a library so that visitors would never know that anything so untoward as women exercising was happening here; the arts building is named after a Gilded Age millionaire who, unburdened after her husband's death, helped to finance the suffragists.

All the while, Aidan listens attentively, and Chloe is both unnerved and emboldened by his attention. She has never before had a boy *really* listen to her, and Aidan makes eye contact and nods his head at the appropriate times and asks questions that flow logically from the things Chloe has just said. As they walk, she notices that Aidan never once slips his hands into his pockets; he keeps them dangling at his side, and in her mind he is keeping them available—she imagines herself slipping her hand into his fleetingly, with the kind of panicked horror she sometimes imagines doing something wildly inappropriate in class, like shouting out in the middle of a test.

As they round the Bowl by Lathrop—and near the inevitable conclusion of their tour—Aidan's walking slows until he brings them both to a stop. It is a natural moment to descend back into the heart of Fall Fest; ahead of them, the columned facade of Trask glows in the autumn light; to their right, a shadowed stretch of pavement leads to the head's residence. Long, low piles of fallen leaves line the road like dunes, and Chloe thinks that she likes that they leave them there for Fall Fest. Later in the day, as golden hour sets in, girls will flock to Head's Road for its highly Instagrammable background.

They are in the middle of a comfortable kind of silence, the sort of sleepy and satisfied quiet she shares with Brie on a Sunday afternoon, when Aidan suggests it: "Want to do the corn maze?"

He motions with a slight tilt of his head and shoulders across the road, where they can see the top of the corn beyond the fence. When she focuses her attention, Chloe can hear a vague chorus of shouts and squeals filtering up the hill from among the stalks. *Here it is*, she thinks, and she has to once again control a burst of crazed laughter—*it was so easy*. She wonders if this could be enough; she starts crafting the story she'll tell herself later, after they walk back to their group, the one she'll work up to legend, the one that will fit the narrative she'd created with Brie this year: he *wanted* to go in the maze with her; he *definitely* wanted to hook up; there was a reason he didn't want to go back for their friends.

To her right, Aidan nudges her gently. "Don't tell me you already did it. I heard that some of the girls race through it as soon as it's finished."

Chloe looks at him with mock horror. "Only the freshmen do that. How uncool do you think I am?"

Aidan laughs, and as he does so he wraps an arm around Chloe's waist, squeezing her briefly. "Come on. Let's give it a go."

The sun has drifted low enough in the afternoon sky to bathe Atwater in a soft orange filter. It will feel like dusk inside the maze, where the corn is tall and dense enough to push time hours ahead. She checks her phone to see that it is a few minutes after three.

"Got somewhere better to be?" It occurs to her that Aidan is a little overeager about a stupid corn maze, but this will be something that sharpens only in hindsight.

"It's supposed to be a surprise"—Chloe's words come slowly, carrying the weight of all that she is debating—"but some of the girls are doing a flash mob at four. I don't want to miss it."

"How long do you think this will take us?!"

His joking puts her at ease. She is being stupid, doing what she always does: avoiding being alone with a guy not because she doesn't want to be but because she is nervous. Her nervousness—her embarrassing lack of experience, she thinks with a hot stomach flip—is forever getting in the way. The only way past it is through it.

"Should we race?"

Aidan grins. "No way. It's way more fun to argue about directions." Like a real couple, Chloe thinks.

The air is cooler among the corn, and quieter, too—the walls on either side of them muffle the noise and flex gently with the breeze, bowing in and out above them. Chloe imagines the maze during the day, empty except for the occasional freshmen duo who race through it: How pure the labyrinth must be. For a while the maze presents no choices—left, then right, then left again—until they are what seems like a comfortable distance in, and an intersection appears.

They speak for the first time. "We'll take turns?" Aidan offers.

"Seems fair."

"Ladies first."

Chloe scans her options. There is, of course, no telling which way is the right way. She tries to imagine herself above the maze—in the clock tower, she thinks—looking down on the road and the entrance and the exit. She has never been very good with directions; she remembers reading once that women tend to give directions by landmarks—left at the church, right by the drugstore, that kind of thing—whereas men tend to use street names and distances. She wonders which applies here.

They turn right.

"Interesting choice."

Chloe raises a single eyebrow in his direction. "Would you have chosen differently?"

"Well, we went left, right, left. This right is heading deeper into the maze. If we had taken the left, we'd be doubling back, turning in on ourselves."

She can barely follow what he says. Again, she has never been great with directions. "Do you want to go back?" It came out with more edge than she'd intended.

Aidan reaches out and brushes her hand, so quickly Chloe considers that he's been looking for an opportunity to do it. "No. Let's keep going."

He does not mention the hand touching, and does not linger that way for long.

Aidan chooses the next turn—left—and at a four-way intersection Chloe chooses straight, mostly because she doesn't want to choose *right* and give Aidan the satisfaction of dictating her choices. The deeper they spiral into the maze, the quieter it becomes—the occasional shout or laugh rings out like a gunshot on a still-clear day—and the more time expands, filling the spaces between the stalks of corn, distorting Chloe's sense of it. It feels simultaneously as though they have been wandering for thirty seconds and an hour. She is hyperaware of the boy next to her, the way he consumes the narrow pathways so that she has to walk slightly behind him or slightly ahead of him and the way he seems so much taller: she has the frenzied idea that he could just jump a few times and determine the correct direction.

Their conversation slows, winnowing to brief exchanges about progress. It seems natural. Chloe admires his focus. At the next intersection—is it the fifth or tenth?—Aidan gestures forward, through another straight. Like in the woods, sun sets inside the maze faster than it sets outside it, but Chloe is reasonably sure that straight leads to a dead end fifty yards ahead. She says so.

"No, I think it turns to the left. See the shadow?"

Chloe peers, and no, she doesn't really see the shadow, but she recognizes the half smile on Aidan's face and, anyway, she isn't stupid. She knows why they came into this maze alone together, why neither of them had pushed to wait for their friends. She feels the same cold-but-sweating flush she has come to expect when she is nervous, and stiffens against the light shaking that will set in.

"I think you're wrong," she says, in a tone she hopes is both firm and coy. She teeters on the knife's edge.

"Only one way to know."

Chloe sighs and shakes her head dramatically before stomping ahead of Aidan, affecting her annoyance to hide her nervousness. Within a few feet of the end, she turns and swings her arm in the direction of the alleged left turn. "See?"

Aidan slows his walk to a gentle sort of lumber. He is close, then closer, until his body is inches from hers. "See what?"

She almost laughs—she feels the giant *ha!* swell inside her chest—because it is so ridiculous how obvious he is now, his face almost slack with the other thing he's interested in. She has the wild thought that she probably could have just asked Aidan to kiss her as soon as they got away from their friends, that she didn't have to do this whole elaborate charade, that this was what he wanted all along.

The kiss is sloppy, teeth bumping, and once or twice Chloe tries to pull away but maybe doesn't do it quite the right way and so Aidan thinks she is doing the thing they do in the movies, the pull-apart-teasing thing. He looks at her without really looking at her before lunging at her again. She moves her face against his until her jaw aches, until she can hear the hinges cracking at the back of her throat, and then places her hands gently on Aidan's chest, one flat palm against each pectoral muscle, and pushes away.

He smiles at her. "That's it?" He reaches for her waist, prodding her gently at her hip, then wrapping his hand more firmly around the softness above her pelvic bone.

"We've still got half a maze to get through," Chloe whispers, and Aidan's nose is against hers again, and this time there is less teeth and more tongue, both of them a little better with the rhythm but also, mostly—and Chloe thought this was the case but she couldn't be sure, she hadn't kissed enough boys to know—Aidan opens his mouth so wide, pushing his tongue so deeply inside hers, that there isn't any risk of their teeth knocking. He is too busy trying to devour her.

The first time he slides his hand from her lower back to underneath her waistband, Chloe takes one of her own hands away from where it moves across Aidan's shoulder blade and gently adjusts his, back onto the soft curve in the middle of her back.

"Come on," Aidan half whispers, pulling her closer. His hips grind against hers, and under the stiffness of his jeans she feels him harden. She lets out a kind of maniacal giggle.

"Someone will see—"

Aidan's mouth is on her neck now, and his hands work in opposite directions: One grips her ass while the other works its way up her shirt. She writhes against him, trying to wriggle space between their bodies without embarrassing either one of them. When his hand reaches the bottom of her bra, his fingers crawl frantically over the mound of her breast before squeezing, hard enough that she reflexively curves forward, her spine flexing convexly, creating an empty space between their torsos.

"Sorry—you just feel so good—"

"It's okay—" She pauses as Aidan slides his mouth across hers, moving from one side of her neck to the other. She kisses him back, like she means it but urgently, changing her strategy from resistance to something she hopes resembles *into it but not right now*. She will promise him it will come later.

She tries to pull away again, but Aidan plays it like a game, some kind of retreat-to-move-forward strategy. She feels the dried husks of corn tickling against her back and becomes aware of her surroundings—of the juxtaposition between their isolation at this dead end and the openness of it all, the dusk settling in above them, darkening their alleyway. Anybody can see them. Nobody will.

Aidan's hands move inside her underwear, the thong she'd picked out excitedly this morning, and as he slips a finger inside her—no one had ever done that to her before—he exhales loudly and whispers, "I want you to get wet for me."

When she thinks about it later, she will focus on this moment, her absurd lack of knowledge and understanding, how she thought that when he said that it was something she could or should have willfully conjured up. She'll think about how he slid his finger in and out of her repeatedly, and how it would be years before a man would use his hands inside her the right way.

She lets him move inside her for a little, and at some point he takes her hand and places it on top of his crotch, and something—had she seen it in a movie? Read it in a book?—tells her to sort of roughly massage the mound that she assumes to be his hardened penis.

Each time they progress, she runs the calculus: Let him do this, get it over with. For a little while, she thinks she can still fairly call it a hookup.

And then they're on the ground, Aidan on top of her, and he's sliding down his pants just enough, and Chloe says that she isn't on birth control and Aidan says, "Don't worry, I'll pull out," and then he's pumping inside her, and she tries moving her hips too because it's so fucking uncomfortable—it hurts—but it's the wrong way, or not what she is supposed to do, because Aidan stops, mid-thrust, and moves an arm so that his hand can anchor her pelvis. She has absolutely no idea how long it lasts. Time protracts. When he pulls out he makes a moaning kind of exhale, like it is a struggle, and pushes himself back enough so that he can come into the inches of ground just below her, between her legs. Chloe looks away, at the gray sky above them and the way that, from this angle, the corn bends into arches.

After he finishes, Aidan lifts himself up and off Chloe, into a standing position from a push-up, his boxers and pants tangled around his ankles. She doesn't want to see it, but when he turns slightly to wriggle into his pants she sees his penis—really for the first time, she thinks wildly—half-erect, cast in the shadow of dusk. It seems both bigger and smaller than she thought it was, smaller than it felt inside of her but bigger—more confrontational, more assertive—than she had imagined one to be. Uglier; alien-like.

As Aidan pieces himself together, it occurs to Chloe that she should, too, and arches her back to give herself enough room to pull her jeans up from where they strain around her knees, keeping her legs as wide as she can to avoid the place where Aidan came into the ground. As she stands Aidan turns toward her, moves a step in her direction, and Chloe freezes: The muscles that flank the vertebrae in her neck tighten, her breath catches in her chest. He brings his face so close to hers that their foreheads touch. In the shadowy half dark of the maze she can see his mouth stretch into a kind of sleepy smile, his eyelids heavy and half-closed.

"We should get back," he says.

Leaving the maze is easy; Aidan either remembers exactly the route they traveled on the way in and manages to navigate the reverse, or perhaps it is just not as complicated as Chloe had previously considered it. She walks a half step behind him, and they do not speak, not as they cross the shadow that angles between the two walls of reedy corn husks at the start, back into the late-afternoon light; not as they cross the street back onto campus, the pavement dusty and strewn with dried leaves; not even as they crest the top of the hill next to Trask that looks down into the Bowl, eyeing the crowd for their original group: Carter-and-Luke and Brie. As they walk, Chloe feels a kind of thick dampness between her legs; she tries to discreetly look down at her pants, panicked that whatever it is might be visible through her jeans.

The scene around them as they cross the Bowl doesn't really dawn on either one of them until they reach their group, which has sort of Venn diagrammed into two: Carter-and-Luke and three other boys stand with their shoulders turned in to one another, a few feet off from Brie, who's joined by Sloane and Blake and Kyla. Each one of them— each of the boys, each of the girls—has their phone out, but they lean toward one another, glancing from their own screen to the one clawed in the palm of the girl next to them. Looking around, Chloe realizes that this is the case across the Bowl: All around them, her classmates are gripped by their screens in a way that suggests something more than a casual and distracted scroll through Instagram. It's something out of a horror movie, where Chloe is the hero not yet aware of the impending doom; something out of an early 2000s teen movie, where the protagonist doesn't understand why the cafeteria's gone quiet. Chloe's stomach drops, and she is gripped with the certainty that what captivates her classmates is a video of *her*, immobile on the ground, Aidan thrusting in and out. It seems entirely plausible that someone watched, hidden in the forest of stalks.

Brie looks up from her screen and catches Chloe's eye, and with one hand waves her over, her palm flapping hurriedly, her eyes wide. Chloe's heart thuds between her ears. She considers running back to her room without a word, unable to confront whatever dictates Brie's urgent waving. But her roommate reaches across the remaining feet between them and grabs Chloe's upper arm, pulling her across the expanse and into their circle of friends. "You have to see this," she hisses, and angles her phone toward her friend.

It's an Instagram post—there's the tidy, upright cursive at the top of the screen, the tiny circular icon to the left—but because it does not immediately seem to be a cell phone video of her on her back in the corn maze, and because she is actively working to slow her thundering pulse, Chloe has to review the content in her friend's hand several times before it really lands.

Centered within the two-inch square are several lines of formal-looking text, typed in a professional sans-serif font, capped on each end by quote marks.

"I think that even a young woman needs to understand what she's getting herself into. I don't mean to imply that it's her *fault*, of course, but I think that it is our responsibility, as educators, to help our girls learn to identify and avoid dangerous situations. For example, I never walk in a parking garage alone at night."

Maybe it's the rhythm of the speech, the comma clause *as educators*, that gives it away. But Chloe knows who the quote belongs to before Brie speaks:

"Can you believe her? I mean, I know it was, like, a different time, but . . ."

"Do we know for sure that it's Brodie?"

Brie snaps her head back, directing her focus away from the screen and onto her friend. "Did you read the caption? You never read the caption!" she groans.

In 2005, a student at the all-girls Tipton School in western Massachusetts accused her former teacher of rape. Asked by local media to comment on the story, Atwater's then-newly appointed Head of School Patricia Brodie implied that the student herself—who, in the course of the investigation, admitted to pursuing a relationship with her twenty-six-year-old teacher—was in part to blame for her trauma.

Perhaps Mrs. Brodie's views have changed. Or perhaps she's simply learned that it's better, with beliefs like this, to not comment at all.

And then Chloe notices one more thing, the puzzle pieces clicking into place.

"Wait," she says, her voice a half whisper: "This is *Atwater's* Insta?" She places an index finger on the icon above the post, pointing at the minuscule drawing of a heron in flight, navy wings spread wide against a fog-blue background. After the yard signs, Atwater had done a slapdash rebrand, wiping the tiny architectural sketch of the clock tower from its logo and replacing it with the school mascot.

Brie nods, slowly.

"How?"

"I'm sure the password is something stupid obvious, like ATWA-TER1813 or something." 1813, the year the school was founded: before the end of slavery, before women could vote, before two world wars. A planet ago.

This crystallizes for Chloe what lurked just beneath the surface of her understanding. Of course the school's social media manager didn't post this; someone hacked into the account.

"I wonder if it was the same person who leaked the newspaper," Brie adds. Louisa wasn't supposed to tell anyone that Mia hadn't really caused the leak, but she'd told Anjali, who told the rest of the staff, including Brie, and thus the news that the *Heron*'s senior art director had taken the fall for a mysterious vigilante had made its way to Chloe. "Makes sense, right? It's sort of a similar . . . approach. Journalistic."

"Do you think it's real?" Chloe asks. "The quote, I mean. How do we know she really said this?"

Brie shrugs. "Louisa already ran off to search for the original source. I'm not sure how many local newspapers keep digital archives from 2005, but—I mean, if it *is* real, whoever posted this was able to find it." She pauses. "But you've gotta admit . . . it does sound like something she would say, doesn't it? I know she's supposed to be an advocate for women and girls or whatever, but . . ." Brie trails off; Chloe nods.

She knows what her friend is saying. It's not just the vague corporate-speak and the noncommittal couching: it's the slight condescension, too, of an adult who does not understand the lives of the people she's serving.

Chloe pulls her own phone from her back pocket—she is briefly surprised and grateful that it stayed put when her jeans were circled around the bottoms of her thighs, just above her kneecaps, so that she couldn't move her legs any wider or adjust her hips beneath Aidan—and thumbs into her own Instagram. She reads the post again, this time in her own feed, a question buzzing inside her brain like white noise. *A young woman needs to understand what she's getting herself into.* There is Aidan's hand on her waist, his drooping smile, his smirking insistence that the path turned to the left beyond the shadows.

"Hey—" Brie says, suddenly, sharply, her neck straightened away from her screen, her chin pointed directly at Chloe. She lowers her voice: "So how'd it go? With Aidan?"

Chloe looks up at her inexhaustible roommate, the way her blond curls shimmer in the afternoon glow, her one imperfection a spot of crowding on the front-right side of her mouth, her canine tooth slipped half behind an incisor.

"You chickened out, didn't you?" Brie asks, searching Chloe's face.

Without thinking, Chloe nods. It is an irrevocable answer, and so it becomes the story she will tell until college, when a new friend will ask—between shots of cheap vodka, the liquor searing across the inside of their skulls—when Chloe lost her virginity, and she'll say: *Sixteen.* A regular age; the safe but true answer—her friend suspects nothing: *Me too!* she says. At thirty, she will try again: first to the man she loves, then to a therapist. But she will find that she has hidden the exact contours of the story deep inside a slowly shifting narrative, like a jagged rock smoothed by the tide, and it will be easier to keep the edges blunted: to let her class ring gather dust in the back of her jewelry box, to tell her classmates at Alumnae Weekends that she lost it in a move, and sure, yes, one day she'll get around to ordering a new one.

To: erin.palmiere@reginaventures.com
From: erin.palmiere@reginaventures.com
Date: Nov 27, 2015, 9:16 A.M.
Subject: A Message from the Board

Dear Atwater Students, Friends, Family, and Alumnae:

I hope that this email finds you enjoying a restful Thanksgiving break, in the company of family and loved ones. To those of you with whom I have not previously corresponded, a brief introduction: My name is Erin Palmiere, and I am President of the Atwater Board of Trustees. I am also the CEO of a venture capital firm, Regina Ventures, and mom to two daughters, Elspeth and Emilia. It is not my intention in reaching out now to disrupt that valuable family time, but rather to provide you with space to process, so that we might all return to school with the clarity of a respite.

The Board of Trustees has retained the services of the consulting firm Jamison Jennings to conduct an evaluation of Atwater's policies and procedures regarding sexual misconduct and sexual abuse. While this evaluation is separate from the facts outlined in the *Hartford Courant* article dated September 26, we understand that the community will draw connections where it sees fit. If anything, the events outlined in the story have provided us with an opportunity to interrogate our school's policies and procedures to be sure that they are both ever-evolving and consistently aligned with best practices.

In my work as CEO of Regina Ventures, I hear dozens of pitches daily from aspiring companies. Each one promises to be the first of its kind: an innovation, something that fills a hole in the market. Pitches are designed to demonstrate what a product can do. But I always look to the future: What will you do, I ask these new inventors and innovators, to ensure that you *keep innovating*? Companies that succeed are those that find the intrinsic motivation to improve.

From its inception, Atwater has been a leader in girls' education. We have remained in this position of leadership not by resting on our laurels but rather via the constant pursuit of betterment; just as we ask our girls to grow, so we must ask the same of ourselves. The retention of Jamison Jennings is a part of this endeavor.

In the coming weeks, representatives from Jamison Jennings will visit campus and establish a line of communication with the community. I hope you will provide them with the same degree of honesty and openness with which I have been met as President of the Board.

Gratefully yours,

Erin Palmiere

Vespers

The whiteboard above the lifeguard chair spells out their morning workout: four hundred warm-up, 1-2-4-8-4-2-1, six by fifty starting every two minutes, four hundred cool-down. It shouldn't take more than forty minutes, Celeste Li thinks, if she's honest with her rest. In the lane ahead of her, Josie—the only other Asian girl on the swim team—is already warming up, and so Celeste begins easing into the water. She likes the way her arms flex as she dips, the way her back arches so that the fabric of her suit stretches taut across her rib cage.

Celeste is not good at swimming, but it's the only sport she knows a thing about, the only lessons offered for free at the local BCYF when she was five or six. She'd wanted to play tennis—"We can't afford it!" her father snapped when she nagged one time too many, angrily shoving his lunch into the small cooler he brought to his job as a call center representative—and still she feels the occasional pang of longing when she walks by the Atwater courts on a spring afternoon, the smack-pop rhythm of a good volley one she'll never compose herself. At school she swims because it's an Atwater requirement to participate in a type of "movement" each semester, and school-sanctioned sports are more socially acceptable than the PE classes Ms. McCredie cobbles together: Zumba, Insanity, pickleball, badminton. In the water she knows she should be thinking about the particular rotation of her shoulder, about how she isn't bringing her arm across her body quite enough, but instead she counts how many strokes she can go without breathing. She loses track of her laps. She decides to stop when Josie stops, because their coach, Joe, considers them roughly the same speed—probably he considers them roughly the same person—and so won't question the timing.

In the locker room, Celeste's teammates chatter away, their post-workout endorphin highs mingling with the anticipation of the upcoming winter break and Friday's Vespers.

"Hey Emma," Brie Feldman says as she detangles her mess of curly blond hair. "Has Olivia picked out an outfit yet? I could totally see her wearing a kind of sleek cut-for-a-lady tux."

Emma pops her head around the bank of lockers between them, an eyebrow raised. "So because she's a lesbian she has to dress like a man?"

"No, because she has a body like a Victoria's Secret model."

"It's true," Emma nods.

"Is she worried that Banks is going to censor her jokes? Because of everything?" For a week or two in the wake of the hacking of the Atwater Instagram, they'd wondered whether Vespers would be allowed to happen at all: there was a rumor—Celeste didn't know who started it—that the school planned to hold the holiday pageant hostage until someone confessed to the misdeed. But then the email came from Linda Paulsen as it always did (*VESPERS INSTRUCTIONS: PLEASE READ*) and the question of whether anyone among them would martyr themselves for the revelry of the student body ceased to be relevant.

"What jokes?"

"The witty banter she'll use to fill the space between performances."

"Nice try," Emma says. She takes on a kind of lawyerly affect: "But you know that I can neither confirm nor deny any rumors about Olivia's participation in the forthcoming Vespers performance."

Each year, the specifics of the holiday variety show—roles in which are the honor and privilege of the senior class only—are a surprise, revealed in real time on opening night. In the two weeks leading up to the performance, the entire school becomes obsessed with sleuthing out the key players and their acts. But it seems obvious to Celeste that Emma's girlfriend is going to be the emcee—Olivia Anderson is funny and charming and universally adored, the exact perfect person for the job—and maybe this is why she never really partakes in the guessing game: her classmates treat the show's particulars like secrets to be discovered, but in

Celeste's mind it's just a puzzle, a matter of piecing together personalities with likely performances.

"It's definitely Olivia," Josie says to Brie, who nods knowingly. Josie has always been better than Celeste at capitalizing on the social opportunities of swim practice; it was too hard, initially, for Celeste to find the exact right moment to chime in—the natural opening in the conversation— and now that she has become the quiet one on the team it would be too strange for her to speak up. She hangs at the periphery, witness but never party to the locker room banter.

"Obviously," Brie says, nodding. "Hey, Celeste—" Brie curves around Josie, arching backward to where Celeste stands in front of her locker. "Did you finish the Bioethics reading yet?"

She says it so quickly that Celeste takes an extra beat to process the question.

"Celeste."

"Yeah. I mean, no. Not yet."

"Ugh, I wanted to copy your annotations."

The purpose of Atwater's electives—the only scenario in which Celeste, a sophomore with average grades, and Brie, a high-achieving junior, might find themselves in the same class—is to provide students with opportunities to study subjects that interest them. In reality, though, electives are by and large treated as freebies: low-input GPA boosters taught by the most preternaturally laid-back faculty (like Mr. Gregory, their Bioethics teacher). Even so, Celeste thinks it doesn't seem like copying annotations would save *that* much time, particularly since annotations are easy to fake anyway.

Nevertheless: "I'll probably do that first," she says, "if you want to come by halfway through study hall . . ."

"Whatever, I'll just do it," Brie groans. "Ugh," she says, pinching a section of hair in front of her face, her irises nearly crossing the closer she moves the ends toward her nose. "The chlorine is *destroying* my hair. I don't understand how yours stays so smooth."

This didn't happen as much at Atlantic Middle School in North

Quincy, where Celeste's classes were filled with Chinese American students like her. Once in seventh grade Julia Lawrence—long-faced with dimples and curly, dark hair; not pretty, but maybe she'd grown into it since—reached forward from where she sat behind Celeste in math and tangled Celeste's ponytail in her fingers, churning it over between her knuckles.

"Your hair is *so* pretty," she said, longingly.

Across the aisle, Kelli McCord—who, because of some strange combination of the timing of her September birthday and the fact that she'd waited an extra year to start kindergarten, was fourteen in seventh grade—whipped around in Julia's direction and snapped: "That's some colonizer bullshit."

Chided, Julia released Celeste's ponytail. Twisting her arm over her shoulder to smooth her hair into place, Celeste hoped Kelli couldn't see how Julia's hands in her hair had made her skull tingle, her shoulders melt.

Next to Celeste now, stepping into her sweatpants, her face turned toward the lockers and away from Brie, Josie shoots Celeste the same look Kelli gave her that day in middle school, conspiratorial and commiserative all at once.

Josie Chen is Celeste's only real friend at Atwater. Celeste gravitated toward her naturally, sensing in Josie another relative outsider. While the majority of Atwater's international students are from wealthy families on mainland China, Celeste understood—from the way Josie commented on the Gucci sneakers, the Vuitton backpacks, the Balenciaga sweatshirts—that Josie's family was middle class in Hong Kong, and that they'd cobbled together all they had to finance her education. At lunch, the girls from Beijing and Shanghai sometimes lapsed into their native languages, but Josie had attended English-speaking schools her entire life and American schools since fourth grade (it was from Josie that Celeste learned that there even was such a thing as a "junior boarding school"). Celeste—the American-born daughter of Chinese immigrants—is on an academic merit scholarship at Atwater; she speaks only minimal Mandarin because her parents refused to use it around her when she was growing up, partly because they wanted Celeste to speak English and partly because they themselves were trying to learn and assimilate quickly. Celeste feels she spends most days at Atwater in a kind of slippery purgatory, and in Josie, she thought she'd found someone who finally understood what it was like: to feel too Chinese and poor to fit in with the American kids, but not Chinese enough—or wealthy enough—to fit in with the students from China.

She hides all this from her mother, who when she calls asks about Celeste's *friends*, plural. Maybe this is why Celeste still tries: that night she thinks about emailing Brie to let her know she finished the reading, but she doesn't want to appear desperate; she writes a draft, deletes it, asks Josie for Brie's number, drafts a text, deletes it. She decides to take a walk across the Bowl to Whitney to see Madame DuBois for help on the French homework, because she's on study hall duty on Brie's floor. When she gets there Brie's door is closed, and this somehow makes Celeste more embarrassed. In the lounge, Madame is presiding bemusedly over Vespers gossip ("Is Mr. Morgan really playing guitar in the teacher performance?" "*I* heard that they're doing that Band Aid song, you know, 'Do they know it's Christmastime at aaaalll . . .'"), a cluster of juniors at her feet and nestled into the couches around her. When she spots Celeste, she holds up a hand and asks in her nasally accent: "Celeste, do you need anything?"

She makes up a question about the journal-entry requirements and hurries back to her dorm.

Like most nights, Celeste has trouble falling asleep. Her window overlooks the small parking lot behind Lathrop. She stacks one pillow on top of another and rolls onto her side, scanning Atwater's still grounds. The ninth- and tenth-grade dorm is shaped like a right-angled U, or an open square, with Celeste's room on the third floor on the longest side. She cranes her neck a bit and shifts on her shoulder. The blinds are drawn on most windows; in some, pink or teal curtains are caught in the sliver of space between the blind edge and the window's side. Some girls line their windowsills: stuffed animals; pictures; small, cheap fans; candles they're not allowed to light. Celeste's own window frame is empty and, even on this early December night, open a few inches. Sometime in late October, the school turns on the central heat and leaves it blasting straight through to mid-April. The rooms bake, swell, radiate off and into one another. On thirty-degree nights the girls throw open their windows and doors, wasting the heat to the early-winter cold.

The new English teacher, Ms. Ryan, lives below her, in the faculty apartment on the second floor at the edge of the U. The kids like her, so far—she's young and pretty, went to Choate and then Yale, and got married over the summer. The girls on her hall like looking at her wedding pictures, and sometimes she brings her dog to class. She teaches freshmen and a senior elective (something about contemporary women writers, which sounds only vaguely interesting to Celeste, whose favorite class is, in fact, Mr. Gregory's), and first impressions of her are that she's *chill*.

Ms. Ryan and her new husband Owen have left the blinds open in their living room, and the white-blue glow of the television cuts through the room's overhead lighting. Celeste watches as Owen pulls Ms. Ryan to her feet, and as she brings her face toward his she slips one hand inside the waistband of his drawstring sweatpants. They're both in T-shirts—the unisex cotton kind you get for free at races or volunteer efforts—and Celeste thinks none of it seems very sexy or romantic, but she doesn't really have any point of reference. When they pull apart, Ms. Ryan rests one hand flat on her husband's chest; she slides the other into his palm, knitting their fingers together. She leads him, arm outstretched behind her, and disappears in the space between windows. The blinds in the next room are drawn, and so Celeste turns over in her bed, into the hot dark quiet of her room.

She feels a kind of swelling somewhere below her navel. She replays the image of Ms. Ryan rising to her feet, the ease with which she kept one hand looped through her husband's while moving the other across and then inside his pants, like it was all second nature. She is surprised by the kind of tucking sensation inside her own pajamas, and—without thinking, impulsively, a thing she has never exactly done before and yet an echo of the way she used to nestle her stuffed animals between her legs when she was eight or nine because something about pressing into them felt *good*, helped her to fall asleep—she folds her hand into her underwear, searching for a way to relieve the kind of tightening there. For a moment or two or three she doesn't think about anything, just the curious way her body feels smooth but also not, and then there's an expanding across her chest and shoulders and she stops, suddenly, pulling her hand outside her pants and squeezing it tight between her thighs, clenching them together, terrified of the edge to which she'd brought herself.

By morning Celeste is carrying last night like a dream of her own—maybe she did dream about it, after—and when she sees Ms. Ryan in the hall before class she smiles at her knowingly, like old confidantes, and is quickly embarrassed. She debates telling Josie what she saw (but not about what she did after); she thought she might do it at lunch, but they ended up sitting with some of the team, and she didn't want to tell *everyone*. Josie would understand that she was watching, not spying; with Josie she could wonder about why Ms. Ryan put her hands inside her husband's pants even though once on the swim bus Celeste had heard Brie say something about *why even bother with that, they can do it better themselves.*

After practice—in the afternoon that day; they're always juggling pool time with the local clubs and masters swim groups who pay Atwater to use its facilities—she catches up with Josie on the way to dinner.

"Hey."

"What's up?" Celeste remembers explaining the greeting to their German exchange students, who couldn't quite get the hang of salutations like, "What's up?" and "How's it going?" Something about their particular unassuming delivery—the idea that they were not really questions—caused Carla and Melanie to kind of choke on their words. Celeste always thought it was interesting that they understood the way the inflection didn't quite match the phrasing.

"Do you think Mr. Morgan is really going to play guitar in the teacher performance? I mean, can you imagine? What an absolute dream. I might spontaneously orgasm in my seat."

Celeste's cheeks flush hot and bright, and she's grateful for the early darkness of a December 6:00 P.M. The word sounds absurd on Josie's tongue—too clinical—and Celeste thinks maybe this is another thing they're getting wrong. She wants to say to her, *Are you sure that's the word we're supposed to use? What about "come"?* But she also wants to ask her, *Has that ever happened to you, have you ever had one, how?* She wants to ask, *Do you think Ms. Ryan had one last night?*

"Speaking of," Josie says, turning to face Celeste so suddenly that her oversize backpack swings away from her side, moving beyond her shoulder and knocking her 105-pound frame slightly off-balance—briefly Celeste is gripped with panic, a wild terror that Josie is going to ask her about last night, as if she can smell it on her—"who did you vote for?"

"What?"

"The Pedophile Playoffs."

Celeste has no idea what Josie is talking about; she stares at her friend, blank-faced.

"Wait, have you not seen it yet? Oh my God—okay, I'll send it to you." She pulls out her phone and tap-taps away, her face glowing in the dark. "Look at your phone."

The link Josie texted to Celeste brings her to an NCAA-style bracket, sixteen entries narrowing in a flowchart to a single name, not yet filled in. In the blank spaces at the outermost edges of the bracket are names, and Celeste absorbs them all at once, her eyes swallowing the sum: *Paulsen, Breslin, Gregory, Zarzynski*—the names of Atwater faculty and staff. The instructions at the top of the page are simple: *Who at Atwater is most likely to fuck a student? Vote your response! Rounds will be updated every eight hours.*

"Whoa," Celeste says, her mind clanging like a pinball machine.

"I know, right? Kinda fucked-up—but also sort of hilarious. I can't believe you hadn't seen it yet."

"Who sent it to you?"

"Brie," Josie says. "I think it's just getting sent around this way—like, person to person," she adds, as if she senses the insecurity at the core of Celeste's question. Josie means it like, *Don't worry, you weren't left out*, but what Celeste hears is confirmation that Josie is her only passage into this kind of gossip.

"Every eight hours," Celeste says finally, counting in her head. "That means the winner will be announced right after Vespers?"

"Mm-hmm," Josie nods, wide-eyed. "Timed for maximum impact. You should vote," she adds, sliding her phone back into her pocket. "My money's on Mr. Gregory."

"What?" Celeste loves Mr. Gregory. He's patient, accommodating, no-nonsense.

Josie makes a kind of groan-growl. "He's such a silver fox."

Here Celeste notices the slight Britishness to Josie's English, a trait her speech shares with some of the other Chinese students who attended English-speaking schools: the curved vowels, the lifted inflection. It's more elegant than the English Celeste's parents speak, dropped prepositions, present-tense only.

"But aren't we supposed to be voting for who's most likely to sleep with a student, not who we most want to . . . you know . . . fuck?" Like "orgasm," "have sex with" sounds clunky and clinical to Celeste, but "fuck" feels off, too—simultaneously indifferent and familiar.

Josie shrugs. "Choose your own adventure, I guess."

Study hall on Thursday night is a total wash, since Friday is a half day, and all the teachers know that their focus will be on that night's Vespers performance. In her room, Celeste opens the bracket on her laptop, waiting for the update. She looks out her window and tries again to count the rows to Ms. Ryan's apartment, but the lights are off. She waits a while like this, her computer in her lap, the names of her teachers spread before her like a kind of map. She wonders, briefly, if they know about the bracket—they can't, she decides; the school Wi-Fi would have most certainly blocked the site.

To vote on the names, Celeste thinks, would be to levy a kind of judgment; she feels as though she holds the fates of her teachers in her hands, that for once—for the first time—it is not the other way around. She looks over the pairings, and finds that she makes her decision differently each time: she votes for Amy McCredie over Linda Paulsen, for example, because it seems both cruel and cliché to vote for the Dean of Students who lives her life at Atwater as if they all do not know that she's gay; she chooses Mr. Morgan over Ms. Edwards for all the reasons that everyone else will surely choose Mr. Morgan: he's young and single and objectively hot—a triple threat, a unicorn on their campus. In Celeste's mind Ms. Hammacher edges out Mr. Hills because her brain cannot place Mr. Hills's endless patience in a sexual situation; when she has to choose between Mr. Gregory and Mr. Clark, Josie's opinion rattles in her memory, and she selects Mr. Gregory against her better instincts. The bottom half of the bracket is a series of teachers she knows less well: Mr. Fink, who teaches Latin, against Ms. Trujillo, a new Spanish teacher and a Dorm Parent in Whitney; the male art teachers—Mr. Zarzynski and Mr. Breslin—face off against one another; Mr. Banks is paired with the bracket's sole write-in spot.

Next to her computer, a new message from Josie bubbles onto her phone.

Did u vote??

        Thinking about it.

Do ittttt

        What'd you put for Zarzynski/Breslin

Breslin duh

        Why

idk he just seems like a cradle robber lol

Anyway my $$ is still on Gregory going all the way

        Did you actually make a bet with someone

lol no I'm just rly into predictions lately

> Vespers will do that to you

Speaking of!

Final predictions comin in hot

> Hah ok

Soph and Ariyana are doing a duet

Kat Foard is doing her own choreography

I think Ayesha is doing the opening

> Mmm bold choice

True, but I stand by it

> Kk

And Olivia MC obviously

> I think it's "emcee"

Nerd

> lol

> Also I feel like that's not a prediction

> Everybody knows

Well u heard it here first

> I didn't . . .

Also we're getting ready together right

The dress code for Vespers is, officially, semiformal, but each year inches closer and closer to the Academy Awards. Celeste and Josie bought their dresses at a consignment store in Hartford; Celeste's is red with a square neckline and a slit up the thigh, and hovers precariously between cheap-looking and '90s supermodel. It cost $17.

> I mean who else would I get ready with

lol same

Celeste types, deletes, retypes. She appreciates her friend saying the right thing, but she knows that's exactly what it is: kindness, or even pity.

omg

Bracket's updated!

Celeste puts her phone down and refreshes the browser window. She scans the names with a kind of heart-thudding delirium, as if the thing she's doing is fatally dangerous. In the bottom half of the bracket—the part Celeste hadn't finished—Ms. Trujillo has advanced against Mr. Fink; Mr. Breslin, like Josie predicted, is into the round of eight, and now faces off against Mr. Banks, who apparently did not face a unified-enough write-in challenge to be spared the humiliation of being among the top-eight faculty most likely to fuck a student.

And Celeste can't explain it, but she feels a vague kind of relief at the fact that Mr. Banks moved on—that no one wrote in Owen or Ms. Ryan. Or maybe someone did, but not enough someones. The image of Ms. Ryan and her husband having sex remains Celeste's alone, a private detail, a secret only she knows.

In the morning the school wakes to the final four, the ballots cast overnight (or, more likely, in the immediate aftermath of the publishing of the round of eight): Mr. Morgan, Ms. Hammacher, Ms. Trujillo, and Mr.

Breslin. Celeste also wakes to a text from Josie, furious that Mr. Gregory lost to Ms. Hammacher. She does not point out that she heard a rumor that Ms. Hammacher actually dated a former student. By the afternoon the Playoffs are as compelling a backdrop to their getting-ready revelry as the pop/hip-hop cacophony that thumps down the hallway, her hallmates shuffling from one room to another, borrowing eyeshadow palettes and hair spray and the good mascara, leaving straighteners and curling irons plugged in by the hallway mirrors for optimal sharing.

Josie sits very still in Celeste's desk chair while her friend smears highlighter on her cheekbones and the tip of her nose and the high points under her eyebrows and draws winged liner at the corners of her lids.

"Honestly you should charge people for this," Josie says, mumbling so as to only minimally move her face. "You know that, like, Collier and Addison hire people to come do their makeup for prom?"

"Mmm," Celeste murmurs, intensely focused. Celeste started wearing makeup in eighth grade, after Kelsey Friedman pointed to a smatter of acne on Celeste's left cheek and said, "I thought Asian people were supposed to have perfect skin?" When her mother refused to use her day off—she worked long hours as a home health aide—to walk Celeste to the local Rite-Aid, she nicked a wad of cash from the bottom of her mother's purse and assembled her own kit of basics: concealer and powder and blush; a stick of black eyeliner and a pink-and-green tube of mascara. She zipped it all into a small pocket in her backpack and applied it each morning on the bus, perfecting a steady hand as she flicked black charcoal along her waterline at long red lights, trying not to dwell on how her mother never mentioned the theft, and how this must have been a sore spot for her, too, the fact that their family had no spending money to spare.

At Atwater she discovered that most girls don't wear makeup on a regular school day, or maybe just a little concealer and a swipe of mascara to look awake, but by then Celeste liked doing makeup, liked marking her face in a neat grid of light and dark foundation before sponging the colors into one another. She started practicing alone at night, after dark, the chatter of a YouTuber directing her: highlighter for day, highlighter for night, cut crease eye makeup, glitter eye makeup, glitter for day, how to do a cat eye on a monolid.

As Celeste combs Josie's eyebrows, fluffing them with a plastic spoolie, there's a shout from the bathroom down the hall—"It's updated!"—and Josie jolts out of her seat, smacking at her phone on the desk, where she announces—they hear it shouted down the hall, too—that Mr. Morgan and Mr. Breslin are the final two.

Celeste does not vote, not again, but not because she wants to take some kind of moral stance on the thing, not because she thinks they shouldn't joke about which teacher might sleep with a student and not because maybe—as she heard one of the seniors suggest over lunch—it's sort of sexual harassment, isn't it, to rank a group of people according to their presumed sex drive? She doesn't vote because she cannot stop calling up the image of Ms. Ryan and Owen together, because she cannot look at the bracket without wanting to scream out that she actually *literally* knows about the sex life of one of their teachers. So instead she lets Josie—who understands the currency that polished, shining hair is at Atwater, who notices the bottles of thirty-dollar shampoo in her hallmates' shower caddies, who once told Celeste, bitterly, that at least they didn't have to be rich to have the hair everybody wanted—smooth her hair in a neat center part and tuck each side behind her ears, sleek and on trend. Celeste closes her eyes and sings very softly along with the pop medley that streams from Josie's phone, the terrible fury of a very good secret nipping at the edges of her focus.

It begins like this: They funnel into the tunnels from their dorms—underclasswomen from Lathrop, juniors from across the Bowl in Whitney—and snake their way beneath the ground to Trask. At the entrance that separates the bowels of Atwater from the century-old halls of the art building, they organize themselves into a long line, two-by-two, 150 students deep—freshmen then sophomores then juniors, so that the oldest among them are the last to enter the auditorium. Waiting, her classmates fuss: they twist their hair behind their heads, sweeping it to one side or the other; they tap gently at the corners of their eyes, heads tilted upward, fighting against the ceaseless migration of eyeliner and eye shadow downward into the circles below; they reach their hands beneath the necklines of their gowns, cupping one breast and then the other to coax them to maximum perk; they drum their almond-shaped acrylics against one another, tap-tap-tapping.

Linda Paulsen oversees the operation, shuttling back and forth between the front and the back, counting students, physically moving them back into place if they step out from their lines. Last year, at her first Vespers, Celeste didn't know what to expect—it's the kind of tradition, like so many at Atwater, that requires experiencing to understand. Standing near the front of the line, she felt like a bride about to walk down the aisle, or a runway model: Should she smile? What if her dress, which was sort of short, shifted with each stride until it grazed and then revealed the bottom of her underwear? She wonders if this year's freshmen—smooth and soft, almost all of them in minidresses, except for Bryce Engel, who is apparently the kind of fourteen-year-old who can pull off an emerald-green silk midi dress—feel like Celeste did then: nervous and curious and excited all at once. Behind her at the end of the line, the juniors exude a kind of superiority, standing tall in the knowledge that next year *they* will be the ones the school waits to watch. Brie Feldman's thick curly hair is woven into an unruly bohemian French braid. Blake Trude's eyes are haloed in smudged black shadow. Sloane Beck's silver dress puddles on the ground behind her.

Standing next to Josie in the middle of the line with the other sophomores—Camilla Frazier in magenta taffeta, Hannah Griffin in cascading ruffles, both of them a little bit bored-looking—it occurs to Celeste that everything about being a sophomore is about biding time between more meaningful stages. As Linda Paulsen opens the door and the line rushes forward—"Slowly, *slowly*," she hisses after them—it seems to Celeste like the whole grade is just passing through.

Vespers opens the same way every year: The lights dim, the curtain rises, and for a few seconds the only thing the audience hears is the opening lines of the first song. The absence of light heightens the senses, attuning them to the voice that diffuses through the auditorium. Celeste feels the skin on her forearms prickle, her hairs standing at attention. For once, the entire school is on its best behavior, hanging on every note, trying to guess the identity of the singer before the light goes on.

Noelle Taylor sings a cappella for the first three verses of the song, all the way until the first "'All I want for Christmas . . .'" The spotlight flips on, the band behind her kicks in, and Celeste's classmates roar so loudly that they drown out the music. At the second "'All I want for Christmas'" Noelle holds the mic out to the audience, who finishes the verse in a cacophonous "'you-*oooo*.'" They sing along for the remainder of the song, unselfconsciously, the audience altogether so raucous that it is impossible to distinguish one voice from another. For a brief moment ("'and everyone is singin' / oh yeah'") it occurs to Celeste that Noelle Taylor probably practiced quite a bit for this performance, hours of rehearsal spearhead by Mr. Banks's sweaty enthusiasm, only to lead the school in a massive sing-along.

As Noelle takes her bow, grinning widely, her sequined gown fanned out at her feet, Josie pauses between whistles to hiss in Celeste's ear to lament her failed prediction that Ayesha Hobbs would open the show: "Damn, oh for one!"

To no one's surprise, Olivia Anderson takes the stage, arm out-stretched, conferring a few additional seconds of glory upon Noelle, which is something of a lost cause because Olivia is a vision. She has, in fact, chosen to wear a sort of tuxedo, but with a nipped waist and tapered leg it's a decidedly feminine suit. She has also chosen to forgo a shirt under-neath the tuxedo jacket, leaving exposed a deep V of gleaming skin. Her collarbone shimmers as she turns toward each side of the auditorium, the light catching on whatever highlighter Celeste imagines she dusted across her chest before going onstage. Celeste finds it impossible to believe that she herself is only two years younger than Olivia. The woman standing onstage in front of them seems a lifetime away.

"One for two," Josie shouts in Celeste's direction.

"I don't think you get any credit for this one," Celeste says, rolling her eyes.

Josie waves her hand dismissively.

Olivia gives the crowd a minute to settle, standing before them with a politician's patience. Her smile is warm and generous. With the nudging of some of the faculty—who bring pointed fingers to their lips or make a sort of patting motion with their hands, hushing the students around them—Celeste's classmates quiet enough for Olivia to welcome the audience to the two-hundred-and-second Atwater Vespers.

"Surprise!" Olivia says. "It's me! I bet you guys had no idea." She winks and pauses for a sort of accommodating laughter before continuing: "I promise the entire show won't be a *Love Actually* cover." She angles her body in the direction of the stage's wings: "Right down to the Black girl in sequins, huh, Mr. Banks?"

Around her, Celeste's classmates' eyes widen and jaws drop in delight. They all understand that Olivia can get away with this joke not only because she is multiracial but also because her success is evidence against the very thing she's mocked: she is the school's diversity-and-inclusion poster child, the story it tells when it wants to say, *Look, see? You don't have to be white to thrive here.*

"Speaking of," Olivia continues, "I do want to take a moment to thank our fearless leader in both on- and offstage drama, Mr. Banks, for putting together this show. You may find us exhausting, Mr. Banks, but I *promise* you that you *more than* returned the favor during rehearsals." Celeste watches the faculty next to her, looking for a stiffening in their body language, any flicker of nervousness that Olivia is going to exploit this opportunity—or, perhaps, the slightest and nearly imperceptible rankling at the word *favor*, loaded as it could be with connotations of sex—but they seem perfectly fine, the light from the stage highlighting sort of bemused smiles. Celeste wonders if any of the Atwater faculty will ever trust her the way they trust Olivia.

"Thank you, too, to the rest of our outstanding faculty and staff, who understand that absolutely zero learning happens this week and adjust their plans accordingly. Let's give them a hand, huh?" She stretches out her arms, clapping in the direction of the faculty section. "We've got a great show for you tonight—some might say the best Vespers in Atwater history. So, without further ado, please welcome Kat Foard to the stage!" The curtain behind her raises, and Olivia—in high-heeled stilettos— glides offstage.

Celeste recognizes the classical music that plays as Kat poses at a single barre positioned to the left side of the stage, at an angle. In third grade, a local dance company visited Celeste's elementary school—later she'd understand as a kind of community service commitment; her entire childhood Celeste attended programs and lessons that were part of *outreach efforts*—and performed an abridged version of *The Nutcracker* for her classmates. The boys squirmed, bored in their seats, until the Mouse King took center stage; the girls twirled on tiptoe out of the auditorium and practiced their balance on the playground jungle gym.

Kat is long-limbed and sinewy like the dancers Celeste remembers from that performance, but she wears joggers cuffed at the ankles and a kind of racer-back top. Even from this distance, Celeste can see that the bun atop Kat's head is secured with a scrunchie. The dance she does is not anything Celeste remembers from that performance almost seven years ago: It's more athletic, more dynamic—a modern dance riff on centuries-old choreography. After a few minutes, the music fades out, and in the space between songs Kat is joined onstage by the rest of the seniors in the upper-level dance course: Emily Malone, Nina Henderson, Gabby Woods, and Tatiana Quirk. They, too, are dressed in what Celeste can only describe as Lululemon-meets-ballet: athletic, not too dainty. Kat anchors a performance whose steps mirror the original. Celeste understands there is probably a statement in the juxtaposition of the athletic attire with the classical dance, but it goes a bit over her head.

Olivia returns to the stage as the curtain drops. "Don't worry, Blake," she says, eyeing the junior in the front row. "I'm sure you'll be able to pull that off next year."

There's some low-toned *oooooh*s as the audience reacts to the barb. Under normal circumstances Celeste thinks that Blake—whose temper tantrums are as notorious as her competitiveness—might have stewed in reaction, but Blake cups her hands around her mouth and hollers at the stage, "Challenge accepted!" and the audience laughs, the tension eased.

"This next duo apologizes in advance for the language, and defers all teacher protestations to Mr. Banks. Please welcome Ariyana Amado and Sophie Wagner to the stage!"

The show goes on like this: music and dance performances intercut with Olivia's emceeing, which is for the most part unobtrusive in terms of material, exactly the kind of confident, easy, non-distracting space-filler Mr. Banks likely requested. Ariyana and Sophie do a version of the Pogues' "Fairytale of New York," not bothering to swap out the references to bums and scumbags and sluts for more school-appropriate language. Olivia makes a joke about the Christian-normative-ness of the show that goes over fairly well. Cate Evers plays the piano and sings Leonard Cohen's "Hallelujah," and by the time she gets to the bit about the flag on the marble arch Josie is weeping, as are most of Celeste's classmates. For her part, Celeste is not sure it counts as a holiday song.

Olivia brings Ashley Witt and Isabelle Baldwin to the stage. Izzy is dressed—unmistakably—as a man, in jeans and a plaid button-down and a Patagonia vest and her hair is slicked back into a curled-under bun at the nape of her neck. Ashley wears dark denim and a leather jacket that looks very expensive. A corner of the stage is reconstructed to look like a bar, and Ashley hops onto it, crossing her dangled legs, as Izzy sidles up to her, resting an elbow on the corner.

Ashley's voice is throaty like a 1940s movie star when she tells Izzy she can't stay.

"'Baby, it's cold outside,'" Izzy answers, and Celeste sees Kit and Blake in the row ahead of her stiffen. "But—I respect your decision," Izzy says, winking at the audience. Laughter rumbles from the audience, mostly from the juniors at the front, who likely have thought more critically about consent as it plays out in the mid-century holiday song than the freshmen have. The duet keeps up the gag throughout the entire song, replacing the male character's insistence with respectful and helpful responses: Instead of whining about the snow and the dearth of cabs, Izzy offers "a hat to cover your hair!" and asks, "the Uber should bring you where?".

Around her, her classmates love the bit. They hoot and whistle and clap, and with every collective approval Izzy and Ashley dig in a little bit more, embellishing, gesticulating, their confidence growing visibly the longer they spend onstage. Celeste cannot stop wondering if Isabelle Baldwin—the Proctor on the second floor of Lathrop, whose room is next door to the faculty apartment—has ever heard Ms. Ryan and her husband having sex, if at night she sits cross-legged on her dorm bed with her head craned toward the wall behind her, her ear attuned to the rhythmic thumping of a headboard. Suddenly, Celeste hates Isabelle Baldwin. When they finish, Josie leans toward Celeste and says, still giggling, "That was awesome, right?"

Celeste shrugs. "It was okay."

"What's wrong?" Josie says, nudging Celeste in the hip.

Celeste can feel the sweat pooling underneath her arms. She wonders if pit stains are forming in half circles in the fabric and clamps her inner arm to her side. "Nothing. Just have a headache."

"It's loud, I know." Josie gives Celeste a little squeeze—one hand curled quickly around Celeste's forearm—and then goes back to clapping wildly for Olivia, who has returned to the stage to introduce the faculty performance.

"Now," Olivia begins, "I know the best part of the faculty performance is—usually—getting to watch our teachers suck at something. Sorry, guys," she adds, shrugging in the direction of the faculty, who chuckle good-naturedly. "But I've got some bad news. This year's performance is actually . . . good? So . . . Let's give it up for the Educators!"

The curtain rises, and in the few seconds of silence that follow they can see that there's a full band onstage and that the teachers who helm each piece are dressed in their nerdiest version of themselves. On the guitar, Mr. Morgan has a calculator and a ruler tucked into his shirt-front pocket; seated at the drums, Mr. Clark wears a lab coat and safety goggles; standing at the mic at center stage, Ms. Trujillo is dressed in a Spain *fútbol* jersey; on the floor next to her spot at the keyboard, Ms. Daniels has stacked a pile of textbooks; and near the back of the set, on the bigger-looking guitar that Celeste assumes to be an electric bass, Ms. Ryan is dressed like a less-stylish version of her regular self, in a slouchy cardigan and Dansko clogs—a loose interpretation of regular suburban English teachers everywhere.

"'It's Christmas,'" Mr. Morgan croons, strumming an uncomplicated chord as he continues: "'Baby, please come home.'"

Mr. Clark (and the drums) kick in, and around Celeste the student body loses its collective mind. Brie turns to Blake, clutching her chest as if in a swoon; Kit Eldridge cups either side of her face, her jaw half-open.

Without taking her eyes off the stage, Josie shouts in Celeste's direction: "If he doesn't win, the game is rigged."

It's not Mr. Morgan, though, who captures Celeste's attention. At the back of the stage, Ms. Ryan occupies a bass player's usual amount of space—which is to say, not much. She sways lightly with the beat, the instrument resting against a jutted-out hip. At the chorus, she leans toward her mic, her neck slightly forward ("'Christmaaas'") before returning to her bass. Suddenly, everything Ms. Ryan does is intercut with what Celeste has seen her do with her husband; the moment plays for Celeste like a scene in a movie where a murderer's confession is spliced together with slash cuts to the act itself. First, the images are contained to exactly what Celeste has seen—the oversize T-shirts, the hand inside Owen's pants, then the palm on his chest, the movement from the living room into the bedroom, Ms. Ryan leading the way—but the longer Celeste is confronted with the image of Ms. Ryan onstage before her, her wavy hair half tucked behind an ear, the more Celeste realizes she has more of the memory:

Ms. Ryan and Owen in their apartment hallway, bare feet against the nubby Berber carpeting, Owen pushing Ms. Ryan against the wall, kissing her neck, his hands working first over her T-shirt and then under it while Ms. Ryan's face tilts back and upward; in the bedroom, Ms. Ryan undresses first, and then Owen climbs on top of her, and Ms. Ryan winds her legs around Owen's waist, her knees toward the ceiling. Her arms wrap around his back, and her nails claw into the space around his shoulder blades, leaving skin-toned not-quite-scratches behind. In this version the lighting is gray-blue and glowing, as if in the predawn; the action is silent. It reminds Celeste of something she has seen in a movie—but she is certain it's real, that this is how it happens.

Suddenly Celeste wishes she could stop the entire concert, wishes with a kind of frantic hunger that someone would pull a fire alarm or that the power would go out or that at this very second an asteroid would career into the Earth. The way Josie bites down on the knuckles of her closed fist; how Sloane holds an open palm to a dropped jaw; the manner in which Blake brings a hand to each temple—it all makes Celeste want to scream: *She's mine, you don't know her like I do, only he and I get to see her like this.*

After the show—after the Songbirds perform "I'll Be Home for Christmas," after Olivia invites the performers onstage for a final bow, after Mr. Banks waves red-faced and sweating to a standing ovation—Celeste follows Josie back across the Bowl to Lathrop, where their classmates sprint from room to room and gather in the lounge for the elaborate spread of snacks their Dorm Parents and Proctors have prepared.

"I'm gonna go put on sweats," Celeste says, a hand on Josie's upper arm, which is already reaching into a five-pound bag of Sour Patch Kids.

"Oh, but—" Josie whines, sucking on a blue candy, "don't you know? It's so *glamorous* to eat junk food in formal attire!"

"Since when?" Celeste asks.

"Since Jennifer Lawrence ate that pizza at the Oscars." Josie pops another Sour Patch Kid into her mouth. "Anyway, I can't promise you there'll be any red ones left."

But instead of going to her room, Celeste walks past her door and to the set of stairs that ladder down the back corner of the dorm. On the second floor she moves with the same kind of wordless viscosity that she does in the pool, all pulse thumping in her own ears, eyes trained on the floor beneath her. When she knocks on the door she does so with a quick rap-rap-rap; while she waits, she brings a hand to her temple, checking where Josie smoothed her hair behind her ears. She looks to her left, to Izzy Baldwin's room, and again calls up the image of the Proctor with her ear to the wall she shares with Ms. Ryan's apartment.

It's Owen who opens the door, in a white V-neck T-shirt and baggy basketball shorts, the edge of navy-blue boxers just visible at his waist, patterned with the gray skeletons of little fish, spiny and bug-like. To an outsider it might seem odd that this adult man—who had to pass a basic background check to live on-campus with his wife but who does not himself have any actual professional ties to the school—lives with 150 teenage girls. But faculty spouses and partners are a regular part of boarding school life, where the private lives of teachers become paraprofessional: even now, as she wonders whether she's thrilled or repulsed by the hair that furs Owen's legs and the patch of chest above the V of his shirt, nothing about the arrangement strikes Celeste as *strange*, not even in this year of yard signs and allegations and Pedophile Playoffs.

"Hi," Owen says finally. "You're probably looking for my wife? I think she's out in the common room with everybody."

"Did you come to the show?" Celeste asks.

"Oh," Owen says. He looks at Celeste directly, curiously. His eyes are gray-green, a kind of kaleidoscopic hazel. "Yes, yeah."

"She was really good," Celeste says.

Owen cocks his head to one side and curls his lips into a kind of half smile, half smirk. "What's your name?"

"Celeste."

"Celeste," he says, nodding, his shoulders slipping slightly back. "Did you know she learned to play the bass just for this?"

"She didn't already know how?"

"Nope." Owen places a hand around the back of his neck and rubs, shaking his head slowly in a disbelieving kind of one-two. "Nothing. She didn't even, like, play the recorder in elementary school music class."

"Wow," Celeste says. She imagines Ms. Ryan as a little girl, her big eyes consuming her soft, small face.

"Yeah. She's always doing things like this. This summer, right after we moved in, our air conditioner broke. We had this crappy window unit, you know? So it was a hundred degrees in here, and I was like, let's just go get a new one. But before I could even google the nearest Target, my wife had yanked the air conditioner out of the window and was sitting cross-legged on our living room floor with a couple of screwdrivers and a wrench. She watched three YouTube videos and had it fixed in like fifteen minutes."

It's almost too much for Celeste, the thought of Ms. Ryan on the wood floor in the summer heat, all exposed skin and sharp angles— knees and elbows and tanned shoulders—sweat beading at her temples, her dark hair pulled back in a tiny ponytail, her focus singular, deter- mined. She imagines the rush of cool air as the unit rumbled back to life, Ms. Ryan standing in front of the vents with her arms outstretched, palms out, eyes shut, and then: Owen behind her, wrapping his arms around her waist, burying his face in her neck as she cranes back, leaning into him—

"Anyway," he says, and Celeste feels her cheeks brighten as the image dissolves, "the point is, the woman can learn to do anything."

What would it be like, Celeste wonders, to be talked about this way? She thinks about how her Peer Educator asked them—in a Hall Meet- ing workshop on "healthy relationships," one mandated by (but without any direction from) Mrs. Brodie in the wake of the newspaper leak—to define *intimacy*: "The sign above the condoms in CVS," Hannah Griffin said, half joking, before they'd come up with better answers—closeness, familiarity. But their Peer Educator wanted them to talk about *communi- cation*, apparently, and anyway the whole thing felt like a case of the blind leading the blind. How could they know? They didn't even like the phrase *sleeping with* as a stand-in for *sex*. This must be it, Celeste thinks now: the marvel of a fixed air conditioner, sex in sweatpants, your spouse singing your praises when you're not even listening.

"I'm sorry," Owen continues: "You probably don't want to hear about all that. Like I said, Allison—er, Ms. Ryan—is probably out in the com- mon room, if you need her."

At the accidental use of his wife's first name, Owen flushes; he crosses one foot over the other, flexing the toes of the crossed foot against the floor, his ankle knocking into the bottom of his shin. Maybe it's the way Owen seems a little sheepish, or maybe it's because he sounded like he was dismissing Celeste but also apologizing—she'll replay the moment again and again in her head, looking for the shrug of his shoulders, lis- tening for the curves of flirtatiousness when he asked *What's your name?*, the impossibility that *Allison* was just a coincidence—but Celeste pulls her right hand from her side and reaches it across the space between them and places her palm on Owen's upper arm, against his outer bicep, right next to where Ms. Ryan had placed her hand on his chest.

As soon as she feels the weight and warmth of him beneath her—as soon as her hand registers how unexpectedly *solid* Ms. Ryan's husband feels—she pulls back, like she's touched a hot stove. She looks up at Owen, whose jaw is half-dropped, eyes wide, head back so that the skin of his neck wrinkles beneath his chin.

She does not look back as she walks quickly back down the hall. Out of the corner of her eye she glimpses the inside of Izzy's room through a half-open door—a mound of rumpled comforter, the gold glow of twinkle lights and a desk lamp, the sophisticated refusal of overhead lighting—and resists the urge to take off running, worried the awkward clacking of her heeled feet would draw attention.

She has a hand on her own door, her fingertips curled around the knob, when someone shouts her name.

"Celeste!"

She turns slowly, bracing herself, sure that it's Ms. Ryan, having chased her down. She imagines what Owen might have said, adjectives clanging in her brain: *weird, awkward, creepy, embarrassing.* But it's not Ms. Ryan who moves toward her down the hall; it's Lauren Triplett, in a tiny black dress with her hair pulled back in a half-up bun, her athlete's shoulders muscular but not manly. Celeste guesses she's on this floor visiting Camilla or one of the other sophomores on the field hockey team—at least, she is certainly not here to see Celeste.

"Just wanted to say that I love your dress," she says, walking closer. "Is it vintage?"

"Oh—yeah." Celeste looks down at her stomach, at the seam that refused to sit flat on her hip bone. "Thanks," she manages.

Lauren stops in front of her. Her eyes flick across Celeste's cheeks, nose, eyebrows, forehead. Celeste resists the urge to bring a hand to the corner of her eyelid, to make sure that her makeup hasn't run, that the concealer by the corner of her nose hasn't caked.

"Your hair looks really, really pretty," Lauren says finally. "I wish I could do mine like that." Smiling, she reaches a hand out and gives Celeste's forearm a little squeeze. "Okay, I've gotta get out of these shoes."

For a moment Celeste stands frozen, watching the freshman stride down the hall with an ease that belies any discomfort in four-inch strappy sandals. She thinks about how Josie has this talent, too—the ability to say the half-true thing, to place all her feelings in a prism of relatability, like the struggle of uncomfortable shoes.

She closes her door behind her, muffling the sounds of vacation eve. It's two minutes to eleven, and the bracket's winner is due to drop. Briefly, Celeste considers its creator; were the yard signs her doing, also? Or did she see them on her way to school—like everybody else—and think, *I could do something like that, too*? Celeste imagines her alone somewhere right now, waiting for her moment to hit Send. What does it feel like, she wonders, to communicate from behind leaked newspapers and hacked Instagram accounts and teacher takedowns? To never be seen but always heard, to choose the terms of your own invisibility?

Celeste surveys her desk. There's a stack of handouts from Bioethics, feedback from Ms. Edwards paper-clipped to her essay on *Jane Eyre*. In the cup that holds her pens and pencils, her pink-handled mini-scissors stand at attention. Hooking the scissors between her thumb and forefinger, she bends to the floor, hiking her dress up to her thighs and folding her legs into one another on the pink shag of her rug. There's a popcorn kernel near her left knee. A long, stray hair snakes through the fibers, its sleek, thick blackness stark against the deep, bright pink.

She follows the curve of her ear with her left forefinger, releasing the hair from where Josie smoothed it into place. She is surprised by her own care, how delicately she holds the two-inch section in front of her face, pinching it between the middle phalanxes of her index and middle fingers. She counts her breaths, listens for the quell in the merriment outside her door. She imagines them together in the hall, foreheads touching over glowing screens, alert to the watchful eyes and ears of the adults in charge. In the quiet she imagines she can hear each strand of hair as it breaks, snapping as the scissors bite. But the cut pieces fall noiselessly, landing like feathers on her thighs.

To: brodiep@TheAtwaterSchool.org
From: breslinr@TheAtwaterSchool.org
Date: Dec 21, 2015, 9:02 A.M.
Subject: Resignation

Patricia,

It is with great sadness that I write to inform you of my resignation, effective immediately. While I have appreciated your support in recent months, and while I maintain my innocence regarding all accusations levied (including those implied in the course of the Vespers weekend), we both know that I cannot return to school in January and continue as an effective educator.

I apologize for the suddenness of this departure, and I realize that such an exit after more than twenty years may be interpreted as a sign of disrespect, ingratitude, or even guilt. I can only say that I hope the winter break will provide you with the space to divine the appropriate messaging, and the time to find a long-term substitute.

Rich

To: breslinr@TheAtwaterSchool.org
From: brodiep@TheAtwaterSchool.org
Date: Dec 21, 2015, 10:18 P.M.
Subject: Re: Resignation

Rich,

I am disappointed although not surprised to hear this. I hope that this decision provides you with the distance, support, and tranquility you crave.

Regardless of circumstance, midyear departures do pose certain challenges. I think that the smoothest way to navigate this transition would be for us to grant you a leave of absence, with your anticipated retirement from Atwater at the conclusion of the school year. Twenty years is, after all, a veritable career. While you are still technically a member of the Atwater community, I would appreciate your continued adherence to our policy of not commenting on the pending lawsuit.

Thank you for your service to Atwater.

Patricia

Retrospectives

The paintings appeared on the first Thursday after break. They hung in classrooms and hallways; above common-room couches and library carrels; on the dining hall doors, in the music practice rooms, and in the gym by the ellipticals. In the arts building, Trask, they were the most prolific of all, reproductions taped to supply cabinets and office doors and even laid flat and tacked down on studio tables, like neat little workstation placemats.

They were portraits of young women, each one comprised of hundreds of tiny drawings of butterflies: smaller and more crowded at the creases of the nostrils, the corners of the eyes, the Cupid's bow above the lips; larger across the cheeks, the apex of the forehead, the point of the nose. Some students said the paintings reminded them of Magic Eye pictures, the dizzying kaleidoscopic optical illusions in which a person could see, if they squinted in just the right way, a cityscape or a cresting wave or a horse in stride. Others said they looked like horror-movie stills, of bodies being buried alive in swarming insects. Most agreed that they seemed to depict rather *young* women—although it was possible that this distinction was less due to artistic intention and more a consequence of context. Everywhere on campus the faces stared at them, girls zipped shut in casts of bugs.

The only upside to the infestation, from Abby Randall's perspective, was that it gave her and Bella Nitido something real to talk about.

The email came in the middle of Christmas vacation. Abby was home in Vermont, most days not even changing out of her pajamas, watching

Netflix underneath a stack of her mother's quilts while her cat—an older, temperamental tabby unironically named Kitty—purred at her feet. It was from her Dorm Parent, Ms. Trujillo, with *Update* typed in the subject line, and Abby knew what it would say before she opened it. Her roommate, Helen, a new girl from South Korea, practically *arrived* homesick, and after a few tearful nights withdrew from Atwater, leaving Abby with a track record of failed rooming arrangements (her sophomore roommate, Haley, who was supposed to be her junior roommate, too, was asked after two years of straight Ds to consider whether Atwater was the right place for her educational journey; it was not) and a double all to herself. Of course she assumed she'd get a new roommate, as assignments shuffled and the usual handful of late-enrolling hockey players (the only Atwater sport that was reliably decent, and the only one that enlisted a roster of PGs) trickled in, but then a week and then two and then a month went by, and it never happened. She spread her yoga mat on the opposite side of the room, played music without her earbuds in, got fully naked when she had to change, no longer shimmying out of underwear beneath a wrapped towel.

Ms. Trujillo knew that this big room had been such a treat for Abby, her email said. But Atwater was welcoming a student back to campus in January, a junior who had previously attended the school but withdrawn for personal reasons, and they needed to put this young woman in Whitney with the other juniors. "You should feel free to reach out to Bella Nitido yourself," the email concluded, and that was when the news went from bad to worse.

Bella left Atwater in the middle of their sophomore year. Before it all fell apart, she was a bona fide member of the group of girls everybody wants to be: her best friend was Sloane Beck, and the two ran around Atwater with their supreme knowledge of drugs and thinness and slept-in eyeliner until spring break, when Bella posted a series of overexposed pictures and videos of herself and Sloane and Blake and Kit and Brie in Bella's room (they could tell by the shibori wall hanging and the Metro-Cards taped to her desk), their heads always cocked at just the right angle, Sloane's hair lazily half covering her face. In one of them, a small pile of Tic Tac–size pills was visible on a shelf behind their shoulders; in another, a disembodied hand passed a joint into the camera's field of vision. Someone shared the pictures with Linda Paulsen, and while the other girls were put on probation, this was Bella's third time breaking a Fundamental Standard. She had to go.

It was kind of a big deal because Atwater doesn't kick people out for ordinary reasons related to drugs and drinking: It takes a higher-order offense, like an *academic integrity violation*, or something that *threatens the community trust*, like theft. Maybe this is why they'd agreed to let Bella back in, Abby thought—maybe they'd realized it was a too-harsh punishment. Or maybe it had something to do with Karen Mirro—everything this year seemed to have to do with Karen Mirro—and how the terms of her expulsion had called into question the seemingly arbitrary execution of Atwater's disciplinary system.

Reading the email, Abby tried to think if she'd ever spoken to Bella outside of structured situations: chem class last year, English the year before that; dorm bonding activities in Lathrop. Otherwise, nothing beyond a hallway head nod or a bathroom-sink smile. It wasn't that Bella was *mean* to Abby, but rather that neither existed in the other's world.

In the end, the move-in had been more survivable than Abby had anticipated; neither she nor Bella died from awkwardness. With Ms. Trujillo's permission she returned to campus a day early to move her things back to her side of the double, and tried not to imagine what her half of the room would look like to Bella Nitido: the used books, the wrinkled comforter, the quilt that suddenly seemed childish rather than homey. When Bella arrived the next day, wearing ripped jeans and a cropped sweater and combat boots, she greeted Abby as if they'd been casual friends for ages. She unpacked without any pomp, piling her textbooks on the floor, stacking jewelry boxes and makeup palettes on her dresser top, leaving her desk bare save for her laptop charger and two slim volumes of poetry: Mary Oliver's *Wild Geese* and *The Essential Rumi*. The lack of fuss seemed glamorous to Abby, so self-assured.

For four days they chatted easily about safe subjects: home, school, family. Bella liked hearing about Abby's house in Vermont; she asked about snow and fireplaces and the size of her backyard. Abby learned that Bella was born and raised in New York, in an apartment on the Upper West Side, and that she spent her summers in the Hamptons. Her brother went to Salisbury, just ten miles northwest from Atwater. When Bella talked about the city it was like she was in love: with jam from Sarabeth's and runs in Central Park, clockwise around the Reservoir, east across the northernmost shore and then south again, past the curves of the Guggenheim. Before she'd come to Atwater the first time, she'd wanted to go to Chapin or Brearley or even Horace Mann—but her parents had both gone to boarding school and so that was the way.

Every conversation with Bella left Abby charged with a kind of hunger, as if every detail Bella shared was a bread crumb; it required all of Abby's restraint to not ask for the entire loaf—to just *be cool*, to act normal, because after all, wasn't this just how all the pretty-smart-rich-athletic girls talked, safe inside the knowledge that people always wanted to hear what they had to say? Maybe it had nothing to do with Abby; maybe Abby could have been anyone at all.

"Like, if you had to be buried in bugs," Bella says on the day the portraits appear, her right hip cocked against the doorframe, her attention trained on a piece of paper in her left hand, "I guess butterflies would be the least terrible, right?"

Abby looks up from her copy of *Gatsby*, hopeful that Bella hadn't noticed how she'd been trying to jut her chin in the air like Jordan Baker, just to imagine what Fitzgerald was describing. "Is that one of the paintings?" she asks, lamely.

"Mhmm," Bella murmurs. "I mean, you've got to admit—they're beautiful."

"Do I?"

Bella looks aghast. Her eyes widen, her jaw drops, and she shoves the portrait out in front of her, so the face crawls in front of Abby. "Look at it! It's, like, fucking Damien Hirst *before* Damien Hirst. If Breslin hadn't ended up teaching, he might have *been* Damien Hirst."

Abby does not know who Damien Hirst is and makes a mental note to google him later. "How's the sub, by the way?" Bella takes AP Studio Art, one of the classes Mr. Breslin taught before his sudden departure, which they'd been informed of via an email from the Dean of Faculty on the last day of break. During his leave of absence, Breslin's classes would be taught by Jessica Abernathy, an alum from the class of 2011 and a recent college graduate, a painter who—according to Ms. Burdick's email—used gloved fingertips to smear enamel paint in barely there layers to create the effect of translucency, of faces seen through fogged windows or wet glass. It only just now occurs to Abby that there's a relationship between Ms. Abernathy's work and Mr. Breslin's: masked faces everywhere.

Bella shrugs. "She's fine."

Abby nods, mostly as a way to fill the space, worried that Jessica Abernathy is not what Bella wants to talk about. She tries again: "Did she say anything about the paintings?"

"No, which is fucking weird, right? I mean, this guy's art is just *all over*, it's this *literal* elephant in the room, and we're just . . . not going to talk about it? Not even from an educational perspective? I mean, we could have done a one-off lesson or some kind of inspired-by exercise, like have us each draw self-portraits in . . . fucking bumblebees, I don't know."

Abby has done activities like this in English class: Ms. Edwards made them write a poem from the perspective of an inanimate object, like "Monologue for an Onion"; this year, Ms. Doyle asked them to write a story in the second person, like Lorrie Moore and Jamaica Kincaid.

"It's actually an interesting question, right?" Bella continues. "What to do with the great artwork of shitty people? Like, we study Van Gogh, who was no fucking hero, and Picasso obviously—"

Abby knows Van Gogh gifted one of his ears to a former lover, but she'd always thought this was an unfortunate result of the artist's depression, not necessarily anything more sinister—although perhaps it would be somewhat traumatizing to receive a bloody ear in the mail. As for Picasso, she didn't know.

"I'm just saying," Bella continues, "for a school that fucking *loves* a 'conversation,' the lack of one about Mr. Breslin is . . . notable."

"Maybe that's why this person is doing these things," Abby ventures, the thought occurring to her only then, in the moment. "These . . . pranks, I mean. I thought that they would end after Breslin left—it seemed, I dunno, reasonable to guess that the goal was to get him off campus? But now he's gone and clearly she's not done. . . ."

Bella nods, slowly. "Did you see that some of his reviews were posted, too?"

Abby shakes her head.

"Yeah, from a couple of his early gallery shows, like when he was a senior at Parsons. And a write-up of some award he won at graduation. Called him *Warholian*. Both 'jarring and whimsical.'"

Abby had initially thought there was a statement in the paintings themselves, one that—lacking any skill in art analysis—she assumed had gone over her head. But now she's not so sure. "Maybe the person who hung these all over wants us to think about Breslin's talent?" She hates the way her voice rises at the end, the way her statement becomes a question.

"And how much it must have meant to the school to have this . . . prodigy on staff," Bella adds. "Anyways, I'm hungry. Wanna go get dinner?"

In a day the paintings are gone, but this rhythm sticks for the new roommates: they start to check in with one another, making their comings and goings mutual, walking downstairs together in the mornings for burnt coffee and past-its-prime winter fruit. Every day Abby is a little slow to get ready, just to see if it's real: to catch the image of Bella lingering, one toe poking out the door, an elbow on the handle—impatient but waiting, nonetheless, for her.

January of junior year is also the official start of the college process at Atwater, although much of the grade begins it long before, with some families—certainly not Abby's—hiring private college consultants as early as freshman year. The juniors are summoned for a weekend-long retreat with Atwater's college advisers, a series of lectures and talks from alumnae and slideshows with crippling statistics (5.4 percent acceptance rates; composite scores in the ninetieth percentile) that Mr. Burke, the head of College Counseling, tries to offer up optimistically. The process involves an individual meeting with Mr. Burke, who asks Abby to rank her college preferences.

"When do you want them by?" Abby asks, leaning over the form, peering up at Mr. Burke.

Mr. Burke, whose soft features and perpetually red cheeks give him the aura of a person always a little put-upon, adjusts his glasses. "Oh, no, I'd like you to do it right now, please." He taps the sheet in front of her, already printed with numbers, one through fifteen.

Fifteen!

"Do I have to fill all of these?"

"Just do the best you can," Mr. Burke smiles, "and we'll go from there. You went on some college tours this summer, right?"

Abby and her mother had, indeed, gone on a slew of New England road trips that summer, just the two of them piled into her mother's old Subaru Outback. They spent a weekend in Boston, visiting Harvard and MIT and even quickly spinning through BU, just in case; before that, they went down to Philadelphia and spent a night at her mom's cousin's in New Jersey between touring Princeton and Penn. They saved Dartmouth for last because it wasn't easily combined with anything else, one lonely trip across Vermont toward the White Mountains.

She nods at Mr. Burke.

"Just you and your mother?"

She nods again, less patiently this time.

"A girls' trip! Like Thelma and Louise," he jokes, as if Abby has ever seen *Thelma and Louise*.

The whole time, their twelve-year-old Subaru sputtering across I-90 or down the Taconic, Abby's mother had been a deluge of enthusiasm. From the passenger seat she rambled about her early twenties, the time on the West Coast, Portland ("Nothing like it is now, I hear") and San Francisco ("Even *less* like it used to be!") and then Los Angeles, how she hadn't had any interest in college ("No regrets, I had you instead!"), but how she was so excited to be doing this with Abby now. When she wasn't talking she sang along to Alison Krauss and Emmylou Harris, folk-country mixes Abby's father made years ago that reminded her of early-summer nights, long and deep blue, swatting mosquitoes on the porch while her parents slowly two-stepped around the kitchen.

She doesn't like Mr. Burke watching her, can't help but feel as though—despite his congeniality, despite the way his shirt collar always seems a little too tight—he will judge her order. His job depends upon his successful stewardship of applications and admissions to the highest achieving colleges, Williams and Middlebury and the Holy Trinity of Harvard, Princeton, and Yale; no doubt he has an opinion about how she should prioritize. Abby skips numbers one and two, and scribbles "Penn" on the third line.

It's the first week in February when Sloane pokes her head into their room, her long, thin brown hair swinging in front of her, Blake visible over her shoulder. Abby and Bella are each sitting on their beds, tapping away at their laptops.

"Hey." Sloane's voice, even in one syllable, is deep and throaty. Before meeting Sloane—in algebra freshman year—it had not occurred to Abby that a voice like that could belong to a teenager.

Bella waves a hand, inviting her friends inside. "Hey, Abby—do you mind if we work together for a bit?"

Abby speaks too quickly and too enthusiastically—"No, of course not!"—and immediately sinks into a humiliated and spiraling despair. She hates her stupid eager self. She hates Sloane, whose presence she reads as proof that Abby is not entertainment enough for Bella. Most of all, she hates how she knows she'd do anything for her roommate's affection.

"Hey," Sloane nods, in Abby's direction this time. Blake follows behind her, taking a seat at Bella's desk while Sloane hops on Bella's bed, nestling in at the foot, her back against the wall. Blake is holding *Give Me Liberty!*, their AP US History textbook. Abby's own copy is facedown on her bed, abandoned for a browse through Facebook.

"Did you do the APUSH reading?"

It does not immediately occur to Abby that Blake is talking to her, and so her response comes out choked, her cheeks flushed. "Just started."

"Takes forever, doesn't it? I need a break every three pages."

"Totally."

Sloane lets out a snort. "Get out of here, Blake. Abby's probably doing *next week's* reading."

Abby is not sure if it's intended as an insult—and if it is, whether it's directed at her or at Blake. Even at a place like Atwater—where it is *cool* to be smart, where the Sloanes and Blakes are also the top of the class—there is still the constant threat of being perceived as trying too hard.

Blake frowns, so briefly that you'd have to have known the frown was coming to see it, before adjusting her face into something coolly judgmental. She looks at Abby, expectant.

"I wish I was that far ahead. Then I could do that mountain of AP Bio we have." It is the perfect response, defiant and unexpected, and Abby has no idea where it came from.

"Don't remind me," Blake groans. She kicks off her shoes and props her feet on the corner of Bella's desk, tilting on the back two legs of her chair. For a few minutes the four of them sit like this, reading—or, in Abby's case, pretending to read while replaying the moment over and over again, luxuriating in the hollow sureality of having passed the test.

Of course, the thing about Bella and her friends—these friends, this circle that seems not to include Abby, because maybe Abby and Bella are inching toward friendship but it would certainly not be the *same* circle of friendship that includes Sloane and Blake—is that the tests come at rapid-fire speed, so that acceptance is a matter of constant appraisal, of keeping up. It doesn't immediately register with Abby, for example, that the water bottle now making its way among the three friends is not, in fact, filled with water. One minute, Blake is sitting lazily at Bella's desk, her pen skating beneath the textbook's too-small print; the next, she's pulling a Nalgene from her backpack, unscrewing the lid, taking a long drag, and passing it on to Sloane. By the time the smell—bleach-like and musky—diffuses to Abby's side of the room, Bella's fingertips hug the bottle, and as she brings it to her lips she peers over the top and gives Abby the tiniest shrug. Not knowing what else to do, Abby smiles.

They go on like this for a while, the turning of recycled pages and the gentle sloshing of the bottle's interior the only noise in the room. Abby wonders what she'll say if they offer her a sip, running over sentences from a chapter about Progressivism while rehearsing options in her head: "No, thanks," is too cold and judgmental; "I'm okay, thanks!" is overeager and shrill; "I'm allergic to gluten" wasn't true, and anyway some alcohols are made without grain, like vodka (right?) and she is not sure which they're drinking. Even *if* "yes" is the nonconfrontational, nonjudgmental option, there is still the matter of which kind of yes. "Sure": Cool, done-this-before; runs the risk of sounding like an alcoholic. "Yeah!": Over-eager, sounds like she's *never* done this before, which is embarrassing and awkward, like owning up to being a virgin. If she leaves the room, Bella might think that she's mad or annoyed. If she goes to sleep, she'll put them in the awkward position of having to be quiet, plus she doesn't like sleeping around a group of awake people, like on buses or trains. She's trapped, a prisoner in her own room, victim to one of those psychological torture techniques where they don't physically harm you but instead make you watch something terrible. Like *Sophie's Choice*, which she hasn't seen, but her mom mentions a lot.

"*Bleargggghh*." Blake lets out an exaggerated groan and slams her book, spine open, on the desk. "I'm so bored by this book."

"I'm so bored, period," Sloane echoes. "This is a waste of good alcohol."

"I don't think anything that makes homework more bearable is a waste, personally." Bella hiccups as she speaks, a response so on-the-nose Abby wonders if it was real.

Blake giggles, and Bella and Sloane follow suit. Finally, Sloane comes up for air: "What should we do?"

"Bowling alley?" One of Atwater's worst-kept secrets is an old bowl-ing alley, hidden in the basement of the school building. A relic of some off-brand discretionary spending in the 1950s, it proved too costly to maintain, and its two lanes sat beneath their geometry and world history classes, the pins that hadn't yet been stolen gathering dust, the wax losing its shine. The door to the bowling alley is usually unlocked; the only breaking involves rule-breaking, as the bowling alley is technically—like the clock tower or the forest after dark or the basement of Trask on weekends and during coed events—off-limits. You can up the ante by sneaking in on a night like tonight, which would also involve (a) being out of bed after lights-out, (b) being off your hall after lights-out, and (c) being in the school building after lights-out.

Sloane pushes her tongue between her lips and blows a raspberry in Blake's direction. Blake giggles.

"Boring," Sloane says.

Blake's giggles morph into full-bellied laughter. "Remember the time you stole Jim's golf cart?"

All three start laughing. Abby watches them openly now, the right side of her mouth curled into a smile, caught by contagion.

"And he was like"—Sloane sits up straight and puts her fists on her hips—"'Young lady, if you bring that cart back here right now—'"

Blake and Bella finish her sentence: "'We don't ever have to talk about this again!'"

It seems entirely absurd and yet also completely inevitable—fated, almost—that an anecdote like this would be true: that these three girls would engage in an almost regular kind of mischief—stealing a golf cart, which seemed so *wholesome* compared to what Abby imagined (cocaine, mostly, and sweaty, glistening, constant sex)—*and* that, when caught, the adults in charge would be so charmed that all consequences would be quickly forgotten. Abby can picture it so easily: the golf cart tipping in the moonlight, their arms spread wide and glowing, long thin fingers combing through the wind.

"He was so worried I was going to crash," Sloane says.

"So was I, honestly."

Blake lets out an exaggerated sigh. "Ugh, it all seems so lame now, doesn't it?"

Sloane frowns and nods, picking up her friend's train of thought: "Like, this girl's pranks are so self-righteous. Stealing Jim's golf cart seems like amateur hour."

"Who do you think it is?" Blake asks.

Sloane shrugs. "I don't know, but she's a genius, for sure. All the shit I've gotten caught for, and this girl manages to *hang pictures all over campus in the middle of the night* and not *one* security camera catches her?"

"She knew how the cameras were positioned, and she kept her hood up wherever she couldn't avoid them." Bella shakes her head. "Like a motherfucking spy."

Sloane and Blake both spin in Bella's direction, their necks nearly snapping. Bella has their full attention—and Abby's, too.

"How do you know that?"

Bella reaches for the Nalgene from Sloane. She takes a sip, and then says: "Paulsen called me in about it."

And Abby can't help it, but there it is again: her insides swell, from her stomach to the back of her mouth, all of her anxiety throttled forward to prevent her from even breathing. All their chatter over the past three-almost-four weeks, the casual but visible ways they'd grown closer, maybe not like friends but definitely maybe like partners, and Bella hadn't mentioned this to Abby, not once.

"Wait, what?" Blake says. "She thought you did it?"

"That doesn't even make sense," Sloane says. "You haven't been here."

"Yes, thanks, I'd forgotten."

"I'm just saying."

"Well, that's what I said to Linda. But she had a theory: she thought there was an original prankster, and that this most recent . . . *incident* was the work of a copycat."

"Why would she think that?" Sloane asks.

"I mean, we all thought they would end, right? With Breslin gone?" Blake reaches for the Nalgene. "We assumed the goal was to get the rapist off campus, if he was actually still here."

Blake passes the bottle to Sloane, who takes a drink and then taps at the corner of her lower lip, wiping away a stray drop. "Honestly, I was on the fence about whether Karen was telling the truth until that man bolted."

Blake shakes her head. "He had to have known how guilty he would look when he didn't come back."

"My question is"—Bella leans forward—"if this girl knew it was Breslin all along, why didn't she just put his name right there on the Atwater Instagram?"

Sloane nods, like she's mulling it over. "Good question."

"Maybe she didn't know," Abby says, surprising herself. She'd forgotten that she wasn't, in fact, directly involved in the conversation: She was supposed to be just an audience. Her cheeks burn. Sloane's eyes narrow. Bella almost smiles, and it's all Abby needs to forge ahead: "Maybe that's why this one feels different, and why Linda would think it might've been somebody new. The initial pranks were sort of random." She remembers learning about guerilla warfare in middle school social studies, the phrase bolded in the textbook. "Like she was just trying to create enough chaos to draw out and then get rid of the rapist, whoever he was."

"And now what?" Blake asks.

Abby thinks about her first real conversation with Bella, the day the paintings appeared, and the reviews that accompanied them. "Well, this one feels like it has a message. The implication is that the school had been protecting its semi-famous faculty member over its students, right?"

"But is he really famous anymore?" Sloane asks.

"No," Abby says, "but at the time he was. In 1995, I mean."

"And once they made that choice," Bella says, catching Abby's eye, "it's not like they could turn around two decades later, when he was sort of a washed-up—but still talented!—has-been and say, 'You know, you're not famous anymore and we're kind of worried we can't trust you around teenage girls, so, you're fired.'"

"Right," Abby agrees. "They had to commit, and then they had to *keep* committing, because otherwise they'd have to admit that they put two decades of art students in danger."

Bella frowns—pulling her lips to one side in a half pucker, a disappointed kind of contemplative gesture—and the high Abby feels dissolves, the buzz of a rapid-fire back-and-forth with Bella in front of Sloane and Blake swiftly replaced by her usual process of internal abasement. How careless she'd been, lumping her roommate into a pile of potential casualties.

"The school will never admit it made a mistake," Sloane says, flatly. "Speaking of, what did you say to Linda?"

"I told her that it was a very traumatic thing to learn that your creative mentor of two years is a rapist," Bella says, dully.

Blake gasps. "No, you didn't!"

Bella exhales. "No, I didn't. Honestly, I didn't really say anything. I didn't do it, and her hauling me in only confirmed that they have no fucking clue who did. So I said that I was happy to be back at Atwater and eager to rebuild the community's trust in me and that I had no interest in jeopardizing any of that."

"Spoken like a true Linda Paulsen veteran," Sloane smiles.

Bella nods. "And she warned me that I'm on, like, super-strict zero-tolerance no-strikes probation or whatever, and basically that I had better watch it."

There's silence for a moment, as Sloane hands the Nalgene to Bella, who takes a long pull, nearly emptying it. She swirls the remainder at the bottom, rotating the bottle in small circles by holding the mouth in her fingertips like a perched spider.

And then Sloane blurts out: "Can I see your tattoo?"

Blake snorts. "What are you talking about?"

"Bella has a tattoo." Abby flushes again, but then Bella smirks at her, the tiniest smile of coconspirators, and Abby wants to stay inside this very specific moment—where she and Bella alone have a secret—for the rest of her life.

"Ha! See! Even Abby knows."

"*What?* You told Abby before us?"

Laughing, Bella wraps her arms around her waist, peeling her sweatshirt up at the hem. She lifts it just to her chest, pulling the edges of the hem up over her shoulders in the back so that the corners of skin between her sports bra and her shoulders are exposed, and then half turns, directing her left side back toward the wall and her right, dotted with three hollowed-out stars, toward Blake and Sloane.

Abby noticed the tattoo the week Bella moved in, although she'd never asked about it. Bella is the kind of girl who is comfortable naked, and at Atwater, *being comfortable naked* is like having sex or drinking casually in the dorms at night: it signals that you are equipped with some kind of superior knowledge. In the evenings Bella takes long showers and sits at her desk in her towel for hours, mindlessly browsing the internet. When she changes she slides out of her towel easily, casting it aside without shimmying on a pair of underwear first. She switches bras like a normal adult person, not putting on a sports bra *over* a regular bra and then unclasping the latter (as Abby does, when Bella is around). She puts on her bra and underwear next to her dresser, by the drawer where those items live, and then strides across the room to her armoire, where she stands for a minute or two while figuring out what to wear.

This means that Abby spends a lot of time figuring out where to look while Bella is naked or half-naked. And the whole business of not looking sharpens whatever she isn't supposed to be looking at, like how Bella always, *only* wears thongs, or how her bra and underwear never match like Abby had assumed they would, or that she likes bright colors, which is also not something Abby would have guessed: lime green, highlighter pink, Valentine's Day red. Or how she has a tattoo near her right shoulder, three little stars, inky blue black.

The tattoo itself is not necessarily an aberration. There have been other Atwater girls who've had them over the years, most of them PGs, girls who were already eighteen. It had been a little bit of a surprise, to Abby, that a girl like Bella has a tattoo—Bella who summers in the Hamptons and whose parents went to boarding schools and then Ivy League universities. For the most part, Bella doesn't talk about her semester at Riverdale, just like Abby doesn't talk about her dad or her mom's increasingly persistent panic attacks or the crumbling house. Abby imagined that it must have pained Bella to admit, after she'd fought so hard for it years ago, that a Manhattan day school wasn't the right choice, after all. But she also sensed that it wasn't the school that didn't fit so much as the being home every day, the daily routine of checking in and out with her parents, the constant being accounted for—none of which Bella would have rankled against had she not come to Atwater in the first place.

There are two other things about the tattoo that puzzle Abby: (1) the design, which seems cliché and a bit uninspired, a tattoo had by a million girls the world over, and (2) the quality of the tattoo, something she hadn't noticed initially but which sunk in, like the artwork itself, the more she laid eyes on it. The edges are blurred, like bleeding ink on wet paper. It is, in other words, and in Abby's opinion, a bad tattoo. Not bad like, your-ex-wife's-name-in-a-heart bad, but just bad.

And now she is watching Blake and Sloane have all the same realizations, at warp speed and with Bella's permission, their noses leaning toward the constellation, able to scrutinize and wonder right up close.

"Do your parents know?"

"When did you get it?"

Bella laughs. "In New York, and I don't think they know, but I guess they could have seen it at some point, just like apparently people around here saw it."

"So, like, does it mean anything?" Sloane asks, leaning back.

"One for the three of us: Me, my sister, and my brother." Bella shrugs. "And I like stars. I think they're cute."

"Did it hurt?"

Bella appears to turn this over for a minute. "Honestly, yeah. But . . . I didn't have it done the traditional way, so . . ." She trails off. The silence holds for a second, as Blake and Sloane each try to wait the other out.

"It's a stick-and-poke, isn't it?"

They turn and stare at Abby. Bella's smile is wide this time, with a raised eyebrow: unmistakably, the look of a person impressed.

"A stick-and-poke?"

"Like a prison tattoo?"

"How did you know?"

When Abby doesn't answer immediately, Bella turns back to Sloane and Blake, Blake with her jaw half-open, Sloane steely-eyed. "A friend at home did it."

"Like, a friend who owns or works at a tattoo parlor tattooed you in his or her tattoo parlor?"

"No."

Something in Bella shifts. She rolls her shoulders back, holds her chin at an angle, slightly upward. One eyebrow slides a millimeter higher than the other; the slightest dimple nestles into her left cheek. It's not pride, exactly, but maybe a look of mischief managed. They are all the kinds of girls who do things for effect: to be able to say they did; to one-up one another in badassery. She's won this round, and she knows it.

"It's a stick-and-poke, like Abby said. My friend Maren—you guys don't know her—did it at home one night when we were just hanging out. She has a few, too, and I wanted to learn how to do it."

"So did it hurt?"

"You wanted to *learn how to do it*?"

Bella laughs as her friends speak over one another. "It hurt a little bit, yeah. I guess it hurts more than getting a 'regular' tattoo."

"Aren't stick-and-pokes, like, extremely unsanitary?"

Bella shrugs again. "I didn't get an infection, so I guess it was safe enough."

Abby imagines Bella, cross-legged on the floor of her Upper West Side bedroom, music lazily streaming from her open laptop, a bra hooked on her closet door handle. It seems totally plausible, to Abby, now that she thinks about it, that Bella would've done it this way. It would have been so ordinary to do it the other way: To make an appointment at some high-end tattoo shop, one in the East Village with a zillion Yelp reviews and an owner profile in the *New York Times*; to walk in on a Tuesday afternoon and ask for three little stars on her right shoulder. The tattoo artist would have humored her, not at all fooled by her fake ID but rather used to a steady parade of lanky girls with perfect skin and American Express cards, and neatly placed the three little stars on her shoulder. The whole thing would've taken less than ten minutes. Worst of all, there wouldn't have been a story to tell.

"So you know how to do this?" Blake is clearly impressed, and finding it harder to hide.

"Yeah, but I've done it only once."

"To who?"

"*Whom*."

"Maren. After she did mine, she let me do one on her forearm."

"She just decided to get a tattoo so you could practice?"

"Well, she has, like, two dozen tattoos, and anyway stick-and-pokes aren't really permanent . . ."

"What do you mean?" Sloane is hungry for anything that will undercut Bella's story.

"They don't penetrate as deeply, so they fade over time. Not like, over six months, but they won't last a lifetime."

Sloane's left eye narrows briefly. "Damn, girl. Good for you." She glances at her phone. "It's late. I've gotta get to bed. Blake?"

"For sure."

"'Night, kids."

"'Night," Bella echoes.

Abby smiles, not sure whether she's included.

Their guests bounce out of the room, leaving the door slightly ajar. Bella and Abby listen for a minute, waiting to hear the judgment Bella's friends will surely save until out of earshot.

"Well"—Bella shrugs at the empty room—"that cat's out of the bag." She pauses, then turns to Abby directly. "How'd you know it was a stick-and-poke? I feel like you're not the kind of girl who hangs out on tattoo Tumblr or Insta."

Abby is not sure exactly what makes her do it. But something about the last hour has both strengthened the kinship she feels with Bella—as though Abby is her greatest ally in her second chance at Atwater. And so she begins to tell Bella about her dad.

"He died when I was eight," she explains, and she is grateful that Bella doesn't try to empathize or offer condolences in any real way. She looks at her roommate attentively, expectantly, as if she knows this essential tragedy of Abby's life is not actually the point of the story.

"I don't remember a lot of the details," she admits, "but it was liver cancer, and there was this window—six months or whatever. He didn't want any kind of treatment, no trials or experiments. He just wanted to spend the time with my mom, and with me, I guess.

"We had always been this trio. Even though he's not my 'real' dad, he and my mom got married when I was two, and he made it official and adopted me and everything. But in those few months I felt like I was always walking in on him and my mom, on these little private moments they'd be having. Maybe they were just conversations about his cancer, or treatment, or maybe it was stuff they didn't want me to hear about the funeral and his will and life insurance and whatever—I don't know, I've never asked.

"Anyway, my dad had a bunch of tattoos. A full sleeve on his arm—a forest sprouting from his wrist, up to the crook of his elbow, and birds bursting from the trees up his bicep—and song lyrics on his chest and a pair of wings on his back, and his brother's initials on his shoulder, and just all over." Abby remembers how she used to trace them, laying on top of him on the living room carpet, their bellies pressed together. "But my mom—despite all her wild-child tendencies, the fact that she had me when she was nineteen, and that I think she's tried every drug under the sun—she didn't have any tattoos, not one. And then one day she did. I noticed it when she was driving, a set of numbers on the inside of her second finger on her left hand. They were small and slightly crooked, bleeding at the edges, raised slightly on reddened skin.

"I guess he gave it to her, one night after I was asleep, and she did the same to him. Just sitting at the kitchen table. The numbers were our zip code, the place where they built a life together, where my mom says she finally felt at peace.

"Later she told me that she wanted to get a real tattoo, that when they had the idea that night she said that she'd make them an appointment at a shop in Burlington, but it was my dad's idea to do a stick-and-poke. He said that he wanted her to have an out. That if my mom ever moved on—which he wanted her to do, even though I don't think she ever will—that the tattoo would eventually fade, that if it made her sad she wouldn't have to look at it forever."

Abby finally pauses here. She does not tell Bella about how the tattoo makes her sad for another reason: It made her feel like there was something between her parents she could never fully know; it shifted irrevocably the way she had previously thought of the three of them as a single unit, all on equal footing, the Three Musketeers. There was her mom and dad—and then there was her.

"Does she still have the tattoo?"

Abby looks up at her roommate and nods. "About a year ago she started talking about having it done officially, making it really permanent."

"But then it wouldn't be the thing your dad gave her."

Abby nods. "I guess not."

It happens on a Thursday two weeks later. Back in her room during a free period, Abby goes to the bathroom before heading up to class. She walks in, pees, does a perfunctory water-only hand rinse before it registers.

Shortly after the special issue of the *Heron* leaked, Mrs. Brodie ordered the plastering of campus with a series of informational flyers. They hung stapled to bulletin boards above water fountains and common-room couches, taped to locker room mirrors and the insides of bathroom stalls—reproduced so many times and displayed in so many places that they became like a kind of wallpaper, absorbed in the periphery but no longer really *noticed*. If someone were to ask Abby, for example, *what to do if someone tells you they've been the victim of sexual assault*, she could not call up the four-item list on the flyer of the same name; she saw it so frequently that she never really *read* it, never allowed the instructions to penetrate.

This is why she does not immediately discern the flyer taped to the mirror above the first sink as an aberration—to Abby it's just another bulletin, another reminder that "Help Is Available at Atwater." But the font is different on this one, not the standard Atwater sans serif, but girlish block letters scrawled in Sharpie; the production quality is lower, not a professional printing job on glossed paper but a photocopy run on a library printer, the toner streaked in even lines.

TATTOOS BY BELLA.

Oh no no no no no.

Perfectly safe! 100% sterile! Long-lasting, but not forever!

And, printed neatly at the bottom: *See Bella Nitido to get stuck.*

Cartoonish doodles backdrop the writing: stars, hearts, a lightning bolt, palm trees, astrological signs. Sample designs.

Abby peeks over her shoulder, double-checking under the stalls, before reaching out and ripping the flyer from the mirror, tearing it where it meets the tape. Like she's disposing of self-incriminating evidence, she carries it with her back to their room before crumpling it and throwing it in their own trash bin, where she can safely see to its removal.

"Did you fucking see this?"

Abby is sitting on her bed, working distractedly through her homework, when Bella bursts into their room. It's the slow and quiet window between classes and dinner, when most of their classmates are busy with after-school sports or clubs or theater. They have the hall to themselves, more or less, Abby who fulfills Atwater's PE requirement with a combination of low-expectation teacher-run classes like yoga and Insanity, and Bella, whose late-arrival meant her schedule would be a cobbled-together one.

She stands before Abby, her backpack still on, the flyer wrinkled between her fingertips and palm.

Abby nods. "There was one in our bathroom."

"Jesus, fuck—" Bella turns on her heels and moves for the door.

"I took it down."

"Oh. Thanks."

Bella generally wears her emotions close. It's part of her whole thing. She keeps her face set with a sort of mild-mannered inscrutability—she isn't exactly hiding, but she also isn't sharing—and since returning to Atwater she's really dug into it.

Now, though, the Bella who stands before Abby has cracks in her. Her eyes are red-rimmed and bright, wetness reflecting in the afternoon light. Her hair has crossed from intentionally messy to disheveled, the roots a little greasy. She picks at her cuticle occasionally between her left thumb and middle finger, making a tiny impatient clicking sound she doesn't seem to notice.

"It was them, right?" Bella asks.

"Sloane and Blake?"

"Yeah."

This seems like dangerous territory to Abby. Corroborating Bella's hunch would be to simultaneously disapprove of Sloane and Blake. On the other hand, Abby might be the only other person who knows about the origins of Bella's tattoo, and therefore the only other person with the knowledge to write those flyers. She gambles: "I think so."

Bella steels herself. Abby watches her jawline tighten, flexing where it slopes up to meet her ears. "Did you see them anywhere else?"

"No—just here on our floor. You?"

"Over in the Student Center bathroom."

Abby lets out a low sigh. "Not good."

"Not good."

"Do you want me to help you? We can split up, I'll go over and check Lathrop while you take Avery . . ." She trails off.

Bella shakes her head, not dismissively but as if she hadn't been listening; in response to something else. "I'm sure Admin knows."

Abby is quiet a beat too long.

"I'm so fucked."

"Why? It's not like it's true." Abby is careful to say it steadily, with no hint of a question's upward inflection.

"It doesn't matter. It's believable enough. And, as Linda reminded me, I'm on the world's strictest probation. She's looking for literally any excuse." She takes a step forward and turns on her heels, slumping against Abby's bed, her backpack perched on the mattress. "I don't get it. I don't know what they get out of this."

"You know," Abby says, slowly, "it sort of reminds me of the paintings." This is the second thing she'd thought, after finding the flyers nestled among the school-sponsored instructions for seeking help: that it also reminded her of seeing their art teacher's butterflied faces plastered around campus. Both made Abby's intestines plummet in her abdomen.

"Except those had a purpose. This . . ." Bella trails off, tracing veins in the ceiling. "This is just a game to them."

It is a revelation to Abby, who'd assumed that the motives were always more calculated, that girls like Sloane and Blake played a particular brand of three-dimensional chess that Abby herself would never be able to learn.

For the first time since becoming roommates, Abby actually believes she and Bella are the same age. She'd always seemed older and worldlier, educated in make-outs and beers and the perks of prettiness. But the Bella in front of her now has flyaways around her forehead and a tiny pimple by her jaw and swollen, puffy eyes, and the whole thing doesn't even add up to the tragically beautiful, ill-fated-heroine thing you see in the movies. She just looks sad.

The next day, Abby tears down flyers in the school building and in the gym and in the bathroom outside the dining hall. At lunch, Bella tells her she found them in the Student Center and in Trask, where they were tacked on the small bulletin boards outside every single practice room and studio space.

At dinner, Bella refuses to leave their room.

"I don't need to make it easy on Linda Paulsen," she explains. It occurs to Abby that Linda is not likely to hand down an expulsion in the dining hall, but she figures it's not really about avoiding the Dean of Students. Bella mentioned earlier that neither Sloane nor Blake spoke to her in English, the only class the three of them had together.

The knock comes during study hall, as Abby is pretending to read, her eyes skirting back and forth again and again over the same paragraph about Daisy Buchanan's voice, too associatively tense with expectation. Linda Paulsen stands at the door, her mouth turned slightly downward.

"I need to speak with Bella," she says. It is not a question.

Abby looks quickly at her roommate, who does not meet her eyes.

"Should I go? I can go read in the common room."

"You don't need to—"

Paulsen interjects: "That would be great. Thank you, Abby."

She closes the door behind Abby, who wanders down the hall to the common room where Ms. Trujillo has tucked herself into a corner of the couch, her knees beneath her, chatting with Tiffany Xu. She looks up at Abby as she enters, empathetically: of course she knows what's going on. Linda Paulsen probably cleared the interrogation with her beforehand.

Abby takes a seat in the armchair in the corner. It sags in the middle and the slipcover needs replacing—it's speckled with suspicious stains—but it has the best view of the Bowl, which glows orange and hazy beneath them, Atwater's own little halo of light pollution.

It hasn't been five minutes when Paulsen's voice interrupts her daydreaming. Whether this is good or bad, Abby can't say.

"Sorry for intruding, Abby. You can go back in now, if you like."

"It's no problem," Abby says, even though it was, of course, a big fucking problem.

With a head nod, Paulsen turns and walks down the hall, toward—Abby imagines—the next offender on her list. Abby waits until she is safely out of sight before standing and returning to her room, ignoring Ms. Trujillo's sorry-about-this half smile on her way out of the common room.

Bella sits at her desk with her neck craned over her phone, its blue light reflecting on her pale skin.

"My mom always says to wait twenty-four hours before sending the angry text or email." Abby imitates her mother's good-natured nagging: "You might feel differently in the morning."

"Well, I'm sure your mother is a very wise woman, but—counterpoint—sometimes rage is worth releasing. Plus, I might have bigger problems in twenty-four hours." She finishes tapping and places her phone with a thud facedown on her desk. She leans back in her chair, extending her long torso, running her hands through her hair, smoothing it away from her face.

Normally, Abby is not one to prod. The machinations of school discipline were between Linda Paulsen and whomever she was rehabilitating. Plus, it is generally better to stay out of these things: The more you know, the more likely you are to appear before Linda yourself. But Abby realizes that in this particular moment, she is probably Bella's only friend on campus.

"So what's the verdict?"

Bella sighs. "Nothing official yet, of course. I have to go before the Disciplinary Committee tomorrow at three thirty. But Paulsen has already called my parents and told them that they need to be here tomorrow afternoon."

"Is that standard?"

"No. And Paulsen reiterated that I was admitted on a 'probationary status' and that 'the terms of my probation were made *abundantly clear.*'"

"Did you tell her you didn't do it?"

Bella shakes her head. "It doesn't matter."

"It has to matter."

Bella looks up at her roommate and almost smiles. It is not a look Abby entirely likes: it seems too close to pity.

"You know, maybe it's for the best. I didn't want to come back here, anyway."

This stings. "Then why did you?" Abby asks.

Bella shrugs. "Why does anyone come here?"

The public school Abby would have attended had she stayed home graduated about forty kids a year. At the ceremony every spring, the principal invites the fourth- and fifth-generation students to stand. In two hundred years, their families haven't left rural Vermont. Their parents work at the ice house and the gristmill and for the highway department.

But this wouldn't have been Bella's fate. Bella is from a place and the kind of family that grants unlimited opportunity. It isn't just that Atwater unlocks doors, Abby knows. The moment she opened her welcome package two years ago, all thick creamy paper in dreamy blues, Abby felt it: this school sinks into your veins.

"'Once an Atwater girl,'" Abby says, parroting Mrs. Brodie.

"'Forever an Atwater girl,'" Bella finishes. They laugh, and Abby is struck by how natural it has come to feel, casual banter with her roommate. She would miss her.

"So . . . are you looking for clients?"

Bella flicks her chin up and wrinkles her forehead.

"I mean, if you're going to get in trouble anyway . . . might as well actually do the thing, right?"

"You're insane."

Abby shrugs. "It's not permanent, right?"

"No, but—don't do this for me."

Abby makes a dismissive *pssh.* "Don't flatter yourself."

Bella is quiet for a minute. "Okay. When do you want to do it?"

"Is now good?"

"Then you won't have any time to reconsider."

"That's the point."

"Okay." She pauses. "Okay. Let me get my stuff. Can you go to the bathroom and grab some paper towels?"

Abby watches as Bella sets up her workspace. It is the most meticulous she has ever seen her roommate, who—she learns—keeps her supplies layered neatly in a small plastic container in her dresser. She makes her desk into their workspace, placing a square of plastic wrap beneath a square of paper towel, tacking down the corners with Scotch tape. The necessities are minimal: a tiny bottle of black liquid, the size and shape of the paint tubes Abby remembers from her childhood; a dish to hold the poured ink; a lighter; a tub of Vaseline; a bottle of rubbing alcohol; a pencil. What appeared to be a coin purse is actually a small sewing kit, from which Bella pulls a spool of black thread and a circular plastic ring of sewing needles. Delicately she slides a needle from its position; with her other hand, she clicks open the lighter. Slowly she twists the needle through the flame, watching it flare neon orange and then black. Returning the lighter to the desk, she finds the end of the thread and begins wrapping it around the needle, near the tip, building a small black chrysalis around the hot metal. The pencil, as it turns out, is carved with a single neat slice, into which Bella slides the needle, holding it in place with a single piece of tape. The whole thing takes less than three minutes. Months later, Abby will think about this moment—Bella's preparedness, her efficiency, the very fact that she had brought the kit to campus—and the facts of the case will suddenly shift for her.

"So. What are we doing?"

Abby hasn't thought about it. In fact, she hasn't ever thought seriously about getting a tattoo. "Umm . . ."

Bella laughs, breaking the intensity that had settled between them. "It's hard to do detail. Simpler is better."

"That's not very encouraging. Are you bad at this?"

They both laugh. "For your information, I'm *excellent* at this, as I am at all things, ever," Bella says. "It's just sort of a primitive way of drawing. Trust me."

"Clearly, I do."

"What matters to you?"

Abby runs through the options. School, but her class ring sort of covers that. Kitty, but she isn't ready to be literally labeled as a crazy cat lady. Home. "Vermont."

"Ahhh," Bella sighs affectedly. "*Home*."

"Whatever, *stars*."

They laugh. "Yes, we're all walking clichés, utterly predictable," Bella waves her hand dramatically. "Okay, okay. What do you think of when you think of Vermont?"

Abby waits. Bella raises her eyebrows.

"Oh, I was just giving you time to make the usual 'cows?' joke."

"I'm serious!" Bella smacks Abby across the shoulder.

Abby looks away from Bella and fixates on their shared carpet. It needs vacuuming. "My dad used to take me fishing in this creek near our house. We'd catch all kinds of trout. Well, he'd actually do most of the catching. I would get bored after a while and pick bunches of wildflowers on the shore. Buttercups and clovers, mostly. When we went home, Dad would make this big show of presenting the fish and my little wilted and crushed bouquet of wildflowers, like even though his fish would literally *feed* us, my crumpled flowers were just as important an addition to the table . . ." She trails off, remembering how he'd throw his arms open wide, fish in one fist, flowers in the other.

"That's perfect." There is no snark or affect in Bella's response.

Abby shrugs. It was.

"Sooo . . . a flower? A fish?" Bella looks at Abby.

Abby wrinkles her nose. "All I can picture is one of those Jesus fish bumper stickers."

"Ugh, no, not like that. I can't be super detailed, but I can handle a little more detail than a single curved line. Where's this going, anyway?"

"Somewhere I can hide it."

Bella snorts. "Chicken."

"Maybe. But only one of us in this room is about to be kicked out of school *again*."

"Touché. How about on the side here?" Bella reaches toward Abby, placing her fingertips on her rib cage below her breast. "It'll only be visible in a swimsuit."

To Abby, it seems as good a spot as any. She nods.

Bella tap-taps through her phone. "Okay, give me a sec." She rests her phone on her desk, next to her work station, and positions a notebook in her lap. She scribbles for a minute, erases, looks back at her phone, bends her head again. Finally she places the pencil on her desk, gives the sketch an approving look, and holds it up for Abby. "What do you think?"

Bella drew the trout as if from above and swimming upstream, its rounded mouth pointing toward the top of the paper, its tail curving to the left. Four fins—two on each side—slip from the fish's abdomen in half circles. It's soft and smooth and graceful. Abby remembers how on a summer morning the fish would sun themselves, suspended against the current, still despite the fury around them. She looks at Bella. "It's perfect."

Bella cracks a wide grin. "Okay," she says. "Let's do this."

To: brodiep@TheAtwaterSchool.org
From: doylen@TheAtwaterSchool.org
Date: Feb 13, 2016, 8:02 P.M.
Subject: Student Voice

Hi Pat,

Hope you're enjoying your weekend.

As the *Heron* adviser, you know that I value a certain degree of activism: journalism, after all, is about holding power to account, and is therefore in many ways a cousin to social and political protest. While I know that the student demonstration that has defined this academic year has made a number of things difficult for our community, we have to admit that there's a degree of irony to this situation: We are a *girls' school*, after all—we pride ourselves on our unique ability to empower young women to speak up, and to instill within them the self-confidence necessary for such a task. What they're doing here might be poorly or misguidedly executed, but we can't deny that we've helped to cultivate a set of values and capabilities that might lead to such behavior.

That said, I thought that Rich's departure in December might bring a natural end to the protest we experienced this fall. I was, obviously, mistaken. I did a lot of reflecting after the most recent incident, trying to understand what exactly our students are looking for in our response. What is the goal of protest if not to spur action?

The answer, I think, lies in part in that very strength we underscore in our marketing: Atwater is a place where young women learn to use their voices, and the student or students behind the events of this year want to make their voices heard. Moreover, at the end of the day, these are teenagers we're working with, and they want to express themselves and have that expression taken seriously and generously.

I wonder, then, if we couldn't present our students with a more intentional space to exercise this skill? In its initial conception, I think that the special issue of the *Heron* was an attempt to do this; I'm not implying that we are to blame for the leak of the paper, but rather noting the kind of opportunities I think our girls crave. I think that the Jamison Jennings interviews are a good step in this effort, but for many of the girls I think JJ is somewhat removed from actual interaction with the school—and, of course, only a very small sample of students have been invited to participate in those conversations. Perhaps providing an open and legitimate outlet for their concerns would prevent them from trying to create their own.

I considered saving this for our March faculty meeting, but I think it needs addressing sooner rather than later. I'm sure you agree.

Happy to discuss in further detail.

Nancy

From: brodiep@TheAtwaterSchool.org
To: doylen@TheAtwaterSchool.org
Date: Feb 14, 2016, 11:08 A.M.
Subject: Re: Student Voice

Nancy,

Thank you for giving this such careful consideration. I must admit that I think you're on to something. I'll take this up with the Board at the next available opportunity, and we'll see what we can come up with.

Pat

To: Class of 2016 <<classof2016@TheAtwaterSchool.org>>; Class of 2017 <<classof2017@TheAtwaterSchool.org>>; Class of 2018 <<classof2018@ TheAtwaterSchool.org>>; Class of 2019 <<classof2019@TheAtwaterSchool.org>>
Cc: faculty@TheAtwaterSchool.org
From: brodiep@TheAtwaterSchool.org
Date: Feb 21, 2016, 7:36 P.M.
Subject: Student Forum

Students,

For many of you, the past few months at Atwater have been disquieting: you might have wondered about the integrity of this school you call home; you may have felt as though the adults in charge were being less than forthcoming; you might have found yourself engaged in rumor and speculation, frustrated by the sense that the full truth was just out of reach. For those of you who have felt this way, I recognize that this must have been a difficult time. You've invested so much in this school, and I understand why the confusion of the previous months might have caused you to doubt whether Atwater was equally invested in you.

Many of you have availed yourself of various campus resources in your quest for understanding. I want to thank our counseling staff and our peer leaders for the ways they have served our community, opening their hearts and offices and dorm spaces to challenging conversations. I recognize, however, that these individuals have had to go above and beyond the call of duty, and that perhaps they have been unable to provide adequate answers to your many questions. To that end, I am inviting the entire student body to a **student forum** on **Thursday, February 25**, at **7:00 P.M.** in the auditorium. Attendance is optional, and study hall will proceed as usual that evening; if you would like to attend the forum, you are required to sign out with your Dorm Parent. The topic of the forum will be **Healthy Relationships and Accountability**, and it will be your opportunity to ask relevant questions of the administration on this issue. Ms. Paulsen, Ms. Burdick, Ms. McCredie, and I will be on hand, and the format will be an open Q+A session. If you have questions about the topic or its makeup, I encourage you to speak with your peer leaders, Dorm Parent, and/ or adviser for clarification and guidance.'

I am often asked what I love most about my job. For me, the answer has always been an easy one: the girls. Wherever I've taught, it has been the students who make the job all that it is—fulfilling, rewarding, challenging, and never (ever!) dull. But at no place and at no time in my nearly three decades of working in girls' education has this been more true than right now at Atwater. Your commitment to and care for our school inspires me daily, and I am so grateful. I look forward to hearing more from you on February 25.

Warmly,

Mrs. Brodie

Field Trip

When Linda Paulsen first suggested that the indefinite revocation of Sloane Beck's sign-out privileges—she lost them in January, after "missing" the bus back from a dance at Salisbury for an extra half hour with a boy named James who was very good-looking but, as it turned out, not very good at anything else—might also extend to the eleventh-grade humanities trip, Sloane was entirely unfazed. *Fine*, she thought. She didn't want to go anyway.

But Mr. Hills felt otherwise, perhaps because to allow his trip—in which he and Ms. Doyle bring their students to New York to visit the Met and the New-York Historical Society and devise an American-culture scavenger hunt in and between both places—to be withheld as punishment was to, conversely, see it as a kind of optional reward: something fun rather than something serious and scholarly. After all, field trips are a rarity at Atwater; the school has every resource it needs, including the money and clout to bring the guest speakers and artists and theater troupes *to campus*. To permit Sloane to miss the trip in such a manner would be to threaten its very survival. Sloane would accompany her classmates, Mr. Hills argued, because her learning experience would otherwise be *greatly* diminished; the trip, when you get right down to it, is a *cornerstone* of the junior curriculum.

On the bus Sloane and Kyla take a pair of seats in front of Blake and Kit and behind Chloe and Brie. It's early, and, in late February, barely light out as they pull through Atwater's gates and rumble along the county road in front of campus, the flattened and snow-dusted roughage of the Darrow farm stretching for acres out the window. Kyla—who can and does sleep anywhere, including on unused mats in the corners of stadiums during indoor track meets—slips in her earbuds and nods off on Sloane's shoulder, her head bobbing against the apex of her roommate's clavicle as the bus thumps over potholes cratered wide by a New England winter. For a while they drive along meandering country roads, tracing the same route Sloane and her father travel to and from Westchester, crossing into New York somewhere after Kent and marching south along Route 22 to I-684, on a ragged tangent toward White Plains.

It's not until Yonkers—another fifteen miles south, where 684 curves into the Taconic—that the notion of the city first seems plausible: where the sleepiness of the Hudson River Valley and its withering suburban sprawl gives rise to waterfront condos billed as luxury living; where the very air seems to change, probably for very real reasons related to smog and pollution and the decreasing elevation of the valley toward sea level but also for reasons that always, inevitably, feel more like magic, like karmic energy. When Sloane's family left Manhattan it was to a place just beyond this radius, so that on a dark summer night Sloane could see the haze of the city over the treetops in their new and impossibly lush backyard but couldn't *feel* it. It was as if her senses had been zapped, her taste buds lasered off before a feast of her favorite foods: Nantucket oysters, a really good burger, rosewater macarons. This is why Sloane didn't really want to come on the trip, because visiting the city had become like some kind of gluttonous feast, all of it opening up again, stuffing her like the last meal of a death-row inmate, so good and so horrible at the exact same time.

Sloane hadn't wanted to go to the student forum the previous evening, either; it was sure to be just another opportunity for the administration to spew the corporate jargon they paid their consulting firm astronomical fees to adopt. But Brie and Kit *had* to go, because Louisa Manning had all but declared their attendance at the forum a *Heron* staff requirement, and they persuaded Blake to go, and if Sloane followed any rules at all, it was that she didn't let the whole of her friend group make plans without her.

As the Atwater auditorium filled and Mrs. Brodie and Linda Paulsen waited for the stream of students to slow to a trickle—the way you listen for popcorn in the microwave, waiting for the three-second lag between pops—Sloane checked her Instagram, where she was alerted to a flood of likes and comments on her most recent post.

She'd asked Ms. Allen to take the video—a common request, a way for Sloane to actually understand how the choreography was coming together, to critique her own execution—and only later, rewatching it at night in bed, did she notice how the early-evening winter light filtered into the dance studio, gold and dusty, and how there were twenty perfect seconds near the beginning. She posted and captioned: Siri, play "Stubborn Love" by The Lumineers. (What would a girl like Sloane do without irony? Without the ability to mean two things at the same time?)

The comments were hearts, blue and gold to match the video lighting, variations on prettyyy and ugh how r u so perfect and then, at the end, from carolinaballerina17: tell me about it, with a little winking emoji. It was like touching a thorn, so quick and instinctive was the recoil: Sloane immediately clicked her screen to black and slipped her phone back into her pocket. For the rest of the evening she had the sense of dissociating, as if she was not really connected at all to either drama: it was only her digital self her former dance partner visited, nothing more than a web of coding in the ether; it was only her body inside the auditorium, breathing by rote the air that soured with frustration and unmet expectations.

At first the questions the students lobbed in Mrs. Brodie's direction were softballs, relatively speaking, although Sloane had to admit that it required a particular brand of self-importance to ask, as Addison did, how to reply when someone who does not go to Atwater inquires about the campus gossip, and that it required even greater self-importance to respond, as Mrs. Brodie did, with a brief vocabulary lesson on schadenfreude. It was Mia Tavoletti—in black jeans and Doc Martens—who changed the tone, when she stood and said, so earnestly it made Sloane physically cringe: "I worshipped Mr. Breslin."

She went on: "He had a way of explaining creativity to me that just worked. He was . . . accessible. He knew how to talk about art in this way that was both specific and generous. He wasn't the kind of art teacher who only spoke in dreamy intangibles. But he wasn't, you know, prescriptive, either. He didn't tell you what to make, but he also didn't let you do whatever you wanted. He always said that what mattered every day was that we had something to show for our time in studio, even if it was shit." She paused then, and Sloane knew she was debating apologizing for swearing. "I just don't know . . . how we're supposed to trust anyone here now."

It had seemed to Sloane like a stupid question. She understood the sentiment, the naivete that lends itself to such heartbreak, but Sloane learned a long time ago that you can't trust anybody anywhere. The question resonated with Sloane's classmates, though, and Blake raised her hand next and said, with enviable elegance, "I think that part of what Mia is getting at is what the paintings suggested."

In that moment, Sloane would have sworn that the crowd collectively inhaled, one sharp gasp. The pranks were non grata; like drugs and sex, they were not to be discussed with the adults.

Blake continued, parroting Bella's analysis from the night they learned about her tattoo, and as she spoke Sloane scanned their section, searching among the juniors for Abby Randall's frizzy hair the way you might press into a bruise to check if it still hurts. (It wasn't guilt Sloane felt; no—what she craved was the high of disruption, to know how much chaos a body could handle.)

"The plastering of campus with Mr. Breslin's work was, clearly, a suggestion that his celebrity was of greater value to the school than the experience of one student. For me, the question isn't just *How do we know who might hurt us?*, it's *How do we know if you'll protect us?*"

Mrs. Brodie did not flinch. "Let me state this very clearly, then. The school will never knowingly retain on staff any individual who cannot handle themselves appropriately with our students," she said, deploying her shield of bureaucratese, her delivery clipped and pointed, the clarity of her statement proof that she'd said all of it many times before: no *um*s, no extraneous pauses, just crisp execution. "And, as I've said, I think that for many years we've relied upon an unspoken understanding of what constitutes *appropriate*. I think for too long we've operated within a good-faith assumption that we all share the same dictionary. Moving forward, we plan to set forth in writing clearer guidelines for student-staff interaction." She then proceeded to explain how, for example, although it is commonplace for students and staff to text, that such behavior is not within "recommended best practices" and that the school was looking into "a number of applications that enable text-like expediency but that capture all correspondence for school records." As she droned on, the students curled back into themselves, slumping, pushing their feet up against the chair back in front of them. Turns out there was nothing to see here, after all: just more proof that the only place their teachers took them seriously was inside the classroom, discussing Nathaniel Hawthorne or debating reparations.

Walking back to Whitney from the auditorium, shoulder to shoulder with Blake and Kit and Brie, a question nagged at Sloane: "Do you really think they were protecting him? Or do you think they just . . . didn't believe her?" she asked her friends.

Blake stopped suddenly, fists balled in her coat pockets. She blinked and shook her head quickly, one-two-three. "Can't it be both? Doesn't one allow the other?"

The bus pulls to a stop in front of the Met steps, blocks wide and set back from the street as if to remind its visitors that it was here first, when there was space for double-wide sidewalks and landmarks that impressed from the ground rather than from the sky. Sloane had seen people on Twitter complaining about the cigarette building on Park Avenue and she remembers, vaguely, when the Gehry building was finished downtown. The buildings grow like runway models, now: tall and skinny and twisting in the wind.

As they'd made their way down the island, her classmates had slowly slumbered into waking, one by one untangling themselves from one another, heads off shoulders and laps, split earbuds disconnected, pillows unfurled from how they'd been bunched against windows. Most of them are too sleepy still to speak, and they primp and stretch and shudder to life with an easy shared silence, a comfortable intimacy. Ahead of her, Chloe fixes her mascara in the mirror of a powder compact while Brie twists her curly and unruly hair into a low bun, loosening it at the nape of her neck and untucking a few pieces of her hair around her ears so that the whole thing doesn't look too fussy. Behind her, Blake stands and rolls her hips in small circles, stretching a dancer's stretch.

They're waiting to disembark when it happens: Chloe angles her screen in Brie's direction; as Brie reaches for her own phone, Sloane hears Blake say, "What is it?", and all around her the juniors tap-tap into their apps.

Briefly, Sloane feels the muscles that flank her ribs tighten, her breath caught in her lungs, everything expanded. Maybe her friends had seen Caroline's comment and wondered who she was; maybe they were now currently clicking through to her profile to examine her painstakingly disciplined grid of dance photos: stretching in the mirror, chewed-up pointe shoes, a new black-and-white headshot for the winter season. Maybe they would look so long and hard at her page that they would fall through it like Alice into the looking glass and the whole of Sloane's life before Atwater would open to them; maybe they would see, if they racked their imaginations, Caroline's hair balled in Sloane's fist or her skin under her fingernails.

"Shit," Kyla whispers, dragging out the vowel in the middle, a long exhale. "Look." She tilts her phone toward Sloane.

It's a Snap story by a user Sloane doesn't recognize, each image a shot of a yearbook photo—she can tell by the whipped blue background, tonally streaked like food coloring in frosting, unchanged in thirty years—cropped at the subject's neck, so that their face is out of frame. In some, a sweep of longish hair drapes over a shoulder, so that blond ringlets or a loose braid enters the frame, but there is no other way to identify the headless girls in the pictures.

A rectangle of text sits at the bottom of each image, centered and nondescript: sans serif against a white background. In 1988, I slept with my math teacher, the first caption reads.

I left my graduation party at Mangino's to hook up with my history teacher in a studio in Trask. We'd been flirting all year.

Mangino's: a very mediocre Italian restaurant in Canaan, the kind of place that uses frozen chicken tenders as the foundation for its chicken Parm. Sloane went there, once, with her advising group freshmen year.

The soccer coach smacked our asses as we went in off the bench. He also refused to buy pinnies for practice, and had us play shirts vs. "skins" (in our sports bras). The girls with the biggest boobs were always put on the skins team.

My Dorm Parent used to write me little love notes on my sign-out card. It was the sweetest and most romantic thing anyone had ever done for me. It may still be.

The cross-country coach groped us under the guise of noting the areas of our bodies that were "weighing us down" (e.g., he would run his hand up and down my inner thighs, slowly, and say, "You don't want these to touch.").

"What is this?" Sloane's voice is a half whisper; she wonders if Kyla notices the catch in her throat. No one has ever said anything like that to her, but she knows how thick hands feel on a small body. She has seen them stretch across leotard-covered torsos and press in, saying, *Tighter.*

"This person—JamisonJennings95—added all of us on Snap. I think these might be from the consultant interviews? Like, based on the username."

Sloane pulls her phone from her jacket pocket and thumbs into her own Snapchat, where JamisonJennings95 has, in fact, added her. She watches the story again, searching among the ribbed turtlenecks and fuzzed alpaca sweaters for any hint about where they came from.

Blake's head appears over their shoulders, her chin jutting between them. "You think this is because of last night? Because of what I asked about the administration protecting Breslin over its students?"

Brie turns from where she sits in front of them. "Gotta be, right? Clearly this person—whoever did this—wants us to know that they can't, or don't. Protect us, I mean."

"Or won't," Blake adds.

"Shh," Kit hisses suddenly, and they realize that Mr. Hills is standing at the front of the bus. He is not the kind of teacher who yells or hushes; he waits, as he does now, for attention to come naturally, with the bemused look of someone prepared for any number of modest-size disasters or disappointments.

"Ladies," he says, "I'm going to ask that you stay together through our check-in. After that, Ms. Doyle and I will distribute the scavenger hunt sheets, and you'll have two hours to find as many things on your list as possible."

"Do we get extra credit?" Coming from someone else, the question might have seemed grade-grubby, but Blake and her Yale ambitions are so perpetually high-strung that she gets away with it.

"Successful completion of the hunt earns you five bonus points on the project or exam of your choosing. Didn't I already go over this?" Mr. Hills pauses to watch his students frown apologetically. "Never mind. Let's just get inside. Follow me, please!" he says, leading the way down the bus steps, his red windbreaker billowing behind him like a smallish parachute.

Sloane grew up going to the Met, of course, like any born-and-raised New Yorker whose preschool experience was managed by a stay-at-home mom: they spent rainy and cold days at the Met but also at MoMA and the Museum of Natural History and, once or twice, the Frick; nice weather called for the Central Park Zoo or Ellis Island and the Statue of Liberty. Sometimes, she thought she could chart her life by her favorite rooms at the Met: like all little kids, she loved the Temple of Dendur, the way it felt like her own private pyramid, the glassy atrium wide and bright with room to run around as the rain made rivers on the walls around them. In fourth grade she'd watched a TV movie about Joan of Arc and developed a paralyzing fear of burning to death—she had nightmares in which, through some medical malpractice, she was mistaken for dead and sent to be cremated—after which Jules Bastien-Lepage's portrait of Joan of Arc, at the top of the stairs through the Great Hall, became her favorite painting; she loved the dead-eyed look the artist had given the future saint, an expression that was supposed to imply her visions but which also looked, Sloane thought, flatly insane.

By sixth grade, it was the French impressionists, for obvious reasons. She couldn't wait to see them in the Louvre and the British Museum and in the Borghese Gallery, all places ballet would take her before she graduated high school. Once she went to Juilliard—if she even went to college, if she wasn't dancing professionally by then—she'd become a Young Member, and her favorite way to see the Met would be by nightfall, at cocktail parties on the balcony bar or at the semiannual galas.

That sort of future seems a long time ago, now, and with it has gone the particular intimacy she used to share with the city. She was surprised by how quickly it left her: how soon she lost the ability to exit a subway station, to emerge from the bowels below and know without straining to read the street signs at both corners which direction is north; how easily she lost the precise patterns of turns in the park that lead to Strawberry Fields or the Balto statue. You don't realize until you leave Manhattan how quickly everything changes. To a permanent resident it might be charming, the rotating cast of characters, but for Sloane the result is that something like retracing the route from her first home on Riverside Drive to the Museum of Natural History has taken on the quality of a fun house, a hall of mirrors: everything is generally the same but not quite.

Chloe nudges Sloane with an elbow as they follow Mr. Hills toward the steps, breaking the trance she'd fallen into. "You probably came here all the time, huh?"

Next to her, Kyla—who knows better than to talk to Sloane about New York—rolls her eyes quickly, a look meant for only Sloane to notice.

"When I was little, yeah," Sloane says, not quite meeting Chloe's glance. She knows that Chloe will interpret this as bitchy, and might even run to Kit or Brie and ask: *Hey, why is Sloane in such a bad mood?* Or *Is Sloane mad at me?* But it doesn't matter. Anyway, most of Sloane's classmates are used to Sloane's spikiness; they've learned how to take wide curves around her edges.

Behind them, Blake is still tapping through Snapchat. "Do you think those are actually pictures of people who were interviewed?" she says, her voice hushed, as if it might be lifted on the city wind and carried to Mr. Hills's ears fifteen yards ahead of them.

Sloane thinks again about Addison last night, the naked narcissism of her question about Atwater's reputation. Blake's question here is almost as transparent: they'd all wondered, to some extent, who among the current students the school would select to join the alumnae and parents and trustees who'd volunteered to participate in the consulting firm's investigation. Girls like Blake and Louisa, who were usually chosen any time the school needed official representation, seemed personally offended as the days and weeks wore on without invitation.

Brie shakes her head, her face half-hidden by a thick chunky scarf. "I don't think so. Why do the headless thing, in that case? Like, if you're going to dox them, just go for it, you know? I bet they're like, a metaphor—bodies that *represent* the girls who've said these things happened to them."

"Why do you care?" Sloane asks, turning to look Blake right in the eye, stopping short.

"Hmm?"

"Do you wish it was your picture in there?"

"Jesus, Sloane—" Blake doesn't even look mad: it's shock, followed by disgust, that ripples across her face.

"Sloane, easy—" Kyla places a hand on Sloane's upper arm. "I think we just want to know where this person is getting their info. Right?"

"Girls?" They hear Mr. Hills's voice carry down the steps from where he stands, an arm holding open the museum door. "A little less chitchat, please!"

"Come on," Kit says, her voice low.

To Sloane's right, north of the steps, vendors set up tables of tourist art: posters of the subway grid; street signs; tiny oil paintings of the skyline, one inch by one inch. To her left, Seventy-ninth Street funnels into the park, the stone wall open like a mouth at the traverse. She hangs back for a minute, and feels her nerves pulse like someone on the verge of doing the irrevocable: she recalls her first shot of vodka, or the first time she slipped a lacy thong from the Victoria's Secret sale table into her purse.

Kyla turns over her shoulder, the last of the juniors to enter the museum. She shakes her head slightly, not judgmentally but like, *Good luck,* and lets the door slam behind her.

As freshmen, Sloane and Blake had tried to choreograph a dance for the spring arts show. It had been extraordinarily high-concept for a pair of fourteen-year-olds, a routine that involved twining their bodies together in a sort of symbiosis, like flames of the sun licking up from a central source. But they hadn't fit together, in the most literal sense; Blake was too tall and too strong, Sloane too tiny and too slight—each time they reviewed the film of their rehearsal, Sloane saw herself as a parasite, gnat-like and clawing. She'd blamed Blake—in the end she called her an attention whore—and bailed on the production a week before the show. They'd never worked together again, and Ms. Allen took to booking the individual studio for them at opposite ends of the afternoon so that one never even warmed up in front of the other. Their friends started calling them *frenemies,* didn't even bother to say it only behind their backs.

Sloane knows that most of their classmates—although they're aware that Sloane has special permission to satisfy both her art and athletic requirements through dance, that she fulfills her volunteer hours providing lessons to four- and five-year-olds for two weeks every summer at a studio in Tarrytown; although they may have heard that an eleven-year-old Sloane danced as Marie in the New York City Ballet's production of

The Nutcracker—consider *Blake* to be the more talented and committed dancer between them. It's Blake who takes the train into New York on Wednesday afternoons for dance; it's Blake who leaves Atwater most weekends for forty-eight hours of practice in her studio in Manhattan. It's Blake's schedule that impresses Atwater faculty and staff—at least those who don't wrinkle their noses at the obvious privilege that affords such a schedule—and that sounds very serious to their classmates, most of whom do not possess any practical understanding of ballet beyond what was accrued in a preschool class.

But Sloane also knows this: that a truly serious young dancer will spend four or five hours a day dancing, every day; that the most promising high school–aged dancers negotiate their academic schedules *around* rehearsal, rather than vice versa, through the employ of an army of tutors or enrollment in a nontraditional high school like the Professional School or, if the dancer is particularly prodigious, completion of an online GED program. Of all of Blake's classmates, it is exclusively Sloane who has the power to crack the veneer of Blake's rigor, of her very identity; it's Sloane who knows that nothing in dance matters except the decision to go all in, to surrender entirely.

This is why their friendship has a kind of simmering tension; their destruction is mutually assured. They both know the truth about the other: that Blake will never be a professional dancer, and that Sloane could have been had she not thrown it all away.

The Upper East Side was never Sloane's domain, although her mother used to take her to Serendipity 3 after a Saturday morning at Barneys when she was very young, and so she turns—as if pulled by a magnetic force—toward Seventy-ninth Street and the park. At the traverse she hangs another right and then a quick left, descending on the footpath and dropping quickly beneath the sidewalk.

Central Park always feels like a kind of insular bubble, a little microclimate in the center of the city. In the summer months it bakes, a crater in the middle of an overcrowded metropolitan, too-tall buildings and millions of bodies trapping heat like an industrialized rain forest canopy; in the winter, the same topography shields it from the wind that whips across the streets between the rivers. Either way, the park—particularly the network of meandering footpaths at the edges, far from the chaos of the reservoir or the boathouse—takes on a kind of eerie stillness.

The paths are mazelike; even when she knew them best she still navigated by an internal compass rather than a mapped route. At the first fork she stays to her left; at the next, she chooses right, until she ends up along one of the drives that only cabs can seem to access. She crosses the road at the boathouse, easing between the stay-at-home moms and model types out for their morning jogs and the middle-aged men with flexible schedules in hedge fund management out for their bike rides. They all look like her dad: soft, round faces; a little bit of a gut spilling over their thighs as they hunch over the handlebars. They ride incredibly expensive-looking bikes, and are each outfitted with all the gear: fingerless gloves and wind-blocking booties slipped over their shoes and yellow-tinted sunglasses.

She began dancing at the School of American Ballet when she was seven, three years and a few months after her very first trip to the ballet. The story is that Sloane exited the theater spinning, twirling across Lincoln Center in tiny sloppy rotations. It is such a devastating cliché that she is not sure it really happened; whatever she did that day, it was enough to persuade her parents to enroll her in classes at a studio around the corner from her preschool, where the teacher encouraged unselfconsciousness among her four-year-old students by asking them to move like storybook creatures: butterflies, mermaids, exotic birds. Sloane hated it. She recognized immediately the pandering; after the first hour-long class, she sat in the back seat of a cab, her body pressed against her mother, her face ruddy with tears and frustration, squeaking between sobs about her desire to do "real" ballet.

The instructors at Little Slippers nodded sympathetically when Sloane's mother explained her daughter's dissatisfaction. They were used to parents who believed their children were exceptional. What they tried to instill, they explained, was an ability to be playful and loose; to work with the body rather than against it. Early childhood lessons that focus on precision yield stiff, anxious dancers. Plus, they added: the truth is that for so many of these girls, dance is only a passing phase. "In five years, it won't matter if she can *jeté*," they said. "But it *will* matter that she has a healthy communion with her body."

So Elizabeth Beck struck a deal with her daughter: Sloane would continue to attend the classes where she swayed her body like ribbons of seaweed *and* she would receive, in the evenings once per week, private lessons from a thirty-year-old waitress who'd recently retired from the ABT corps, her Achilles tendons so rigid with scar tissue that they creaked like door hinges when she walked. What Annie told Elizabeth, after just three lessons with Sloane, was that her daughter was not at all at risk of being too precise. "She's fearless," she explained. "It's like she's desperate to know what her body can do, what shapes it can make. She's too curious to be anxious."

Shortly thereafter Sloane withdrew from classes at Little Slippers and into a full week of private lessons, a routine she maintained until first grade, when her teacher at the time suggested Sloane attend open auditions at the School of American Ballet, a feeder institution for the New York City Ballet and where Sloane would meet Caroline Keegan.

Although she was a year older—a chasm in elementary school growth and maturity, and an even greater distance in ballet skill—Caroline was small for an eight-year-old, a little soft in the cheeks still, with dimples that lingered like shadows after she'd relaxed her smile. She hadn't started dancing until the year before; Sloane still remembers the pang of territoriality she felt at this reveal, the unfairness that a girl so late to the game could be at her approximate skill level. In the end they both made the cut: Sloane would dance with the six- and seven-year-olds, Caroline in the eight- to ten-year-old group, and for both of them the door to a different kind of future opened just the tiniest bit wider. (Of course their daughters were exceptional, their parents thought—how foolish of them to have ever doubted it.)

And then when Sloane was eleven and Caroline twelve—still small for her age, still waiting to see whether puberty would thwart her ballerina dreams—they were chosen to dance as Marie in NYCB's production of *The Nutcracker*. That fall, six days a week for eight weeks, Caroline and Sloane danced together in private rehearsals, hours and hours and hours just the two of them and the children's ballet master, a dark-haired, fair-skinned woman named Maureen who was surprisingly warm and patient with her two young steads. They were prickly around each other initially, their fifth- and sixth-grade brains imagining their sixteen- and seventeen-year-old selves vying for the same spots in the SAB-NYCB apprentice program. But the exposed vulnerabilities of hours of training a day will bond you to a person, and by the end of their *Nutcracker* run in December, Caroline and Sloane were best friends.

For a while she stands just across the street, in the triangular patch of park where Broadway and Columbus intersect, pigeons hooting at the ground around her. She thinks it looks as it has always looked: smooth and polished and still.

There's no reason for her to go any farther, but there was no reason for her to come all this way in the first place, and so she flicks her head quickly to the right before hop-stepping across the street, not bothering to wait for the light to change. She comes to a standstill in the middle of the three-sided quad, near the fountain but not quite at its edge, listening to the water gurgle over the sound of the Upper West Side's thinning traffic.

Her memories of Lincoln Center blur together in the way of routines: she has scampered up these steps so many times that she is not sure she can pick out any particular day. There are moments that should stand out, but they are ones that were recorded elsewhere—in playbills and on the pages of the *Times* and in a documentary about child professionals—and reflecting upon them has the uneasy opacity of remembering a long-dead relative, one who exists around the house in family photographs: Does she remember them, really, or does she only remember the pictures?

What has always, always struck Sloane most about Lincoln Center is its absolute tranquility; something about the way it sits far back from the street—like a Greek acropolis, imposing, the kind of place that makes you triple-check with yourself before entering—makes it seem preternaturally untouched. (It is also not *itself* a tourist attraction—it *houses* the attractions; on a nonperformance day no sightseers crowd its sidewalk, lingering and selfie-taking.) And so when a figure emerges at the edge of Sloane's vision, in the space between the opera house and Fisher Hall—no doubt performing a cut-through to Broadway Sloane herself has walked a thousand times before—she notices. The woman wears loose-fitting joggers, cuffed around the ankles, and has shrouded herself in a large blanket scarf semi-tucked into a mid-length puffer jacket. She wears the kind of mid-height Nike sneakers only very skinny people can pull off.

Despite the inevitability of it—of course she would be here, in the middle of the day in the middle of the week—Sloane is surprised to see her, like someone whose impossible wish has come true. Her stomach somersaults. Sloane thinks about the way the Instagram comment—knowing, empathetic—might have latched like a harpoon, reeling her in across two states and over rolling midsize mountain ranges until she was close enough that all she needed was a final push.

After the *Nutcracker*, Sloane and Caroline were funneled into a different channel, even at a place like SAB: they were repeatedly called up to perform child roles in various NYCB performances, and their schedules were increasingly removed from the regular division progression and replaced with semiprivate lessons and rehearsals. They started working with Michael, a twenty-four-year-old soloist and teaching fellow with sandy hair and mottled blue eyes like overripe blueberries, on original choreography, in some kind of allegedly mutually beneficial relationship that allowed the girls to receive individualized instruction and that gave Michael the opportunity to hone his choreographing style.

Sometimes she thinks it didn't actually happen, that's how hard she's worked to suppress this one memory above all others. But of course it happened, and watching Caroline stride across the black-and-gray pattern of the plaza in Sloane's direction brings it rushing back, her brain flooded: Caroline's arm in her fist, the dull thud of her head against the glass; the neat smack of Sloane's body against the synthetic tile of the studio floor, her wrists behind her, instinct nurtured over a thousand falls taking over even in this absurdly unlikely scenario. Before that: Caroline and Michael, their faces close; Michael's hand on Caroline's waist, then his knuckle at her chin, lifting her lips toward his; a kiss that seemed to unfold over the course of an eternity.

Sloane would never have said that she had a crush on Michael. When she'd hear the older girls say he was *hot*, especially his longish hair, she'd nod and smile, but to imagine Michael in this way was an absurd mental exercise. What she and Michael and Caroline had was a closeness that transcended such a regular description. But on the walk home that night she replayed the image over and over and over, trying to discern exactly how wide Caroline's eyes had been, to figure out whether she smiled like she knew what was coming—was it curved at the edges, like a smirk?—or like she was nervous, her front teeth gnawing slightly at the inside of her lip? She couldn't remember; each time her mind rewound the tape Caroline's face shifted, a chameleon inside Sloane's head. And Michael: Did he reach for her chin tentatively, cautiously, only after the tacit approval of his hand on Caroline's hip? Or did he reach his hand to her face possessively, with the confidence of experience?

By the next day, the sight had inked itself on the insides of Sloane's eyelids. It set up camp deep in the pit of her stomach. At thirteen, she had not yet experienced heartbreak, and so she could not identify the maelstrom of jealousy and self-loathing and obsession she felt as anything except outright fury. In class that morning—it functioned as a kind of tune-up, no new skills, just reminding the muscles and tendons what they had to do—she took her usual place against the barre in the back corner, next to Caroline. They'd known each other for more than six years, nearly half of Sloane's life, but as they rotated through plié squats and calf raises she found herself looking at Caroline as if they'd only just met, the entire history of their relationship reengineered through this new revelation.

"You're being weird," Caroline had said at one point, almost dismissively. She fiddled with a bobby pin at the nape of her neck, one of the ones she used to secure the small flyaways she hated.

Had this gulf between them been there all along? Sloane wondered. And what about her own relationship with Michael—had she imagined it? All the times he'd placed a palm tenderly on the small of her back; the way he'd take her hips in each of his hands, rotating her pelvis forward under the guise of moving her body into precisely the correct position but doing it with such *care*, a kind of gentleness she'd never felt with the slew of Russian women who'd trained her before this; how he'd take a seat on the floor as she stretched after class and wrap a calf in his hand, sliding her tiny body closer to his, dropping her foot into his lap and rubbing it, kneading the knots in her aching arches. She drew herself a spectrum of affection, placed Caroline at the very top. Where did all this other touching land?

Sloane still couldn't say who'd been off-tempo that afternoon in rehearsal—whether it was her timing or Caroline's that caused them to collide, knocking them off-balance and sending their bodies crashing onto the floor. They were exhausted, too, the day long and the choreography complicated. It wasn't unusual for the competition between them to flare in little spats, laser-like glares and snarky digs. Maybe to Caroline it had just seemed like an escalation, if a disproportionate one. Sloane still remembers the way she popped up after falling, then the feel of her palms against Caroline's chest, the stunned way Caroline stumbled backward into the mirror. Sloane is not sure why she didn't stop here—it was enough to shove someone; that alone was something she'd never done.

As Caroline teetered into the mirror, Sloane advanced. She pushed again, harder this time, and the back of Caroline's skull collided with the glass. She dropped to the floor, in a kind of defensive and pained crouch, one hand against the back of her head, her opposite forearm curved up and over her body like a shield. Sloane started kicking at first, weak thumps that seemed inconsequential in her pointe shoes, furious at the irony that the shoes could inflict so much pain on her own feet but none on another body. She reached down for Caroline and pulled at her, shrieking *Get up get up get up.* Had she wanted her to fight back? Or was she trying to erase it, to have Caroline stand to prove that she was fine? The longer Caroline stayed down the harder Sloane pulled, clawing at Caroline's arm, her tiny soft nails pushing deeper and deeper into her friend's smooth skin.

Michael pulled them apart, in one swift movement extricating Sloane from Caroline and pulling Caroline to her feet. He held them like that for a moment, one ninety-pound body in each fist, both of them panting, both too shocked to cry. Where he gripped Caroline's arm just below her wrist Sloane could see thin jagged lines rapidly purpling, tiny blossoms blooming beneath the skin.

"What the fuck, Sloane?" Caroline shouted, one hand still cradling the back of her head.

Michael released Sloane and moved to Caroline, leaning close to where her skull curved under toward her neck, his nose inches from her softest parts.

"Get out," he said to Sloane. "Go home."

"I'm sorry—" Sloane mumbled, as if by reflex.

The school had spoken to her parents by the time she walked in the apartment door. They would be asking Sloane to withdraw. A whole future folded in on itself, crumpled as easily as a paper fortune-teller, origami crushed into garbage. Her mother told her Caroline needed six staples. Sloane wondered why the mirror didn't break.

Caroline is barely ten yards away now, too close for Sloane to avert her eyes, too close for her to flee. She halts, her stride pulled up. "Sloane?" she calls.

Sloane waves, as if it's the most natural thing in the world that they should run into one another here. People are always saying how small New York really is, aren't they? "Hey, Caroline."

Caroline crosses the remaining space between them. She puts her hands in her pockets, burrowing into herself against the cold. Sloane searches her face: Is she angry? Afraid? "What are you doing here?"

Sloane pauses. "Just out for a walk," she answers.

"Are you guys on break this week?"

"Huh?"

"Aren't you still at Atwater?"

"Oh, no. I mean, yes, I am. But no, we're not on break. I'm here on a field trip, actually."

Caroline frowns, clearly puzzled.

"Anyway—how are you?"

"Me? Fine. Busy. You know how it is."

"Hey—congrats on Juilliard." The price of this congratulations is, on the one hand, complete humiliation: it admits a certain attentive following of Caroline's Instagram, where she recently posted about the acceptance in an infuriatingly noncommittal caption that suggested she might not actually *enroll* at the famed conservatory (presumably—Sloane understood, although surely most of Caroline's followers did not—because it might make more sense for her to begin dancing professionally). On the other hand, acknowledging their Instagram relationship—that they did not unfollow one another after the incident, that they've each maintained a degree of investment in the other's life—is acknowledging that Sloane did, in fact, see Caroline's comment on her post; it makes possible the idea that they could cease haunting one another, that the phantoms of their usernames could be made solid.

"Oh, thanks." Caroline cracks her neck slightly, a graceful twist back and to the side. "I don't know if I'll go, which is sort of a hard thing to explain to most people. . . ."

Caroline doesn't say this like she's humblebragging; she says it like she's legitimately sad, like she's been searching far and wide for someone who might understand how difficult it is to navigate each precarious transition in a ballet career, for someone who understands the cost of a single miscalculation.

Sloane nods. "What do your parents think?"

Caroline shrugs. "I think they'd like me to get a degree. But they sort of leave me to my own devices now. I guess they think"—she sighs, searching the sky above them—"I've earned it."

In their first summer in the new house in Westchester, Sloane's mother found the shed exoskeleton of a cicada nymph perched on the railing of their two-story porch. Amber-colored with lobsterlike claws and a massive, swollen abdomen, it fascinated and repulsed Sloane: she convinced her mother to let her keep it, and she perched the shell on its haunches on her desk lamp. It weighed nothing. It could be crushed by an errant breeze. Most of the time that summer Sloane herself felt made of air, only the remnants of the thing that shrieked and clicked when the sun went down. She still feels that way, sometimes.

"You know they fired Michael, right?" Caroline says, suddenly.

Somehow, she doesn't collapse in on herself. Her shell withstands the blow.

"What?"

"You didn't know?" Caroline looks away again and shakes her head. "I guess I shouldn't be surprised. They did a really good job keeping the whole thing under wraps. You know how this place is about PR. Still . . . you of all people . . ." Caroline trails off.

"Why? What happened?"

Caroline's eyes narrow. When she speaks, she cocks her head to one side. "He was kind of a creep, Sloane."

Sloane feels completely detached from the news, from this entirely sudden realization that her ballet career was thwarted by a pedophile. No one had ever flipped the image this way; when her parents made her go to therapy, she never explained the inciting incident. The therapist laid her assumptions onto Sloane and her outburst like a lithograph: Dr. Leahey had seen the movies; she knew how competitive and jealous ballerinas could be. Sloane was an easy one, the case closed as soon as it was opened.

"Did a parent complain?" It is the smallest detail, but Sloane finds herself ravenous for the logistics. *How* did it happen? *Who* sounded the alarm? Her craving for the facts is unbearable, the deepest kind of aching hunger. She thinks of Karen Mirro and her curly blond hair, reaching across the decades to tell her story. She considers all that they don't and will never know.

"You saw him, Sloane," Caroline says, shrugging. "He was so handsy, always telling us we were beautiful, rubbing our shoulders, massaging our feet—" She sounds almost weary, like someone who's had to explain this part of her life a thousand times before. *My Dorm Parent used to write me little love notes on my sign-out card.* Sloane understands, now, how something can be simultaneously catastrophic and banal; ruinous but ordinary.

"But there must have been something that put them over the edge." Sloane scans Caroline's face, searching, waiting. She wonders if all this time Caroline understood, if Caroline doesn't actually blame Sloane for the series of tiny centimeter-wide scars that ladder up the back of her scalp. Maybe it's Caroline who's sorry: for not having told sooner, for not having said, *No, this was all his fault.* Maybe she heard about the scandal that has plagued Atwater this year, and she thought of Sloane and said to herself, *Jesus, what are the chances? Everywhere you go, this kind of thing.*

But all Caroline says—her phone slipped from her pocket, distractedly checking the time—is: "He became a liability, I guess. Anyway, listen, I gotta run. It was really great to see you, though." She holds her arms wide and pulls her old partner into a quick embrace, their jackets squishing against one another but their bodies ultimately still inches apart. "Text me the next time you're in the city. We'll get coffee or something." She smiles and gives Sloane's arm a quick squeeze before darting down the steps and across Columbus, her body easing between a gap in the traffic. Sloane follows her until she can no longer be sure which shapeless coat is hers.

Sloane's phone is lit up with messages: from Kyla, from Chloe, from Mr. Hills. They've gathered on the Met steps and have noticed her absence. They're supposed to be leaving, walking across the park as a gaggle to the New-York Historical Society.

Where r u? Chloe asked, then sending again: ???

Tried to cover for u, Kyla wrote. Hills is freaking.

I'm fine, Sloane thumbs back to Kyla. I'll meet you guys at the Historical Society. I know where it is. She doesn't wait for a reply. She's in trouble; it is what it is.

It's a fifteen-minute walk, one block over and ten up. She crosses

Sixty-third, where Caroline dissolved into the lunch crowd minutes ago, then crosses again so that she can walk along the park side of Central Park West. She passes a few dog walkers, each with a fistful of leashes, guiding an improbably well-behaved pack. Their work is one of New York's greatest mysteries. As she walks she wills herself to replay her conversation with Caroline, to try to discern the exact tenor of Caroline's voice—but she finds herself unable to concentrate, her mind drifting to the wreckage of her failed or failing relationships: with Caroline, with Blake; most recently with Bella. With her parents. With ballet. All of it has left her like this very island, windblown and steely.

She thinks about the night her parents told her she would be attending Atwater, sitting at their new dining table in their big and impersonal new house. The plan had been for her to continue dancing in a new studio while attending Chapin. That evening, her mother began by saying that they just wanted Sloane to be happy and healthy. Sloane remembers her mom's wide eyes, the outsize smile, the desperate pitch in her voice: It was how you talk to someone who's experiencing a psychotic break. Atwater was a very lush, expensive, more socially acceptable version of institutionalization. *They think dance made me go crazy,* she'd realized. But what she never understood was why they had to leave New York, too, if they were just going to send her to boarding school. It never made any sense: her mother loved the city; she would pull Sloane in for a hug as the hot air from a subway grate exhaled on her shins and say, "Do you know how lucky you are to grow up here?" The truth flickers briefly, something Sloane can only begin to see, the world of parenthood mostly an abstraction to her: the place where their daughter was hurt had been ruined for her parents; they, too, felt a kind of betrayal. Knowing what they knew about Atwater now, did they feel they'd upended their lives for nothing? Or are they just grateful that at least *this time* it was somebody else's little girl?

To Sloane's left, the well-preserved faces of prewar buildings stand at attention, imposing and serious; above her, the naked trees stretch their branches in knobby fingertips. The bustle of the intersection at Seventy-second offers contrast, a chaotic and lively hubbub: three food carts, filling the air with the sour haze of sweating meat; a cop on mounted horseback and two on foot, their hands resting on the weapons at their hips; a man balancing on a pedicab calls to a pack of tourists at the opposite corner.

Next to her, where the path widens to accommodate a sidewalk that curves down into the park, a street musician takes a break, repositioning his fingers and his bow. Sloane gazes into his case, strewn with a few dollars and tattooed with peeling stickers. He's young, only twelve or thirteen, if Sloane had to guess: an entrepreneurial kid using the practice time his parents set aside to make a few bucks.

"Shouldn't you be in school?" Sloane says to him.

The boy shrugs and grins, his hair flopping across his forehead. "Parent-teacher conferences."

"Lucky you."

"Shouldn't *you* be in school?"

Sloane laughs, digging into her pocket. "Hey, you want my dollar or what?"

The boy raises his eyebrows, scheming, before resting his bow against the strings. He takes a breath, purses his lips, and starts to play.

It takes Sloane only a few beats to recognize the music as a Bach suite. She has danced to it a hundred times before, routine practice music. She listens for thirty seconds, then forty-five, her eyes closed to the city around her. She feels the beat inside her ankles and wrists, her head swaying with the rhythm of choreography ingrained like a second language. Her shoes are not made for dancing: They're heavy and clunky, a thick-soled nineties throwback. But she can make do.

She drops a dollar into the boy's case as she stretches out her arm, steadying herself, waiting for her cue. And then she begins.

SETTLEMENT REACHED IN ATWATER SUIT

By Amanda Lucas
Updated April 16, 2016, 7:46 A.M.

FALLS VILLAGE, CT—The Atwater School has reached a settlement with the former student seeking damages for the school's handling of a sexual assault allegation, according to a joint statement released by both parties. The settlement amount owed to Karen Mirro, 38, and the exact terms of the agreement remain undisclosed.

In the statement, representatives for the school made clear its intent to perform a "rigorous evaluation and retooling of (its) practices to ensure an environment that prioritizes respect and healthy boundaries." Additionally, Atwater announced in January that it has retained the services of Jamison Jennings to perform an assessment of school policies and procedures surrounding misconduct and abuse. The firm's findings are expected in June.

"Ms. Mirro's motivation was never a financial one," Mirro's attorneys said in the statement. "She was motivated by future generations of Atwater alumnae and alumnae families, who deserve the full protection and compassion of the adults with whom they have bestowed an immense amount of trust."

Connecticut's statute of limitations for rape cases—among the most stringent in the nation—prohibited Mirro from bringing a criminal suit against her alleged rapist or the school. In the same statement, Mirro expressed hope that the suit would "bring to light the necessity that Connecticut join a growing number of states in expanding its statute of limitations for crimes involving sexual assault."

Mirro's case is one among a proliferation of sexual abuse cases at private schools across the nation, a trend that—victim advocates say—suggests a long-standing culture of institutional nontransparency and retaliatory behavior. Although Title IX has offered protection against sex-based discrimination since 1972, and all states have had mandatory reporting laws since 1967, private and independent schools have historically been subject to a lower level of rigor in their compliance due to lesser oversight than that faced by public schools. Furthermore, federal and state laws have struggled to address the role of power and trust in consent, guidelines that could offer additional protection to college students and high school students above the legal age of consent.

With the promises made in its statement, Atwater hopes to play a role in changing the landscape. "Since its founding, Atwater has been a leader not only in girls' education but also in teaching and learning broadly. Ms. Mirro has started a conversation from which we will grow and innovate, and we are grateful."

Prom

By the time the morning light creeps in, Emma has been awake for hours. In fact, she isn't entirely sure she's sleeping anymore, period: she spends most nights in long stretches of wide-awake, stare-at-the-ceiling fitfulness, so long and so frequent that when her alarm finally rings it comes as a relief. It occurs to her on those nights she must be sleeping some, surely she falls in and out, a person can't go this many days without any sleep whatsoever—but her own memory says otherwise.

Next to her, Olivia shifts her weight slightly, nestling herself closer to Emma, who can feel her girlfriend's warmth on the sheets between them. It has to be said: Olivia is incomparably beautiful. Stop-you-in-your-tracks, normal-people-don't-look-like-this, sticks-out-even-in-L.A. beautiful. It is the kind of beautiful that flattens a person, distills them only to one thing—an irony, in Olivia's case, because her beauty is the product of a marriage between the daughter of Korean immigrants and a Black man from South Carolina, a story that is inextricable from the complicated history of America.

But Olivia doesn't like to talk about that, neither her multiracial heritage nor the entirely original beauty it bequeaths her. When a person tells her how striking she is, Olivia replies with a thin-lipped smile, one that widens the eyes just enough so the complimenter feels as though their opinion is appreciated. She cocks her head, sometimes reaches a hand out to touch their forearm. "Thank you," she says, and that's it.

Once, in that shimmering space between when they were not a couple and when they were, Emma asked Olivia, in bed, her hands near her hair but not touching it, how she had learned to take a compliment like that. Everyone Emma knew—herself included—had a way of politely rejecting praise. The first time Emma had heard Olivia merely say *thank you* it had struck her as rude.

At the time Olivia had smiled at Emma and moved her hands to her face. She held her gaze for a moment, so closely and unblinkingly that Emma could see the shadows of her reflection in Olivia's irises. And then she kissed her, slowly, until the question evaporated from Emma's lips. Only later, thinking about the smile, would Emma realize that it was identical to the one Olivia used with a stranger: *Thank you.*

Tonight, Olivia will be perfect. She will look effortless. She will do her hair and makeup and nails herself and it will be as if she had a professional glam squad. Collier and Addison, who will have actual glam squads come to campus, whose dresses appeared in fashion magazines with the descriptor "Price Upon Request," will look like the thousands of dollars they've spent.

In bed, Emma turns away from Olivia, eyeing where her dress hangs against her closet door. It's fine. When Olivia picked out her own dress, Emma told her to pick a few options for her, too, and she'd decide from among the narrowed selection. It's black with a deep V and squared-off shoulders that finish in elbow-length sleeves, sharp and modern. When she told Olivia which one she'd chosen, her girlfriend said simply, "Knew it," and Emma still isn't sure what it said about either of them. How much can you tell about a person based on her prom dress?

She untangles herself from the sheets carefully, so as not to disturb Olivia, who could sleep until lunch if anyone ever let her, and tiptoes across her room to her desk, where her phone lies overturned. No messages. Some Snapchat alerts—she hates Snapchat, actually, but since some of the Jamison Jennings interviews were leaked on the platform, she's worried she might miss out on something if she quits it. She scrolls through Instagram, where no one has posted anything interesting in ten hours. She is in the gentle coma of social media consumption when Olivia sighs across the room, dramatically announcing her awakening.

Emma rotates slowly back toward the bed, placing her phone on her desk behind her. "'Morning, beautiful," she says. It's time to start the day.

At breakfast, they grab their usual table in the corner in the lower dining room. The light is good, and the trickle of girls is slow and quiet. They share the *Times*, which Atwater has delivered in addition to the *Courant* because it's paid for by an alum whose last name is also the name of a major publishing house. They linger over coffee, the paper divided between them like a middle-aged couple in a suburban dramedy, when Collier and Addison make their entrance, both in their college crewnecks (Pomona for Addison, Williams for Collier) and tapered joggers and Birkenstocks with marled camp socks. Olivia drops her paper slightly and gives them a head nod, which the girls perceive as an invitation.

"'Morning," Addie chimes, maneuvering through the chairs and tables between them like a biblical figure parting the seas. They post up next to Olivia and Emma, Collier resting a hand on Emma's chair, Addie leaning into the table next to theirs.

"Excited for tonight?" Collier asks with her usual New York indifference, not sounding excited at all. In fact, Collier is from Greenwich, but at Atwater Emma quickly learned that—although they are not the same thing—young people from Fairfield County operate as if they are from New York.

Addie doesn't wait for an answer. "You're coming to my parents' place after, right?" The Bowlsbys' Litchfield estate sits empty most of the year, except for Parents' Weekend and the occasional visit—they come to a couple of Addison's tennis matches every fall, and sometimes Addison's mother "makes a trip out of it," using Connecticut as a hop-step on her way to Europe. In other words, the home is basically Addison's, and Addison is therefore the only one in the senior class with the resources (chiefly, a house within driving distance) to throw an actual after-prom party, like they do in the movies or, Emma assumes, regular suburban high schools all over the country. Like they might have at the high school she would have gone to in Cincinnati, had she stayed, had middle school been bearable.

"I think so," Olivia says, which is news to Emma, because while they'd talked about Addie's party she wasn't aware they'd reached an "I think so"-worthy consensus. She flashes Olivia a look but doesn't say anything else—it's not worth escalating here, in front of Addie and Collier and the sparsely filled dining hall.

"You *have* to. You're not worried about getting in trouble, are you?"

Olivia tilts her chin down and raises an eyebrow, like, *Are you fucking kidding me?* They all know that after-prom is one of those moments where the school very deliberately turns a blind eye, and that this trend will continue even this year, when the growing consensus has been that the Dean of Students is going a little bit crazy in the face of her inability to catch the person responsible for the Snapchat and the Instagram and the paintings and, most recent, the flyer placed neatly in each of their physical mailboxes that implied that Mrs. Brodie's relationship to her husband—who is twenty years older and was her professor in graduate school—prevents her from responding to allegations like Karen Mirro's with sensitivity and empathy.

"Good. I mean, I know you guys always do your own thing, but everybody is dying for you to come. It's our senior prom!" She gives them each a little squeeze on the shoulder.

"Wild, right?" Olivia says, her mouth curled up in one corner, her delivery just flat enough that only her girlfriend will notice. Emma almost snorts into her coffee.

Addison smiles, unfettered. "Okay, I need caffeine. And eggs! I'll see you ladies later!" Both she and Collier give a little wave before leaving the table.

"So—we're going to Addie's?"

Olivia props her feet against the edge of Emma's chair and pushes slightly, tilting her own chair onto its back legs. It's a fidgety behavior that on anyone else would read as immature or adolescent; because Olivia is Olivia, it's *casual,* ironic. "I figure we should, right? It's the right thing to do."

Olivia is always saying a version of this when Emma doesn't want to do something. *We should make an appearance. We don't want anyone to be offended. We should go—it's the right thing to do.* They had their first real fight about exactly this, last year when Emma didn't want to go to the winter luau because, in her opinion, it was stupid and heteronormative, busing boys in from Westminster and Salisbury for a *pool party*—but Olivia had been firm on *making an appearance*.

"I'm a Peer Ed," she'd explained, her voice even, her eyes unblinking, standing in Emma's doorframe in a high-cut one-piece swimsuit and frayed jean shorts: "I have to go."

No you don't, not technically, Emma had thought.

"It's important that I participate in school bonding activities," Olivia said, before turning on her heels and striding out of Whitney. Emma joined her, sheepishly, an hour later, sidling up next to Olivia as she tangled her ankles in the deep end.

"I'm sorry," she'd said. "I know this is important to you."

"It's not important to me," Olivia said, her tone betraying the slightest edge of frustration. "I just have to do things like this. I have to try to be a part of the community."

"For Proctor, I know." Emma knew that Olivia had her eyes on being named Proctor, and although to Emma it seemed like a foregone conclusion—everybody loved Olivia—Olivia wasn't taking any chances. But Olivia just shook her head, and neither of them said anything else about it.

A year later, Emma knows that this is less a bug of Olivia's personality and more of a feature. Even if she does not particularly prize her friendships with Collier and Addison (for example), she *does* value her position at the top of all of Atwater's various hierarchies—and has a keen sense of how to maintain her status. "We only have a month left here," she's saying, her coffee cradled in one hand. She has this particular way of holding it: with the base of the mug resting flat in the palm of one hand, the fingertips of the other hand dancing around the rim. It's delicate, oddly elegant, inimitable.

"Don't lean back like that," Emma says, rolling her eyes. "You'll fall and crack your head open. Didn't your mother ever tell you that?" Dr. Anderson is a literal brain surgeon at Stanford Med. Although Olivia likes to pretend that she did not have the same kind of immensely privileged upbringing that Collier and Addison had, the truth is that she grew up in a sunlit craftsman in Atherton, with a plunge pool in the backyard and dinners served al fresco, under conical cypresses and craggy oaks and a lemon tree that even occasionally bore fruit.

Olivia lifts her feet from Emma's chair and tips forward slightly, easing the front legs of her chair back on the ground. "She was too busy operating on strangers' brains to worry about mine." This is not true. Olivia's parents, despite their very busy professional lives—Olivia's father is also a surgeon at Stanford—are endlessly attentive to both Olivia and her older brother, Anthony.

"So what's the plan for the rest of the day? I figure we have to start getting ready around fourish, which would give us"—here she looks over Emma's shoulder to the clock that hovers above the dining hall's back door—"six hours of uninterrupted Netflix."

Emma swirls the remainder of her coffee, watches it dance up the sides of her mug. "Actually—"

"What, you got big plans today?" One of the most wonderful things about Olivia is that she could spend all day, every day with Emma. She doesn't need alone time, has never needed "space," has a knack for coexisting, like it's some kind of inherited gene. *Look,* she'd said when Emma sent her deposit to Michigan, *you can fly from Detroit to New York for less than $200 round trip.* It is also terrifying, a thing that makes Emma feel the tiniest bit guilty, somewhere deep inside her, in a place she doesn't visit very often.

"Well, I was hoping to steal a few hours today to finish my econ project . . ." She trails off. It's a version of the truth, anyway.

Olivia cocks her head. "So, how about *you* finish your project while *I* watch *Friends* in your bed?" This runs right up against one of the few things they've ever fought about, and Emma feels a pang of guilt at the fresh reminder that Olivia so willingly ceded her ground. It's Emma's room that has become *theirs*; Olivia has a single, too, but because she's a Proctor her room is in Lathrop. Emma bristled at spending the night in the underclasswomen dorm; something about the obvious curiosity of the freshmen, the way they allowed their eyes to linger as they walked past Olivia's open door, both girls curled into one another in Olivia's bed, made Emma feel like an animal in a zoo.

"It's good for them to see a happy, healthy—and, yeah, *not straight*—relationship!" Olivia had argued, somewhat indisputably.

"But," Emma had said, running her hands up Olivia's inner thigh, moving her lips toward her neck, "I just have a really hard time doing this when there are a bunch of fourteen-year-olds around."

Olivia laughed. "Oh, really?" she asked, and then every night after check-in made the walk across the bowl to Whitney, even in the rain, even in the February cold.

Now Emma just hesitates.

"I know, I know—me, your bed: it's so distracting." Olivia smiles.

Emma laughs, relieved, grateful for the out. "It's true. I feel like I should put in a few hours in one of the library carrels."

"I don't know how you get any work done in those. It's like solitary confinement."

Olivia is right—it's not the pin-drop silence of the carrels that Emma loves but rather the fact that there is hardly ever another person using them. The hardest thing to find at Atwater has always been true privacy; in the perpetual dimness of the library stacks, a person has it in troves.

"Is that okay? I can finish my project in a few hours, then join you for a few episodes of *Friends* before we start getting ready?"

Olivia stands, stretching her arms above her head, gazing out the bay window in front of them. When she turns back to Emma, still sitting, Emma is struck by how unbothered she is, totally at ease. She leans over, one hand on Emma's shoulder, and touches her lips to Emma's forehead. "Sure thing," she says. "You know where to find me."

The carrels are arranged in small diamond-shaped clusters, four to a set. Emma chooses the quad at the far end of the floor and sets up her work space in the cubicle that positions her back—and her computer screen—to the wall. Even in an empty room, she doesn't like the possibility of someone reading over her shoulder. She does a quick look around before tapping into Tumblr.

She joined Tumblr in eighth grade, before she came to Atwater, when she knew she was gay but wasn't ready to say so in the real world. (It would be two more years before she'd say it out loud to her parents, armed with a photograph of Olivia, tall and deeply tanned on the sands of a beach in Santa Cruz with her hair blowing in the ocean breeze. "This is my girlfriend," she'd say, turning her phone screen toward her mother, who would sigh: "Well, this is the time to figure these things out, I suppose," adding, after a beat, "She's very pretty, though.") In the space between her middle school swim season in the fall and when her club team picked up in January, she took the bus home, where she first met Laurie. Laurie dressed like a punk-Goth but in a way that suggested she was borrowing from an archetype: she wore band T-shirts and combat boots but never once did Emma catch her listening to the Ramones or Green Day. She liked to write poetry in the notes on her iPhone and upload it to her Tumblr in a typewriter-style font. The afternoons that December stretched long and languorous, and one day, bored and curious, Emma logged in, too.

Right away it provided her with a kind of anonymity that she did not have on Twitter or Snapchat or Instagram. She didn't know anyone besides Laurie on Tumblr, and so she followed accounts based on how they presented themselves. Unlike the forums she ghosted—watching but never posting on Reddit and Empty Closets—here she felt she could participate without revealing too much of herself; here she could communicate in JPEGs and GIFs. She didn't intend for it to be a secret—so many times she thought about showing Laurie on the bus—but the longer she went without telling anyone, the more it became her private life. Sometimes she wonders if Laurie will find her on the platform—if one day some algorithmic magic will cause them to like or reblog the same post. It's possible.

Her notifications light up, a satisfying little bubble of tallied alerts. Beyond-the-binaries liked a string of posts from the past week. Lezbian-librarian posted a new quote, set in a sort of contemporary calligraphy:

an Emily Dickinson poem about stepping from plank to plank. Something about the final lines—or maybe it's the typeset, "This gave me that" in small, narrow capital letters, "precarious gait" in flourished cursive—gives her the deep-bellied sensation of being *seen*, seems to fill her up and empty her out at the same time, like a meditative breath, and so she clicks the arrow square to reblog. It doesn't really fit next to the GIF of Anna Kendrick imitating Kristen Stewart or the image of soft, manicured hands linked at the pinkies against a millennial pink background, but Emma is not very good at Tumblr. She envies the users whose pages look like baby websites, sleek aggregates of carefully curated content, not a single post off brand.

She wishes she had more time to check her messages, more time to spend in the right-angled ether that is her DMs. She had been on Tumblr for six months or so before she received her first message, and when it appeared in her inbox she'd been gripped with a mild panic: she didn't know anybody on here; who'd found her? But 525600minkas just wanted to say hey, I like ur vibe, and so Emma said thx, thinking it would end there. But then Minka started asking Emma about regular things, and Emma answered, briefly at first—only the basic details—until she felt more comfortable. Minka was fifteen and lived in Kentucky, which was cool because it meant they were in border states; it didn't take long before their conversation wandered into one about their sexuality. From Minka Emma learned that a person could identify as *queer,* broadly, that it was okay to not necessarily be more specific, because specificity was just a construct like everything else. Margo_on_the_gogo messaged in response to a piece of Mary Oliver poetry Emma blogged: MO is the best, she said. From Margo Emma learned that a person could define as asexual, which was not something Emma knew about at thirteen, and still seems a little bit fuzzy in her mind, if she thinks about it too hard.

She still talks to Minka and Margo, but also mcphillivanilli and rbg-is-my-homie and annasbananas and a dozen more. It wouldn't be entirely true to say that these people feel as real to her as her friends at Atwater or her friends from home—real, three-dimensional, breathing and heart-beating people she's touched and smelled and tasted, even—but they do feel *real* to

Emma, like she's communicating with characters from her favorite books. In some corner of her brain she knows that she has invented them, each and every one, taken what they've told her about themselves and put a body and eyes and voice and height and smile to their usernames. When they type "haha" or "lol" she hears their laughter, high and giggly or low and throaty. Each time she meets a new user she is consumed by the task of rendering them real, of molding them from the clay of their digital selves.

Although it is barely 3:00 P.M. when Emma returns from the library—and the first vans will not leave for the private estate that is hosting Atwater's prom for four more hours—Whitney has descended into some kind of controlled chaos. Music thumps from every other room, and as she moves down the hall her ears catch alternatively diva pop (Whitney Houston's "I Wanna Dance with Somebody") and synth-laden Robyn ("Call Your Girlfriend") and swagger-inducing Nicki Minaj ("Bang Bang"). The cacophony is enough to induce a seizure, Emma thinks. The hallways swell with the heat of a hundred warming straighteners and curling irons and blasting blow-dryers; the windows in the first-floor common room are literally fogged with humidity. Her classmates race from room to room, most half-dressed, some in bathrobes or wrapped in towels. It smells like hair spray and perfume and just-finished showers.

Upstairs, Karla and Priya and Addison and Collier have fully monopolized their end of Whitney. There are piles of shoes in the hallway. Priya has positioned herself in front of the only full-length mirror on the hall, palettes of eyeshadow at her feet, gently buffing dimension onto her eyelids. Behind her, in a black lace thong and a matching strapless bra, Collier does a badly executed version of the "Single Ladies" dance, barely in step with the music that thunders from Addison's room.

Collier spots Emma before she can do anything about it. She shouts her name, louder than she needs to, announcing her arrival to the entire dorm, and Emma is suddenly grateful for the cover of music and blow-dryers and running showers. "Towne!"

Collier has already started drinking, Emma thinks.

"I told your girlfriend—" she lowers her voice as she draws closer to Emma: "Come pregame with us. Sixish."

Emma tries to say something noncommittal, but Collier cuts her off.

"Shh! Olivia already said you would grace us with your presence."

"Ah, well—in that case. I better start getting ready."

"Seriously! You're way behind. Olivia said you were working on your econ project? Did you finish?"

"Not quite," Emma says, before making her exit. "I'll see you in a bit."

The door to her room is open, and Olivia sits at her desk, scrolling through a Spotify playlist. "Freedom," from the new Beyoncé album, thrums in the background. As Emma fills in the doorframe, leaning against the left side, Olivia doesn't even look up.

"Song requests?"

"Well, I know we love her, but you're, like, the eighth person on this hall playing Beyoncé and every single one of you is playing from a different album. It's like a mash-up gone wrong."

"No such thing, my dear, where Queen Bey is concerned." She stands, and Emma notices how her T-shirt hangs over her chest. When Olivia kisses her, she lingers before pulling away. "Did you finish your project?"

Emma shrugs. "Not quite."

"Well, we've been having much more fun here."

"Oh yeah?"

"Mm-hmm. First of all, Collier and Addison have been drinking since noon. They went to get their nails and hair done and came back smelling like fancy prostitutes. Second of all, I didn't want to watch *Friends* without you—"

"—thank you—"

"—so I watched like three episodes of *The Good Wife*, and I am afraid to tell you that I will be leaving you for Archie Panjabi."

Emma, whose hand is at her girlfriend's hip, pulls Olivia closer. "She's not really your type, is she?" she asks.

"Do I have a type?" Olivia asks, playfully.

Emma steps squarely inside the room and swings the door shut behind her. Olivia smells like lotion and the perfume her mother gave her, something complicated and adult that she says reminds her of a family vacation in Japan. Emma didn't like it at first, but now the smell is indistinguishable from a million memories.

Olivia presses Emma back against the door, moving one hand behind her head, ensuring her aggression is playful and not hurtful. She steps away, slipping easily out of her boxer shorts and T-shirt so that she is completely naked. She moves to the bed, stretching herself out, waiting for her girlfriend to catch up. Instead, Emma climbs over Olivia, pressing her lips on her collarbone, the place where her rib cage arches to its highest point, the soft spot to the left of her belly button.

The first time Emma went down on Olivia, she had only a rough idea of what to do. She'd tried to read about it online, first in the euphemistic language of women's magazines and then in forums, where if you looked hard enough you'd find more clinical instructions. Neither of them came; it was six months before Olivia gave Emma an orgasm, a shuddering that was not immediately identifiable to either of them, not until the feeling grew in duration and intensity and they both could trace that first quivering to a kind of infant pleasure.

The dress looks better than she remembered. Emma is not thin and lanky like her girlfriend; she has swimmer's shoulders, broad and muscular, and swimmer's boobs, too—small, not much to write home about. Dresses tend to make all these things more noticeable, what with their plunging necklines that are supposed to hang over cleavage or thin straps that are supposed to enhance a delicate bone structure, tethered over protruding collarbones like cables on a mountainside.

But Olivia has managed to pull Emma's hair back into a kind of low and messy bun, with little wisps of hair pulled loose next to her ears, and she's contoured Emma's eyelids with black powder and dabbed highlighter—despite Emma's protestations that highlighter is not for white girls—on her cheekbones and the tip of her nose and the highest points of her forehead and across her clavicle and the result is, remarkably, that Emma is wearing the dress rather than vice versa.

Olivia is not even wearing a dress. She's wearing a kind of jumpsuit, also with a vague 1970s vibe, with wide legs and a neckline so deep it nearly grazes her navel and a tie around the waist that Olivia positions just so. It's from a brand that's based out of San Francisco; at one point, Emma made her way to the company site, and, as far as she could tell, they design exclusively for six-foot-tall, one-hundred-pound twentysomethings. Their models all looked a little like Cara Delevingne.

They stand like birds on a high wire, perched delicately at angles: Karla is propped against the edge of Collier's desk, a hip half on the hard wood corner; Priya leans next to her, one arm stiff and flat-palmed on the desktop; Collier and Addison rest against Collier's neatly made bed, the comforter smoothed underneath them. The delicacy with which they stand is both due to the heels in which they each teeter—four or five inches, some with sturdier platforms but others pencil-thin—and the desire to preserve the perfection of their dresses, to not add a single crease or wrinkle until the photos are done.

Karla deejays from the MacBook on Collier's desk, clicking through a playlist titled "Getting Ready." It's a mix of Top 40 and nineties and early-aughts throwbacks, with a heavy emphasis on the pop queens: Britney, Mariah, Lady Gaga, all songs chosen by the people before them. Next to the laptop are two water bottles, each half-full with a liquid whose precise color and opacity is difficult to determine through the tinted polycarbonate of its container. It does not matter: it is, surely, some combination of clear liquor (vodka, probably) and juice or an otherwise sweet and alcohol-free beverage, like Crystal Light.

Priya, looking a little bored, her eyes not yet shining the way Collier's and Addison's are, thrums her nails against the desktop, a specific plastic trill. "Let's play a game," she says.

"Which one?" Olivia asks, by way of agreement.

"Something that doesn't involve any kind of mess," Collier says, likely remembering the time they all tried to play flip cup by shoving their desks together in the middle of the room. It smelled for days, a stale and sour rot they tried to hide from their Dorm Parent with open windows and bottles of Lysol.

"What about ten fingers?" Karla offers, toggling between songs (she lands on TLC's "Waterfalls," slowly windshield-wiping her shoulders to the opening beat).

"What are we, in eighth grade?" Addison laughs.

"Don't we already know everything about each other?" Priya asks.

"That's why it's *fun*!" Karla explains. "You've gotta get creative."

They look at one another, trading eye contact around the room. It's not exactly tense, but there's the sense that they're sizing each other up, particularly Emma and Olivia, who do not, in fact, know everything about the other four, and about whom the other four know relatively little truly personal information. The longer Emma and Olivia dated, the more Emma came to realize that so many of Olivia's friendships were a kind of one-way street: while so many of their classmates claimed to *absolutely adore* Olivia, they never seemed to show any real interest in Olivia's life. Emma asked her about it once, after an hour spent listening to Olivia counsel Collier through a breakup with her at-the-time boyfriend.

"You're always asking Collier and Addie about their lives, but they never ask you about ours," she said, and Olivia replied simply, her chin cocked to one side with that curious smile of hers: "What would I tell them?"

Now Emma knows that Olivia engineers her conversations this way: all listening, no sharing.

Nonetheless, it's Olivia who breaks the silence: "I literally haven't played this game since middle school, so I need a refresher on the rules."

Karla smiles, setting her drink on the edge of her desk. "Okay, so, when it's your turn, you say something you've never done, like, 'Never have I ever . . . shoplifted—'"

"That's a lie," Priya interjects.

"Shh! I'm just giving an example!"

"Well, that's a bad example."

"Okay, fine. Um, never have I ever . . . hooked up with someone more than five years older than me," Karla says, shooting Priya a pointed look.

"And if you've done the thing, then you put a finger down and take a drink. So, Priya will be putting a finger down and taking a drink."

Olivia whistles. "Damn, girl," she says, although Emma can tell she's not really impressed at all, that she's just playing along.

"Whatever," Collier asks, "that's not even scandalous anymore. It only counts if he's twice your age and your teacher." Next to her, Addie bursts into laughter, a dramatic *bah!* Emma stiffens, unsure about the joke.

"First of all, he was seven years older than me," Priya says after rolling her eyes, "and second of all: I know we're supposed to think there was something weird about Brodie dating her grad school professor, but—"

Oh, Emma thinks. They're not talking about Karen Mirro and Mr. Breslin. They're talking about the flyers that landed in their physical mailboxes last week, a single piece of paper printed with a page of the *New York Times* Vows section from 1978 announcing the marriage of Elliott Rhodes and Patricia Brodie. The stunt hadn't landed like the rest, in part because it lacked the choreography of the previous pranks—most students only checked their real mailboxes when they were expecting care packages from home, and so the release was too subtle, initially just a trickle rather than a swift and sudden drop—but also because it required a little too much *thinking*. The announcement said that Brodie and her husband met at Columbia, but additional googling was needed in order to suss out, as Louisa Manning did, that Elliott Rhodes was Patricia Brodie's professor, and then still more analysis to understand the insinuation behind it all.

"Obviously it worked out for them," Collier says, and Addie nods. This is the other reason the maneuver hadn't quite hit the mark, especially among the upperclasswomen: Mrs. Brodie's relationship is a staple around campus, as much a fact of Atwater's existence as the clock tower or the Bowl; more important, their marriage seems like a good one. Mr. Rhodes seems to know that at Atwater he is an accessory to his wife, and carefully selects his contributions to the school accordingly: he never eats in the dining hall, for example (although plenty of faculty spouses do), and only in the middle of a blizzard might you find him working out in the Atwater gym rather than at the YMCA in Canaan; for years he has made his space within the community not by taking from its resources but instead by making himself useful, lining the athletic fields or weeding the gardens outside Trask or setting up hundreds of plastic folding chairs before graduation. It isn't that he seems like a good guy (although he does; most of them see him like a kind of benevolent grandpa), but rather that he seems supportive, that his decades-long marriage to his wife seems legitimate. What did it matter that he was her professor? There he was, leaf-blowing her school's sidewalks. Clearly, there was something real between them.

"I just feel sort of bad that her marriage got dragged into this, honestly," Priya says. "They're so cute, you know? Obviously they love each other."

"I don't think the flyers were trying to say that they don't," Emma says, surprising herself. When she speaks, she notices a numbness around her lips and has to bite the inside of her cheek to prevent herself from smiling inappropriately. She's drunk. "I think the idea was that it makes Brodie biased in some way."

Next to her, Olivia nods. "Like, she can't fully participate in a conversation about power and consent because it, like, fucks with her own origin story." The two of them had talked about it the night they found the flyers. Emma bristled at the suggestion that Brodie lacked nuance, that she couldn't hold her own love story in one hand while making space in the other for the reality that girls are sometimes exploited, manipulated, made to feel as though they have freedom of choice when, in fact, they do not. They all had problems with Patricia Brodie—this year in particular—but Emma believed that, at the end of the day, she was a smart woman.

"I'm not saying she's not *smart*," Olivia had said. "I just think even smart people engage in self-preservation."

"Do you mean you think it's not possible for them to have fallen in love in 1978?" Emma had asked, genuinely curious.

"No," Olivia sighed, exasperated. "Or, I don't know. I think that part of the conversation this year has been about power dynamics. Think about the Jamison Jennings interviews and the girls who said they fucked their teachers. They didn't say they were *raped*. I bet some of them were eighteen, just like Karen was. But the idea is that the relationship was inherently imbalanced, right?"

"But Brodie was a grad student at the time, not a high school senior," Emma said. It was strange to think of themselves in this category, that of the potentially-taken-advantage-of.

Olivia shrugged. "I'm not sure it matters. Teachers have influence and power by nature of their position. If Brodie accepts that basic principle, she calls into question her own agency in 1978." At Atwater, a student learns that words like "agency" have sociological definitions. But it's in Northern California, in a house where the *New Yorker* comes every week, that a girl learns how to use them in regular conversation.

Now Collier frowns into her drink. "The whole thing just felt like a cheap shot."

"Agreed," Priya says.

"I mean, sure—" she adds, "the first time I saw Mr. Rhodes when I was a freshman, I thought, *whoa*, he's, like, *a lot* older than her."

In spite of herself, Emma nods. It *was* noteworthy.

"But, like," Addie jumps in, "not every relationship with an age gap is inherently fucked-up, you know? My point is, *love is love is love*, or whatever, even if it doesn't always look the way we expect."

Olivia wraps an arm around Emma's waist, curving her fingertips around the place where her torso narrows. "That's what I always say," she says, and then she pulls one hand to the side of Emma's face—careful not to disrupt the hair she sculpted into the perfect messy bun—and brings them together. Her kiss is not indulgent—their tongues barely meet, their lips open for just a moment.

"Ugh, you guys are adorable," Collier says thickly.

"But also so *basic*," Karla says, making a *blech* sound.

Addie starts laughing. "It's true! Like, in this room, you are the only two going to prom with a *date*. Ugh, how mainstream."

When the Supreme Court made its decision last summer, Olivia sent Emma pictures from San Francisco: pride flags draped outside city hall, rainbows saturated in the California light. In Ohio, the yard signs and window placards would linger for months: EVERY CHILD DESERVES A MOM AND DAD; MARRIAGE IS BETWEEN A MAN AND A WOMAN. None of them will ever fully understand Emma because her life outside Atwater is like science fiction to them; her hometown is full of aliens. Her girlfriend is pressed into her still, their hip bones stuck together, yet Emma feels anxiety balloon at the top of her sternum, in the little hollow of her clavicle. Her friends think they sidestepped a hard and confusing conversation by walking into an easier one about social norms, because in this corner of Connecticut—and in the places the five of them grew up, Silicon Valley and Brentwood and Washington, DC—it really is as simple as *you love who you love*. But of course it has never been that simple or easy for Emma at all.

"All right, all right," Olivia says. "You think we're basic? How about this: never have I ever . . . had a Pinterest account."

"Fuck you." Collier laughs, taking a drink.

"I can do this all day," Olivia smirks. "Never have I ever had a Pinterest *fail*."

"Okay, okay, you've made your point!"

Karla makes a mock pouting face. "Pinterest can be very useful when you're redecorating! Plus, that's two turns in a row."

"I still think Coll should drink, though," Addison says.

Priya sets down her glass with a dramatic gulp. She wipes her lips with the middle part of her index finger, tapping at any liquid caught in the hairs above her lip. "All right, I've got one," she begins. "Never had I ever"—and here Emma can't be sure, she'll replay the moment over and over in the weeks to come, but she swears that Priya looks directly at her—"had a Tumblr."

"Oh, why, because Tumblr is for *les*bians?" Olivia emphasizes the *z* sound at the end of the first syllable.

"Hey!" Priya shouts, pulling an arm from her side and extending a long manicured pointed finger at Emma. "Knew it!"

Olivia rotates her shoulders, drops her chin, and raises her eyebrows. Emma does not entirely meet her gaze; she looks at her girlfriend, then back at Priya, then down quickly into the depths of her cup, where the liquid swirls in a viscous circle.

"You didn't know about this, did you?"

"I did not," Olivia says, and her voice is light, teasing, as though she's waiting for the punch line.

"Show us!" Collier whips out her phone and starts tapping.

"Oh, no, no, no, it's stupid—" The same mild drunkenness that gave Emma the courage and false sense of camaraderie to lower her finger now causes her to sweat, to swing from insouciance to paranoia.

"Wait a minute," Priya says, "this isn't like a *past tense* thing, like you *had* a Tumblr? You *have* a Tumblr? You didn't delete it?"

It takes Emma a beat to process, to realize what Priya means, the fact unraveling before her quickly—and she is struck with the familiar shame of being not quite savvy enough.

"What's your handle?"

Emma looks at Olivia, eyes wide, pleading, willing her girlfriend to understand—but of course Olivia thinks it's a joke, a relic from middle school. She has no idea.

"Don't look at me like that!" Olivia throws her hands up. "You think I'm not just as curious about the angst-ridden blog posts of a curious and questioning preteen Emma?"

Emma had a friend in elementary school who had the remarkable ability to make herself vomit on command. It was a stunt she saw her pull more than once: in the hallway after morning snack, because she wanted to go home; on the playground during recess, because Mrs. Mooney was yelling at her for throwing the four-square ball directly in Jackson Plowman's face, knocking his glasses off and causing them to crack against the blacktop, and she didn't want to get in trouble. Puking is a great elicitor of sympathy.

She sighs.

"Ryderdietownie, with a *y* and an *e*, like Winona Ryder."

Olivia raises her eyebrows. "Winona Ryder?

This is not close to the worst of it. "I had just seen that movie *The Private Lives of Pippa Lee*," she offers. "I was obsessed with it. With Robin Wright and Julianne Moore and Blake Lively?"

"And you didn't know you were gay?"

"I had a hunch."

"Aha! Got it!" Collier shouts. "Ooh, boy."

All five of the girls crowd around Collier, who holds her phone out from her body far enough for everyone to have a view. Emma does not join them. She knows what they see.

"Wait—"

"Scroll up," Addison says. "You updated this today!"

Emma thinks of the photo of the gold necklace: Two linked Venus symbols, the circle at the top of each transformed into a heart. The pendant falls against the wearer's baby pink T-shirt. She remembers, with a hot flush of fresh humiliation, the meme about the Disney character from the nineties: it's a kind of meter, placing her character in various stages on a scale from femme to butch. At the time, she thought it was funny.

"Old habits die hard," Emma says.

Addison hoots. "I thought this was, like, some embarrassing middle school secret!"

"It was," Emma says. "It is."

Collier and Karla pull away from the phone. Karla leans toward the mirror anchored on Collier's closet door, tilting her face slowly from side to side, confirming that she looks as pretty as she suspects she does. Collier finds her own phone, scrolling mindlessly while she finishes her drink. That their attention is short-lived does not surprise Emma, not really, but now that the group has begun to move on she does feel a vague kind of disappointment, the same feeling she'd have at a birthday party when a friend would open her gift—a gift Emma had selected painstakingly, the gift that was the perfect combination of the friend's desires and their shared inside jokes—and nonetheless move on to the next present. The party was supposed to stop; she could not be outdone.

"We've gotta go. The bus leaves in five," Addison says suddenly.

"I've gotta pee first," Priya says.

"Me too," Emma agrees, if for no other reason than to reassert herself into the normalcy of the conversation, to not let on that anything at all is wrong.

In the darkness of a rural Connecticut 8:00 P.M., the estate that hosts Atwater's prom glows, sending an aura into the night sky. It announces its existence before the bus has even turned down the half-mile private road, buffered by split-rail fencing on either side, an incongruous nod to the home's nineteenth-century establishment. The alumna who owns the house is a hotel heiress, although since she served as the treasury secretary to a Republican president some administrations ago it is more polite to refer to her by her own accomplishments, rather than the fortune that was bequeathed to her.

Access to the main house is limited to the catering crew and event staff and Atwater faculty; students are limited to the tent, the gardens, the pool, and the high-end "luxury portable bathrooms" that Atwater rents for tens of thousands of dollars and furnishes with designer hand soaps and little bottles of mouthwash and tampons. (This expense, too, is made possible by the property owner, who was perfectly fine with Atwater students using the house bathrooms despite Atwater's misgivings about letting its students have the run of an empty seven-thousand-square-foot house.) Last year, both literally drunk and a little bit punchdrunk, giddy with the openness of their romance, Emma and Olivia had wandered from the tent Atwater pitches on the long expanse of flat and golf course–perfect lawn that extends from the back of the main house and explored the property. They counted three additional houses, not including the pool house or the (empty) stables.

On the ride to the estate, Olivia was quiet. Emma tried once or twice to chatter about the game—*Actually I wouldn't put it past Priya to have slept with, like, somebody's dad*—or their destination—*Do you think they'll have avocado fries again this year?*—but Olivia's answers were monosyllabic. As the bus grinds to a halt now and opens its doors with a mechanical exhale, the music inside the cabin mingles momentarily with the music that thumps from the party itself, filtering through the clear spring night, over the chimneys and peaked windows of the Georgian mansion that towers before them. It presents as a backbeat to the central notes: heels crunching against the gravel of the driveway; the clang and clatter of chefs and cater waiters moving between the main house and the tent; the shouts of their classmates from the dance floor and garden beyond. The excitement is enough to ensure that no one notices the way Olivia does not reach behind her to help Emma down the bus stairs, or the way she keeps a half step in front of her as they make their way across the driveway and through the gardens along the side of the house, canopied by century-old willow trees, or the way she does not ask Emma for her opinion before choosing a seat at a table near the edge of the tent.

There are always twice as many girls as boys at Atwater dances, but for some reason the ratio always stands out more at prom, perhaps because of its more traditional trappings. Other "dances" are really more like the local YMCA's Kids' Night Out: there's dancing but also activities both structured and unstructured (air hockey in the student lounge; poker tables at Casino Night) and fried food served from under the fluorescent lighting of the Lathrop Snack Shack. On those nights, Emma's classmates huddle and hunt in packs, removing themselves from coed scenarios conspiratorially, plotting next steps and next texts in an effort to secure a hookup before the night ends and the visiting buses depart. Over the years—particularly since they started hosting it here, at an estate that might as well be Litchfield County's Versailles—prom has become for Atwater students something like Ringing or Vespers: something just for them.

"Guys!" Karla gasps from two tables away, clutching a cocktail napkin in one hand. "They did the avocado fries again! With the aioli!" She takes a bite and makes an exaggerated groan, a food-induced orgasm.

"You know that aioli is just a fancy word for mayonnaise, right?" Priya snarks.

"The French are better at everything," Karla says. She turns on her heels and snakes through the tables back to where the cater waiters enter the tent.

"I think Priya gets bitchier when she drinks," Emma says, leaning her head toward Olivia.

"Mmm." Olivia makes a noncommittal mumble and nods her chin once.

"Liv. Can we talk?"

"We are talking." It's a petty, childish answer that is so atypical for

Olivia that Emma feels as though the earth beneath them is suddenly molten.

"Liv. Please."

"This is not the right time," Olivia says, and for the first time since standing in Collier's dorm room Olivia looks Emma directly in the eyes.

"It's never the right time!" Emma hisses, and the words escape her lips before she is sure what she means by them.

Olivia tilts her head slightly.

Emma looks at her feet, feeling the way the edges of her sandals press into the curve of her outermost metatarsal. "I just—I mean that we—" She pauses, searching: "I mean that you don't like people to know that we ever fight. We always, like, put on a little bit of an act when we're in a crowd."

It's the first time Emma has ever seen Olivia's jaw do anything that resembles dropping. Her lips part slightly, her eyes widen—but it's the tiniest flash, only the briefest loss of control. Olivia swallows, purses her lips, and then says, very evenly: "I can't believe you would have the nerve to say that to me right now."

And suddenly Emma remembers: her phone, facedown on Collier's desk, left behind when she went to the bathroom. "Liv—" she begins.

Olivia shakes her head, the smallest one-two, and turns and makes her way out from under the tent and into the gardens. Emma follows her, her heels sinking into the soft and still-wet spring earth. Of all the New England seasons, spring is her least favorite for the way it's so unsure of itself: it lacks the conviction of summer or winter, ferocious in their extremes; nor is it fall's mirror image, because fall is perhaps Connecticut's best-defined season, with its leaf peeping and carved pumpkins and corn mazes and mornings marked by frost melting on the grass. Spring's defining characteristic seems to be that it comes and goes before you can be sure you're inside it.

They wander past the gardens to the pool area beyond, which is sanctioned off by a double layer of intruder protection: hedges manicured at right angles stand in front of iron fencing, whose arrow-like tips barely peek above the boxwood. The pool is still covered—a disappointment every year, when someone suggests as the party winds to a close that they should all jump in, gowns and hair and makeup and all, only to discover that no one in Connecticut opens their pool before Memorial Day—but the caretakers light the patio for the evening, likely to prevent anyone from accidentally falling onto the blue tarp that stretches across the pit. The patio is bordered on three of its four sides with slate benches built into a small rock wall; it's the kind of decorative touch only incredibly rich people would consider, like refrigerators built to blend into the surrounding cabinetry. Olivia takes a seat facing away from the main house, her back to the tent and her classmates. Emma joins her, but is careful not to slide so close to her that even the excess fabric from their gowns might touch. For a little while, they don't say anything: they try to decipher the music as it evaporates into the air; watch as their classmates wander in pairs and quartets across the lawn to their right, either not noticing Olivia and Emma or sensing, even through the giddy veil of a pleasant drunkenness, that they do not want to be bothered.

When she cannot stand the quiet between them any longer, Emma says, "I'm sorry." It seems like a safe bet, a way in.

"What are you sorry for?" Olivia directs her words out toward the tarp-topped crater ahead of them rather than at Emma.

"Keeping the Tumblr a secret. I don't want to keep secrets from you."

Next to her, Olivia rubs her temples, her head in her hands, propped up by her elbows against her thighs. "I just want to know," she says, "is it just an online thing? Or have you, like, met in real life, too?"

The dread descends thick and heavy like childhood fears of monsters and murderers at night. Terror mushrooms inside her. In the darkness Emma feels her face flush from her nose to the tips of her ears, all the way to the helix piercing Olivia gave her sophomore spring, the two of them up late on an April night, looking for excuses to extend their minutes together. Olivia had held an ice cube to Emma's ear, catching the melt in the palm of her hand. Again: the image of her phone, facedown on Collier's desk corner. She sighs through her nose. "When I went to the bathroom, right?"

"What?"

"You kept looking at my Tumblr when I went to the bathroom."

"Seriously? That's the approach you're going to take here? I was *snoop-ing*?"

"No—" Emma pauses. She really didn't mean it that way; she was just curious. Later, she'd want to be able to explain how it all happened.

"So who is she?"

From under the wisteria-cloaked willow across the lawn, her class-mates giggle, high-pitched and bubbling. Above them, Emma finds Orion, first by the three stars that mark his belt. It's the only constellation she can reliably pinpoint, easier even than the Dippers. She decides to start at the beginning, with middle school and the bus and Laurie. The internet was her safe space, she explains, it helped her discover who she was—to name the things she could not yet name—and then it gave her a place to be that person before she was ready to be that person in front of everybody else. It was like a virtual dress-up bin: she logged on and became Emma, Lesbian, like how politicians on television have their party affiliation next to their name. If it didn't work out—if she was wrong about being gay—she could just delete it, disappear Lesbian Emma with a few clicks.

It was Harper who talked her through the coming-out. They started messaging eight months or so into Emma's Tumblr life, after trading likes and reblogs. "It wasn't anything at first," she explains. "We just talked, for a long time—for years. She's a little bit older than us—"

Here Olivia, who has been listening wordlessly, interrupts: "Does she go to Michigan?"

The question surprises Emma. "No—Liv," she stutters, "that wasn't about us at all. You know that."

Once or twice in the application process, Olivia had remarked that she didn't understand why Emma wanted to head back into the Midwest—to her the states that buffeted the Great Lakes were all the same, the college towns they housed irrelevant, mere islands in a conservative wasteland—but Emma sensed that it wasn't just coastal elitism: it was all part of her ability to prioritize their relationship, her keen sense of how to *work at it*; Olivia didn't *need* Emma with her at Barnard or even in New York, but didn't a train ride away seem more manageable? Now Emma had exposed the nerve again, awakened her girlfriend to the suspicion that her college decision wasn't about returning to her roots but was, instead, about running away. (In reality, it feels more complicated than either of these desires, a confusing need for a reclamation of sorts.)

"I don't even know where Harper goes to school," she adds.

If Olivia senses that this is a lie, she doesn't let on. Her expression is unchanged: lips pressed together, eyes expectant, jet-black in the glow of the patio lights.

Emma forges ahead: "I just meant, she had some things figured out. She helped me talk to my parents. She helped me decide to come to Atwater. She was my advice columnist, my therapist, my mentor. Sophomore year she helped me figure things out with you. I hadn't ever had a girlfriend—you know that. I didn't know how to flirt or . . ."

"How to have sex?"

"Yes, that, too. We talked about everything. At the time, I just . . . wanted to be a good girlfriend. I still do."

"When did it become something more?"

The truth is that there's a part of Emma that still, even now, despite a message history filled with flashes of skin that are not Olivia's, bristles at categorizing her relationship with Harper as something more. It was never real because that was the point, their founding principle. "I didn't mean for it to happen," Emma says, a line borrowed from Hollywood, but she's serious nonetheless.

"I believe you," Olivia says, and the sadness Emma feels is unlike anything she has experienced before. They are quiet for a minute, and Emma has the sensation of being within the eye of the storm: The calm is momentary; magical, impossible if not for the laws of physics.

"She doesn't look anything like me," Olivia says, finally. "Is that—is that what you like?"

And Emma feels her entire body slouch into itself, a sudden emptiness that reminds her of all the times she thought about telling her parents she was gay—just imagining the conversation caused her to feel like an urn of disappointment, a vessel for her parents' sadness. In so many ways, Harper is Olivia's physical opposite: her thick black hair is half-shaved, so she's constantly sweeping the longer side back from where it curtains in front of her right eye; her skin is milky pale, almost vampire-like; she does not wear dresses or makeup and often wears a binder.

Emma is attracted to Olivia—of course she is. And she loves the way Olivia feels like home, safe and warm. But with Olivia she feels like she's only acting the part of one half of a model couple—a sensation that's heightened by the fact that they practically live together, every day playing house. Their classmates think it's cute and romantic, but Emma knows what they don't: that this kind of intimacy has its own challenges, a relentlessness that doesn't allow a person to hide. Olivia has come to feel like a half measure; Harper, on the other hand, is *thrilling*, her entire persona a dangerous suggestion: that it's possible to live fully, to not give a fuck.

But of course there's no way to say any of this, so instead she tells Olivia: "You're beautiful."

"I know," Olivia snaps. "People tell me all the time. Everybody tells me all the time."

Emma starts to speak, but Olivia puts up a hand. "So was I—was I just your cover? Are you just with me because I make it okay? Because I complete some picture you have in your head of this perfect gay couple? If you were with me, then nobody would give you a hard time about being gay?"

Emma thinks again of her mother: *She's very pretty*. It had felt like a kind of victory. But her mother is in Ohio, in a suburb of Cincinnati where people still say things like *That's so gay*.

"I don't know. I thought everything would be different here. But it still . . . it was still hard for me."

Olivia tilts her head slightly back. She brings a knuckle underneath each eyelid, blotting her mascara and eyeliner where it threatens to melt. When she levels her chin again, she looks directly at Emma. "Do you think it isn't hard for me?"

She thinks about Olivia's parents, her exceptionally petite Korean mother and her towering and broad-shouldered Black father, both of them Northern California transplants; the pictures Olivia sends her from holidays at home, dinner tables laden with orange-red tofu stew or grilled peel-and-eat shrimp but also tikka masala or stir fry or oysters fresh from Tomales Bay, as if even the food Olivia ate every night could represent the way she grew up in a house that understood the breadth and depth of the human experience. She wants to say this, she wants to say that Olivia is lucky, but what she says instead is: "Everyone loves you. They never stop telling you how perfect you are."

Olivia shakes her head. "Do you know what else people say? That I'm so *exotic*. That the way I look is so *interesting*. Freshman year—do you know how many times someone said to me, 'You're so pretty—where are you from?' Like, I'm from fucking California, asshole."

It will be years before Emma understands. She'll be in her late twenties, living in Seattle, a science teacher and swim coach at a prestigious prep school that will have more in common with Atwater than she presumed, before she realizes that for all the ways that she herself was pretending—to be a little less edgy, a little less butch—Olivia was also pretending: the whole persona she'd built at Atwater—of model citizen, Head Proctor, liaison to the administration—was a matter of painstaking restraint. It was that tight-lipped half smile she offered whenever someone told her how beautiful she was.

For now, Emma just feels as though Olivia has said something about race that she—a white girl from the suburbs of Ohio—can't entirely access. It's supposed to be empathy but it feels like a trump card. "I don't know how to respond to that," she says, in the end.

Olivia sighs. From the speakers Emma can hear the twang of autotune, the unmistakable drawl of Miley Cyrus's voice against an overproduced backdrop. Emma likes Miley Cyrus, actually—so does Olivia. They bonded early in their friendship over the Miley backlash, which they both felt (and still feel) was entirely unwarranted.

"I'm just saying," Olivia says, "that you're not the only person who's pretending to be a little bit less."

That night Emma takes the first bus back to Atwater. Olivia offers to make an excuse for her—she blames the weed that Izzy Baldwin brought, the joint they passed in the semidarkness behind the stables. It's believable; Emma has never been able to metabolize the drug, and their friends know this about her. Together she and Olivia make a little bit of a show of it, Olivia asking if Emma's sure she doesn't want Olivia to go back to the dorms with her, Emma insisting that Olivia *go have fun!* Collier and Addison tug on Olivia's elbow, making pleading pouty faces, desperate for the all-star of the senior class to make an appearance at their after-prom party. It occurs to Emma—fleetingly, bitterly, a fraction of the idea dislodged from some corner of her brain and drifting to the forefront like a melting iceberg—that Olivia is, in a way, their mascot. She tries to grab on to the thought—to wrestle with how they could be casually, subconsciously racist or homophobic like Olivia says but also outwardly adoring—but something—the fog of the weed and the alcohol, the emotional trauma of the evening—prevents her from doing so.

Whitney is quiet. The halls are scattered with the aftermath: Straighteners left to cool, cords snaking across the carpet; eye shadow palettes and brushes poking out from half-zipped vinyl makeup cases; abandoned stiletto heels, one in the pair fallen on its side dramatically. It still smells like perfume and hair spray, but mixed now with the mustiness of a two-hundred-year-old building; it reminds Emma of the Macy's on Kenwood, where her mother would drag her for Christmas shopping—a Ralph Lauren sweater for her grandfather, a scarf and some Clinique for her grandmother, the same things every year. The store itself was old, and on the right day if you entered through the men's department you smelled instead of perfume and candles the faint stink of a deteriorating carpet, dust, bathroom cleaner.

Her laptop sits on her unmade bed, half-covered by abandoned clothes from earlier today: a sports bra, a sweatpants leg. She picks it up and leans against the edge of her mattress, holding her computer open as she half stands, the front edge of the keyboard pressing into her abdomen.

Make sure u send me a pic, Harper wrote. She sent it after they'd boarded the bus, after Olivia had looked at her account when she'd gone to the bathroom.

Emma positions her laptop on her desk, tilting the screen so that the camera is slightly downward-facing. She takes a few steps back and squats slightly, angling her torso forward, allowing the fabric to gap away from her chest. With her left hand she pulls gently at the bottom of the dress's deep V, and then again shifts her thumb slightly to the left, so that the fabric barely grazes her nipple, which is hard, hard, hard. With her free hand she clicks the shutter on the screen; before sending it, she looks carefully: there it is, the tiniest glimpse of the outer edge of her areola.

Look closely, she types, as if there was any chance Harper would miss it.

While she waits for a reply, Emma begins brushing out her hair, tugging at the bun Olivia swirled and pinned at the nape of her neck. It's half-undone when Harper responds, a tangled mess of bobby pins jammed into the bottom of her skull.

I wish I could see that for real.

Emma squints. She knows instinctively what Harper means. They've been hinting at it for months, edging closer and closer to the suggestion, nervously composing messages that asked for more without letting on that either one of them thought this *wasn't* "real."

Harper goes to college in Vermont, four hours due north from Litch-field. There's a bus from Hartford that takes double the time, an all-day trip. It's always seemed insane, improbable, *unrealistic*.

You could, Emma types. I could be there by tomorrow night.

To: erin.palmiere@reginaventures.com
From: erin.palmiere@reginaventures.com
Date: May 13, 2016, 9:18 A.M.
Subject: A Message from the Board

To the Atwater Community:

It is with mixed emotions that I write to inform you that Patricia Brodie will be retiring at the end of this school year. She informed the Board of this decision at our last meeting.

Mrs. Brodie—as so many of you know her—joined the Atwater community as Head of School in 2004. In her twelve years in this position, our school has grown and thrived in unprecedented and unparalleled ways. Under her leadership, we've retained the highest enrollment since our founding; our bicentennial campaign was our most successful fund-raising effort in our history. Through her vision, we: designed and implemented a more individualized curriculum, including expanded elective course offerings and the senior independent study program; expanded our varsity sports program, adding to our roster crew, squash, water polo, and ice hockey; critically refurbished and enhanced our infrastructure, including updates to the Inez and Marshall Emmons Field House and the addition of the Burgess Center for Science, Technology, and Engineering; added at least one full-time faculty member to each major department, tightening our overall faculty-student ratio by 30 percent. Each of these developments has helped to bring Atwater into the new millennium, into an era of education that prioritizes individualization and hands-on, problem-based learning, and that prepares our young women for leadership in an entrepreneurial economy.

In fact, Mrs. Brodie has built a career and a lifetime out of innovating and self-starting. She earned her MEd. from Teachers College when Title IX was in its infancy, unregulated by the Department of Education and under frequent litigation that sought to chip away at the meager protections the earliest form of the law afforded. She began her teaching career at Brearley, and in the subsequent years would traverse the nation, working for some of the country's finest educational institutions.

She did much of this with her husband of almost forty years, Elliott Rhodes. An accomplished scholar and professor emeritus at Columbia, Elliott has also become a fixture on Atwater's campus, an honorary member of the maintenance department (we've seen him snowplowing the track), theater department (where he's helped with set design), and history department (more than once in his decade on campus, Mr. Rhodes taught a senior elective). Both Elliott and Patricia are looking forward to spending more time together in retirement. We are so grateful for all that they have brought to the community, and we wish them the best in their next adventure.

A leadership search is a ten-month endeavor, necessitating the formation of a search committee, the retention of an executive search firm, and feedback from a wide variety of constituents. Given the timing of this announcement and our reluctance to abbreviate the search process in any way, the Board has made the decision to appoint an interim Head of School for the coming academic year, with plans to name Atwater's sixteenth Head of School in the early spring of 2017. We look forward to your input in this undertaking, and are excited for this next chapter in Atwater history.

Gratefully yours,

Erin Palmiere

Senior Prank

Dusk is settling long and pink across Atwater's grounds, and Bryce Engel sits cross-legged on her twin bed. Her window is thrown open, and below her she hears the cacophony of her classmates soaking up this warm spring night. For the seniors, it's one of their last on campus, and she imagines without looking that the majority of the revelers are from the class of 2016. She thinks she can hear Karla Flores's big, generous laugh.

They leave for the senior retreat tomorrow, three days on a lake somewhere in Vermont, while the rest of the school stays behind for exams. Honestly, Bryce thinks this is one thing Atwater gets really right: all spring, the seniors are a distraction; they've been accepted into their dream schools—Harvard and Princeton and Williams and Middlebury—and so all they have to do each day is not *fuck up hugely*. They can let their grades slide a little. They can break all kinds of minor rules a little more flagrantly: they can "forget" to sign out when they leave campus for lunch; they can be a few minutes late to class.

Anyway, this means that for the month of May there's a little bit of controlled chaos on campus, and for Bryce—who began organizing her exam notes in April—this is an annoyance. She'll be happy to have them gone tomorrow, leaving her a whole day to study for her world history exam in peace.

She puts her computer down for a second and shimmies off her mattress, sliding her toes as she does through the hard plastic of the flip-flops she keeps near her bed at all times—the floors are dirty, and as much as she'd like to rid herself of this particularly obsessive quirk, she cannot stand the thought of placing her bare feet directly against the floor; she can imagine the way the dust and dirt would nibble at her soles, microscopic grains of sand itching at her skin—and shuffles across the room to the window, thinking she'll slam it shut. On move-in day she gave the bed under the window to Lauren, because her mother said that although it sounded romantic to have the bed under the window the reality was that *that* meant *your* bed was the one that dust and rain and bugs filtered onto first, and it was more of a nuisance than it was worth. She pauses to listen, her hands on the sill, the music drifting up to her in an indistinct medley: summertime outdoor stuff, Edward Sharpe or Dave Matthews or maybe Belle and Sebastian.

"Bryce!"

For a confusing second or two she thinks it's coming from outside, and her face flushes hot and red, as if she's been caught spying. But no— it's just someone outside her door.

"Bryce!" The voice hisses again. "You there?"

The girl at Bryce's door is six feet tall and lanky like a model, her arms and legs long, graceful extensions of herself. She's wearing ripped black jeans and an undersize black T-shirt.

"Hey, Mia," Bryce says, one hand still on her doorknob. "What's up?"

"How's it going?" Mia Tavoletti says as she takes a step forward, push- ing easily into Bryce's room. She does a tiny circle in the space between the beds, then chooses Bryce's desk chair. She drags it a few feet away from her desk, but doesn't turn it around to face the center of the room before sitting. Instead, she sits down backward, resting her chin on the top of the chair's back. She whips her head around for a second and eyes Bryce's still-open computer.

"Ahhh—studying?"

Bryce nods. "Trying to," she says, and then immediately regrets the dismissiveness in her tone, the way she failed to mask the slight annoyance at Mia's interruption. She *is* annoyed—but she's also curious about Mia's presence in her room, flattered at having captured the attention of an up- perclasswoman, especially one as indifferent and self-involved as Mia.

Unfazed, Mia taps at Bryce's laptop, scrolling back through her notes, scanning the eight-page document. "Shit, these are thorough," she says, arrowing down. Bryce looks for the contours of disbelief in her observation—an echo of the backhanded way people are always saying to her, "Smart too, huh?"—but does not immediately find them. The notes, after all, are not necessarily evidence of intellect: they're proof of hard work, of grit.

"I've heard it's traditionally a tough exam."

Nodding, Mia lightly taps shut Bryce's computer. "Speaking of traditions," she begins, "I missed out on a very important one this year."

Bryce first met Mia when she joined the *Heron*'s writing staff in the fall. It was a decision that had puzzled Bryce's mother, who'd had her daughter's Atwater cocurriculars mapped out from infancy: tennis in the fall, lacrosse in the spring; Key Club, for volunteer work; student government (if she played her cards right, Lillian Engel knew, her daughter could be student council president, and then from there a natural choice for an alumnae Board position). The *Heron* was a ragtag enterprise, one of the few underfunded and overlooked ventures on campus. They did not have a digital platform, not even a website; their room was a basement lair where students chipped paint from the walls like they might pick at their cuticles when bored. The couches sagged and smelled. More than once, they'd found the sand grains of mice poop at the edges of the carpeting. Most important: no one really read the *Heron*, anyway; it might have not existed at all. For these reasons, the *Heron* attracted a similarly ragtag group of students, each of them idealists in their own way, looking for a place to direct their fledgling talents.

Bryce liked Mia, and—along with the rest of the staff—saw her dismissal from the *Heron* in the fall as a great injustice. In the room, her absence was felt immediately: Hard-to-impress and cynical, Mia had a grounding effect on all of them. Plus, she knew her way around the software. In her place Bryce had picked up some of the duties of art director; Anjali knew a bit of Adobe, also, and so between the two of them they could piece together an issue. So far, though, they'd yet to produce one that had the polish of Mia's design.

"You see," Mia continues, "due to the manner in which I was summarily dismissed from the *Heron*—"

Bryce feels her pulse quicken, her cheeks flush. She hates the way she blushes, the way her Irish descendants handed down this one revelatory trait, a smack of rosacea that gives away her secrets.

"It's fine, I was proud to take one for the team," Mia says, waving away Bryce's self-consciousness. "Anyway, because my firing was immediate, I was not granted my *God-given* right to induct my replacement. You see, typically, an outgoing member of leadership"—she uses the shorthand for the *Heron* staff members who make decisions: the editors in chief, the art director, the Opinion editor—"mentors their successor through a kind of . . . *editorial* test to ensure that she can handle the pressure or assignments of the role."

"An editorial test?" Bryce repeats skeptically.

"Okay, okay, sure, it's usually a little bit of light hazing. Last year, when Louisa replaced Madison Hubbard as coeditor, Maddie made her write a feature article on the feminist politics of Taylor Swift's girl gang. It was weird and hilarious and—because it's *Louisa*—thoroughly researched and reported. She agonized over it."

Bryce slowly nods. "So you want to give me my . . . edit test?"

"I want to formally pass the baton, outgoing art director to incoming art director." She smiles and adds: "Well, I guess I'm no longer technically outgoing."

"But why should a mandate from Linda Paulsen get in the way of your senior bucket list?" Bryce says, half teasing. It was always hard to find her footing with the older girls, hard to keep up with the banter while still showing deference.

"I knew you understood me. Due to the unusual circumstances of my departure, you and I are just gonna have to come at this a little bit differently."

"How so?"

"Well, funny you should mention our esteemed Dean of Students. She let something very interesting slip when I was on the receiving end of one of her lectures this fall. See," Mia continues, "among this institution's numerous fine traditions was this long-since abandoned one: the senior prank."

"Why was it abandoned?" Her mother never mentioned a senior prank.

"Something about a petting zoo, but I couldn't get more than that out of her. Anyway: I have a plan to revitalize the senior prank, and I could use an extra set of eyes and hands. And *you* can have an opportunity to prove to me that you have the creativity, resourcefulness, and ability to focus under pressure required of the *Heron* art director."

Bryce thinks about it. The truth is that she doesn't know Mia very well, that after she was kicked off the *Heron* they ceased spinning in the same orbit—it wasn't unusual for a senior and a freshman to have little in common besides their shared cocurriculars; in fact it would have been *more* notable had Mia and Bryce developed a friendship outside of the *Heron* room. They kept in regular contact through most of the fall, as Bryce stepped into Mia's old role on the newspaper staff—she often texted her or dropped by her room during study hall to ask for pointers on certain aspects of layout—but by December she'd run out of legitimate excuses to talk to Mia. Finally, she says: "But it wouldn't be the *senior* prank if I helped."

"That's the brilliance of it, right? No one will ever suspect you." Mia stands from her backward-facing seat, swinging her right leg around to meet her left, and in two steps is next to Bryce. Her perfume is heavy and musky, not at all like the floral and fruity sprays most of her classmates wear, and Bryce wonders if that's a Mia thing or a senior thing, the wisdom to wear a more complicated scent. "I'll be back after lights-out. That gives you three more hours to study."

At 10:42, Bryce finally puts down her history notes. Technically, it's past lights-out, but their Dorm Parent, Ms. Daniels, goes to bed at precisely 10:32 and so everyone on their hall knows it's safe to turn the lights back on around 10:34. Her roommate, Lauren, has been asleep for an hour, her body curled toward the window and away from Bryce's desk lamp. Lauren would never—has never—asked Bryce to turn off a light or to make less noise, which is not to say that Bryce is disruptive but rather that in Lauren's mind she cannot commit even a minor annoyance. She likes Lauren, really, but the best parts of her—her sarcasm, a certain hardiness and pragmatism Bryce chalks up to hailing from the wilds of upstate New York, which Bryce imagines to be farmland or forest exclusively— she keeps hidden from the rest of the student body. In school she does not speak unless spoken to; at meals she lets one of her friends (Bryce, Tessa) dictate her choice. She has spent the entire year learning how to be at Atwater by following the cues of the freshmen she presumes to be more informed. Bryce has always been the one her friends follow, steal-ing what they could—braided ponytails for tennis, nails lacquered with Essie's Ballet Slippers, high-waisted bikinis last summer—in an effort to capture what they could never: Bryce's delicate wrists, her cheekbones, her straight hips and flat stomach no matter what she ate or how little she exercised. All of this is why she can't help the creeping sense of pity she feels for her roommate, the disappointing patina of a person who isn't quite what you'd hoped.

Mia Tavoletti, on the other hand, moves through Atwater with the confidence of someone who understands who she is. She has a cru-sader streak, but she doesn't want to be known as one—she seems not to do anything at all for attention or validation. Bryce thinks about this—how a person could end up that way, the curiousness of someone who slices through the world without a hand to guide them—as she changes into something a little more nimble: she swaps her sweatpants for leggings, her dad's Princeton crewneck for a quarter-zip athletic top; she laces into a pair of sneakers, one of the new ones her mom bought her in January for "winter workouts," a not-so-subtle reminder to frequent the gym in the off-season. As she waits for the minutes to click forward, she flips through her flash cards, slipping ideologies into her subconscious.

"Dressed for the job, too, I see?" Mia announces her arrival, smirking, her small lips thinning as she presses them together.

"You know, I don't have to do this. It's not like Louisa has someone else in mind for art director."

"*What?* I'm being serious! You look like a ninja."

Bryce raises an eyebrow. "So, what do I need?"

"Just a sense of adventure."

Most of Bryce's classmates entered Atwater's tunnels for the first time on the evening of their first Vespers, when they funneled into Trask from the bowels below. Initially conceived as insurance against a student who might use a Connecticut winter as an excuse for missing class, the network of underground channels linking the dorms to one another and the school building was the genius invention of Atwater's second headmistress, Edith Jordan; now, due to some combination of fluctuating financial resources and a sense that Edith Jordan's understanding of feminine fragility was somewhat Victorian, the tunnels are kept locked most of the year. The school officially opened them on just two occasions each year: Vespers and Alumnae Weekend, when visiting graduates delighted in recapturing a sense of their high school mischief-making.

This is how Bryce ended up in the tunnels when she was just eight years old. It was the same year her parents got divorced, and Bryce guesses now that Lillian thought the trip would be a fun girls' weekend, a bonding opportunity for the two of them: a preview of all the excitement her daughter's future still held, regardless of whether her father was a permanent resident in her house. On that Saturday afternoon, Lillian slipped away from lunch—her eyes red-rimmed and watery, her hair flattened at the roots, her teeth faintly purpled, little fractures Bryce would come to understand as symptoms of too many glasses of wine—and tugged her daughter across the Bowl into Whitney and down to the basement, where a heavy and cracked wooden door opened into a pitch-black hallway, so dark her eyes refused to adjust. Bryce stood at the threshold, her hands in tiny fists, her eyes trained on her mother's calves thinned by shadow as she stopped to slip her feet out of her stiletto sandals. Her bare feet caved inward, so flat that she couldn't help pronating.

"Come on," Lillian shouted, and the empty corridor repeated the command: *Come on come on come on*. And she stepped out the halo of light into the darkness, her shoeless feet so quiet and soft against the cement that it was as if she had disappeared entirely.

It was Bryce's father who taught her to swim, who carried her in the pool first with his arms and then with just the tips of his fingers and then with his hands outstretched, always an inch away; it was her father who taught her to ride a bike, his palm flat against her upper back; it was her dad who walked her into school on the first day of kindergarten, hand in hand. Lillian didn't know that her daughter wasn't brave.

"Bryce!" *Bryce Bryce Bryce*. Her father called her Little Bee, short for *his little bumble bee*. He made buzzing noises at her when he got home from work, chasing her around the kitchen island. Lillian never called her anything but Bryce.

With her eyes shut, choosing her own darkness instead, she ran down the hallway, her sneaker slaps echoing in the corridor. Her mother shrieked, laughing wildly, until Bryce caught up with her, her chest smacking into her mother's hip.

"Watch it!" Lillian snapped, shoving her daughter off.

Finally they reached an intersection, and light glowed dimly from a spare bulb at the ceiling center. A set of cubbies lined the hall to their left—"That's the way to the art building," her mother explained; the hall to their right was more properly lit, and on the walls Bryce could see the sketches of a pattern.

As she followed her mother to the right, the markings clarified, each line made more distinct as her eyes adjusted. It was writing: hundreds of hand-scribbled messages. Names. Numbers. Doodles: hearts and clovers and rainbows. Her mother stopped short suddenly, and extended a pointed finger to the wall, tracing up and down as if searching a crossword.

"Here!" she cried out, finally, and pushed her forefinger into the concrete. "Bryce, look."

Lilly Lowell, it said, in a tight and jagged handwriting that only slightly resembled the wide loops that signed Bryce's school permission slips.

"When you come here, your friends will want you to sign your name near theirs, near your class. But you can sign wherever you want."

Whether it's the bravery of age and familiarity or actual minor electrical renovations, the tunnels don't seem so dark to Bryce, now, following Mia through a lock-picked door in Lathrop's basement ("Sometimes I just get the hot security guard to open it, but I didn't want to involve him in this," Mia said, her nose close to the keyhole). There's an orange glow that fuzzes every twenty yards or so, from bulbs at intersections or exit signs over doorways, and it's light enough inside the tunnels to see that behind the scratches of signatures—like hieroglyphics inside an ancient tomb— the walls are painted a sort of milky yellow; the writing itself seems more childish and playful than menacing: GO HERONS! FAB 4 EVER. PENNY WAS HERE.

At the first intersection, Mia takes the tunnel to their right, heading toward the school building.

"Where are we going?"

"It's safer if you don't know the plan," Mia says. "If we get caught, then they won't be able to wring it out of you."

Bryce rolls her eyes. "We're not spies."

"But Mrs. Brodie is *kind of* like the CIA, isn't she?" Mia pauses at the door at the tunnel's end, thinking. "I still sort of can't believe that she's leaving," she adds.

The email announcing Brodie's retirement had come from the President of the Board, and included a lengthy recounting of their Head of School's many accomplishments both at and before she came to Atwater. It made no mention of Karen Mirro or Mr. Breslin or the tumult of the year; it was as if the circumstances were completely normal, entirely coincidental. There was only the vague insinuation, at the very end, that the timing was inopportune—normally a Head announced her retirement a year in advance, and continued to fulfill her duties while the school performed a search for her replacement.

"I mean, it's not entirely her fault, right?" Mia continues. "It all went down way before she was Head."

Bryce considers this. "But she still kept him on staff," she says, carefully.

Mia shrugs. "I'm not defending her, I don't think. I'm just saying that I think she was at the end of a long line of . . . buck-passing, you know? I think a lot of people knew Breslin was sleeping with his students, and firing Brodie just feels more symbolic than anything else."

Bryce is still turning this over when Mia says: "You know there are cameras around school, right? Have you figured out where they all are?" Without waiting for a response, she continues, her voice at a clip: "Anyway, some of them are decoy cameras, just meant as deterrents. If you spend enough time at the security desk watching the monitors you can figure out which are real, but there are a lot and I forget sometimes. I'm, like, ninety percent sure the one on the other side of this door is fake. But keep your head down just in case, okay?"

Bryce's heart pumps in a kind of way that seems to come from the bottom of her sternum, deep in her gut. She can feel her skin pulsing with the beat, giant echoing thumps that must be loud enough for Mia to hear.

Mia puts her hand on the doorknob, then turns over her shoulder one more time, angling her chin slightly up so that Bryce can see her eyes. "Having fun yet?"

They enter the schoolhouse in the basement wing, a dusty and dark corridor secretly beloved by the teachers whose classes take place in its outdated rooms. It's where the *Heron* staff convenes in its crumbling and cavernous room; Bryce also has English down here, in a classroom with lab tables stacked end on end, puzzled into a square that theoretically works and facilitates discussion like a Harkness table. The basement classrooms are unfussy, unstuffy, not at all the crown-molded and twenty-foot-ceilinged stereotypes of those on the first floor. The carpet peels up at the corners. The chalkboards never fully erase.

Together they hustle along the corridor, shooting for the stairs at the opposite end, where they ascend two flights into the world languages wing. The second floor holds an old dance studio that the school uses for

health classes and interdisciplinary workshops and independent studies—
Sloane and Blake use it most afternoons for their ballet practice, although
never at the same time. Basically, it's a forgotten room, no good even for
weekend hookups or drinking because of its location. But this is where
Mia leads Bryce, to a closet at the back of the studio, where she pulls out
an overstuffed duffel bag and hooks it over her shoulder. She clicks the
closet shut, and motions over her shoulder for Bryce to hurry behind her.

Mia leads Bryce back to the southern entrance of the school building and into the administration wing, where the offices of Mrs. Brodie, Linda Paulsen, and the College Counseling staff sit beyond a set
of glass-paneled and gold-lettered double doors. The senior sets down
her bag and begins riffling through it; when she stands, she's clutching
two giant boxes of maxi pads. "I'm gonna need your help. There's two
more of these in there—grab 'em?"

"Seriously?"

Mia stares at her. "Put your hood up, too."

The spring-loaded glass doors move with an eerie silence, cutting
through the still air as quietly as the ghosts they are. Bryce follows Mia
down the hall; together they walk more slowly than before, peeking in
and out of offices, waiting (maybe) for the inevitable blare of an alarm.
A daytime visit to the admin wing usually means trouble or, at the very
least, discomfort and stress, and so tonight it feels more forbidden even
than the tunnels.

Mia stops at Mrs. Brodie's office, setting the boxes of pads on the
floor. She gets right to work, tearing quickly at the box top; the pads are
so tightly packed that when she pulls one the surrounding three come
with it. She tears open the wrapping, tosses it aside. "Fuck, this is gonna
make such a mess," she says as she peels away the backing. "Pull the garbage bin over, will you?"

As Bryce reaches for the waste basket, Mia presses the first pad
against Mrs. Brodie's door, applying pressure for a few seconds. It reminds Bryce of when they were taught how to use a pad in middle school,
and the health teacher stuck them to her arms and forehead in an attempt
to lighten an awkward lesson. It's absurd; hilarious. Mia leans back to

admire her handiwork, keeping her hand a length away from the door, waiting to see if the stick takes. It does, and Mia exhales. "Fuck yes. I wasn't sure this was gonna work. Are doors like underwear?"

"Metaphorically," Bryce says, "a little bit."

Mia snorts a laugh. "Come on, we gotta cover this thing. Make it neat—rows of them, side by side. That way we'll get the most coverage. I want this motherfucker leak-proof."

And for a few minutes they work in a diligent silence, pasting the pads in tidy rows, their rhythms syncing, tearing and peeling and sticking at the same time, and Bryce's adrenaline is calmed by the manageable task at hand. She read something once about a depressed polar bear in the Central Park Zoo, and how the key to the polar bear's depression was that he lacked "manageable tasks"—he was bored, basically—and that the path to contentment for humans and zoo animals alike is via a series of manageable tasks.

Bryce positions a final pad in the bottom corner of the door, and then lets her crouching body fall back into something half-seated. Mia had turned over the trash bin to use as a footstool; Bryce watches her finish the top row, then jump off her stool and walk backward for a better view.

"Sorta can't tell what they are, can you?"

"It looks like those cushioned walls you see in psych wards on TV." This is probably the truest thing about the door: it looks like it was designed for you to run into it.

"Well, that works just as well."

"So . . . why pads?"

"For three years, Flawless has been lobbying Atwater to put pads and tampons in the bathrooms. At first we wanted free ones, and when the administration said that would"—here she puts on a sort of vaguely British affect—"'amount to a not-insignificant expenditure,' we campaigned for dispensers instead—you know, those things you see in public bathrooms."

"Yeah, I'm never clear on whether or not those work."

"Yeah, me neither. Anyway, so we said fine, we'll pay for them, but you should have them all around campus. And we did this research, polled the student body, made the argument for reliable access to *feminine care* and our role, as a girls' school, in setting the standard for that right . . . and they just said no. 'The Health Center always has tampons in case of an emergency,' they said, which, yeah, we know, but the Health Center can be out of the way, and by definition that sort of misunderstands what a period emergency looks like."

There are so few people who know this about Mia, Bryce thinks—how *noble* she is, how morally righteous. With her black-on-black clothes and her good-but-not-outstanding grades and her lack of really *close* friends, Mia always seems sort of above it all: just passing through. In so many ways the pads on the door is classic Mia: weird juxtaposed with virtuous; hilarious with high-minded; deadly serious but also superficial.

"This school—they say they're all about empowering us, but the truth is they have a very narrow view of what that looks like. And if our empowerment comes at any kind of cost, then we can forget about it." She inhales deeply. "And I don't just mean financial cost, like, dollars spent or whatever. If it costs their image, then that's an issue, too."

"Well, if their image is tarnished, then so is their bank account," Bryce adds.

Mia nods, reaching a hand out to flatten a pad that curls at the side.

"Why not have somebody from Flawless do this with you?"

Mia turns over her shoulder, and Bryce senses she's disappointed in the question. "I didn't want them to be able to sanction the club," she says, as though it's the obvious thing. "A mysterious rogue defector is best."

After packing up their things—they leave the wrappers in the admin trash can, but otherwise try to make the area look undisturbed, so everything looks normal at first—they head back across the main floor up the stairs again.

Bryce does not remember the first time she came to Atwater; she was too young for the memory to stick, and by the time she was old enough for a visit to settle into permanence she had traveled to the campus enough times that it felt like visiting a relative. She didn't always understand why, of all things, she had to go with her mother to Alumnae Weekends and fund-raisers—she had a nanny, after all, a rotating cast of them, soft-featured and brown-haired graduate students from Yale, working on their Ph.D.s in public health or sociology, on-call help who picked Bryce up from school or practice and helped with homework and dinner and dishes and bedtime when her mother (who did, in fact, have a graduate degree in psychology and who was, in fact, in private practice in Greenwich, where she worked mainly with the mothers of girls with whom Bryce played tennis) was too busy or too tired or, maybe, Bryce came to understand when her mother kept hiring nannies even when Bryce was twelve and thirteen and old enough to do a lot of the nanny's tasks on her own, when she just wanted another adult in the house.

Lillian brought Bryce to Atwater because it was the greatest thing she had ever done in her life, Bryce now knew. Looking at the pictures of her mother in the old yearbooks and in the graduation and society photos on the walls, tall and thin and soft-focused, her hair long and honey blond, a kind of classic American beauty that could and would withstand the shifting whims of decades and generations, the Lilly Lowell who went to Atwater in the eighties—a decade before Karen Mirro—was a girl with unlimited promise and potential: student council president, captain of the tennis team; a boyfriend at Westminster; accepted to Barnard and Wellesley and Bryn Mawr. Loved by all her teachers, the envy of all her classmates. *Perfect.*

But then life had become a disappointment for Lillian, as it is for so many girls whose high school careers are extraordinary. She got her degree in psychology, and after a couple stints as an in-house therapist at various rehab centers, she found the demands of corporatism too stringent, too inflexible; it was because her ex-husband was a hedge fund manager that they had the capital for Lillian to start her own practice, just a few clients at first, recommendations from friends, a list she could keep as small as she wanted provided she could cover the lease on her office space and that she could keep her office itself decorated in whatever style was de rigueur. (Whether her wardrobe—tailored staples from Theory and

Vince, sensible but chic flats from Chanel and Prada, hair by Kérastase, always—counted as a work expense was up for debate, and so the budget varied from month to month.) The arrangement allowed her to say that *at least she still worked,* something many of her friends and Bryce's friends' mothers could not say, *at least she had purpose,* but it was a small existence, a modest career, one that hovered at the edges of a hobby, smelling like sacrifice and resentment and an angry yearning for what might have been.

She did not have an M.D. or a Ph.D. She did not lead a team of psychologists in a hospital or a rehab facility. She did not perform her own research. She did not speak at conferences. She was not, by any measure, *wildly successful.* She made low-six figures every year. And then her marriage fell apart, and she became a middle-aged Connecticut divorcée with a middling therapy practice and a stubborn wrinkle between her eyebrows. It wasn't a failure, exactly, it just wasn't what anyone saw in the future of the senior who once charmed the President of the Board of Trustees into *personally* funding and hosting the first senior retreat on her Hamptons estate.

Of course Lillian never said any of this to Bryce, and in fact it would be years—Bryce would be in her thirties—before her daughter would really see how the hints of unhappiness that vignetted their existence had coalesced together into one shroud, before she would see her mother at seventy and understand the mountain of dissatisfaction that shadowed their life. For now, all Bryce knew were the average and prickling constraints of a mother who saw her daughter as a piece of her own résumé, a reflection of herself, one last chance to get it right.

The clock tower announces Atwater from a half mile out. It crests above pine and oak and birch trees, the tallest building at the school's highest elevation. Officially, the only people with access to the purely ornamental tower—there's no bell that tolls each hour, nothing to maintain up there beyond keeping the bats out—are members of the maintenance team, but some students, over the years, have successfully badgered a beleaguered and good-natured facilities worker until he says he's *headed up there anyway, so sure, why not.* The occasional clock tower view pops up on social media, and the jealous! comments flood in.

Bryce has never been, but she knows how to get there, and she recognizes where Mia's leading her before they reach the door that hides in plain sight. It's at the end of the hall on the third floor, between a few offices and some storage closets and a last-resort bathroom. "Have you been up here before?" Mia whispers, sort of absentmindedly, jiggling the door handle.

Bryce shakes her head.

Mia lets out a low whistle. "You're in for a treat."

Immediately Bryce feels the night air tumbling down the shaftway. The staircase up the clock tower is impossibly narrow. Mia wears the duffel bag like a backpack, the handles looped over her shoulders, and still it rubs against the drywall on both sides. The tiny flights switchback on one another, and Bryce's suspicion that they are not only narrowing but also steepening is confirmed when they reach the final flight, little more than a ladder.

Mia goes first, and Bryce waits for her to clear the landing at the top before beginning her ascent. She's never had a thing about heights, but ladders provoke in her some other primal fear, and she imagines a sort of nonviolent tumble, her foot missing a rung and plunging through, knocking her off-balance. She steps gingerly, foot-foot-hand-hand, until her head pokes into the night sky.

She expects Mia to be busy implementing the plan, but as Bryce ungracefully slides her body chest-first onto the (weakly supported, clearly deteriorating) floor, she sees the senior standing at the ledge, her hands gripping the barrier at her waist, surveying the little world below them. Bryce joins her, and for a minute they don't say anything. Beneath them is their bubble, the Bowl at the school building's base the bottom of the convex curve. Lathrop is to their right, where they spot a number of lit windows violating lights-out; the same is true to their left, in Whitney. Lampposts ring the Bowl and the roads that arch away from it into parking lots and Professorville, radiating orange haze. Beyond their artificial border to the west, where the long, low, purely ornamental rock wall briefly swells to an always-open iron gate, the world switches suddenly black, acres of sprawling farmland that is tended to with the course of the sun.

"'Look, Simba,'" Mia growls, "'everything the light touches is our kingdom.'"

Bryce laughs, a low, whispered *ha*, because she is aware that she is supposed to. But the truth is that she is mesmerized by the view, by the way the campus below them looks like an island in a sea of darkness, like flying over the middle of the country at night and seeing, suddenly, the lights of a city clustered like burning stars. It is as though Atwater is the only civilization for miles; as though the universe does not exist beyond the Bowl. But this feeling Bryce has is too delicate—too embarrassing, too humiliatingly sentimental—to put into words, and so she says instead: "What's the plan, Mufasa?"

"Mufasa ends up dead." Mia squats at her duffel bag and slowly unzips. She twists and pulls; with a final tug she's thrown back two steps and Bryce can see what she had crammed like vacuum packaging into the bag: a life-sized stuffed heron, at least three feet long, with stiff, yellow legs attached to a blue-gray body. Its wings are stitched flat against its trunk, a bird that cannot even pretend to fly. "So," she says, standing and turning to face Bryce, shaking the heron by its disproportionate neck. "How should we kill her?"

Bryce stifles a laugh; Mia's delivery is perfectly deadpan, a restrained mix of melodrama and sarcasm. But she knows, too, that despite her inflection Mia is completely serious: This is a long-standing Atwater annoyance, that the mascot for their historically progressive all-girls school is a *Lady* Heron. In her four years, Mia, a star soccer player, had led or cosigned petition after petition to remove the "Lady" from their title, calling it—alternatively and simultaneously—"unnecessarily gender normative," "midcentury misogynist," and accusing the heron of extolling "outdated definitions and expectations of femininity." This is also—it occurs to Bryce—why Mia had been only moderately careful about the cameras and the entire notion of getting caught. Any symbolic destruction of the school mascot would point directly to its most vocal opponent. In other words, Mia was prepared to pay the price.

Bryce extends a hand toward the bird, fingering its coat gently. It's a high-end toy; it reminds her of the stuffed animals she admired at FAO Schwarz as a child, horses as big as ponies (and sturdy enough to ride, too), giraffes tall enough to graze the ceiling, each so realistically rendered that the store might as well have been a zoo. The heron Mia holds is cloaked in feathers, hundreds of soft synthetic approximations of the real thing. She pinches one between her thumb and index finger and tugs lightly at first, then harder. It comes loose. Her breath catches: "Oh, shit—sorry," she whispers.

Mia's eyes widen. Her lips peel into a smile. "Genius." Still clutching the bird's neck in one fist, she reaches a hand to its belly and tugs, as Bryce did, pulling another feather loose. And then—with surprising calm, like a child picking petals from a daisy—Mia extends her arm out of the tower, into the open air above the roof, and releases the feather from her hand. They watch it drift on the imperceptible breeze, shrinking smaller and smaller in the distance and darkness.

Together they set in on the bird, plucking and yanking, pinching at her faux feathers and releasing them—individually at first, then by the fistful—over the ledge, onto the roof and the sidewalk below. The destruction threatens the toy's integrity, and as she begins to bald, small bits of stuffing poke through the holes created by their tugging, so that what they toss out of the clock tower becomes a mix of fluff and feather. The heron withers before them, naked and sagging.

Mia peers over the railing, and Bryce follows suit. The debris litters the ground at the steps of the school building, a tiny blast radius of animal destruction. Mia eyes the bird, its ultrathin ("Ultrafeminine," she'd griped) neck tight in her fist. And then she lifts its shriveled remnants out into the open air and lets go, releasing the toy to its scattered plumage. It lands noiselessly, splayed at the center of its own wreckage. Surveying their handiwork, Bryce thinks suddenly of a story she read about a young woman who jumped from a parking garage roof, and how surprised she was to learn that the woman's body wasn't obliterated on impact: the damage remained inside, broken bones and ruptured organs contained by thick skin. At the time, Bryce had double- and triple-checked the facts, obsessively searching for just how much force a body could withstand. If they'd thrown a real heron from the roof, it occurs to Bryce, there might not have been any splatter at all.

Of course, if they'd thrown a real bird from the tower, it might have just flown away: they'd have freed it, instead. She wonders why neither of them thought of this, a version of protesting the Lady Heron that involved deliverance rather than death.

"Now what?" Mia asks.

"Hmm?" Bryce says, jolted from her trance.

"What's next?" the senior says.

Bryce feels the space around them tighten. She begins to shiver, and bites the inside of her mouth against the shudder. "Huh?"

Mia squares her shoulders against Bryce's, and Bryce—who is not short, who is an average five-foot-five—is suddenly aware of how tall Mia Tavoletti is. It makes sense, in a way, that she is as certain of herself as she is: there would be no way for her to pass through this world unnoticed, no way to shrink against upward-gazing eyes. "I know it's you."

When she was a child and in trouble, Bryce would do this thing where she would just refuse to talk to her mother—a version of the silent treatment, applied in reverse. Her mother would scold and shout and wave her arms wildly, pointing, hollering in increasing decibels, and Bryce would just stand, stone-faced, waiting for the torrent to end, for her mother to run out of gas. What she knew then—although she could not have explained it, had only the vaguest sense—was that what her mother wanted most of all was someone to shout *with*, an equal in argument. Her daughter's muteness triggered a reminder that she was alone in this business of parenting, in living.

She considers ignoring Mia. She could just move past her, down the staircase, through the tunnels, and back into bed. But before Bryce can move, Mia continues: "It started with the newspaper, when I—unwittingly, turns out—took the heat for Louisa. I knew that the person who published the special issue had to have been on the *Heron* staff. I considered for a little while that it *was* Louisa—that she was lying to me—but it just didn't fit. She's too . . ."

"Goody Two-shoes?"

"I might've gone with 'Nervous Nelly,' but yeah. She's too afraid of getting in trouble. So then I went through the list, starting with the seniors. Hitomi? No way."

This is correct. Hitomi is the daughter of diplomats, quiet, focused, ferociously smart. Bryce nods.

"Right. Anjali?" Mia cocks a head to one side, nods. "Maybe. She was pissed off enough that I could've imagined her doing something stupid."

Anjali has a hot temper. Bryce bites the inside of her lower lip, pulls her shoulders back.

"The juniors." Mia ticks them off on her fingers: "Brie? Can't imagine her caring enough. Kit? She *does* have that kind of West Coast hippie, social justice warrior thing going on—but, like everybody else, I knew—I assumed—that the person who published the paper was also the person who made the Pedophile Playoffs and the Snap story. I was looking for someone who wasn't just a hot-tempered campus avenger but somebody who was *disciplined*. Committed."

"That's not Kit."

Mia laughs. "No, it's not. So that leaves you and Macy."

"And obviously it couldn't have been Macy."

"I mean, I love that kid, but she can barely tie her shoes in the morning without having a panic attack."

Poor Macy. Once, Bryce had come across a quote from Virginia Woolf: "I thought how unpleasant it is to be locked out; and I thought how it is worse, perhaps, to be locked in." It remains for Bryce the most illustrative sentence she has ever read about mental illness. Macy is locked in, a prisoner in her own mind. It must be a terrible way to live.

"And I figured that the clues had to come from somebody who *knew*," Mia continues. "Somebody who had the insider information about Karen Mirro's lawsuit and Mr. Breslin and the school . . ." She searches for the right word until she lands on one borrowed from the same corporate lexicon that has plagued them all year: "*bureaucracy*. It had to be someone who was connected. Maybe someone whose grandmother was a Trustee. Someone whose mother is angling for her own position on the Board."

Bryce bristles at the use of this word to describe her mother, feels instinctively embarrassed at the obviousness of her mother's wants. "Angling" makes Lillian sound cunning and calculating when Bryce knows her mother to be flailing wildly, desperate. It was this desperation that opened the private doors of the school's scandals to Bryce, her mother's obsessive need to talk about her alma mater, to ramble on and on during car rides and over dinners about all the Atwater gossip. It was both a compulsion and a nervous tic, her constant dissecting of the school's decisions ("As soon as this thing resurfaced over the summer, they should have asked Rich to take a leave") and worrying over the reputational cost ("They needed to get out in front of this, control the narrative") and engaging in all kinds of affirmations, manifesting that this was a survivable scandal. *Bryce,* she'd said one night over winter break, a piece of roast chicken stabbed at the end of her fork, golden skin molting off the slick meat, *just remember that everybody is hiding something.* She paused, shoved the chicken into her mouth, chewed. *Trust me. I'm the one they tell.*

"Well, when you put it that way," Bryce says finally, "I'm surprised that no one else figured it out."

"Yes! Ha!" Mia lets out a kind of cackle that echoes in the still air.

"Shh!" Bryce hisses, reflexively ducking beneath the rail of the tower, out of view to someone below.

"Sorry!" Mia whispers. "I *knew it!*"

All year, Bryce had imagined versions of this conversation. She knew that the publishing of the *Heron* would be the key to her identity—that someone would be able to cull the newspaper masthead for the person closest to the school's secrets. Sometimes Bryce savored the irony: that the one thing that should make her immune to expulsion—her family's *connectedness,* as Mia had phrased it—would also be the root cause of it. She wouldn't have known all she knew without her mother and grandmother, without the legacies whose paths had made Atwater Bryce's destiny.

"So what else is there?" Mia asks.

"What do you mean?"

"What's one thing you didn't get to do yet this year? I want to help."

That's up to you, Mia had said. And something else begins to crystallize for Bryce. "Wait—is the edit test—is that even real?"

Mia shrugs. "Yes and no. The bit about Louisa is true; you can ask her. But it's not, like, a Vespers-level tradition or anything."

It wasn't the *Heron* hazing Mia wanted in on, Bryce realizes. That was just a ruse; a ploy to get her out of her room. Bryce knows that Mia works so hard to keep an arm's length from the intensity with which she cares about the things she perceives as injustices, using humor (maxi pads on the Head of School's door, for example) and a sort of blasé affect (she told Louisa she *didn't even care about the newspaper anyway*) to soften her edges. When Mia looks at Bryce, she sees some kind of kindred spirit: someone else who knows what it is to have to temper your outrage, to never fully claim the things that eat at you. What she wants, Bryce realizes, is to feel a little less lonely inside her fury.

But Mia has come to her at the wrong time, Bryce's wings scorched from flying too close to the sun. She tugs at her ponytail, pushing it higher up on her head. "I think I'm done," she says finally.

Mia cocks her head to one side. "I don't believe you," she says, quickly.

Bryce shakes her head, the smallest one-two. "I crossed a line with the last one."

She thinks about the way Lauren slapped the marriage announcement down on her desk, smacked beneath a flat palm. *I mean, this seems a little below-the-belt, doesn't it?*

Mia lifts her palms up like, *Meh.* Like, *What did you expect?* "I don't think you were wrong. I just think it was too hard. I think we thought we wanted a head to roll and then when it was served to us on a silver platter we were sort of like . . . man, that's a fucking head."

Bryce laughs a little, in spite of herself, in spite of the fact that it's her miscalculation they're talking about. "I should have stopped once Breslin left," she says, although she's not convinced she means it, or that she could have. She just knows it didn't feel *good* when they announced Brodie's retirement; it felt heavy. She eyes the heron splayed on the ground three stories below them, and thinks about how you don't always see the lines until you've crossed them. *That's a fucking head.*

"No," Mia says. "I mean, he had to leave, obviously. But that's what's so hard about this, right? I'm not just mad at him. I'm mad that I ever *met* him. I'm mad at the whole system that allowed him to seduce and then rape a student and then keep his job for twenty more years, so that one day he would be my teacher and I would look at him every day for three years like, holy shit, you're the guy who made the butterfly faces, you're a fucking genius, teach me everything." She shakes her head, sloughing the disgust from how it settled in her brain like dust. "I think that's what you were trying to do, with the paintings and the interviews—you were trying to say that it wasn't just on him." She pauses again, taking a breath. "It was like this perfect storm, right? We've been living inside the section of the Venn diagram where a culture that protects men like him overlaps with one obsessed with prestige and status and reputation. How were you supposed to know how to tackle all of that at once?"

And although this sounds true to Bryce it also seems too straightforward, too intentional and too morally unambiguous. If Mia wanted Bryce to draw a straight line between the school's cover-up and her behavior this year, she couldn't do it. Nor could she say—entirely—that she did it because she sensed that she was communicating something on behalf of the student body, and that with each subsequent act the feeling that she had more to say for them only intensified, like she had something to live up to but that that something was like the edge of an exponential curve, never meeting the asymptote. No, if Mia wanted to know how it happened, Bryce would have to say: *It just did.* The newspaper just presented itself. What she couldn't have imagined before hitting Send was the gratification, how good it would feel to say *Hey, this is bullshit*, without anyone saying back—because they couldn't, because there was no one to say it to—*You'll understand later.* This is why she doesn't think she could have stopped herself after Breslin resigned: she wanted that feeling *all the time.* The yard signs acted as both her inspiration and her scapegoat: They gave her a blueprint but also muddied the waters; she knew that her actions would be lumped together with the events of Opening Day, and the hunt for a single vigilante rather than many might provide her cover.

How can she say any of this to Mia? How can she tell her that there was something greedy and not at all altruistic about what she was doing? It wasn't just about safety *(get the rapist off campus)* or justice *(how do you hold a whole culture accountable?)*—it was more personal than that.

The wood beneath her feet is worn and fraying and soft, as though it might melt beneath them. She thinks about her mother, smudging at an oily fingerprint on a wineglass, saying, *Everybody has skeletons, Bee,* using the name only her father used.

"You know what my mother told me when I was picking my classes for this year?"

"Hmm?"

"She said that I had to take photography, not Drawing and Painting."

Mia laughs, a single puff of the chest, a knock back of the head. "That's fucked-up."

"The thing is, she thinks that Atwater is the greatest thing she's done in her life. It's like she peaked at eighteen." It's a joke, sort of, but her voice is hollow and it doesn't quite land. "I want to be proud of this place like she is, but I'm also afraid that it's all I'll ever be. You know, an Atwater Girl."

"Sometimes it feels like a trap, doesn't it?"

Bryce nods. In the fall, the thought of anyone knowing all this— about her mother, about what she'd done; that the girl on campus who seemed to be the epitome of that tag line, a multigenerational legacy from a wealthy corner of New England, pretty like a J.Crew model, was, in fact, a traitor—made her break into a cold damp sweat, moisture condensing even on the tiny blond hairs above her lip. She didn't think she'd ever be able to explain it, and that even if she could, no one would understand. It will be years before she can look back on this moment and realize that the Venn diagram Mia described had a third circle overlapping the other two: the portion of a culture that takes and takes and takes from girls, all the while refusing to recognize them as whole people. She will remember this conversation and know that they didn't only want to be seen. They wanted to feel like they mattered.

But for now, it's enough to have Mia just listen, to sense that what they are feeling is the same thing, for her to nod, *Yes, yes, me too.*

"Come on," Mia says finally. "I know what we should do."

A river of bubblegum-pink liquid stretches out at Bryce's feet. The smell—antiseptic, like a hospital—mingles with the stink of going-cold fried food, a nauseating combination. The ease with which Mia assembled a DIY slip-and-slide inside the main room of Atwater's student center seemed to mean only one thing—that she had done this before—and Bryce found herself wondering, as she watched the senior splash jugs of industrial soap across the floor, liquid smacking and spraying like shrapnel against chairs and couch backs, whether this, too, was a kind of tradition, a piece of random mischief transformed over the years into a rite of passage. She can't imagine her mother having done this.

"Stop being such a chicken!" Mia shouts through gasping breaths, positioned at the door at the opposite end of the room, holding it wide. "It works, I promise!" Under her arm she clutches a food tray, sticky rivulets of soap streaking down its smooth underside and dripping onto the floor at her feet.

Bryce inhales deeply, a yogic breath. She closes her eyes and thinks about how Mia launched onto her tray like a surfer diving into a wave, her chest smacking against the hard plastic. As a spectator Bryce's skepticism had vanished in an instant. But at the same time, tennis is not the kind of sport that teaches a body how to absorb a blow, and Bryce's last thought—rocking back on her right heel the same way she does when she's preparing to serve—is *This is going to hurt.*

She uses her arms to catch the tray, breaking her fall slightly before her chest smacks into the plastic. Soap sprays on her face, onto her eyelids, the tips of her flyaways. It's over before it registers, the lip of the door functioning as a speed bump at the end of the road. She wonders if she kept her eyes closed the entire way. When she stands, soap dampens her shirt and the edges of her thighs. The dry rectangle where the tray pressed against her body blurs like a Rothko.

Mia has her hands braced against her knees, trying to contain her own laughter. "You. Looked. Terrified," she says between breaths.

Bryce frowns, narrows her eyebrows into one another. She picks up her tray and marches back to the beginning of the stream. She pauses, picks up the last remaining bottle of soap, and tosses more onto the floor, greasing the slide. They go again and again and again, until the soap has slipped to the edges of the floor and out the door, until their clothing is heavy with wet and their ribs and hands ache with latent bruises, until Mia wanders out into the center of the parking lot, her tray tucked under her arm like a canvas. Bryce follows her. Out from under the aura of the building lights and lampposts, they can begin to see the stars that blanket a New England night.

"It wasn't just that I wanted to help, you know," Mia says, finally. "With your mischief."

Bryce looks at Mia. In the darkness she can't see the earnestness that creases the senior's brow, the way her eyes flare with a kind of urgency.

"I just think it's pretty chill, what you did this year," Mia continues. "And I didn't want to leave without telling you that."

She sighs then, a satisfied kind of exhale, and Bryce appreciates all that she is trying to communicate. It would be too much to expect her to say it precisely. Instead Mia looks skyward again. "You know, the truth is, I don't hate it here."

"Me neither," Bryce agrees.

"It's got work to do," Mia murmurs, like an afterthought. "But it's not all bad."

"I know," Bryce whispers. And she does. Later that night, tucked into her bed at four in the morning, Lauren sound asleep in the bed across from hers, Bryce will think about this, the sentimental denouement at the end of an adrenaline-fueled night. She'll put it next to how Mia went quiet in the tunnels, her steely determination every step of the way. She'd never imagined that Mia Tavoletti might love Atwater as much as her mother does, as much as her grandmother. But now she understands. Now she will want to say to her mother: *This is what it is to love a place.* She'll want to tell her: *You have to want it to be better.*

To: erin.palmiere@reginaventures.com
From: erin.palmiere@reginaventures.com
Date: June 1, 2016, 5:07 P.M.
Subject: Jamison Jennings Report

To the Atwater Community:

On November 27, 2015, I wrote to inform you that the school had retained the services of the consulting firm Jamison Jennings to perform a cultural assessment and to evaluate our institutional response to allegations of sexual misconduct.

Attached to this email are the firm's findings. Their report makes clear that Atwater's efforts to prioritize the safety of its students have not been without failure, even if those failures have been impacted by changing social norms. It pains me to share this, as I'm sure it pained many of our community members to reveal this information in the course of the investigation. That said, I write to you today with no less pride in our school than ever before: your participation in this investigation, your candor with relative strangers, and your trust in the process demonstrated the extent to which we share in a common faith; we believe in our school, and we are invested in its future.

If you are an Atwater graduate, you know that we never stop learning. This report is but one unit in an ever-evolving curriculum. These recommendations will inform our work moving forward, including our search for Atwater's sixteenth Head of School. I hope that you will continue to participate, and I vow to continue to listen. If you plan to be on campus this weekend for Commencement, I invite you to find me to share your input.

Yours with optimism and gratitude,

Erin Palmiere

In November 2015, representatives from The Atwater School contacted Jamison Jennings to initiate a conversation about the school's desire to explore its policies and procedures regarding allegations of sexual misconduct. In a changing landscape, the school sought to receive recommendations for twenty-first-century best practices. Our research affirms our initial hypothesis: although Atwater's legacy has been defined by innovation, it has failed to stay a step ahead of a challenging coupling between shifting cultural norms and the inherent hazards of the boarding school environment. We are optimistic, however, about the school's unique capacity to appropriately address such a challenge.

Methodology

The first step in our investigation was a *cultural assessment*. To best serve the school, we needed to understand its habits and mores. The core of this work depended upon one-on-one conversations with members of the Atwater community. We sought to speak with a wide range of constituents, from current and former faculty and staff to current and former administration to alumnae and alumnae parents. With the help of school administrators, we also compiled a representative selection of current students, and with parent/guardian permission, interviewed eight of those chosen.

In total, Jamison Jennings conducted fifty-three interviews with various Atwater community members. We also reviewed thousands of pages of physical documentation, including: emails, text messages, personnel files, and personal notes. In some cases, physical corroboration of various rumors offered in interviews could not be found. In other instances, School communication was essential in supporting our understanding of community culture and norms.

Findings

We believe in the importance of *context* in understanding and evaluating our findings, both at Atwater specifically and in the broader historical moment. Nearly every individual we interviewed affirmed the quality of education offered at Atwater, and many spoke specifically to the inherent value of a boarding school community, which they felt results in more individualized, empathetic educational experiences. On the other hand, however, many community members wondered whether the boarding school setting causes a blurring of traditional boundaries in a manner that creates confusion regarding appropriate behavior for students and faculty alike.

On several occasions, interviewees described relationships between students and faculty that they believed to be romantic or sexual. In each instance, we sought to corroborate the information through additional interviews and documentation. In total, we found five former faculty members to have been credibly accused of engaging in inappropriate relationships with students.

Four of the five relationships described are believed to have occurred in the 1970s and early 1980s, when the cultural understanding of appropriate romantic and sexual relationships differed vastly from today's. All are believed to have been understood as consensual at the time. In our opinion, the extent to which the school was involved in cultivating an environment that fostered such relationships does not exceed the parameters of the cultural moment itself. Indeed, the community members who described these relationships by and large called upon the benefit of their own hindsight: individuals who were aware of the relationships described coming to the understanding that they may have been inappropriate only afterward, sometimes quite recently.

The remaining accusation has been entered into the public record via local news reporting. In 1995, Karen Mirro, then eighteen and a senior at the school, alleged that she was raped by a male faculty member in his on-campus apartment following a months-long romantic and physical courtship. The school's handling of the case at the time reflected a lack of meaningful guidelines to follow under such circumstances. While we do not believe that school officials at the time made a conscious decision to protect a distinguished faculty member, we understand how a lack of transparency could contribute to a fear of retaliation. Responsiveness to these kinds of allegations should not be left to administrative discretion.

A clearer process was and is necessary to ensure students and staff alike are heard and protected.

Recommendations

We believe that in matters of sexual misconduct, the nature of a boarding school community is both a weakness and its greatest strength. The benefit is that these communities tend to function *as such*, and are uniquely equipped to collaborate in the manner required for cultural change.

In this effort, it is important that the school assess both its response to alleged misconduct and its efforts to prevent misconduct. In the former, the school should swiftly establish a set of in-house policies on top of state and federal mandatory reporting and Title IX guidelines, e.g., a clearer, more explicitly delineated sexual harassment policy inclusive of an extensive anti-retaliation clause and an accessible avenue for confidential reporting; the establishment of a committee inclusive of school personnel outside administration (e.g., school counselors; a representative selection of faculty) that must convene in every instance of alleged misconduct.

Preventative work, however, is the key to creating lasting change within a community. Programming that helps students and staff alike to develop an understanding of healthy relationships, including education in sexual literacy and affirmative consent, will be the most beneficial in establishing a climate of respect. The school has made clear its intention to assume leadership in sociocultural change. We suggest that it utilize the Head of School's retirement as an opportunity to carry out this mission, and that it invest in a progressive leader with a proven track record of prioritizing student safety.

Finally, our investigation underscored the extent to which the Atwater community is one consistently willing to do the work, and we advise the school to capitalize on this asset with the same ingenuity and inventiveness that has defined its operation for two centuries.

Commencement

The email comes from Linda Paulsen in mid-January, as it always does, with the subject line *PLEASE READ: GRAD DRESSES*, as it always says. If a member of the graduating class had thought the events of her senior year might have given the school cause to reexamine the dress code for Commencement, she would be disappointed: the contents of the email are more or less unchanged from the previous year. Per tradition, graduates of the class of 2016 are invited to purchase their own dress for Commencement. Atwater also maintains a small "closet" of gowns donated over the years; students may borrow from this collection for the occasion on a first-come, first-served basis. All dresses—whether they are chosen from the closet or purchased independently—must be approved by the Dean of Students by April 15. Should a student choose to purchase her gown rather than borrow one from the school closet, she should be advised of the expectations. Dresses should be no shorter than three inches above the knee and no longer than the ankle. They should be made of a single-texture fabric, e.g., silk, silk crepe, or satin, which is to say that embellished (e.g., beaded) fabrics and/or lace and lace overlays are not permitted. Plunging necklines are also not permitted, with the definition of "plunging" at Ms. Paulsen's discretion. All dresses should be, of course, paper-white.

Collier Ludington has just the right kind of buzz. It's midmorning on the first Saturday in June, and she and the forty-seven other members of the class of 2016 are gathered inside Trask, in an old sculpture studio near the back of the building. Outside, it is a perfect late-spring morning; the forecast calls for early-evening thunderstorms, but for now it is warm and bright, the sun cascading from spotless skies. Linda Paulsen wrangles her students like cattle, literally poking and prodding them when they dare to leave their confined space. The last thing she needs, she says, is for one of them to be in the bathroom when it's time for the procession to start. The whole thing will fall apart! Like a house of cards! Like dominoes!

Collier wonders if Paulsen knows that probably a third or even half the students around her are also lightly buzzed, or a little high, or blissed out on benzos, if they're hard-core like that. She probably does. She has been doing this for a long time. They keep it together, and that's all that matters. Collier considers that of the things young women learn at Atwater, keeping it together while a little bit drunk may just be among the most valuable. On the other hand, it's not like she wouldn't have picked this up at home, had she gone to Greenwich Academy or even Greenwich High School. Her mother and grandmother have the talent in spades.

But she didn't go to GA or to Greenwich High, and not because the latter is a public school (GHS is so well-resourced that it may as well be a private school). She came here, and in an hour or so she will be the fourth generation in her mother's family to graduate from Atwater. Third-gen graduates are not uncommon at Atwater, but fourth gen is rarified air. Her mother had a slate of paper-white dresses shipped to the dorms from Neiman Marcus before Linda Paulsen's email—*PLEASE READ: GRAD DRESSES*—dropped in Collier's inbox. Like the dresses themselves, an Atwater graduation every three decades is a family tradition. She chose a wrap dress with a high slit and cascading ruffles along the neckline from the shoulders to her waist in both the front and back. It's a little bit bohemian, something that she might have expected Addison to wear. Her mother had been surprised by the choice.

"Really?" she'd said over the phone the night Collier tried them on.

"She looks great, Mrs. L," Addison hollered from where she sat on Collier's bed, willing her voice into the speaker across the room. Collier wondered: Who will do this for her next year—be her casual ally, her easy and constant company?

"It's just—" Meredith Ludington lowered her voice: "I threw that one in as an afterthought."

Honestly, the white dresses are embarrassing, Mia Tavoletti thinks as Mrs. Brodie welcomes the community to the 202nd Atwater Commencement. It's true that Karla Flores is killing it in that one-shouldered, trumpet-shaped gown that accentuates her teeny-tiny waist, and that Olivia Anderson is—as always—a vision, and that Mia's own dress, an early-nineties silk-satin slip dress bought for $78 from a vintage store online, is perfectly fine, but for the most part her classmates just don't look like themselves. She remembers sitting in the back of the student rows as a freshman at her first graduation and watching the seniors—none of them she knew well, but she could call up their names easily now, still: Delaney Mathis and Lidey Preston and Tatum Walsh—clop across the stage to shake hands with Mrs. Brodie and accept a single red rose, cradled in plastic and a few sad sprigs of baby's breath, from the Dean of Faculty. Even Tatum Walsh, who looked like a Tatum, the kind of girl she expected to meet at boarding school, tall and tan with glossy brown hair that always seemed to catch the light, looked ridiculous that day in her paper-white gown. Nobody that isn't a wedding dress designer makes a decent paper-white gown, and at her first Atwater graduation Mia understood what her mother meant when she said something looked *cheap*. None of the dresses fit quite right; the fabrics were too stiff or the seams stitched too thick, and so on this day—their graduation day, the crowning achievement of four years of toil and turmoil—the seniors looked suddenly like little girls playing dress-up.

But the poor tailoring was really just a superficial appraisal, one that hooked her attention while she honed a more sophisticated critique. By her sophomore year (Bea Corbin, Francesca Murray, Annika Stern) she'd developed a line of thinking about the white dresses. The whole connotation was off: purity, chastity, fetishized notions of innocence. Atwater— one of the finest schools for young women in the entire world, educator of CEOs and Pulitzer winners and MacArthur Geniuses and senators (but no presidents—yet)—dressed its graduates as brides on their graduation day.

She wrote editorials in the *Heron*. She drafted petitions that even members of ***Flawless refused to sign. She had meetings with Mrs. Brodie and Ms. Burdick and Linda Paulsen herself, each of whom listened attentively and made empty promises to visit the issue at the next faculty meeting. This year, she'd lost track of this particular battle—maybe they all had, or maybe Mia had thought that the thing would take care of itself: that the school would realize that this year was not the year to force its young women into wedding dresses. But like everyone else Linda Paulsen plowed forward undeterred; the email came regardless—*PLEASE READ: GRAD DRESSES*—and Mia was told in no uncertain terms that she would find herself a paper-white dress or she would not walk across the stage with her classmates on the first Saturday in June.

Like the rest of her classmates, Anjali Reddi had become obsessed with sleuthing out the identity of Atwater's Commencement speaker, whose name—according to tradition—is kept under lock and key until the weekend-of. Much like the roles of the Vespers performers, the students delight in the guessing game, trying to trick faculty members into giving it up—*just raise your left eyebrow if it's Oprah*—and hounding the children of Board members, who might have some intel. Anjali tried exactly this with Bryce Engel, whose grandmother stepped down two years ago after a decade on the Board, going so far as to take the freshman out for a coffee "study date" on a Sunday afternoon in May—but little Bryce with her freckled nose seemed to have genuinely no idea.

Mostly because of the Oprah fantasy, the speaker selection is always a little bit of a let-down, which is not to say that Atwater's alumnae themselves are let-downs but rather that the pool of dream candidates is not rich with Atwater-adjacent individuals. Personally, Anjali had been rooting for a Supreme Court justice. Instead they'd been blessed with a writer, a woman in her mid- or late-thirties with pale skin and a blunt cut and wooden clogs peeking out from beneath her academic regalia. She's

a cultural critic whose work primarily focuses on feminist issues, Anjali
reads from the program in her lap, and her writing has appeared at or in
all of the major places: *The Atlantic, The New Yorker, New York Magazine,
The New York Times.*

It is also tradition that relevant members of the senior class are invited
to an evening tea with the Commencement speaker on the eve of graduation. Because Anjali is coeditor of the *Heron* and because the speaker is
a journalist, Anjali was an obvious invite, and so she spent her last official
night as an Atwater student in Patricia Brodie's living room perched on a
stiff and scratchy floral settee, bitter tea balanced in her palm, angling for
the attention of a writer whose work she'd crammed-read hours before.
Also in attendance: Collier Ludington (student council president); Hitomi Sakano (top in their class, although Atwater did not officially rank);
Olivia Anderson (everyone's favorite, and—Anjali was cynical enough to
know—a diversity twofer, multiracial *and* gay); Addison Bowlsby (Collier's best friend); Karla Flores (who was heading to Georgetown in the
fall, the writer-in-question's alma mater).

From her quick pre-tea research, Anjali knew why the school had
invited this particular speaker: she'd written widely about sex and consent, about reproductive rights and equal pay, about gender parity in the
workforce. She had a book coming out in the fall, a "deeply reported exam-
ination" (according to one reviewer) of the sex lives of young women (they
never orgasmed! Young men always do!). Her invitation was an obvious
PR stunt, one more Band-Aid on a gaping reputational wound. And yet,
in spite of herself, in spite of the cynicism that had calcified around her
this year like a hard shell, Anjali had been excited to meet this woman.
She seemed like the kind of person they could talk to. Her writing talked
about sex in a way that wasn't plainly clinical; she seemed to use "oral sex"
and "head" interchangeably.

Maybe it was because Mrs. Brodie was there. Maybe it was because
the school was surely paying her a large honorarium. But the writer—a
journalist!—had asked them the same questions as everyone else: Where
are you going to school? What do you plan to major in? And what do you
want to do with that? *But don't you really want to know if we've ever had an*

orgasm? Anjali had wondered, wildly, simultaneously embarrassed at the ludicrousness of her interior thoughts.

Anjali picks at a cuticle, tugging at a snag of skin she should have manicured away. Her dress has sleeves, fluted ones that flower like calla lilies from the crook of her elbow. The fabric puddles in her lap. The writer's speech is indistinguishable from the speeches Anjali heard at her first three Atwater graduations, none of which she can remember in all that much detail. Do well but do good; be the generation of women leaders we need; do not forget the people who helped you along the way, thank your families, call your mother from time to time.

The conferring of degrees happens in a kind of two-step process: first, they are called up by row to the stage, where they stand in a line at the base of the short staircase; next, they are called by name to mount the temporary platform and receive their diplomas from Mrs. Brodie and a rose from Ms. Burdick and to shake hands with the speaker, a writer whose speech was just fine. Kat Foard is in the first part of this process, waiting for her name to be called—the President of the Board is at the Ds, now ("Cecily Davidson . . . Lucy Dawn . . . Claire DiNuzzo . . .")—facing the audience and thinking about where to put her hands. She chose a dress by a smallish brand out of Venice Beach for the way it reminded her of something she'd danced in, once: A U-shaped neckline not unlike a leotard, with a waist seam cut at the base of her rib cage, stitched into a basic ankle-length ball-gown skirt. She fights the urge to fiddle with the single piece of jewelry she wears: a simple gold cross dangling from a chain at her neck, a Confirmation gift from her grandmother.

She had debated wearing the necklace this morning, putting it on, then taking it off, then putting it on again at the last minute. She wears it every day, although not during dance (because it gets in the way), but most days it stays tucked underneath her shirt. It's not that her classmates have never seen it, or that she only ever wears tops with highish necklines, but rather that she isn't *typically* wearing something that exposes as much of her sternum as this dress. Standing in Trask, waiting to process in, Kat noticed her classmates staring at the pendant on her chest.

You can be a lot of things at Atwater, Kat thinks: There's a GSA and a club for students of color and a Torah study group (JDate, officially, but "Jew Club" for short, in what Kat guesses is an effort by its members to be ironic in an anti-PC kind of way) and a Kabbalah study group; there's Veganomics, for students who are either actually vegan or just vegan-curious, and Glutoxic, for girls on gluten-free diets; Breathe is for girls interested in meditation. But there is no Bible study group; if you want to go to church on Sunday, you take a cab into town and a separate one back. There are a handful of other girls who wear crosses, Kat has noticed, but she gets the sense that they are family heirlooms or otherwise sentimental gifts, baby rings from baptisms and charms gifted on First Communions.

It's been hard this year in particular to be the girl who wears a cross not as a piece of inheritance but as a personal reminder. Kat actually believes, and not just in God and heaven and hell and all that but also generally in the mandates of the Catholic Church. (She thinks it's a little bit manipulative to call abortion *murder*, but she doesn't think it should be legal. She thinks that birth control as in *the pill* is complicated but condoms should be okay; after all, wouldn't widespread use of condoms lead to fewer abortions? Which is worse?) Everybody knows that Kat is waiting until marriage to have sex, and so in a year when everyone has wanted to talk about whether it was okay for a twentysomething teacher to have sex with an eighteen-year-old student, not a lot of people have wanted to talk to Kat.

The thunderstorms aren't supposed to start until that evening—five or six—and Priya Sandhu knows that for the next few hours the air will thicken steadily until it cannot hold another invisible drop. Under the reception tent the air is already damp and heavy, the tarp above and around them acting as a kind of trap for the increasing humidity. She spots her parents right away: her father's turban, her mother's head scarf. They

stand next to one another, motionless, shallow half smiles on their faces
like wax figures. Her father's temple gleams. The glass her mother holds
sweats with condensation. A low-level anxiety reverberates somewhere at
the bottom of Priya's diaphragm, just below the seam of the empire-waist
gown she ordered from Anthropologie as soon as the email from Linda
Paulsen landed in her inbox.

Priya's parents—despite the fact that they live in London—had
made the trip to Atwater every Parents' Weekend, dutifully meeting
with each of Priya's teachers as concerned and involved parents do. They
always bring gifts: teas, chocolates. When they visit, Priya finds herself
acting as their chaperone, translating her mother's accent, countering
her father's reservedness with bubbling conversation. "They're so sweet,"
her teachers would say, without ever learning to pronounce her mother's
name—they were always *Mr. and Mrs. Sandhu*, while Collier's mother
was *Meredith!* And Addison's mom was *Eleanor!*—and her friends were
no better, never extending an arm for a handshake like they did with
Hitomi's parents (*Maybe he's not allowed to touch a girl,* Priya could see
them wondering; *Maybe her scarf will slip off her shoulder—it looks so delicately placed*). In an American school in a liberal state, Priya knew what
her classmates saw when they looked at her parents, the debates they'd
have out of earshot about *servility* and *subservience* and *patriarchal con-
ceptions of modesty*.

The only option is to overcompensate, to try to temper the way her
parents landed. This afternoon she will help them socialize over the
trendiest foods—poké, bibimbap, California cheeses—never letting her
guard down, making sure that both of her parents' hands are at all times
occupied so that the question of a handshake is never raised, making sure
to steer the conversation toward topics in which her mother can participate (reality television, the new Indian restaurant in Hartford, weirdly—
inexplicably—American football), making sure that they spend at least
twenty minutes talking to Hitomi's parents, who—because they are a
diplomat and the wife of a diplomat—are perfectly adept at carrying on
a conversation with two Indian expats. She knows that no one will mention Karen Mirro or Mr. Breslin or Jamison Jennings because people will

make assumptions about her parents' conservativeness; to talk to them in particular about a sex scandal would be to violate some unwritten code of polite conversation.

After she's put her parents in an Uber, after she's made excuses for why they can't attend the parent cocktail party that night ("Early flight tomorrow!"), after she clicks through the afternoon's conversations, unfolding and refolding them like little paper sculptures in her mind, searching every crease for a misstep, after the adrenaline buzz of preventing her own embarrassment winds down like a sugar crash, the worst part will come. Washing her face, pinching her eyelashes to rub off her mascara, she'll feel a hollowing deep in her gut, so acute it causes her to brace herself against the sink, and she'll wonder: *Was I mean to them? Do they know they embarrass me?*

For much of the afternoon, the flat-bottomed clouds with the slate-gray undersides hung over the hills in the distance, tethered for reasons related to pressure and altitude to the valley beyond. As the day wore on, the winds lifted them from their position and pushed them toward Atwater until they melded together into one great darkening storm cloud over campus. A breeze lifted the underbellies of the leaves around the Bowl so they seemed to shimmer. And Olivia Anderson and the class of 2016 gathered on the schoolhouse steps for one last tradition before the rain broke.

Senior Smoke is, in Olivia's California-born and doctor-raised opinion, the most ridiculous of the Atwater mores, dumber even than the stupid white dresses, because at least the weirdness of the white dresses is right out there, unmistakable, undeniable. The tradition that calls on the graduates to share a cigar on the afternoon of their graduation day is something else, something that seems to Olivia equally antiquated but in a more confused way. Every year, the girls post pictures from the steps, hips jutted to one side, cigars perched between two fingers at O-shaped mouths. Trying so hard to say, *We're not the ladies you think we are.* Staged irony. Faux self-awareness. It would be better if it was weed, honestly, because the worst part about the whole thing was the subconscious riff on cigars as symbols of masculinity. They weren't breaking any barriers by smoking cigars in white dresses. They were just getting Instagram likes.

There are more girls there than Olivia was expecting—twenty or twenty-five of them, the usual suspects like Collier and Addison and Karla but also some of the model citizens like Ashley Witt and Hitomi Sakano. Mia Tavoletti dangles her legs from the stone ledge that runs at a diagonal up the steps with her lips—as it happens—wrapped around the end of a vape pen. She watches as Mia holds for a second, her chest beneath her white slip dress projected slightly outward, then exhales, releasing a cloud of milky vapor that briefly wreaths her head before evaporating into the air. The smell lingers, and Olivia smiles to herself.

This is just like Mia, she thinks: a joint would be too ordinary for someone who's always so determinedly ahead of the curve.

Olivia stands at the edge of the ledge near Mia. "Hey," she nods.

"What's up?"

"Smoke before your smoke?"

Mia laughs. "Hey, this isn't smoking." She waggles the pen in front of Olivia. "Happy to share," she adds.

Olivia puts up a hand. "I try to break no more than two school rules simultaneously," she says, counting in her head: the dress (sort of); the cigars (technically).

"Fair enough." Mia pauses for a second to take another hit. "Cool outfit, by the way," she says when she looks at Olivia again.

Olivia's dress is, actually, if she says so herself, pretty cool, and partly because it's not *really* a dress: It's a mullet dress. Pants in the front, skirt train in the back, with a bustier top, Olivia's "gown" pushes the limits of Paulsen's dress code. But she informed the Dean of Students that she had every intent of wearing it regardless of whether she granted her permission, and—to Olivia's astonishment—Paulsen backed down. It wouldn't have surprised Olivia if Linda Paulsen did not exactly keep up on trends in designer dresses; she imagined her seeing the choice not as protest but rather as just buying what was available.

"To be honest"—Olivia flicks her chin up, gesturing toward Mia's dress—"I'm a little surprised that the president of ***Flawless is actually going along with this patriarchal bullshit." She says the name of the club exactly like the song title, *asterisk-asterisk-asterisk-Flawless*.

Mia sighs and lifts her chin skyward, appraising the blackening above. "I know. I let us down on this one."

At that moment Olivia spots her ex-girlfriend in the sea of girls circling around Collier and Addison, who distribute individual cigars from heavy wooden boxes. Emma catches her eye.

"Someone once told me that it's important to pick your battles."

"Yeah," Mia says. "Sometimes I think that's just what we tell ourselves when we're exhausted."

Olivia lets out a low laugh. "Well, it's been an exhausting year, hasn't it?"

"You're tellin' me."

"Cigar?" Collier has materialized in front of them, the box extended in front of her like a host on one of those 7:00 P.M. game shows. Mia slides the pen into her bra so that the slim white metal protrudes only slightly and at an angle at her dress neckline, and lifts the tiny log of tobacco from the box. Olivia follows suit. "Wait to light them until after the pics! The smoke is too hard to photograph."

Olivia has never held a cigar before. It's both heavier and lighter than she was expecting, and smells like rotting fruit: honey-sweet but also earthy.

Someone yells over the group: "Hurry! Let's get the pics before the rain!" Olivia's classmates stack themselves on the schoolhouse steps with the expertise of girls who've posed ten thousand times before. They jostle for the inside positions (the middle photographs skinniest); the lower rows sorority-squat; the girls at the ends cock their arms at their hips. Mia stays on her perch; Olivia leans against the railing, moving herself just inside the frame. The photographers are some obliging juniors: Blake and Brie and Kit, each juggling four or five or six phones.

They are still and silent long enough to hear thunder rumble in the distance.

"Hurry!" Ashley Witt shouts, and the group disperses, and Olivia realizes that several of her classmates have come prepared with lighters. They cluster in random groups, leaning inward, small sizzles issuing forth as the cigars catch.

Next to her, Mia holds out a lighter. "Light?"

It tastes like ash. She holds it inside the back of her throat and feels her eyes begin to water. She realizes she is making the same rookie mistake she made the first time she smoked weed, and not actually inhaling. Next to her, Mia pushes tiny smoke rings into the space in front of them.

"I can't decide if I'll miss it," she says.

Olivia tilts her head and blows outward. Together they watch the exhalation diffuse, blossoming like a three-dimensional Rorschach. A single raindrop cuts through the cloud, then another. One lands on her temple, tiny and ghostlike, and as she reaches a single fingertip to her forehead to wipe away the phantom wet Olivia realizes that neither of them will miss Atwater, not exactly. Instead what they'll feel is a very particular kind of ache, one that will spasm at random intervals—in the shower, on a bad date, in the middle of a college seminar—and when it does they'll know: this is the longing you feel for a place that's become a part of you. This is the yearning you carry when you never really leave.

Acknowledgments

I spent most of my twenties teaching at boarding and independent day schools, the majority of them all-girls. We live in a culture whose regard for young women is both conditional and changeable, and yet every day I watched my students insist upon the validity of their experiences. Teenage girls are wise, bighearted, and relentlessly optimistic, and it is very likely I learned more from them than they did from me.

To my agent, Lisa Grubka, a handler with all the calm and compassion of Frank Langella's Gabriel, the toughness of Margo Martindale's Claudia, and the wisdom to know when to use which (and the good humor to tolerate these random and logically shaky tangents): Thank you for . . . *gestures vaguely at new life*.

My editor, Sarah Cantin, is extremely fucking good at her job. Were I writing this story, I could not have conjured a kinder, savvier, and more professional ally. Thanks as well to Katie Bassel, Erica Ferguson, Erica Martirano, Sallie Lotz, and Hannah Nesbat, who gave this book its title. And at John Murray in the UK, my gratitude to Becky Walsh, Charlotte Hutchinson, and Emma Petfield.

Hilary Zaitz Michael at WME championed not only this manuscript but also my desire to write for television (when there was yet very little tangible evidence I could do such a thing); what a person wants most when navigating a new landscape is to be taken seriously but also with generosity, and she and Scott Goldman at FKKS have this talent in spades.

Lisa, Sarah, Hilary, and Scott each brought with them to Atwater a veritable army. Thank you to everyone at Fletcher & Co., WME, FKKS, and St. Martin's Press who believed in these girls and fought for their space in the world. And to Jessica Rhoades and the team at Pacesetter: Thank you for understanding this story, for wanting to give it a broader audience, and for helping to tell it in rich, new ways.

The transition into this new career would not have been possible without the support of my therapist. Good therapy with the right fit is transformative, and yet the fact that I am able to pursue treatment is a privilege. Mental health care should be accessible to any individual who needs it, and I hope that one day such a system will prevail.

I am eternally grateful to the many professional (and paraprofessional) communities and work families that have sustained me over the better part of the last decade. Lizzy DiNuzzo, Jon Hickey, Allison McCann, and Julian Stern read and provided essential feedback on as many pages as I could send, and in so doing made the wilderness a little less lonely. Steady employment paid my bills but my colleagues fed my soul, including Steve Brown, Tim Fitzmaurice, Claire Mancini, Cristi Marchetti, and Tesha Poe.

Donna Inglehart gave me my first teaching job but always called me a writer. From Meg McClellan and Kathleen McNamara I've received a master class in mentoring (and personhood). Judy Richardson's office in Margaret Jacks ranks among my favorite places in the entire world; all I can say about her is that I had wandered very far from writing and myself by the time we met, and now here we are.

Thanks, for that matter, to everyone in the Stanford American Studies and Creative Writing programs, including Richard Gillam, Adam Johnson, and Angela Pneuman. It is impossible to think that I was ever worthy of their attention, tutelage, encouragement, and empathy.

I have always felt similarly undeserving of the loyalty of my closest friends. Maria DeMatteo, Erin Hatton, Maria Malone, and Julie McPhillips: Whether we met at twelve or twenty-five, it has been a gift to grow with you.

My cousin, Kristen Layden, fits into every category in this section—

friend, teacher, teammate, collaborator, family; it would be simpler and truer to merely say that she is the glue.

Gabby and Nina Armstrong are also more than my cousins: they are my inspiration, and the best people I know. So much of the first draft of this book was written or nurtured in their home in Lake Placid, and so much is owed to the entire Armstrong family—to Nina and Gabby but also to Karen, Shayn, Neil, and Peeves: for the naan pizza and funfetti cake; for loving and caring for Canfield like their own; for the training outpost; for a teary walk around the lake when I was certain this would never happen.

In fact, I have been exceptionally fortunate to live my life inside a big, generous family. My maternal grandparents, Henry and Jeannette Boehning, taught me to be compassionate, unselfish, and devoted—in teaching and in life. My dad's parents, Ed and Kay Layden, raised a family of storytellers. Thanks as well to Chris, Julian, and Julie Boehning; Janet, Kevin, and Tim Layden; Peg, Sam, and Todd Palmiere.

My parents, Joe and Sue Layden, opened every door for me. All of this begins with them. My brother, Max, has always been my number-one fan: I believe in you, too, Bud.

Finally, to my husband, Brian: The book was the dream; meeting you was better.